Praise for *Mur*

'Coles's feline wit and infectious enthusiasm for ecclesiastical trivia make for a very moreish read'
Daily Telegraph

'Written in Coles's customary wry style which owes much to the work of Alan Bennett' *Daily Mail*

'Richard writes beautifully . . . a delightful piece of detective work set in a religious order. The atmosphere is so intense, you can almost smell the incense on the page' *Irish Mail on Sunday*

'A village that could rival Agatha Christie's St Mary Mead and the TV murder hotspot of Midsomer for its ever growing body count' *The Herald*

MURDER AT THE MONASTERY

A Canon Clement Mystery

The Reverend
RICHARD COLES

W&N
WEIDENFELD & NICOLSON

First published in Great Britain in 2024 by Weidenfeld & Nicolson
This paperback edition first published in Great Britain in 2025
by Weidenfeld & Nicolson,
an imprint of The Orion Publishing Group Ltd
Carmelite House, 50 Victoria Embankment
London EC4Y ODZ
An Hachette UK Company

The authorised representative in the EEA is Hachette Ireland,
8 Castlecourt Centre, Dublin 15, D15 XTP3,
Republic of Ireland (email: info@hbgi.ie)

1 3 5 7 9 10 8 6 4 2

A CIP catalogue record for this book is
available from the British Library.

ISBN (Mass Market Paperback) 978 1 4746 1 2722
ISBN (eBook) 978 1 4746 1 2739
ISBN (Audio) 978 1 4746 1 2746

Typeset by Input Data Services Ltd, Bridgwater, Somerset

Printed in Great Britain by Clays Ltd, Elcograf, S.p.A.

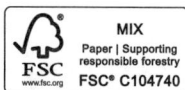

www.weidenfeldandnicolson.co.uk
www.orionbooks.co.uk

For Johnny

And so we are going to establish a school for the service of the Lord. In founding it we hope to introduce nothing harsh or burdensome. But if a certain strictness results from the dictates of equity for the amendment of vices or the preservation of charity, do not be at once dismayed and fly from the way of salvation, whose entrance cannot but be narrow. For as we advance in faith, our hearts expand and we run the way of God's commandments with unspeakable sweetness of love . . .

The Rule of St Benedict

Prologue

By night, seen from the moors that surrounded it, the Abbey of Sts Philip and James at Ravenspurn looked like a liner in the middle of the ocean. You could make out a long silhouette with what could pass for a bridge and fo'c'sle and a pair of masts against the starlit sky. There was also, very faintly, a cranking, whirring sound that suggested steam turbines, only it came not from the abbey, but from a small granite building with a steep slate roof that stood near the edge of its grounds. The monastery was originally a Victorian Yorkshire wool baron's mansion, built above the soot-stained valley where his fortune had been quickly made, and quickly spent on a house that rushed to display a summary of English architecture as if it represented the fullness of a civilisation's achievement. The effect now was of pompous ugliness, but half a century after it was built, when the owner's successors were unable to maintain it, a newly formed religious community bought it and converted it for their use, with a church and cloister added at one end, a guest house and service buildings at the other.

To those who lived there now, a ship alone on the ocean by night was a fitting metaphor. It was an ark for the faithful few, called by God to a life of prayer and service, preserved in their fragile craft from a restless sea of strife and sin and change.

Its captain was the abbot, Father Aelred, his officers the senior monks, with a crew of forty brethren, and some temporary passengers, visitors, all now abed and asleep; and while there was hardly a comprehensive menagerie of the beasts of the Earth, there was a chicken coop and run outside, and a fox loping across the lawn in front of the main house, while Scholastica, the monastery cat, crouched under a rhododendron, watching.

Not all were abed and asleep. A couple of lights burnt even in the stillness and silence of that hour, like lamps fore and aft. Aft, along one of the corridors where the brethren lived out the part of their lives that was private, one was awake and alert. He was sitting at the plain desk in the plain room lit by a table lamp, and he was carefully opening a large brown envelope that he had taken that morning from the table where the post was laid out for collection after breakfast. He was opening it carefully because it was not addressed to him and he had no business opening it at all. He worked away at the gummed flap with the tip of a letter knife. Eventually it gave and he reached in and pulled out the contents.

It was a glossy sheaf of A3 pages with a spiral binder at the top. It was, as he thought it would be, a calendar to be hung on the wall, with a page for each month of the year. But this would not be hung on any wall in the abbey. It would be reserved for private use, the most private, intimate use imaginable.

Two young men, blond and beautiful, like an advert for an Aryan identical-twin brotherhood, stared out from the cover. They were in ripped and worn jeans, wide leather belts, with studded leather jackets over bare chests, arms folded, hips forward, and the promise of more anatomy available within the straining seamed denim.

BROS, with the letter S back to front, was printed above the year 1990, 'Official Calendar' scrawled in yellow freehand.

He leafed through it, page by page, turning it one way, then the other, admiring the ingenuity with which the unarguable charms of the Aryan brothers were displayed. When he had finished, he unpeeled a Post-it note from the yellow block on his desk and stuck it over the face of either Matt or Luke, he was not sure which. Then he wrote on it.

'*When will I, will I be FAAMOUS?* Never. If I were you, I would avoid publicity, for if your weaknesses were to be revealed, then it would not be fame but notoriety that would follow.'

He slid the calendar back into the envelope, pressed down the gummed flap and fixed it with a strip of

Sellotape. That would give him a nasty surprise when he opened it, he thought, but a salutary surprise. He was only doing his job, opening the way to salvation; and sometimes people needed a push. Then he went downstairs and left it on the table outside the refectory for the addressee to collect later. He smiled at the thought of him opening it and finding his message stuck over that handsome face.

At the other end of the becalmed ship, the light burning fore was in the monastic library, where the exceptionally studious sole inhabitant had paused his research for a moment to admire a photograph he had found of the Empress Elisabeth of Austria-Hungary. She was young, dressed magnificently in a tiara and veil, holding a fan, and looking out at an angle like a more coquettish King Ludwig of Bavaria, the Fairy Tale King, her adored first cousin. There was suddenly a lump in his throat.

Her story was tragic. She had married Franz Josef I, Emperor of Austria and King of Hungary, in 1854, an unhappy marriage that produced a son who shot his lover and then himself. Ludwig, her cousin, died mysteriously in 1886, and then in 1898 she was assassinated by an anarchist by Lake Geneva.

His eyes suddenly glistened at the thought of her sad life. And then they narrowed at a solecism in the text, often repeated, but always wrong. She was not known as 'Sissi', but 'Sisi'. The extra 'S' seemed, if not *lèse-majesté*, then careless, and the empress should at least be spared that, with her wretched marriage, her lovers, her heartbreak, her murder.

But this would not do. He recovered himself, took off his glasses and wiped his eyes on his sleeve, but it was not really suitable for the task. He tugged a handkerchief from his pocket, which brought with it a little shower of cherry menthol Tunes and a Chap-Stick, which he struggled to retrieve from the floor. He inspected the handkerchief, found a clean part, and wiped his glasses.

He put away the book with the picture of Sisi and took another from the shelf he had annexed for his own use. He kept on it the selection of books he had taken from the monastery library's history section, and from the university's more extensive library too, where he had a reader's ticket, and where he had spent many hours, days, weeks, poring over long-unopened books from unvisited shelves, researching his esoteric subject, and on the way becoming a rather unusual polyglot so he could read the primary sources.

What a long way he had come! But the way was hard and stony. This volume was unusually demanding, an edited collection of the correspondence of Admiral Horthy, Regent of Hungary during the Second World War. His unsolicited letters to the Führer advising against entering into a pact with Stalin betrayed a rather naive overestimation of the value of his counsel. Written in an archaic Austro-Hungarian German, he thought. Then he felt pleased with himself for having mastered enough of the language to detect the nuances.

He yawned, a yawn which started small but ended large, as he leant back in the chair and stretched. He was more tired than he thought, for it was long past bedtime and he could not be sure if the text in front of him was unfocused because of his smeared glasses or simply fatigue. It was Matins in just a few hours, so he made to close the book but then stopped. He looked. Squinted. Took his glasses off, wiped them again with his handkerchief, and looked again.

There, in the margin, in faint pencil incompletely rubbed out, were some notes, and again faintly, some underlining in the text. He squinted again and held the page up to the light. Who had been reading this book? Who had been looking at exactly the texts he was interested in? Then he remembered there was a magnifying glass in the librarian's desk so he went and fetched it and looked again.

His eyes widened.

I

Canon Daniel Clement wasn't sure if he had been dreaming or in a sort of reverie when the rising bell roused him. He looked around the unfamiliar room. Not completely unfamiliar, for he soon recognised it as a guest room at Ravenspurn. It had a plain little chair and table, with a Bible on it in a version that was once trendy but now out of fashion. There were still two wire coat hangers hanging on a row of pegs and, saddest of all, a tired brown towel with a tiny little bar of Lux placed on it, an inadequate flourish of indulgent comfort.

The bell that usually roused him each morning rang from the tower of St Mary's Champton where he was rector, but not this morning. This bell was tinnier but more clamorous, and grew louder. It was a handbell, rung by the hebdomadary making his way down a dreary corridor of chipboard and strip lighting. Hebdomadary – sounds like a sort of camel, Daniel thought, but it was a job, a duty rotated each week between the novices of the Abbey of Sts Philip and James at Ravenspurn. One of the duties of the hebdom, as they called them, was to get up even earlier than usual in order to wake the others, monks and guests, half an hour before Matins.

It was half past five in the morning, Daniel's normal hour to rise ever since he, too, had been one of the brethren there, a novice known as Brother Crispin. After three years he'd had to choose whether to continue and become fully fledged as a monk or leave and live out his vocation in another form. 'The world, not the cloister, for you, Crispin,' said Father Aelred in his last interview. 'It would be like having Rudolf Nureyev in the chorus line if you were to stay.'

But here he was, twenty-five years later, not as a novice but as a visitor, a country parson, and a Canon of Stow, a dignity the bishop of that diocese had conferred upon him for helping him swerve 'a sadness'. He had always come back, in one way or another – or rather, he had never entirely left, and he knew a part of him would be forever there.

He switched on the light, a 40-watt single bulb under a useless shade, and got out of bed. It was narrow and not very comfortable, and now in his late forties, he knew the ache in his shoulder would not be easily soothed. The ache in his heart, he thought, would never be soothed. He stretched, and at the apex of his stretch the exchange of words that had made him pack a bag, leave his parish without notice and drive through the night to Ravenspurn returned, unbearably. He collapsed in on himself like a winded fighter in slow motion.

'I love Honoria.'

Three words, spoken to him by Detective Sergeant Neil Vanloo, confessing his secret passion for the daughter of Daniel's patron, Lord de Floures.

This came as a complete surprise, but it was not what upset him; it was not that an attachment between a policeman and the daughter of the grandest landowner in the county might be seen as scandalous; it was not that it came on the night Daniel had solved a terrible crime and caught a depraved murderer.

It was that Daniel secretly loved Neil Vanloo, and that he had thought the handsome young policeman's confession would end in the longed-for declaration of his secret love returned.

'I love Honoria.'

Three words that in an instant undid all his hopes, slashed his heart and wrecked his happiness.

But not his composure; he had barely flinched, not that Neil would have noticed, for he threw his arms around Daniel in gratitude for what he thought was his patience and sympathy. It was a good job, Daniel later thought, that he was wearing his thick cloak over his cassock, for he had been stirred so obviously by the anticipation of Neil's passionate embrace.

A matey hug, not a passionate embrace. Admired, not desired. Friend, not lover.

He had promised he would not tell anyone. He had

promised he would talk to Honoria. He was *so happy* that Neil had finally met someone and fallen in love, and said he hoped, too, that the day would indeed come when he could do his friend the greatest of honours by marrying him to his bride.

Neil had left with the brio that unburdening yourself brings, a brio so intoxicating he did not for a second pause to think about the effect his confession had had on his friend.

Daniel had stood absolutely still. The kitchen had been almost in darkness, lit by a single candle on the dresser, for on Bonfire Night a day earlier, someone had tried to burn the rectory down with his mother, Audrey, inside it. She had been rescued, along with their dogs and their puppies, but the hall of the lovely Queen Anne rectory was wrecked, and the effects of smoke and soot and water had made the ground floor uninhabitable. How fitting, he thought, that he should be standing alone and in darkness in his ruined home.

For the first time since his father died, he had cried. He cried again as the rising bell clanged more faintly from the floor above.

Audrey Clement rose two hours later in the vastly more comfortable hospitality of Champton House, where Bernard, Lord de Floures, had provided accommodation for her and Daniel and the dogs after the fire. It was not a squeeze, for Champton House was so large and rambling that not even Bernard knew how many bedrooms they had; twenty decent, and many more on the attic floors, where the sixty servants who ensured fires were lit, tables were laid and washstands replenished once lived. Guests, like fish, begin to stink after three days, as the proverb has it, so Bernard had accommodated the rectory refugees in the grandest part of the house, a separate wing from the family apartments.

Audrey had been put in Queen Charlotte's Bedroom, so named for the queen consort of George III, whose visit in the early 1760s was the reason for the construction of the entire wing. This was before her husband lost his wits and the queen, blithe and congenial then, had somehow impressed her personality on the room. It was handsome rather than grand, with a sort of exalted *gemütlichkeit* – perhaps a risky thing, Daniel thought, to offer for a queen's accommodation – but it could have been hung with leopard skin and carpeted in rushes for all Audrey cared. She was sleeping in a queen's bedroom, an actual queen.

There was a tap at the door. 'Come in?' she said in a voice which she had not intended to be queenly, but it must have sounded so, because Honoria, bringing her a cup of tea on a tray, had to smother a laugh.

'I've brought you tea, Audrey, I don't know how you like it.'

'I take *déca*, dear,' she said, 'decaffeinated coffee . . .'

Honoria, who knew perfectly well what *déca* was, and that Audrey had probably acquired that affectation on a day trip to Dieppe, said nothing.

'. . . but tea is fine, and so *kind*.'

Honoria put it down on her bedside table. The sound of yapping came from behind the bathroom door. 'Do you need to let them out?'

'I think I should, really.'

'Let me do it.'

'Thank you. I'll get up.'

'Do you have everything you need?'

'I think so, dear. The dressing gown is rather fun.'

'It's a bathrobe,' said Honoria, 'you can get out of the bath and straight into it, no need to towel.'

'And what an advertisement for the Motcombe!'

The monogram of the Motcombe Hotel, where Honoria worked in 'events', was stitched in royal blue across the breast.

'We did order rather a bundle,' said Honoria.

'And the toiletries too? When I went into the bathroom I felt like Howard Carter opening the tomb of the boy pharaoh.'

'Honestly, Audrey, they come by the D. Did you sleep well, by the way? After everything that's happened?'

'Like a baby,' said Audrey. 'In a queen's bed!'

'When you're ready come down and I'll make you breakfast. It's in the family breakfast room – do you know where that is?'

'I don't.'

'Come to the kitchens and Mrs Shorely will direct you.'

'I don't know where they are either.'

'Well, if the staircase is in front of you, go to the left of it and you'll find the door to the service wing. Keep going. Follow the smell of kippers.'

'Smoked herrings!' She clutched her chest.

'Huh?'

'I was just nearly kippered myself when the rectory burnt down.'

'I'm so sorry, Audrey, I didn't think . . .'

'I'm joking.'

'Oh, phew! But you must say, Audrey, if you are feeling at all peculiar. You might be in shock.'

'The Blitz was a shock, Honoria. Not a singed rug and climbing through a window.'

'OK. I'll see you at breakfast.'

Audrey opened the bathroom door and Cosmo bounded out, barking at the intruder, followed by Hilda and the puppies, who tumbled and slithered on the parquet floor between the wall and the fringe of a Persian carpet, which was still lovely, if a bit threadbare and stained.

'Oh dear,' said Audrey, peering into the bathroom. 'I think that's a deposit on Queen Charlotte's bathmat.'

'May I leave that with you?' said Honoria.

'You may.'

Honoria scooped up the puppies and held the bedroom door open with her foot so Cosmo and Hilda could follow. Audrey watched them follow her into the surprising vastness of the space beyond the door, which slowly closed.

★

Neil Vanloo let himself out of the back door of the tiny warrener's cottage, which stood in the park a quarter-mile from Champton House. The cottage, a one-up one-down, had been built in the seventeenth century for the man responsible for providing the estate with rabbits, or rather that end of the estate more humbly fed than those who dined on deer. The last warrener had retired three hundred years ago, and the cottage was now used for overflow guests. A lean-to at the back provided a kitchen and bathroom for the single parlour on the ground floor. Above, and reached by steep stairs, was the upper room with a large bed and a lovely view across the park to the house, close enough to be admired, far enough away for whoever was staying there to be unobserved. Neil was now a regular, because there he had been conducting his affair with Honoria ('at it like rabbits' he liked to think) for weeks now. This was the reason for her frequent returns to Champton – how easy it was for her, he thought, to take as much time off from her 'job' as she liked – not to connect with her patrimony, but to connect with her policeman. And a very vigorous and frequent connection it had turned out to be. This had come as a surprise to her, and to her brother and confidant Alex, normally a sound predictor of her passions, for a detective sergeant from Manchester was not her idea of a match at all. He compared so favourably with those that were, however, she had started to wonder if she had been brainwashed all along.

Neil had fallen in love with her the moment he had seen her. He was not the first to do this – Honoria had been captivating ardent young men and charming everybody else since she was a teenager – but she was the first to produce in him physical and ontological desire simultaneously. She not only made his pulse quicken, but also hit him like destiny. Neil had experienced desire before – sticky bus-shelter desire in his adolescence in Oldham – and he knew about destiny because he had grown up in the Moravian Brethren, an ardent Protestant sect, and around the same time as his bus-shelter stickiness he had experienced New Birth into the life of Jesus Christ, his Lord and Saviour, which had put paid for a while to erotic exploration on the transport infrastructure of late-industrial Lancashire.

As his horizons broadened so did his experience, and his sex life, but this was the first time the physical and the ontological had come together in such a fissile way, and he could not think of Honoria without simultaneously experiencing a rush of blood and imagining her streaming with light, like Blake's *Albion Rose*.

The Honourable Honoria de Floures! Saying her name out loud sounded like John Betjeman sung by the Stone Roses, his Lancastrian flatness drawing out the last syllable of her fragrant name. The Manc and the aristocrat, who would have guessed it? It could never have happened had they not met when he was sent to deal with the horrible murders at Champton last year.

He looked to the left and right. No one was about,

save the rabbits, which scattered when he started the car. The affair was a secret, shared only with Alex and Nathan — Honoria's brother and his lover — and now Daniel.

Daniel: he smiled as he drove slowly through the park and felt a surge of love for his friend, another unlikely affinity. Daniel had listened without judging when he told him last night about his secret love, and wished him and Honoria well, and the tears that had begun to appear in his eyes told him Daniel, too, was deeply moved.

Maybe the time had come for him and Honoria to declare themselves, to go public? He had said this on an impulse the night before, but she did not think so. Her father was still coming to terms with the recently revealed news that his eldest son and heir Hugh was marrying a 'squaw', a Canadian vet with Mohawk heritage. Only a year had passed since he heard the even more indigestible news that his second son, Alex, was not only a 'pansy' but was having an affair with Nathan Liversedge, the 'gippo' grandson of his shady gamekeeper. Perhaps discovering that his daughter — and obvious favourite — would also not make the suitable match he hoped for would be a disappointment he could not bear?

Neil reached the gates to the park, which opened automatically — 'Open sesame!' he said, in a little fantasy of supernatural command — and noticed that the lights were on in the south lodge, where Alex and

Nathan spent their nights, but not yet on in the north, where they spent the days. The course of their relationship had hardly run smooth. It started illegally, was clandestine for years, survived a murder investigation, enforced exile, a double arrest on suspicion of murder, a notable disharmony in age and class, and the almost universal disapproval of all sides. If they could find a love nest, even if it were literally on the edge of the park, then why not Honoria and him?

'Something's gotten hold of my he-a-art,' he sang as he drove through the gates and out into the village.

2

Daniel washed and shaved in the sink in his little room. He was used to the perfunctory grooming that monastic life afforded, although now his nose wrinkled at some of the older brethren who seemed to have given up altogether. He did the best he could, dressed in his cassock as usual, but then took the blue scapular he had worn as a novice – a sort of long apron that hung from neck to ankles, front and back – and threw it over his head. It made him look like the monk he had once wanted to be, typical of monastic dress in undifferentiating the brethren. They were who they were by virtue of their corporate identity, not as individuals.

This was one of the aspects of the life that he liked most, not having to be someone in particular. Even your name was surrendered; when Daniel had chosen Crispin, patron saint of shoemakers, it was to honour his forefathers, who had been in that trade for generations, and because of the thrilling speech at the Battle of Agincourt given by Shakespeare's Henry V. When he told Father Aelred, then the novice master, what he had chosen he'd said, 'Well, if you think "happy few" at least you're half right . . .'

The mirror above the sink was fogged with steam so he wiped it with the scapular, and with a shock saw not the face of the novice he used to be looking back at him, but a man approaching fifty. His hair was greying, his cheeks had a blush of rosacea, and although he could still fit the cassock he had worn back then, his neck was becoming jowly and the bags under his eyes looked like they belonged to a minor marsupial.

He slipped out of his room quietly, not wanting to disturb any other guests unused to the early hour, and went downstairs to the corridor which connected the guest house to the rest of the monastery. He should really have left the building and walked to the church along the path that skirted the outside of the abbey to join any other visitors going in through the south door, the one for those coming in from the world, opposite the north door, which admitted those from the cloister. But he had lived there once, and though he was no longer a member of the community, he wanted to retrace the steps he had taken when he was. He walked along the silent corridors, feebly lit by bare lightbulbs, past the hooks hung with the monks' choir robes, until he reached the double swing doors into the church. To the right there was a holy water stoup.

He dipped two fingers into it and signed himself with the cross.

He pushed open the doors and stepped into the darkness of the church, like an astronaut opening the hatch to limitless space. The first thing he noticed, as he always did, was the difference in the acoustics – the swish of the closing doors, dampened on the cloister side, echoed on the church side like a whisper in a horror film – then the difference in temperature, and as his eyes grew used to the darkness the dimensions of the building began to reveal themselves to sight.

It was huge, the size of a small cathedral, only the proportions were different. Instead of a big nave there was a big choir, furnished with tiered wooden stalls facing each other. At the west end, high above the back of the church, he could make out the pipes of the abbey organ on its balcony, the rose window behind it dull and flat before the first light of dawn. At the east end there was the sanctuary where the high altar stood, and behind it a large chapel forming an apse. Another altar stood here and on it was what looked like an over-dressed pedal-bin, the tabernacle. Inside it, in a silver chalice, the consecrated bread of the Eucharist was kept. For Anglo-Catholic Christians, this was the very presence of Jesus, and the entire building, indeed the entire community, was founded and ordered around it. It was lit with a single candle, one that burnt always, the one source of light in the dark church, and the one source of light for the world if you wanted to be theological about it.

Daniel moved through the church with more confidence than most people would in a dark building, but he knew his way around, as surely by night as by day, a habit he had taken with him into the churches where he had later served, for a parson's life also began early and finished late.

He was not entirely alone. An occasional sniff, or the clearing of a throat, emerged out of the darkness from the places where the early risers among the brethren came to pray individually before the first service of the day. When he was a novice Daniel had grown to love this time before Matins, getting up so early that he almost met himself going to bed, and Father Aelred eventually told him to regulate himself more carefully. He loved it still, and every morning, when practicable, he went to church in the darkness of the predawn, or the brightening dawn when summer came around, and prayed what he always prayed in the twenty minutes before they opened for business.

He reached into the pocket of his cassock and took out the *metanoi* that was with him wherever he went. It was a knotted circle of string, the size of a bracelet, strung with plain wooden beads separated by knots with a small wooden cross hanging from a tassel. It had been given to him by a monk visiting from Romania, his friend Paisie. For more than twenty years now he had started each day as Paisie started it, saying silently on each bead the Jesus Prayer: *Lord Jesus Christ, son of God, have mercy on me, a sinner.*

He moved towards that tiny point of light at the east end, which the rising sun would outshine soon.

A smell of tobacco smoke crept across the stone floor, which Daniel instantly identified as Father Gregory's, who was somewhere in the gloom praying too. He was able to identify most of the brethren from their smell, their gait, their breathing, for so much of their lives was spent in silence and in darkness that you became as familiar with the sound of arrhythmic footsteps, their preferred tobacco, their body odour, their sniff, as you did with their appearance. Neil had once asked Daniel how he had acquired his Sherlockian powers of observation; living in a monastery, he said, in the enforced silence of a cloister, where you learn to make your way by other means than speech and vision.

Daniel settled onto his stool facing the tabernacle. His knees, a quarter of a century on, complained at the angle and he shifted the seat to find a kinder one. When he was comfortable, he held the first bead on his *metanoi* between thumb and forefinger and started to pray, knot by knot, each prayer slow, measured, geared to his breathing, which slowed too, and as his mind and body stilled, he drew the silence of the abbey church around him. The silence, like the stillness, was imperfect. There was the faint thump and whine that was always there, and the occasional gurgle of the radiators, the whine and rattle of a milk float on its rounds, and the far-off sound of a car alarm wailing. But these were distant, beyond the silence he wore like a habit when he prayed.

In that silence he could normally tune in to the frequencics he needed to, among the hiss and static of daily concerns, but sometimes he could not because the hiss and static were too loud. When that happened it was a matter of discipline, like running through exhaustion in a marathon, not that he knew what that was like, but Neil did.

He shifted along the string, bead by bead, on each one calling to mind his sins. His love for Neil he knew was not sinful, although the Church, its long tradition and nearly everyone he knew would disagree. He knew his resentment that Neil did not love him as he loved Neil was sinful, definitely, but he had been hurt, and when we are hurt we respond ungenerously.

He had never felt this way before. He had never wanted to feel this way before, but the urge to . . . give himself, was it that? . . . had been so powerful, and so obvious, he thought its return was inevitable. So to have that not only refused but not even recognised had wounded him. He hoped he had not flinched; he was sure Neil had not noticed the blow he'd inflicted, but keeping that to himself would come at a cost, he knew. And he could not put on a brave face to everyone, not to Neil, nor to Honoria, nor to Alex, nor to his mother. He felt a surge of grief and anger, and his thumb slid off the bead.

A cock crowed, waking to another day of business with the monastery's hens. How enviably simple that must be, he thought, to wake without consideration, to mate without discrimination, to sleep, to wake again, to mate again. Cock-a-doodle-doo. And then it crowed again, and it made him think of betrayal.

Daniel collected himself, and started his work again – 'Always, we begin again,' Father Aelred liked to say – and he made himself on each bead send prayers to God for the welfare of his parishioners, for the safety of those in trouble, prayers for those to whom prayer was owed, and for his friend Paisie in Romania. The *metanoi*, he understood now, connected them across the thousands of miles between Champton and Iaşi, between his comforts and privileges in a vision of English pastoral and his friend's privations and danger in the wobbling Eastern Bloc.

Suddenly a bell started tolling, sounding all the louder for the silence encircling it. It was the bell for Matins, and so habituated to it were the brethren that they stopped whatever they were doing and turned to head towards the rows of hooks in the cloister where their hooded cowls were hanging.

In the darkness of the chapel Daniel heard Father Gregory stir and grunt as he rose from his seat against the wall and started shuffling towards his stall in the choir. The double doors to the cloister creaked open and closed and there followed the faint squeak of a wheelchair heading there also, for the older monks who could not manage the processions took their places before their brethren arrived. Daniel got up too, his unflexed knees complaining now, and went to find a seat in the pews at the back of the nave, a couple of them already occupied by guests who, in the self-effacing discipline of Christian living, had competed fiercely to take the humblest place.

He wanted to sit down in an inconspicuous seat where he would not be observed. He liked to be left alone in church when he was not on duty, and he was worried he could burst into tears without warning and then someone might practise their compassion on him.

He saw a chair against the wall behind the pews and was about to sit on it when a man appeared and hissed, 'This one is TAKEN . . .' and then saw the collar and added '. . . Father.' The man was slight and wiry with wild white hair mirrored by a wild white beard so he looked in the half-light a bit like a dandelion clock. In between the two, Daniel could make out a cross little face. He would normally yield out of habit in any encounter like this, but resistance rose within him and instead he looked at the angry man without saying anything. After a two-second stand-off, the man nodded resentfully and retreated. Daniel sat. Then the lights in the north transept were switched on, and the lights on the altar and over the choir, enough to see where you were but still maintaining the shadow and silence of the predawn. Then there was a faint swishing, like a distant scythe to the corn, and two by two, in the black cowl of the community, the brethren processed in, perfectly in step, for they did this every day, and every week, and every month and year, round and round, in common life until they died. You never know a monk or nun, thought Daniel, until you see them in their community.

As they stepped into the choir they tilted their heads back so the hoods fell onto their shoulders to reveal their faces, monkish anonymity yielding to familiarity — in the lead were Father Paulinus, who sat in the precentor's stall, and beside him, the occupant of the succentor's stall, Father Dominic. They looked, thought Daniel, like Battery Sergeant-Major Williams and Gunner 'Lofty' Sugden from *It Ain't Half Hot Mum*. Paulinus was tall and imposing and walked with purpose. Dominic beside him looked his junior, which he was, although older than Paulinus, with thinning grey hair that had been brushed like a schoolboy's. He had a slightly flinching manner — flinching from Paulinus? — and a forehead that looked corrugated with worry. Daniel recognised also Father Cuthbert, Father Crispin (who had arrived after Daniel had left and taken the name he no longer required) and Father Chad, looking even more corvid than he had twenty-five years ago, smoke-scented Father Gregory, then Brother Joseph and Brother Charles, and some novices he didn't know wearing the blue scapular instead of the black, and last of all the abbot, Father Aelred, his confessor and friend, with the pectoral cross on his chest, the only sign of his rank. Abbots of Ravenspurn used to wear a gold cross, a beautiful and historic jewel that had been owned by a martyred English abbot of the dissolution of the monasteries, but Aelred found it too grand and chose another made of four nails, forged from iron.

There was a rustling as the brethren settled into their stalls and found their office books, marked up with ribbons for the prayers of the day. One of the novices, charged with minding the guests, handed Daniel a book with a slip of paper, on which were printed the commemorations of the week. He doubted the Dean of Westminster would be able to decipher the encoded instructions to find the relevant place in the book, so bespoke were the customs of Ravenspurn, but once learnt they were never forgotten, and Daniel already knew that today was the commemoration of William Temple, Archbishop of Canterbury during the Second World War.

Normally such a person would not merit too significant a rejig of the provision for the day, but Temple was such a significant figure he was afforded a dignity equal to Pope Gregory the Great. So Daniel turned up the special texts for bishops, the Collect, the readings, the hymn, and settled back in his pew pretending not to notice the other guests turning forwards and backwards as they tried to work out how to join in. 'Don't,' would be his advice, if asked, 'leave it to the pros, sit back and enjoy the flight,' but Church of England people think it their sacred duty to join in with everything as if it were *Songs of Praise* and get shirty if provision is not made for them to do so.

'*Oh Go-o-d make speed to sa-a-ve us,*' sang a single voice.

'*Oh Lo-o-rd make haste to he-e-lp us,*' the monks responded. Some of the keener guests joined in, one irritatingly half a second behind the others, and they bowed their heads with the brethren on the '*Glory be to the Father and to the Son and to the Holy Ghost . . .*' and stood straight again to sing '*. . . As it was in the beginning, is now, and ever sha-all be, world without end. Ame-en.*'

Audrey stood on the grand staircase of Champton House that led from the upper floor to the hall. It had once been a courtyard, but in the improvements of the Georgian era the outside had been made the inside, to provide a splendid space for the theatre of power and influence that the de Floures family enjoyed at the time. As she carefully made her way down the staircase she decided it was almost too grand, better scaled to horses than to people, and she imagined them galloping up and down the steps like they did at Sandhurst, was it? Or at Westminster Hall for the Coronation Banquet? She wasn't sure, but this was apt, for on the wall opposite an equestrian portrait of Charles I looked back at her. It was surrounded by portraits of de Floures ancestors, recognisable in their different centuries from the repeating characteristics of coppery hair and blue eyes, a pedigree as traceable as the Champton short-horns painted in the reign of the Georges and hung in the Rudnam Room.

Audrey knew her way to that but did not yet know how to find the working sections of the house, where splendour gave way to utility and Mrs Shorely presided. So she sniffed the air, detected a suggestion of burnt meat, and followed it.

The smell led her to the kitchen, where Honoria was standing in front of a double Aga so ancient it was crusted with overspilled brown Windsor soup from the last visit of Queen Mary. She was prodding a big frying pan, in which something not unlike bacon sizzled in lard.

'Breakfast Slices,' she said. 'Awful stuff made from the leftover parts of pigs, but Mrs Shorely thinks they're fine. They're not.'

Audrey had eaten snoek for king and country. She could manage a Breakfast Slice for Bernard.

'We're through there,' said Honoria, pointing with a fish slice to the door opposite. 'There's tea and coffee and toast.'

Lord de Floures sat at the head of the breakfast table, which had no cloth to cover it, though the cutlery was magnificent, in what was once the servants' hall. He was fifty-eight and florid, dressed exactly as his father had, in tweeds and a regimental tie, and was reading *The Times* when Audrey came in. 'Dear lady,' he said, 'allow me . . .' and leapt up to gallantly pull out the chair on his right, not only to afford her an honour, but to spare them both having to look full face at each other.

'So kind, thank you, *hmbmmhm* . . .' said Audrey, using the indistinct sound she used instead of his Christian name, which she did not yet dare use.

'Tea, coffee?'

'Coffee, please.'

He took a stainless-steel pot from a hot plate and poured with just enough of a suggestion of labour to indicate his unfitness for the task.

The door banged open and Honoria reversed in carrying three plates, waitress style. Bernard winced to see it.

'Breakfast' – she turned to face them – 'is served. Do help yourself to toast.'

What looked like two cat's tongues, untimely ripped, lay across Audrey's plate.

'Thank you, dear,' she said, 'such a treat!'

There was the sound of approaching footsteps from the corridor and Mrs Shorely appeared in the doorway holding two envelopes. 'M'lord?'

'Yes, Mrs Shorely?'

'Note for you.'

'From whom?'

'The rector, I think. And another for Mrs Clement. Left on my desk.'

She took one to Audrey and, without breaking her

slow, regular stride, took the other to Bernard and went right out again.

Bernard opened the envelope with his unwiped knife, which left a thin smear of butter along the edge. Audrey ripped hers open with a finger and there was silence while they both read the notes inside.

Then Bernard said, 'Called away! Will be gone for a few days. And written in evident haste. I wonder why? Does he say why?'

Audrey said, 'No – the same, he's been called away. Must be an emergency of some kind. And he'll be incommunicado! That's very unlike him.'

Honoria frowned.

Audrey said, 'Any idea, Honoria?'

'I don't think so. I can't remember if I saw him after the service last night . . .'

'I didn't see him,' said Audrey. 'But it was All Souls – and if someone was upset afterwards he would have dealt with that. Theo walked me back here and was bidden to supper with Alex and . . . Honoria, you didn't see him?'

'I went straight to Alex's . . . Dad, you didn't see Daniel?'

'No. I had the sandwiches Mrs Shorely left out and a Cup a Soup. Normal Sunday supper. Then I went to my study until bedtime. Didn't see anyone.'

'I don't want anything after a Sunday lunch,' said Audrey. 'I was in bed by nine – sheer bliss.'

They sat in silence, save the crunching of toast and

the dainty clatter of silver and china too good for the occasion. Only Honoria knew who Daniel had seen after the service: Neil Vanloo, who had joined her in the warrener's cottage later, more excited, she thought, to have received Daniel's blessing than to see her.

3

Breakfast in the monastery was always silent, for the prohibition on talk which began after Compline in the evening prevailed until breakfast was cleared away. This was one of those austerities that was in reality a blessing, for, as Father Aelred had once observed, if anything could raise murder in the placid heart of a monk it was a refectory chatterbox.

Daniel thought of this as he took his place at the end of the table reserved for guests. The refectory was the largest room in the monastery, with plain white walls curving into the ceiling over a floor laid with boards, which made the space acoustically lively, and something whispered in a corner could sound unnervingly close in the other corner. There was a table at one end on a low platform reserved for Aelred, or Abbot Aelred as he was properly known, though Daniel kept forgetting that. Aelred's was the place at the centre of the top table, in a chair marked out for distinction by having arms. To his right and left sat honoured guests and senior monks on chairs without the luxury of arms. Two lines of tables extended from each end of the top table, where diners sat on long benches. The arrangement was shaped like a croquet hoop, appropriately he thought, for the lawn beyond the big window was set for croquet, a pleasingly monkish pastime, he'd thought, until he'd played it and discovered how it could turn unusually vicious.

The refectory was about half full, monks arriving with their rhythmic swish, guests more hesitantly, wondering what to do in the unaccustomed silence. There was a repertoire of gestures the monks used when they were obliged to be silent, a sort of sign language which they deployed to communicate with each other and to chivvy guests when required, practical rather than ceremonial, for there was no religious ceremony at breakfast, no procession in, no sung grace. Daniel crossed himself and moved his lips piously in a gesture of thankfulness before sitting down.

He had poured himself a mug of coffee and then went to the temperamental machine that passed two slices of Mothers Pride on a wire conveyor between two heating elements, producing either a warmish, sweaty result after one pass or cinders after two. He had chosen the second, and was pressing fridge-cold butter onto a slice when he was joined opposite by a huge Orthodox monk. Romanian, he thought, for Ravenspurn had for many years enjoyed a cordial friendship with a monastery in Transylvania and bearded monks from that distant place were regular visitors.

With his old friendship with Paisie in mind, he smiled at his opposite neighbour, who did not smile back. Monks of that tradition were not noted for pleasantries, partly because monks have little use for them, and partly because it is not very Romanian. His friend Paisie had been baffled by English habits of courtesy and comedy. 'Why do you have to make a joke about everything?' he had once asked Daniel, who, most unusually, had no answer.

The monk had brought to the table a black coffee, which he had poured into a bowl, and a plate laden with inaccurately toasted bread. Daniel, silent but courteous, pushed into his reach the jam and the marmalade, home-made, and the Marmite, which came in a catering-sized tub. The monk looked at this stiff black paste with curiosity. Then he took a knife and helped himself to about a quarter of its contents, smearing it thickly on a slice of toast as if it were chocolate spread, which Daniel supposed he thought it was. He held up a hand in warning, but the monk ignored him, admiring this chocolatey treat, and took a huge bite.

If the refectory had not already been silent it would have fallen silent at that moment, for everyone was looking to see what effect a mouthful of Marmite would have on the monk.

It had none. He just chewed and gave no indication of surprise at all.

★

Champton St Mary was waking up. Neil Vanloo's white Escort, bound for Braunstonbury Police Station, passed Miss March's bronze Vanden Plas, parked outside Elite Fashions, the dress shop near the post office of which she was the new proprietor, or proprietress, as she preferred. It was already lit, for Anne Dollinger, Miss March's assistant, had arrived and put the kettle on, as she had done every working day for the previous proprietress, Stella Harper, until she was murdered.

The post office was open too, or rather the fags-and-mags end of the shop, where Mrs Braines switched between her twin roles of shopkeeper and public official. Her paper boy, Christian Staniland, had just returned from his round: *The Times* and the *Telegraph* for the big house and the rectory, the *Mail* for the Staveleys and the Porteouses, the *Guardian* for Jane Thwaite, the *Express* or the *Mirror* for the cottages on Death Row, as it was called, where former employees and tenants of the estate enjoyed the very last benefits of the de Floures' waning *noblesse oblige*. Christian had stopped at Gilbert Drage's for a mug of tea so brewed it could have tarnished diamonds. It had been fortified with a dash of Clan Dew and supplemented with a Player's No.6, a twin treat, which made Mr Drage's angry and unintelligible conversation endurable.

He said, 'I didn't know what to do with the rector's *Telegraph* and *Times*, Mrs Braines, with the fire and that, so I gave them to Mrs Shorely along with his lordship's, because they're staying at the big house.'

'All those years in the cubs paid off, Christian,' said Mrs Braines. 'I'd give you a badge if I had one.'

'But the rector's gone away, Mrs Shorely said. Unexpected, in the middle of the night.'

Mrs Braines looked up from her *Radio Times*. 'Gone away?'

'Yes, left a note for his lordship and for his mother.'

'I wonder what that's all about,' said Mrs Braines.

The door rattled open and the bell above it dinged. It was Dora Sharman with her little Jack Russell Scamper.

'Norah,' she said, 'I ent 'ad my *Mirror*.'

'Christian,' said Mrs Braines, 'what happened to Miss Sharman's paper?'

'I didn't have one.'

'Well, why didn't you say summat?'

'I don't mark them up, I just deliver them.'

Mrs Braines looked under the counter and produced a *Daily Mirror*, '14 Main' written across the top in thick 4B pencil.

'Here it is, Dora.' She tutted at Christian as if it were his mistake rather than hers. 'And the rector's gone AWOL.'

'AWOL?'

'Yes, Jean Shorely told Christian that he was called away in the night. Left a note for his lordship and for his mother.'

'Where to?'

'Nobody knows. Maybe it was something to do with the parson at Badsaddle?'

Dora thought for a moment. 'Doesn't sound like him at all.'

'No, I was just thinking the same, he's like clockwork.'

After breakfast the brethren gathered in the common room to read the papers and mark the end of the Greater Silence by discussing matters of the day if they wanted to, or just to sit in a personal continuing silence. Those to whom small talk is torture need not defend or explain silence in a monastery. Daniel was sitting in an armchair and picked up an untouched *Daily Telegraph* from the table, which made him suddenly start, for back in Champton his mother, whom he had abandoned with his moonlit departure last night, would be doing the same, turning first to the Court Circular to see what lay ahead for HRH Princess Alexandra, the Hon. Mrs Angus Ogilvy, or the Earl of Snowdon, or which ambassador would be presenting his credentials at the Court of St James's. A tut of frustration sounded behind him. He turned to see a monk, tall, in his sixties, with very short greying hair and narrowed eyes. It was Father Paulinus, the precentor, who led the singing of the psalms.

'Did you want the paper, Father?' asked Daniel.

'You beat me to it, Father,' he said and forced a smile. 'Take it, please.'

'No, you are our guest. It's yours.'

Daniel nodded, and started to read the front page, but instead of leaving him to it, the monk stood looking at him.

'I think you are Crispin?' He pronounced it Creespeen.

Daniel put the paper down. 'I was once,' he said. 'You are Paulinus? I remember you, of course, but you were not living here when I was.'

'No, I was at our sister community for a time. In Rhodesia, as we called it then. But I remember you from when I came back for chapter. Or rather, I remember your chant. It is very fine.'

'Thank you,' Daniel said. 'Yours is finer.'

'*Il miglior fabbro!* But that is no compliment.'

'No, I suppose not.'

'If I had done my job properly you would not have noticed anything special about me at all.'

'Forgive me, Father, I hear chant so rarely now, when I hear it done properly it moves me very much.'

'Ah, thank you.'

Daniel indicated the chair opposite. 'Will you join me?'

'I will.' He flicked the back of his scapular to the side and sat down.

Just as he did so, the succentor appeared, Father Dominic, who hovered at a distance too close to ignore but too distant to be involved.

'You wanted something, Father?' said Paulinus, with a note of irritation.

'So sorry to bother you Father, Father' – he nodded at Daniel – 'but what hymns do you want for St Willibrord, only I'm printing the slips and I need the numbers.'

'I am sure you are capable of choosing some hymns for the feast of a missionary.'

'Well, yes, but because of the connection with here I wondered if you might want something special?'

'He is a missionary, Father, not an apostle. It is not a day of obligation.'

Father Dominic stammered a bit. 'N–n–no, but I wanted to get it right . . .' He made to go but changed his mind, then changed it again, and was caught in a nervous pirouette.

'Are you all right, Father?' Paulinus asked.

'Yes. No. Not really.'

'What is the matter?'

'The novices are . . .'

'Tell me about the novices later.'

'And then there's . . . something nasty has happened, but you know about that.'

'I don't.'

'I think you do.' Dominic half muttered this, as if it were something he had to say but did not quite dare to.

Paulinus said, 'What did you say, Dominic?'

Dominic shook his head.

'Something disagreeable in the post? Bad news? A picture in the paper?'

Daniel saw Dominic was trembling, so he said, 'You're busy, I'll leave you to it—'

Paulinus interrupted. 'What hymns would *you* choose, Father?'

'I wouldn't dream of interfering . . .'

'In the parish, for the feast of a missionary saint?'

'We don't really go in for things in that way in the parish,' said Daniel, 'but for Mission Sunday we usually have "From Greenland's Icy Mountains" because the congregations love it. I hate it.'

'Then we shall have it here too, in honour of your visit.'

'Oh no, I don't think it would be suitable . . .'

'And I will tell everyone it is your choice.' He laughed but in rather a mean way. 'And you will play the organ for us, yes?'

'If you would like me to.' He glanced at Father Dominic, the precentor's deputy.

'Good,' said Paulinus. 'So, Dominic, we will have "From Greenland's Icy Mountains" as the processional hymn at Mass and choose something suitable for the Post Communion, and something for first and second Vespers.'

'But . . .'

'Thank you, Dominic. I need to speak to Father Daniel now.'

Dominic went red, then gave the nearest he got to

41

an outburst. 'Father, there are matters we need to discuss, and you must, really must, deal with it sooner or later, and—'

'Later, Dominic. Thank you.'

The succentor fell silent. Then he nodded and went away.

'He frets about the novices. He frets about *everything*. But especially the novices. It is the schoolmaster in him.'

'He looks like a schoolmaster,' said Daniel, thinking of his own prep school and the jittery men back from the war who would sometimes explode with mysterious rage to the delight of their schoolboy tormentors.

'Yes, an Old Calcottian. I understand that is rather something to be. He went as a boy, left to go to university, then came back as a master. Imagine that! He could have been a Mr Chips and spent his whole life there, then one day be found dead under a newspaper in the senior common room.'

'But he didn't. He came here.'

'Yes.'

'I wonder why.'

Paulinus said, 'Oh, the usual.' Then he seemed to check himself.

'The usual?'

Paulinus was silent for a moment, then with a note of reproach said, 'You would have to ask him about that.'

Daniel nodded at the implied rebuke, although he knew he had been enticed into the fault.

'You like to ask questions, Father,' Paulinus said. 'But then you are a famous detective.'

'I'm not a detective.'

'We read about you in the paper – when was it?'

'Ascensiontide.'

'*Viri Galilaei, quid statis aspicientes in coelum . . .*'

Daniel recognised the quote, from the antiphon for Ascension Day – '*Men of Galilee, why do you stand looking up to heaven?*' 'They weren't looking up to heaven in Champton, I'm afraid,' he said, 'but behind them, into a dark past.'

'So how did you bring that to light?'

'It started as an argument about a lavatory. And then a murder, and another murder and another.'

'And another.'

'You heard about that?'

'It is in the paper.'

Daniel said, 'Oh Lord . . .' and started to leaf through the pages.

'Not that paper, one of the tabloids, I don't remember which. One of our guests – Colin? Looks like a gnome? – brought it in to show us.'

'I think I encountered him this morning.'

'He's a scholar, of sorts. One of our long-staying guests. And has . . . How to put this? Inexhaustible curiosity.'

'I see.'

'Teenager murdered. Man arrested. Your curate.'

'Associate vicar.'

43

'You can see how that might arouse curiosity. And they mention you too. The Sherlock Holmes of the parish clergy.'

'Silly thing to say. I just saw what was in front of me and worked it out. Anyone would.'

'But it was you who worked it out. More than once. To what do you attribute this?'

'I hadn't really thought about it.'

'Yes, you have.'

Daniel thought for a moment. 'It was here. I learnt how to look at things. How to listen. Didn't you?'

'Yes, of course. But I live here.'

'So?'

'If there were a murder at Ravenspurn, there would be forty suspects; you know?'

Daniel smiled. '"*By this shall all men know that ye are my disciples, if ye have love one to another.*"'

'John, thirteen, thirty-five. It was the original motto of the community, but after six months they changed it to Matthew, twenty-four, thirteen.'

'"*He that shall endure unto the end, the same shall be saved.*"'

'Yes. You have not forgotten your studies?'

'My studies?'

'I read your paper on Matthew, twenty-four.'

'That puts you in a very exclusive club, Father.'

'The omission of "or the Son" in the Fı manuscripts . . . I forget the verse.'

'Twenty-four, verse thirty-six. You are a text critic?'

'Not especially, but I find the problem fascinating. And this sort of problem especially.'

'This sort of problem?'

'Why something is *not* there rather than why it *is* there. You think it a later addition?'

'Yes. But I can't remember why. A tension between the external and internal evidence. As I recall it came down to how much weight you gave to the number and distribution of manuscripts that omitted it and how much you gave to a scribe altering a text from theological necessity. It was a long time ago.'

'You do not keep up with your studies?'

'Not in any formal way. I don't have time.'

'But you still have the skills, I think. Looking to see what is not there rather than what is there?' He smiled.

Daniel thought for a moment. 'Yes, I suppose so.'

'I would like you to give a seminar to the novitiate.'

'A seminar? On what?'

'New Testament textual criticism.'

'Don't you have brethren better qualified than me to do that?'

'No. And you are such a *novelty*, Father.'

A novelty. Was that a jibe or a challenge? 'I don't know if I am even qualified to—'

'Yes, you are,' said Father Paulinus. 'I have a session with them this afternoon at three. And then we could have tea?'

'I suppose I could set out the basics . . .'

'Excellent.'

'I'll need handouts. Could someone do some photo-copying for me?'

'Give it to Dominic, tell him I said to.'

'All right.'

'The seminar room, then – you know where that is? Next to the library? – at three.' He stood up briskly, nodded, and was gone.

At the lodges on either side of the great gates that opened into the park at Champton House there were fitful signs of life. In the north lodge, which Alex de Floures, Bernard's second son, had commandeered for his use when he was home, a curtain flicked open. It was what he called the day pavilion, the lodge in which his sitting room and dining table and kitchen and studio were located. On the other side of the drive, in the south lodge, was his bedroom and bathroom and dressing room, and there he lay, still asleep. His boyfriend, Nathan Liversedge, unofficially promoted from his original post as assistant gamekeeper, was awake beside him. Nathan got out of bed and went for a pee. They had drunk too much last night and gone to bed too late. He pulled on a dressing gown tightly around him, tying its cord, and stepped into two sheepskin slippers left neatly in front of the night storage heater, then half ran across the drive to the north lodge. This caused the automatic mechanism that operated the park gates to crank into action and they swung wonkily open as if to admit a ghostly visitor.

46

He tapped on the door – 'Theo, it's me, Nathan!' – and went in before waiting for a reply. Theo Clement, Daniel's brother, was standing in the tiny 'drawing room' wearing nothing but a pair of white boxer shorts printed on the right leg with a logo Nathan recognised.

'Morning,' said Theo. 'I feel like shit.' He was holding a bowl half filled with last night's crisps and crunched a mouthful. 'Past their best,' he said, 'but maybe you've come to make me breakfast?'

'What's that on your boxers?'

'Oops,' said Theo. 'I was very drunk and off my tits and—' He looked down. 'Oh, you mean that?'

The logo showed two men's heads in silhouette printed in a roundel at the centre of the star.

'It's the Communards, I think. Well, not the actual Communards but their logo. I got them at one of their gigs – Hammersmith Odeon. Clever bit of merchandising.'

'Good gig?'

'Marvellous, I think. To tell you the truth, I was off my tits then too. I don't actually remember buying the pants. I woke up somewhere with them on. It was quite a complicated night.'

'So was last night.'

They had stayed up very late, drinking and experimenting with the magic mushrooms Theo had acquired for Bonfire Night.

'Yes. I'm surprisingly hungry, though.'

'I think we've got bacon,' said Nathan, 'and an egg.'

'Any coffee?'

'Tea.'

'Then tea, please.'

'Are you in a rush?'

'For what?'

'Do you have to be back in London anytime soon?'

Theo thought for a moment. 'What day is it?'

'Monday.'

'Nothing much on this week. Lunch with my agent. A voice-over on Wednesday. Maybe Thursday. Am I outstaying my welcome?'

'No. Not what I meant. I just wonder how people like you . . . live.'

'I'm an actor, Nathan. An artist, like Alex. It's not like a regular job.'

'He doesn't need a job.'

Nathan picked his way through the debris of the night before, collecting the ashtrays most urgently in need of emptying on his way to the kitchen. He moved in Alex's spaces, Theo observed, with more assurance and delicacy than he used to. Not that long ago he looked like a stevedore who had wandered into the Wallace Collection. But now he knew the difference between soft-paste and hard-paste porcelain and what a porringer was. Would Alex go off his own creation if he lost his rougher edges?

But that was some way off, he thought, when he saw Nathan hacking away at a loaf of bread. 'I'm not looking for cucumber sandwiches with the crusts cut off, Nathan, but this' – he picked up a slice the size of a breeze block – 'is a bit Stone Age. Try it like this.'

He took a breadknife, positioned it like a carpenter would his saw, and gently pulled it to and fro over the crust until it broke, then cut off a slice so thin it looked like lace.

Mrs Shorely put her head round the servants' hall door.

'Telephone for you, m'lord.'

'At this hour?'

'It's Bob Achurch.'

'What does he want?'

'I couldn't say, m'lord.'

Bernard, irritated by the interruption, made rather a show of getting up and followed Mrs Shorely out.

'It never stops,' said Audrey to Honoria. 'Piccadilly Circus!'

Honoria got up. 'I'll leave you alone, Audrey,' she said. 'I have to get going.'

'Before you do, Honoria, I wonder if you have any idea where Daniel may have got to?'

'Me? No. Why would I? Milk?'

'Yes, please, just a drop.' They both knew Honoria's reply was defensive. 'Only . . .'

'Only what?'

Audrey put down her cup. 'I don't want to overstep, dear, but is something . . . going on with Daniel?'

'What sort of thing?'

'I don't know. I do know his absence is completely

out of character. And you are so close. And with Neil.'

How Honoria's blush clashed with the red of her hair.

Bernard came back in. 'That was Achurch,' he said. 'Opened the church this morning for Matins but no rector. Doesn't know what to do. I don't suppose . . . you?' He looked at Audrey.

'Surely you, as patron?' she countered.

Bernard's temper flared. 'Do I look like I can tell my fucking psalm from my fucking epistle? That's why I have a rector. Where the hell is he?'

4

Daniel had gone for a walk. It was a cold, bright morning and a very faint scent of woodsmoke loitered in the air. He had been up for a couple of hours already, but the world beyond the monastery wall was only just stirring. The first buses of the day were heaving up the hill, a too-cheerful DJ wittered on from someone's wireless; beyond that was the building rumble of traffic on the new motorway, but not enough to drown out the perpetual whine and thump in the background.

Monk of habit, man of habit, he took the same route round the monastery grounds that he had taken when he was a novice. It went through the kitchen garden and the orchard, where the hens, liberated like the prisoners in *Fidelio*, clucked and scratched wherever they liked. He had looked after them when he was here – Scots Dumpies, chosen because they were a traditional breed, slightly comic with short legs and a waddling gait, and looked sober in black and grey. They were under threat also, required rescue, which appealed to the monks' charity, and were good both for laying and for meat, which appealed to their appetite.

The hens kept the monks in eggs but were not long destined for the pot because the more tender among the brethren had started naming them after saints and the thought of wringing the neck of Gertrude of Nivelles or Christina the Astonishing became impossible. They were allowed to run and scratch in the orchard and the gardens but ate everything that grew and annoyed the gardeners, and eventually there was a stand-off between the poultry novices and the nursery novices, and a chapter was called to settle it and a compromise reached. A run was built for them, fenced off from the rest of the gardens, with plenty of room for them to enjoy what people now called a free-range existence in a time when most hens were kept in awful battery farms that made Daniel think of Belsen. But despite the summoning call of the cockerel, there were no hens to be seen that morning; the run was deserted, the coop unstirred.

Beyond lay the silence of the Calvary, where departed brethren were buried, and beyond that a meadow and the woods, full of bluebells and ramsons in the spring, but now almost leafless and smelling of deciduous decay.

He turned and looked behind him to see the monastery, builded as a city that is compact together, as one of his favourite psalms had it. The community of Sts Philip and James had been started by half a dozen earnest and well-connected Anglo-Catholic curates in Oxford, who moved to Ravenspurn to witness to Jesus in the industrial North. The industrial North, had it been consulted, may have wondered about the usefulness of this, but as the years went by the community grew, built the enormous church, and was granted the dignity of an abbey. It was one of the first the Church of England had recognised since the dissolution of the monasteries, but nobody really knew how to do monasticism, so they made it up as they went along. This is not unusual in the Church of England, which began by making something up as it went along.

The monastery prospered in donations and vocations. At its height, when men returning from combat after the Second World War found that civvy street no longer served, it had built new wings to accommodate a swelling novitiate. Of the seeds sown, some fell on stony ground, some on thorny; some went mad, but some put down roots and the abbey had become a fixed feature in the life of the Church of England, restoring a dash of Catholic character to a Reformation experiment, like a tot of brandy in a cocoa.

In practice this meant gorgeous liturgy, fine scholarship, good preaching and a sort of ecclesiastical campery unique to the Anglo-Catholic tradition. That campery had here reached a high point. The sacristy, where its lovely and historic vestments were kept, was referred to as 'the boutique', the Comper altar with riddel posts and hangings as 'the Wendy House'; drag names were unofficially conferred on new brethren with their saints' names: Dark Mavis, Wobbly Wendy, Gloria Monday. When Daniel was there he had completed his thesis, that impenetrable work on a New Testament text, which earned him the name Trude the Obscure. There were still some of his cohort around, now serving in the Dales parishes of North Yorkshire, or the cathedral chapters of Wells and Truro, and one in the House of Bishops, who called him Trude.

The far side of the woods sloped down to border the monastery's land, marked by the river, which flowed fast down from the moor, so fast that industrious brethren seventy years ago had built a hydro-electric turbine to provide the community's light and power. This was the source of the perpetual thump and whine, heard faintly but distinctly wherever you were in the monastery grounds. Everywhere but here, close to, for the rushing of the water obscured it.

'Christians have always been innovators,' Father Aelred liked to say, but innovative new technology was imperfect, and the monastery's ancient wiring produced a light so dim and unreliable it would have irked a medieval monk transcribing the Epistle to the Galatians by tallow candles.

The machinery was housed in a stone and slate turbine house that looked like a small Cornish tin mine. Inside it was more Frankenstein's laboratory, with a panel of dials and switches against the wall and then a conglomeration of cogs and wheels connected to what looked like a giant ammonite's shell. In it was the turbine, driven by the force of the water tumbling down the moor and pounding into a water wheel beneath them, nature and machinery and electricity combining to create that relentless sound – so relentless the brain edited it out of consciousness. When Daniel was a novice one of his duties was to mind the turbine house under the supervision of the *custos lucis*, or the Prince of Darkness as the novices called him, and he had grown so used to it that even now, twenty-five years later, he did not notice the noise until he did.

Daniel pushed open the door and surprised a portly young man. He was in his twenties but with a fogeyish look, in old-fashioned round horn-rimmed glasses that made Daniel think of Billy Bunter, the Owl of the Remove, and wearing the blue scapular of a novice. It was gathered around his waist, but only just, by a leather belt, notched on a hole that had been crudely added to the row provided when the distance it enclosed grew too great. Little holsters and pouches and straps hung from it, holding a selection of screwdrivers, spanners and pliers. The ensemble seemed unfittingly butch for a man who was so startled to see Daniel he gave a squeak of surprise while his hand fluttered to his breast.

'Oh,' he said, 'you made me jump, Father!' sounding slightly reproachful.

'Daniel,' he said, raising his voice to be heard above

the whirr of the turning wheel and the rush of water below.

'Yes, I know, Father. You're the famous rector of Champton. I recognised you at Matins.'

'And you are?'

'Brother Bede. I'm one of the novices.'

'I was a novice here too. In fact, I used to assist the *custos lucis*.'

'*Custos* what?' said Bede.

'*Custos lucis*. The keeper of light. Don't you have one now?'

'I wish we did. There aren't so many of us now. Father Paulinus – he's the novice master – is in charge. Oh, *charge* . . . just noticed that.' Bede gave a little laugh.

'How many of you are there now?' Daniel asked.

'Six. Seven if you count the postulant, Darren. Darren!' He rolled his eyes. 'That will have to go.'

'What were you before you were Bede?'

'Adrian. Dates me, doesn't it? What were you when you were here?'

'Crispin. After the patron of shoemakers.'

'We have another Crispin now. What a load of cobblers.'

Daniel smiled politely at a joke he had heard many times before. 'Why Bede?'

'Historian, like me.'

'Church history?'

'No, modern. At Magdalen. Are you an Oxford man?'

'Not really,' Daniel said.

'The other place?' Bede gave a sectarian grimace.

'*An*other place,' replied Daniel.

'Where?'

Daniel was beginning to be slightly annoyed by the novice's demanding curiosity. 'Why do you want to know, Bede?'

'God, not the LSE?'

Daniel said nothing, for he did not want to satisfy Bede's nervy desire to mark him by a checklist of things of which he approved and disapproved. It was not unusual for novices of Ravenspurn to do this, because so many of them had entered a world of greater distinction than the world they had come from and felt the need to express their credentials for being there. He often thought it peculiar that so many who had elected to live the monastic life, and therefore rejected worldly prestige, should jostle on that ladder. He changed the subject.

'What's your field?'

'*Götterdämmerung.*'

'The opera?'

'No, the Dual Monarchy after Trianon,' said Bede.

'How very unfashionable.'

'I hope so. Are you an historian?' Bede asked.

'My academic field, when I had one, was New Testament textual criticism. In fact, I'm talking to the novitiate about it this afternoon. So brace yourselves.'

'Where did you do that?'

'A lot of it here,' Daniel replied. 'I wrote most of my thesis in the library.'

'I don't know how you found the time. I never seem to get a minute. Too busy being Martha rather than Mary. And keeping an eye on this.'

Bede turned and looked at the dials on one of the panels. It made Daniel think of someone visiting a patient in intensive care looking thoughtfully at the screens around the bed as if they understood what they meant.

'It's been a bit of a beast lately,' said Bede. 'It keeps cutting out, so I'm keeping an eye on it. Father Paulinus thinks I have a natural gift.'

'*Ora et labora?*'

'Oh, yes, prayer and work, the twin themes of our life. It will take both I think to ensure a steady supply of current. And there'd better not be a power cut tonight. It's *Birds of a Feather* after Compline. Are you watching it?'

'I think my mother likes it. It's new?' Daniel asked.

'Yes. The brethren love it. It's like *EastEnders* only not so tragic. Are you staying in the monastery?'

'The guest house.'

'I'm sure you'd be welcome in the calefactory if you want to watch it with us,' Bede offered.

'I'm on retreat. Or I'm meant to be,' said Daniel.

'Oh, forgive me, Father, are you observing silence?'

Daniel shrugged. 'I rather thought I was. But it isn't turning out that way.'

'Oh, I'm sorry . . .'

'Don't be sorry. I'm not the rigorist I used to be.' When he was a new novice he was so punctilious about keeping silence he had tried to use sign language if necessity required him to pass on a message, until one day Father Aelred said it was more distracting than watching Marcel Marceau trying to raise the alarm in a fire.

Brother Bede seemed displeased by this confession of slacking. He nodded and turned without a word back to the panels.

In Champton St Mary, Miss March and Anne Dollinger were preparing to open for business. Elite Fashions, the new iteration of Stella's High Class Ladies' Fashion, was smartly situated in the row of shops opposite the gates to Champton House. Some of the customers were already known to Miss March from her former shop, March & March of Stow, selling shoes in the shadow of that city's great cathedral.

Not all, though, so she decided that Anne, Stella's faithful lieutenant in both the shop and Champton's Flower Guild, should be kept on when she took over after Stella fell victim to a poisoned slice of walnut cake. Anne's continued employment was partly a charity, for she was grief-stricken following that dreadful event, and partly in Miss March's self-interest, for who the customers were, but also how things worked, whom to talk to at the wholesaler's and when the van came. The benefits this conferred, however, were balanced by costs, and Miss March, who had run the shoe shop with crisp efficiency, had felt obliged to be clear about where the boundaries lay between employer and employee.

Anne was meek by nature and had found it easy to mould to Stella's command, but Miss March was not Stella, and when those boundaries had to be clarified Anne shied away like a faun, which Miss March found more irritating than resentment. She had almost lost her temper when Anne brought her a mug of Lift for elevenses one morning rather than the cup of Camp coffee she preferred, 'because Mrs Harper found it refreshing and there's the end of a jar to finish'.

'I am NOT Mrs Harper,' said Miss March, reminding herself of the new Mrs de Winter in *Rebecca* imposing regime change on Mrs Danvers as Anne whimpered and reversed back into the kitchen.

This morning they were awaiting the delivery of dresses from Tricoville, which Miss March thought a little flimsy and incorrect as the autumn turned to winter, but Anne had been adamant that they would sell. There was some paperwork to prepare and suddenly, from nowhere, Miss March recalled doing the same with her father at the shoe shop, awaiting the van from Tricker's with its cargo of Oxfords and brogues and a Derby boot that Mr March thought might catch the eye of the better sort of countryman. He had been right; they had sold very handsomely indeed. Perhaps that was why she suddenly felt a stab of grief. It was two years since he had died of a heart attack after confronting some yobs in the street, a loss still so enormous and so painful she could only admit it in fragments, but it was always there, waiting to overwhelm her, and it did at that moment. She made no sound, but tears began to flow down her face, as unlikely as water from the rock at Meribah, for she seemed invariably composed.

It was unfortunate that Anne Dollinger appeared from the kitchen at that moment with her coffee. Miss March had her back to her.

'Miss March? Your coffee?'

'Just put it down on the counter, would you, Anne?'

'I think we are going to need to reorder gloves—'

'Not just now, Anne—'

'Only the van's coming this morning and we can catch him before he leaves if we call now . . .'

Miss March took a handkerchief from the sleeve of her grey cardigan and tried in as unobtrusive a way as possible to dab at her face.

'Oh,' said Anne, 'are you . . .?'

For her distress to be revealed to Anne Dollinger was bad enough, but when she turned to face her, Anne was so surprised and so affected by her tears that she said, 'Kimberley, whatever is the matter?'

Distress yielded instantly to fury. 'I beg your pardon?'

'You're crying.'

'What did you call me?'

'Kimber— I'm sorry, Miss March.'

But it was too late.

★

Honoria was at the south lodge. She was waiting for her brother to wake up properly. The room was stuffy without being warm, stale with cigarette smoke, and smelled of debauchery. She pulled the curtains apart and hoisted the sash window, so infrequently opened it made a grinding sound, and a draught of piercingly cold air rushed into the room.

'Fuck off, darling, would you?' Alex said, but slowly lifted himself up on his pillows. He was wearing his favourite T-shirt, Julien Temple's half-naked cowboys, and she thought again how ill-suited punk fashion was to his genetic inheritance. 'Get Nathan to make me my coffee,' he said, 'and pass me my dressing gown.'

She took it from the hook and threw it at him. 'I'm coming back.' Then she crossed the drive and let herself in to the north lodge.

'Morning,' she said. 'You both look disgusting.' She opened the curtains and half opened the windows. Theo and Nathan recoiled like vampires from sunlight.

'Thank you,' said Theo. 'Is Alex awake?'

'He is now, and he wants his coffee. Nathan, he wants you to make it.'

'It's nearly done. He's partic'ler,' said Nathan and went into the kitchen.

'*Partic'ler*,' said Honoria. 'It's like an episode of *The Archers*. Looks like you made a night of it.'

'I found some leftover magic mushrooms. And after

all that drama last night . . . A quieter night at the house, I hope?'

'There's been a little drama this morning.'

'What's happened?'

'Your brother has gone missing. Called away in the middle of the night, left a note for your mother and Daddy.'

'The police? Something to do with the murder?'

'Don't think so . . .'

'Neil would have said something, wouldn't he?' Theo said.

Honoria looked at him. 'How would I know?'

Theo said nothing.

'And he's gone *away* – away away – but didn't say where or for how long. Does that sound like Daniel?'

'That's not him at all. Perhaps he's finally done something spontaneous?'

'Oh, that's not good,' said Honoria.

'Isn't it?'

'I don't want spontaneity from Daniel.'

Theo thought about this for a moment. 'There is a real person in there, you know? With feelings and desire and uncertainty.'

'Stop it, Theo . . .'

'Don't we all?'

'You'll be telling me next there was once a sweet-heart but the match was forbidden by her father, or she was eaten by a lion, or became a nun . . .'

'It was Daniel who took the veil, not the sweetheart.'

'What do you mean?'

'He was a monk for a while. Didn't you know?'

'Oh, yes, I think I did. Somewhere up North. Didn't last?'

'Only a couple of years.'

'Did he jump over the wall?'

'That's actually a saying, you know, when a monk doesn't qualify or whatever they call it. He jumped the monastery wall. But it wasn't so startling. He just turned up one day and said it wasn't his vocation after all and he went back into the parish.'

Honoria looked thoughtful. 'Does that happen a lot?'

'Jumping the monastery wall? I suppose it must, or it wouldn't be a saying.'

'Doesn't sound like Daniel.'

Nathan appeared in the doorway with a mug of coffee. 'Hon, do you want to take it to him?'

Daniel's walk took him back through the woods and up a hill to the dry-stone wall built along the ridge, which overlooked the fields beyond the monastery's land. It reminded him of the outer wall of a medieval castle, a line of defence between those settled within and the invaders without. In the dark ages monasteries had been fortresses, protecting learning and civilisation from marauders who cared only for the cheap treasure of gold and silver, not the lasting treasure of heaven. He thought the same in his own time, when thieves came by night to strip the lead from a church's roof when they could walk in through the door by day in front of everyone and receive a gift worth immeasurably more.

Weak sunlight was breaking through the thready low clouds, making the river flash and the colours of earth and evergreen perk up. He thought of the devil taking Jesus up to the mountaintop and showing him the Earth and offering it to him if he would only . . .

It was not only marauders that needed to be kept out. It was the temptation of a life lived beyond the wall, out in the world, with its sweetness and its bitterness, and its possibilities of change and of glory and of wounds. That had to be left behind when you entered the cloister. At their first meeting Aelred had said choosing this life meant unchoosing all others, for it demanded everything. No comfort, no delight, no freedom, no intimacy. Give it everything and what did it give you? A stony road to a hill, on top of the hill a cross, but beyond it a life transformed. That made perfect sense when he was a young and earnest student, full of piety and passion.

He remembered, with sudden clarity, his first visit.

He was sitting on an uncomfortable armchair upholstered in a plain worn canvas, with a slightly crispy antimacassar that gave a genteel note to the utility feel not only of the furniture, but also the room, a small office, lit by leaded windows, hung with unlined curtains. There was lino the colour of oxtail soup on the floor, and the walls looked like skin on a custard. The door opened and he stood up as a monk in a black cassock and scapular came in. He squinted through his glasses at Daniel and then at the door. He moved the sliding label on the outside to show OCCUPIED, then closed the door and sat down in the armchair opposite.

'Sit down, my dear,' he said in an Old Etonian accent. 'I am Father Aelred. And you are Mr Clement? From King's College London?'

'Yes, Father.'

'And what brings you to Ravenspurn?'

'I think I should like to try my vocation to monastic life.'

'Oh, how marvellous. And what makes you think you might have a vocation to *our* monastic life?'

'Recommended, Father. And there aren't that many Church of England Benedictine monasteries.'

'There are two,' said Father Aelred. 'Hartley Mauditt and us. Have you tried there?'

'No, I think I like the sound of here better.'

'The sound? Goodness.'

'And the dean thought it a better fit.'

'Oh, yes, dear Sydney. He would be very keen for you to try us out. But what about you? What do you think?'

'I think I might be a monk.'

'Why?'

'I like plainsong. I like prayer. I like monasteries.'

'And you could see yourself in this monastery singing and praying?'

'Yes. In theory.'

'And in practice?'

'I expect it's not just about singing and praying.'

'I expect not,' said Father Aelred. 'Really, it's about lots of things. Everything. And if you choose this – perhaps this chooses you? – then you must unchoose everything else. And if you do that, then at that moment comes the death of who you were before. I sometimes think of us as the walking dead.'

'Aren't we baptised into the death of Jesus so we can rise with him into new life?'

'Isn't that a lovely image? And how that might make you want to sing and pray! You can do that anywhere, of course. I wonder what else there may be that makes you think you should sing and pray with us, here?'

'I'm not sure I could put it into words.'

'Such an interesting answer. Because you cannot or because you do not want to?'

'I don't know.'

'You see, it surprises me that people still want to come to places like this. This world seems so full of enticements and possibilities. Everything opening up, a new era is upon us – the Beatles, Ban the Bomb, cheese and onion crisps. It is the Age of Aquarius, or so I was told by a Gnostic who was here the other day. You are twenty-two? Twenty-three? Why don't you want to be part of that?'

Daniel thought for a moment. 'I'm not sure it's for everyone.'

Father Aelred sighed and looked out of the window, which was fringed, Daniel noticed, by pink roses. 'If I were twenty now I think I would want to be part of that.'

'Forgive me, Father, but I can't really see you doing the Twist,' said Daniel.

'Perhaps not, but like most people who have lived a very buttoned-up life, Mr Clement, I imagine in age what an unbuttoned youth would have been like. And who I would be if I'd had one.'

Daniel felt suddenly self-conscious in his dark suit, his only suit, worn for high and holy days, a ruthlessly knotted college tie around his neck and shiny black Oxfords on his feet.

Father Aelred looked back at him. 'But my generation was formed not by peace but by war. My father came home from the first war silent. He never spoke about it. I wish I had spoken to him before he died, but . . . he never spoke about anything apart from cricket. And then I was a padre in the next war. I buried I don't know how many young men after Salerno. I dug graves for some of them too. What I remember most clearly was the ghastly sound of shells whistling through the air. And then . . . BOOM!' He extended his hands in a sort of explosive gesture. 'We lost some boys to our own artillery, you know?' Then he was silent for a moment. 'So when I came back I came here. It made sense. It has to make sense, you see, Mr Clement. Not just singing and praying.'

'I think I could love people if I were here,' said Daniel.

Father Aelred looked at him. 'Yes, that makes sense. If you can't love people the other way.'

They sat in silence. Then the bell rang to summon the brethren to church. Father Aelred got up and said, 'We had a vine dresser staying here a while ago – imagine, a vine dresser in the 1960s? – and we decided to plant a vine and asked for some advice about where we should put it, and do you know what he said? He said, "Dig where the shit is." May I give you a blessing?'

Honoria was sitting at the end of Alex's bed, facing him, topping and tailing like they used to do in the nursery. He had hoisted himself up sufficiently to handle the mug of coffee his sister had brought him. It steamed in the barely heated bedroom, now colder because of the draught from the open window.

'Did you tell Theo?' she said.

'Tell him what?'

'About me and Neil.'

'I can't remember *everything* I say,' said Alex.

'I asked you not to tell anyone. Especially not Theo.'

'Why did you tell me, Hon, if you didn't want others to know?'

'I thought perhaps I could rely on your discretion.'

'Oh, please!' Alex took another sip. 'I don't know if I told Theo or not. God knows what I said last night.

God knows if he'll remember. But, darling, if I guessed, why wouldn't he?'

'Because you're the expert in keeping secret love affairs secret. Theo would give his clap clinic results to the milkman.'

He took a sip of coffee. 'Why is this suddenly so important?'

Honoria thought for a moment. 'Daniel's gone AWOL. Left a note for Daddy. And another for Audrey. He was called away in the night, doesn't say where, doesn't say why, doesn't say when he'll be back.'

'That doesn't sound like Daniel.'

'No, it doesn't. And how could someone have contacted him in the middle of the night?'

'It's the kind of thing Daniel *would* say if he was being punctilious about not disclosing something he could not disclose. So boring when he does that.'

'That's what I was thinking. But there is *something*. Last night Neil told him about him and me.'

'Why? Where?'

'After the Evensong *in memoriam* thing. Neil said he needed a word in private – isn't it awful when someone says that? – so they went to the rectory, all wreathed in soot and water damage, and he . . . confessed.'

'I suppose Daniel *already* knew. Mystically.'

'No, Neil said he had no idea. Actually he was flabbergasted. So he told him all about it, how we got together, the assignations, declared his undying love for me and all that. And Daniel was so affected he embraced him. A hug! From Daniel! Gave him his blessing, literally. And Neil came running home like a little boy who'd just seen Father Christmas.'

Alex took a cigarette from the pack on his bedside table. 'Thought so.'

'Thought so what?'

'Come on, Hon.'

'Now *you're* being mystical.'

5

Daniel had a vague unfocused fear that one day he would go back to Ravenspurn and discover that its attraction had gone, like a magnet that had lost its powers. It had never happened; even when he felt most distant from the cloister, he only had to smell boiled celery, carbolic, the unlaundered smorgasbord of an old monk's scapular, to fall back into its routine. It was more a regime than a routine, he thought, a rule of prayer and work and leisure and sleep, timetabled by the horarium and mapped by the boundary wall, the cloister, the church, the Calvary, the vegetable garden. The constraints gave a paradoxical liberty, freedom from the necessities of earning a living, providing for a family, going to the golf club – stone walls do not a prison make, nor iron bars a cage.

There were those at Ravenspurn who already knew about the deprivation of liberty. They came and went, appearing in the refectory, or working in the fields and gardens and workshops, people who did not come to church and had no obvious connection to its life. They were former prisoners, disowned by their past, with nowhere to go on release. Once a guest on retreat had recognised a temporary resident, a man who had committed a notorious crime, and whose release had been luridly reported by a newspaper. The two were put on garden duty together, but the guest had refused to work alongside him and went to see the then abbot. He complained that he did not want to 'live and sleep and *pray* next to someone evil', to which the abbot replied that neither did the other man so they might as well get used to it. 'Sinners all, sinners all,' said Father Aelred in the sing-song way that meant there was no more to be said.

Daniel was in the crypt chapel, beneath the church, where he sought to follow Our Lord's injunction to find an inner room and pray there.

He had spent all his years of ministry soliciting invitations into other people's inner rooms, to see what troubled them, what strengthened them, but mostly what they were most anxious to keep behind a locked door. You get a knack for this, and Daniel had acquired a reputation as a confessor with an almost supernatural ability to see into the contents of a troubled soul. In reality, it was simpler than that. People tend to mess up their lives in the same ways – sex, money, violence, addiction – and the effects create patterns of behaviour, which become recognisable. Occasionally a visitor sitting on the Sofa of Tears in his study revealed something unpredictable. Sometimes he would pretend to tidy things up at the back of the church to be near to the person who sat alone there for too long, and a surprise would come from them.

Physician, heal thyself. So much easier to open the door to another's inner room than to open your own. He sometimes thought confessors became confessors to silence the knocking and rustling from their own inner rooms. Our determination not to hear may for a while keep them where we want them, but most people sooner or later surrender and open the door. What do we find?

We fear we will discover a horror, like the Monster of Glamis, a terrible creature we lock away in a secret chamber, but keep alive because we think we have to. There was a story that a new Lady of Glamis heard about the legend of a monstrous figure confined some-where in the castle – the true heir it was said – but no matter how thoroughly she looked she could never find the hidden room. So when her husband was away she got the servants to draw all the curtains in every room. Then she got on her horse and rode round the castle. One window was uncurtained. She never found the room it belonged to.

Daniel liked this story. The uncurtained window was a nice illustration of how a disrupted external pat-tern can reveal a hidden inner truth – when people were not telling him what they needed to tell him the eyes usually betrayed what the tongue did not. But what he liked most about it was what the story did not tell.

In the legend the room was undiscovered, the monster undisturbed. In his ministry people sometimes did find the room and open the door, and what they found was not a monster but themselves.

Daniel had opened the door of his inner room and found on the other side his own self looking back at him, in itself enough to wrench the heart, but what caused him to lose his composure was what he was wearing – not the sober vestments of a cleric, but the motley of a clown.

Ridiculous.

He let out a breath that was almost a sob.

'Are you all right?'

Daniel pretended to cough. He turned and saw a man standing behind him. It was the man with the white hair and beard from the stand-off at Matins. He was dressed in the sort of clothes worn by people who have no idea about clothes – or who have not had to think about what they wear for so long that they wear anything.

'I didn't want to disturb you, but . . .'

'I'm fine, thank you,' Daniel said, 'just a bit . . . verklempt.'

'The charism of tears. One of the *rarest* of the gifts of the Holy Spirit.'

'Not that, no. Not one of my gifts *at all*.'

'My name's Colin.'

'Daniel.'

'We got off on the wrong foot this morning. May I?' Colin sat down before Daniel could reply. 'The Bishop of Durham has the charism of tears. He cries when he preaches. Have you ever seen it? It's rather affecting.'

'No. In fact, I find it unnerving.'

'Not one for the gifts of the Spirit?' Colin enquired.

'Not the showier ones, no.'

'Oh, yes, the showier ones. That's part of it, I think. Margery Kempe – you know who I mean?'

'Yes,' said Daniel with a note of impatience.

'She cried buckets,' said Colin, not noticing, 'but tears were a sort of mark of authenticity; they gave her authority. If you were a fourteenth-century woman in Norfolk, no one really took any notice of you. Not an issue for the Bishop of Durham, of course.'

'Perhaps. I'm not so sure now. About people noticing the Bishop of Durham . . .'

'They said it was his doubts about the Resurrection that caused the lightning to strike York Minster . . .'

'Well, yes, the sillier kinds of newspaper would notice that,' said Daniel.

Colin seemed quite rehearsed on this subject. 'All the same, I thought it extraordinary that one of the most senior bishops of the Church should describe the Resurrection as a "conjuring trick with bones".'

'He didn't say that,' Daniel interjected. 'He said exactly the opposite, that the Resurrection was *not* a conjuring trick with bones. And he wasn't then the bishop.'

'All the same, all the same . . .' muttered Colin.

Daniel decided to change the subject. 'Are you interested in Margery Kempe?'

'Not especially. She crops up.'

'In what?'

'My research.'

Colin the scholar, Colin the long-stay guest with the inexhaustible curiosity. He looked, Daniel thought, like Bernard's antisocial cat Jove with his fur up in a hostile frizz.

'You're an academic?' Daniel asked.

'Yes.'

'Church history?'

'Systematics,' Colin said.

'Oh, at King's?'

Colin smiled. 'I'm an independent academic. Published, I might add. My field is the relationship between spiritual authority and political authority.'

'An enormous topic.'

'Yes, but a fascinating one. I've been working on Queen Liliuokalani of Hawaii. Are you aware of her?'

'Barely,' said Daniel, aware that he was about to learn more.

'Brought up by Presbyterian missionaries – rather a mix, actually. After she lost her kingdom in 1893, she became Church of England, or the Hawaiian version of it. Some say she later became a Mormon. Have you noticed how often deposed monarchs become terribly religious?'

Daniel thought about it for a moment. 'Yes, I have. Lose a kingdom in this world, set your sights on the kingdom of the next?'

'Yes. It's why the pope granted himself infallibility, I think. Because he lost the Papal States and had to make up for it somehow.'

'That's a rather colourful way of putting it.'

Colin took that as a compliment and gave a little nod. 'And your field?'

'I don't really have one,' said Daniel. 'It was New Testament, but I'm a parish priest now.'

'Actually, I knew that. New Testament textual criticism. You're giving a talk to the novitiate this afternoon. It sounds fascinating.'

'I find it fascinating.'

'I wonder if I might come?' Colin asked.

'I'm sure that would be fine. Perhaps ask the novice master, Father Paulinus?'

'I notice you wear the novice's habit, Father.'

'I was a novice here, years ago,' Daniel explained.

'So what brings you back?'

'Oh, you know, a twitch upon the thread.'

'Isn't that from *Father Brown*?' Colin asked.

'It is.'

'My favourite priest-detective. Obvious, when you think about it.'

'What is?' Daniel asked.

'A priest as a sleuth. It comes with the job, don't you think?'

'So they say.'

'Well, you would know, Father,' Colin went on. 'I mean, you get everywhere. You see the best of people and the worst of people. You constantly have to work out why things happen. Or don't happen. Everyone confesses things. But perhaps that is only in the Roman Catholic priesthood?'

'Not that different, at least in the senses you just listed.'

'But you, I think, do not have the same relationship to people – with marriage, children, vicarage life. The Roman discipline removes all those distractions. You are alone in the world. And that perhaps sharpens your focus, or I imagine it . . . are you all right?'

The gift of tears.

'So sweet of you,' said Audrey, her words rather lost to the yapping of Hilda, the mewling of the puppies and the hissing of Jove, who had retreated to a higher shelf in Bernard's bookcase.

She and Mrs Shorely were standing in the doorway to the study. Mrs Shorely was holding the whelping box, now puppy nursery, in which the three were squirming while in transit. Hilda, anxious, was circling the study, a security sweep, Cosmo behind her.

'I'm not fucking Crufts,' Bernard muttered.

'*So* sweet, only I simply have to get to the post office and Honoria's gone out and Mrs Shorely has to do the bedrooms. I shall be no time at all!'

'What am I supposed to do with the fucking cat?'

'Keep it well away, if I were you. Nature red in tooth and claw!'

Audrey gave a little wave and as she went to leave Jove shot past her, a streak of white, as Mrs Shorely closed the door on Cosmo's sudden barrage of yapping. 'The old Adam,' she thought, but had no time to worry about the eternal enmity of dogs and cats, for she had to get to the post office to be absolutely sure to catch the next post. She was not sure how it worked with the collection and delivery of post at the big house, and she did not particularly want Mrs Shorely to see on the hall table the address on the front of the envelope – *The Abbey of Sts Philip and James, Ravenspurn, Yorkshire.*

'There goes your mama . . .' said Alex, looking out of the window at Audrey's briskly walking figure passing through the park gates and into Main Street.

'Which way?' said Theo, checking his boxers from reflex lest more of him was on show than he could bear to countenance if his mother were to suddenly appear.

'Post office, I think,' said Alex. 'She's holding a letter. I hope she's not still offering clairvoyancy by correspondence.'

'That's too good, isn't it?' said Honoria. 'But I don't understand why she thought it a good idea.'

'Money,' said Theo, once he'd ascertained all was safely gathered in. 'Or lack of it. They're very hard up.'

'Are they?' said Alex, sounding surprised.

'Yes. I know it's a struggle for you to understand, Alex, but most people don't have inherited wealth to spend and estates to replenish it.'

'I *so* adore it when you go all lefty. And in your Communards pants. I just thought . . . wasn't your father a manufacturer of some sort?'

'Shoes. Boots and shoes. Family firm. Went up the swanny. Nothing left now. Mum has a small pension and Daniel gets a pittance for a stipend.'

'I thought our parsons lived rather well.'

'In the old days. When there was such a thing as a good living. Not now. They all get paid the same and it's barely enough to run a lawnmower, let alone a Queen Anne rectory.'

'But what an irony,' said Honoria, 'that while no one comes to church and the parson starves, Audrey should be raking it in providing supernatural services through the post.'

'Not any more. I think there was rather a show-down,' said Theo.

'With who?' Honoria asked.

'Daniel. Mum said she'd never seen him so angry.'

'Daniel angry? I can't imagine what that looks like.'

'It's not exactly volcanic, but you can tell because he blinks.'

Nathan said, 'So that's why he's gone.'

Theo looked surprised. 'Oh . . . yes, I hadn't thought of that. Maybe.'

'A fall-out with Audrey?' said Honoria, mugging a sceptical look.

'What else could it be?'

Daniel normally found that prayer came to him quite naturally. As a parish priest he had managed to preserve enough of the monastic discipline he had acquired at Ravenspurn to feel he only had to turn on a tap and it would flow. Occasionally the flow was unsteady, the tap reluctant to budge, or giving forth a dribble rather than a spurt, but it had always produced something.

Now there was nothing. He had dutifully sung the psalms and canticles at Matins, he had knelt in silence and alone in front of the sacrament, he had repeated and repeated the Jesus Prayer, he had slowed his breathing, he had made intercession for those people he was obliged to pray for, but there was nothing. It was not even the right kind of nothing, the nothing that answers a dishonest prayer. His prayer was heartfelt, heartbroken, and he wanted more than anything the strange returns that surprised and challenged him. Nothing. It was as if he were deaf, mute, sightless.

After half an hour of this he decided to go into town

to seek its distractions. He went to his room in the guest house and changed out of his cassock. He paused for a moment, then decided not to put on a dog collar but a normal shirt, because he did not want to stand out, he did not want to represent anything. He remembered how differently he had felt when he was first ordained and would wear his dog collar to put the bins out, so excited to be seen in this new role. What he could not see now was what others saw plainly: that he was no less clerical in mufti, for he had become so habituated to the role that he would still look like a vicar if he put on a tutu and a sporran.

Ravenspurn itself spread along the valley south of the monastery, a little town that could never really grow much, for it was hemmed in by moors and the river and the railway and the canal. It had crept a little over the lower slopes, a few streets of Victorian terraces when the wool mills arrived, a ribbon of council houses beyond them when the Second World War receded, but it had hardly changed at all, he thought, from when he had first seen it twenty-five years ago.

At the bottom of the hill the town began, tentatively at first, with the garage – more a sort of shanty than the neon-bright ensemble that sat on the outskirts of Braunstonbury. Its little fleet of second-hand Escorts and Granadas looked unfashionably boxy even to Daniel, who normally would not be able to tell a Datsun Cherry from a Hispano-Suiza. There was a bus stop, an Indian restaurant – that was new – and then a little parade of hairdresser's, off-licence, post office and a shop that seemed to be selling window frames. 'DOUBLE GLAZING' shrieked the sign on the van parked outside – a home improvement his mother secretly longed for as they shivered in the draughty rectory, but he did not mind a draught to preserve the elegance of its windows, even if they were rotting, and his mother would sooner sit naked than admit that it would take more than an extra jumper to check the creeping cold.

The Co-op had upgraded itself to a 'superstore', which promised, Daniel thought, temptations beyond the expectations of its thrifty clientele. The architecture was peculiar, like a warehouse pretending to be a Tudor market square, and he went in past corralled shopping trolleys that looked like they were tethered to each other with reins. Inside there were exotics – yoghurt, courgettes, orange juice – alongside potatoes and mince and marrowfat peas; so much choice he felt for a moment like one of the Romanian monks seeing the menu at a Golden Egg for the first time. Against his better nature, which was trying to enforce the disciplines of retreat, he bought *The Times* and took it to the café he used to visit when he was a novice on his day off, the Kozy Korner.

He loved it then because it was a reminder of the world outside the monastery, where people who were not obliged to tune their lives to abbey bells went for a mug of tea and two slices and talked about Don Revie rather than Polycarp of Smyrna. It wasn't busy, but he found a little table at the back, left his paper there and went to order a tea.

Once he'd sat down, he looked at the news without really looking, his eye falling only on an article about the demonstrations in East Germany, people on the streets in terrible clothes and haircuts, shaking the unshakeable regime of the German Democratic Republic. Another anticipated the rather less momentous debate about the ordination of women scheduled for the General Synod of the Church of England the next day. Less momentous but rancorous and divisive in Daniel's world. Whatever the Synod decided it would not settle the matter, and he feared that the Church's sad divisions, far from ceasing, would only deepen. What would that mean for him, with friends and loyalties on both sides of the argument? The thought of his no-longer-steady world being shaken again was too much and he put the paper down.

'Crispin? It is Crispin?'

A woman was looking at him from another table. She was in her seventies, he thought, but her hair was blonder than nature allowed and she was dressed in a lilac shell suit, which looked unusually athletic considering the rasp of her voice. It was the voice he recognised.

'Alma?'

'Hello, love,' she said. 'I knew it were you. You're famous now. I should ask for your autograph.'

'Alma, how lovely to see you.'

'What brings you back to Ravenspurn, my lad? Sorry, I should call you Father.'

'Call me anything you like, Alma, but Daniel is my name now. Can I join you?'

'I'll join you. On the naughty table.' She gathered her packet of cigarettes and lighter and house keys and dropped them on the little table Daniel had chosen at the back so they spread like tokens thrown by a witch doctor divining the future.

'So, why?' Alma asked.

'I'm just visiting.'

'Trying to get away from all the hoo-hah in your parish? Poor little lad. I hear his throat were cut from ear to ear.' She drew her finger across her own, which had grown more wattled, Daniel noticed, than when she had worked as a cleaner at the monastery when he was a novice. But he could think of nothing to say.

'Horrible, horrible thing. Are you OK, love?'

He started to cry.

'Oh, now I've gone and made you cry. I'm sorry, love, I should have thought.'

'Please don't be kind to me,' he said and waved his hand as if he were batting away the surge of sadness that had enveloped him.

'I'm getting you another tea.'

She went up to the counter and Daniel tried to compose himself, but he could not stop. Tears came and his shoulders shook and there was nothing he could do about it, except to jam himself into the corner and turn away from the embarrassed glances of the ladies of Ravenspurn, distracted for a moment from their vanilla slices and fat rascals.

'Are we to have cake?' said Alma, reappearing with two mugs of tea. 'Yes, I think we are. Nellie's parkin could raise Lazarus.'

He took the mug of tea and slurped it like an accident victim being treated for shock. It was so sweet he almost choked, and that was enough to stop the sobbing by the time Alma returned with a plate and two slices of parkin.

'Butter or as it comes, love?'

'As it comes.'

The parkin, a sturdy sort of gingerbread, came apart in Daniel's fingers. He thought for a moment of breaking the consecrated bread of the Eucharist and it made him start to cry again.

Alma said nothing until the wave of sadness subsided. 'What's going on, love?'

Daniel started to say something but could not find the words, so he stuffed a piece of parkin in his mouth instead.

'Oh, I know what's wrong with you. Someone's gone and broken your heart, haven't they?'

'I don't know, Alma.'

'Yes, you do.'

'I feel so ridiculous.'

She sat back in her chair. 'You're not looking your normal unruffled self.' She took a cigarette from the packet, lit it, and squinted at him through the curl of smoke. 'But there was always something about you that needed a bit of ruffling up.'

'Was there?'

'You could be a right pompous twat sometimes, Crispin. Most of the novices were until it wore off. If it wore off. Are you going to have the rest of that?' She jabbed her cigarette towards his leftover parkin.

'Yes. No. I'm not really hungry.'

'That's because you're heartsick. Is it the first time?'

'Yes. There was . . . a crush . . . when I was at university. But nothing like this.'

'Who is he?'

Daniel flushed. 'I . . . I . . .'

'Do I look daft? I've been cleaning at Ravenspurn abbey for forty years. It's not Hull Kingston Rovers.'

Daniel nodded and took a few seconds to compose himself. 'It's someone I met because of work. We became friends. Just friends. And then something changed. I didn't notice it at first. And then I found I was thinking about him. And we started seeing each other outside work, but it was all perfectly innocent and then it . . .' He felt another surge of sadness and waved his hand again in a pointless gesture of defence.

Alma suddenly looked alert. 'Not the one who murdered his lad?'

'No! No, no, no . . . It's the policeman who arrested him. We met when the first murders happened. He was the investigating officer and we had this unusual affinity . . . we solved the murders. And then he started giving me driving lessons.'

'And it were all accelerator and no brake?'

'Somewhere along the way it changed. I didn't see it coming. I didn't mean it to happen.'

'That's nothing new. Copper and a parson, though. Interesting new line-up for the Village People.'

'No, nothing has happened. My feelings for him are not reciprocated. I only just found out. Last night.' His mouth twitched again. 'I'm such a fool. I thought he felt the same way. And he did. Only not for me, for someone else. I made a terrible mistake. And now I'm . . .'

He started to cry again.

'And now you've been ruffled up a bit. Welcome to the world, Crispin.'

'I can't pray, Alma. I can't think. I can't read.'

Alma took a piece of his parkin and chewed it thoughtfully.

'I'm from Hull, did you know that? I worked in a factory in the war and met a Yank. Ken, a GI. From Providence, Rhode Island. Like the hens. He were lovely, looked like Gary Cooper. Then he had to go away to fight the Germans and so I gave him a night to remember. Next to the water chute in East Park. There were an air raid that night and they dropped a bomb on the Savoy picture house while we were going at it. He pledged his undying love to me, went off to liberate the Rhineland and I never saw him again. He left me in the family way. I had a baby in a home for unwed mothers in Batley. Couldn't go back to Hull after that – the shame – and the brethren took me in here and gave me a job.'

'I'm so sorry, Alma.'

'I'm telling you this for two reasons, love. Well, it's the same reason. In the long run it's not what causes your heart to flutter that matters, it's doing right by people. And not judging them.'

He started to cry again.

'You've just barked up the wrong tree, love. Sort yourself out. Move on, and don't give yourself a hard time. You should know that better than anyone. But it's so often the way with you lot. I could never understand why you were so hard on yourselves. Chapter of Faults and all that.'

'I'm so sorry to inflict this on you,' Daniel said through his sobs. 'You only came in for a cup of tea.'

'Don't be silly. And get a nice boyfriend. Our Donna, maiden of the parish, answered an ad in the *Reporter* and joined the lesbians. Moved to Hebden. Now she and Trish run the library.'

Daniel laughed.

'See,' said Alma, 'I've made you laugh, you're on the mend!' She flicked open her cigarette packet and tore off a strip of white card from the inside of the lid and scrawled a number on it. 'Here's my number, Crispin. If you're down, love, give me a ring and come round. Skip Compline and come t'pub, have a laugh. OK?'

'OK.'

6

Audrey was quite breathless when she got to the post office. It was a longer route than she was accustomed to, through the park from the big house rather than the rectory, and in her haste she had set off at more of a lick than was wise. She paused for a restorative moment in front of the door, painted in the puttyish shade the Champton Estate preferred, before pushing it open and making the little bell over it ding to alert Mrs Braines to the arrival of a customer.

No need, for Mrs Braines was already at the counter – shop, rather than post office, for she could lean on that when confidence required it. She was leaning sympathetically towards Anne Dollinger, who was sitting on a high stool pressing a sodden tissue to her cheeks, which were flushed from crying.

'Morning, ladies!' said Audrey, pretending nothing was out of the ordinary.

'Mrs Clement,' said Mrs Braines with a nod. 'Shop or post office?'

'Post office, please.'

Mrs Braines moved from one counter to the other.

'A first-class stamp for a letter. It absolutely MUST get there as soon as possible.'

'There's a collection at noon. Where does it need to go?'

Audrey paused a moment and said, 'Inland, dear. When will it get there?'

'Tomorrow.'

'Not today?'

'We're the GPO, Audrey, not Concorde. But you could always send a Telemessage.'

'A wire?'

'No, we haven't done those for twenty years, but it's like one. You phone up British Telecom and dictate it. They deliver it.'

'I don't want to dictate it to anyone.'

'You'd better post that then. First class.'

'How much?'

'Twenty pence.'

'Four bob! For a stamp?'

'Haven't you got any left over? From your little business? Not so little, mind – the postie was bent double going up and down Church Lane.'

Audrey flinched. News had evidently arrived at the post office, and therefore all Champton, of her exposure as the correspondence medium Caduceus, whose mantle she had taken on with the death of the foundress of that particular cult, Mrs Hawkins of Upper Badsaddle Manor.

'That's quite different, Mrs Braines. A business expense connected with my duties as executrix of the late Mrs Hawkins's estate.'

'So I heard. Will you be continuing in that line?'

Audrey gave Mrs Braines one of her stoniest smiles.

'With you here cranking the parish pump so reliably, dear, the Oracle at Delphi would soon be out of business.'

Mrs Braines gave her stoniest smile in return and fetched the thick, battered stamp folder from a shelf. 'Your stamp,' she said and produced a single red.

Audrey licked it with a deliberation that made Mrs Braines think of Dora Sharman's Scamper anticipating a chew.

'Shall I take it for you, Audrey?' she said, slightly craning to see if she could make out the address on the front.

'No need. I'll pop it in the box myself. Peace of mind. Oh, and a poppy, please. Two poppies.' She put some coins into the collecting tin next to the little tray of poppies for Remembrance Day.

'Do you want pins for those, Audrey?'

'No need, dear.'

She turned to go before Mrs Braines could reply but Anne's mysterious distress made her pause, and in an instant she had to weigh the benefit of making a magnificent exit against the benefit of discovering its cause. It was not a difficult calculation to make.

'Anne, whatever is the matter?'

Anne shook her head and turned away.

'Will that be all, Mrs Clement?' said Mrs Braines, looking pointedly at the door.

Audrey put a consoling hand on Anne's shoulder, which caused her to flinch. 'Anne . . .?'

'I'm fine, thank you, Audrey.'

Audrey withdrew her hand and gave a little sigh, as if this were a mildly irritating lapse of Anne's, rather than a righteous rebuff, and left with a shake of her head.

She thrust the stamped envelope into the post box, almost ran over the zebra crossing, and went directly to Elite Fashions. The door dinged its own peculiar peal and Miss March emerged from the curtained section at the back of the shop.

'Mrs Clement? What may I do for you?'

This rather threw Audrey, for she had called in only to see if she could find out why Anne was in tears in the post office. 'Um, now, there WAS something . . . oh, yes, can you recommend somewhere where I may get my winter coat reproofed?'

'Yes, we could look after that for you. Or perhaps I could interest you in something new?' She went to a rail and took out a coat of restrained splendour. 'This is lovely, midi-length tweed by Jaeger. Very smart, very you.'

'I'm afraid, Miss March, my funds are suddenly rather depleted.'

'I see. In that case let us see what we can do with

your old coat. I'm sorry to say it may take some time, for I find myself suddenly rather depleted too – of staff.'

'Oh, I just saw Anne Dollinger in the post office in floods of tears. Isn't she meant to be with you?'

'Not any more. I'm afraid I have had to let her go. Just now as a matter of fact.'

'No?! Not fingers in the till?'

Audrey instantly regretted asking so nosey a question, but it couldn't be helped, and as it happened Miss March, who had after all rescued her from an arsonist's deadly enterprise on Bonfire Night, was in an unusually receptive mood.

'I could have forgiven that.'

'Then whatever has she done?'

'She was . . . overfamiliar.' She pressed the palms of her hands against her skirt as if to smooth away a crease.

'Goodness! How so?'

Miss March shook her head.

'Anne may be clumsy sometimes,' Audrey went on, 'but overfamiliar?'

'She . . . she addressed me by my Christian name. I did not entrust it to her. I barely knew her and she is – was – my *employee* . . . and . . .'

'Yes?'

'I never use it. I don't like it. It is not a Christian name at all.'

'Whatever is it? Jezebel?' Audrey knew perfectly well what her name was because she had seen it written in Miss March's own hand on a wreath at Mrs Hawkins's funeral, but she now wanted Miss March to reveal it and be condemned from her own mouth.

'It is . . . it is Kimberley.'

There was silence for a moment.

'Oh, my dear,' said Audrey, 'I am *so* sorry.'

'It was not my wish to be named after a South African diamond mine.'

'No.'

'But my father's uncle died during the battle to lift the siege of Kimberley in the Boer War.'

'I see. How very sad.'

'My father held him in high regard and always wanted his sacrifice commemorated in some way. Years and years later I came along and the opportunity presented itself.'

Audrey winced. 'Thank goodness it wasn't Mafeking.'

Miss March looked at her sharply, but Audrey did not notice.

'Miss Mafeking March . . . Sounds like something from the Light Programme—'

'But you see,' Miss March interrupted, 'without staff I may not be able to expedite orders as swiftly as I would like. It is only right that I should tell you.'

Audrey had a flash of inspiration. 'I wonder if I might make a suggestion.'

'By all means.'

'You are suddenly short-staffed. I am suddenly short of funds. Perhaps a mutually beneficial opportunity presents itself?'

Miss March thought for a moment. 'Are you familiar with shop work?'

'No. But I am familiar with shops. And this shop especially. And if Anne Dollinger can do it, I'm sure I can.'

Miss March said nothing.

'And I can absolutely assure you there will be no risk of overfamiliarity with me.'

Miss March thought for a moment longer, then said, 'Mrs Clement, this may indeed be to our mutual advantage. May I think it over? Perhaps I could telephone you later?'

'Of course. I shall be waiting by the instrument!'

The shop bell gave what sounded like a tinkle of triumph to Audrey as she left. She crossed the road again and paused outside the post office to enjoy, in anticipation, her double victory: discovering the cause of Anne's misfortune and, by it, adding to her own good fortune. She made her way down Main Street towards the rectory, forgetting in her exalted mood that it was uninhabitable, and that her temporary billet lay in the opposite direction.

Miss March stood in the window, motionless between two mannequins, looking like a mannequin herself were it not for the appearance of a slow, thin smile.

Crestfallen, Honoria thought to herself; such an apt expression. Neil, whom she had summoned to the warrener's cottage at what he called 'dinnertime', was still in the kitchen but half out of his trousers before she made it absolutely clear that the only lunchtime quickie happening that day would be a Penguin and a cup of tea. The disappointment this caused appeared instantly on his face; elsewhere, the effects of anticipation took a little longer to wilt, but wilt he did.

'To be honest, I was hoping for more than tea and a biscuit. We *are* finishing up a murder inquiry.'

She frowned. 'It's important. Daniel's gone missing.'

'Missing?'

'Not exactly missing; AWOL. Left in the middle of the night – called away according to the note he left for Daddy – and no one knows where or why.'

'Could be an emergency. Something confidential?'

'Maybe so, but it's not like him, is it? He left a note for Audrey too, but no address, no telephone number. Do you think it might be because of the murder?'

'That he's gone off somewhere? No. Did he not leave a note for me?'

'No, not that I know of. Do you think he might be in shock, or something?'

'Daniel? In shock?'

'Maybe not. But what then? You're his best friend, Neil. Aren't you his *only* friend? Don't you have any idea?'

'He didn't say anything to me, but that's not unusual.'

Honoria sat down at the kitchen table and unwrapped

her Penguin. 'You were the last person to see him. Your revelation at the rectory.'

Neil pursed his lips. 'I told you all about it. He was quite . . . taken by it, I think. But he didn't say anything about going away. Maybe he didn't want to—'

'Spoil the moment?'

'I don't mean like that. Can I have one too?'

She slid a Penguin across the table to him.

He sat down and took it and looked thoughtful. 'A *Penguin*,' he muttered. 'When you feel a little p-peckish, p-p-p-pick up a *Penguin*.'

Honoria felt something Antarctic move within her.

Three o'clock chimed gently from the clock outside the library, like someone politely pretending to clear his throat, thought Daniel, and at that very moment Father Paulinus said, 'Let us pray.'

The novices sitting at tables facing Daniel in the seminar room were already sitting still and in silence, the custom at the abbey, so the exhortation to pray merely made them shift very slightly in their chairs in acknowledgement.

'Heavenly Father,' said Father Paulinus in accented English that made Daniel think of Arnold Schwarzenegger in *The Terminator*, one of his mother's favourite films, 'who caused all holy Scriptures to be written for our learning: help us so to hear them, to read, mark, learn and inwardly digest them that, through patience, and the comfort of your holy word, we may embrace and for ever hold fast the hope of everlasting life, which you have given us in our Saviour Jesus Christ, who is alive and reigns with you, in the unity of the Holy Spirit, one God, now and for ever . . .'

'Amen,' they all replied.

'My brothers,' he went on, 'we are most privileged today to have with us Father Daniel, rector of Champton St Mary in the diocese of Stow as you will know from the newspapers, but better known to us as a former novice of this community. As Brother Crispin he also wrote here a most distinguished thesis on a problem in New Testament textual criticism, and even though you have been, I must say, remiss in attending my Greek for Fun class – in fact, *because* you have been so remiss – I have asked him to talk to us today to open—'

There was a knock on the door.

'Come in,' said Father Paulinus a little crossly.

It was Colin. 'Sorry I'm late,' he said, and, with the exaggerated choreography of someone trying to slip in without causing a disturbance, caused more.

'Look who's here,' muttered one of the novices.

'Mr Cummings,' said Father Paulinus, 'this is a class for the novitiate.'

Colin, elbows slightly out, eased himself into the chair next to Brother Bede, who, with his own exaggerated choreography, shifted six inches to the side.

'Ah,' said Colin, as he unpacked his satchel and stacked a Bible and a notebook and a pencil case on the desktop, 'Father Clement invited me.'

Daniel was thinking of a reply but before he could Paulinus said, 'And so you are here . . . as I was saying, Father Daniel will open our hearts and minds and spirits to the glories and mysteries of Scripture. We are so grateful, Father, that you, at least, have joined us.'

There was a polite murmur of affirmation from the class. It was a small but unusually mixed group. Brother Bede in his round glasses looked attentive with a notebook and a fountain pen – a well-used Osmiroid 75, piston-filled, in French Blue, with chrome fittings, Daniel noticed – and on the next table there was a jolly-looking freckled man about the same age with black curly hair and an expression of absent-minded geniality. A brace of novices sat at the next, a little florid man in his late forties or early fifties, about Daniel's age – old for a novice, he thought – who looked at him from over the top of his half-moon spectacles, and next to him an even slighter black man, very neat and composed, one of the exchange novices from South Africa, where Anglican monasticism had put down unlikely roots. At the next table, and of necessity solo, was a man who looked like Friar Tuck, barely contained by his cassock, so broad his scapular looked more like a tie than a pinafore, and so roly-poly it occluded all other characteristics and you had to look again to work out his age and demeanour. Sitting at the next table was a pale-faced young man with glasses that looked like they had been borrowed from an astronaut. They were shaded darker at the top of the lenses than at the bottom, which made him look a bit sinister. Darren, thought Daniel, then noticed he was wearing a cassock but no scapular – Darren the postulant. It was him who had muttered when he saw Colin at the door. Next to him was the huge Orthodox monk whose sang-froid when he chewed down on half a jar of Marmite had made such an impression at breakfast.

Daniel got up. 'Good afternoon,' he said. 'I gather from Father Paulinus that you are not all accomplished in New Testament Greek – yet – so I thought we could look at one or two problems in the text, which I think are fascinating and constructive. Father Paulinus, do you have the handouts?'

'Handouts?'

'Yes, I asked Dominic if he could photocopy a passage from Matthew for me. Are they not here?'

'Nothing on the table when we arrived,' said Bede.

'Oh well. Do you all have Bibles?'

They did.

'Do any of you have Greek New Testaments?' Brother Bede raised his hand with his index finger pointing up, like a child, thought Daniel, at primary school. 'Good, necessary for the textual apparatus. That's the section at the bottom of the page, which tells us what we need to know about the versions of the text the editors have chosen, and their variations, and the evidence for them.' The faintest shift of mood in the room told him his fascination with the subject might not be virulently infectious. 'Let us turn to Matthew, chapter eighteen, verse fifteen. Would someone care to read?'

Bede's hand went up again.

'Perhaps verses fifteen to seventeen?'

Bede nodded. He turned some pages in his Bible and then started to read. '*Ean de hamartese eis se ho adelphos sou—*'

'In English, please, Bede,' said Daniel.

Bede said, 'I don't *have* an English New Testament with me . . .'

'Neglectful of you, Brother Bede,' said Father Paulinus, which made the man in the half-moon glasses smile. 'It is a Bible class . . .'

'And I have a Bible, Father, a Greek Bible, and knowing Father Clement's scholarship, I—'

'We are not all Greek scholars, Bede. Brother Anselm, perhaps you would read?'

The jolly-looking monk with freckles started to read.

'*If your brother sins against you, go and tell him his fault, between you and him alone . . .*'

There was a knock at the door and Father Dominic came in with a sheaf of papers. 'So sorry to be late – photocopier had a paper jam and it took me ages to fix it.'

'Ancient wisdom thwarted by new technology!' exclaimed the Friar Tuck monk.

Daniel said, 'You raise an interesting point, Brother . . .?'

'Augustine.'

'Christianity has always been an enthusiastic adopter of new communications technology. For example, and immediately relevant to our discussion, the codex. Would you pass those round, Father?' he said to Dominic. 'The early Church expanded as it did partly because of the development of the codex – pages bound together in a volume. More portable, and more easily accessible and indexed than the scroll.'

'Yes, turning pages,' said Paulinus, 'rather than unrolling and rolling a parchment scroll.'

'Then there was printing, which put the Bible in the hands of the people. Then radio and television, mass communications,' Daniel continued.

'Thora Hird,' muttered Augustine.

'Augustine?'

'Thora Hird, *Songs of Praise*, Harry Secombe. The great Christian apologists of the television age.'

'And photocopiers that don't work,' said Dominic as he distributed the papers.

'But the advantages!' said Paulinus. 'Think what you can do with the codex! Binding pages together in book form! Or imagine a calendar, one for the wall, perhaps. Spiral bound, so you can turn over the pages month by month . . .'

Dominic dropped a photocopied sheet, which swished unevenly to the floor.

'And no loose leaves to blow away in the wind!' said Paulinus.

'Does everyone have a sheet?' said Daniel. 'Thank you, Father Dominic.'

Dominic nodded and left.

'Right,' said Daniel, 'Anselm, you were reading?'

'From the beginning?'

'Yes, please.'

Anselm scanned the handout until he found the text. '*If your brother sins against you, go and tell him his fault, between you and him alone. If he listens to you, you have gained your brother. But if he does not listen, take one or two others along with you, that every word may be confirmed by the evidence of two or three witnesses. If he refuses to listen to them, tell it to the Church; and if he refuses to listen even to the Church, let him be to you as a gentile and a tax collector.*'

'Thank you, Anselm. Tell me, what is this passage saying?'

Bede put up his hand. Daniel ignored it. 'Anselm?'

The monk looked back at him genially. Daniel wondered if he were capable of any other expression. 'Well, it's Our Lord giving instructions to the Church, I suppose? If someone does you a wrong, sort it out with them, and if that doesn't work, take along another novice or two . . . or friends . . . and if that doesn't work take it to the Church community, and if that doesn't work, then you . . . ah . . . ask them if perhaps they're not *quite* the right fit for . . .'

'Not quite the right fit?' interrupted the man in half-moon glasses. 'It's excommunication!'

'You are . . .?' asked Daniel.

'Brother Placid, Father, and . . .'

'No,' said the Romanian monk, 'not excommunicated – he is *anathematised*.'

'We don't have that distinction here, Brother Nicolai,' said Placid over his half-moon glasses. 'Actually, we can't really excommunicate anyone in the Church of England, let alone anathematise them.'

'How do you deal with evildoers, the wolves, the goats, the ravening lions?' asked the Romanian.

'Ordain them,' said Placid.

Daniel said, 'What I'm interested in is what has gone wrong here. Or, rather, *who* has been wronged.'

'The man who brings the complaint has been wronged. We don't know how specifically. Maybe someone coveted his ass or short-changed him at the shop,' said Anselm.

'There's a textual variant here. You know what that is?' Daniel asked.

Without being invited to speak, Bede said, 'It's when two manuscripts, or more, have different versions of the same verse.'

'Yes,' said Daniel, 'and there's an interesting one here. Verse fifteen – if your brother sins against you, go and tell him his fault . . .'

'*Ean de hamartese eis se ho adelphos sou . . .*'

'Thank you, Bede. Anyone know the variant?'

No one answered.

'It's "if your brother sins *against you*" – *eis se*. In some early manuscripts, some would say the strongest – the great fourth-century uncials, Codex Vaticanus, Codex Sinaiticus—'

'Stolen!' said Brother Nicolai.

'I beg your pardon?'

'Codex Sinaiticus! From the monastery of St Caterina in Egypt!'

'Rescued, not stolen,' said Placid. 'It was being used as lavatory paper by the monks before Tischendorf realised what it was . . .'

'I don't want to get into an argument about that for now,' said Daniel. 'It ended up in the British Library – how it got there is complicated . . .'

'Yes,' said Father Paulinus, 'looted by a German adventurer, sold to the tsar, stolen by the Communists, then acquired by the British . . .'

'. . . and one of the Bibles commissioned by the Emperor Constantine after he accepted the lordship of Christ . . .' said Brother Nicolai.

'Not really,' said Colin. 'He accepted Christianity as *one* of the official religions of Empire, with the Edict of Milan in 314, a very important milestone in the history of Church and state, which is my academic field . . .'

'It was 313, I think . . .' said Anselm.

'That was the Battle of the Milvian Bridge, which preceded it, or so the legend goes . . .' said Colin.

'No, definitely, 313,' said Bede, 'February actually, promulgated by Constantine and Licinius . . .'

'But 313, 314, these are not the really significant dates,' said Colin. 'Galerius anticipated the adoption of

Christianity in 311, but it was the Edict of Thessalonica in 380 that eventually made Christianity the official religion of Empire.'

'But Constantine converted on his deathbed,' said Bede, 'Pentecost 337, at Nicomedia.'

'He accepted the lordship of Christ for the Empire,' said Nicolai.

'Thou hast conquered, O pale Galilean!' said Anselm, in a voice like Henry Irving.

'That was Julian the Apostate, not Constantine, dear,' said Augustine, 'and it was 363, the Battle of Samarra.'

'It's all a bit more complicated than that,' said Colin.

'Colin is the expert in this field, so perhaps we could move on?' said Daniel.

'Expert?' said Bede. 'Yes, I suppose so . . . in his way . . .'

'It is my field, Bede,' said Colin, colouring.

'You certainly put the hours in,' said Darren.

'What do you mean?'

'Twenty-five years, was it?'

'It has been the work of my life.'

'Nothing much else to do between slopping out and cocoa.'

'Brethren!' snapped Father Paulinus. '"Hearken continually within thine heart, O son, giving attentive ear to the . . . oh, *előírásai* . . . of thy master" . . . from the Rule of our Holy Father Benedict.'

The novices were at once quiet. Bede put his hand up.

Father Paulinus looked at him. 'What now, Bede?'

'Precepts. *Előírásai* means precepts.'

Father Paulinus blinked and said, 'Yes, it is the first sentence from the Rule, the *first*. So perhaps, Bede, even you could turn an attentive ear to the master?'

'Thank you, Father,' said Daniel. 'Putting arguments about the acquisitions of manuscripts to one side for the moment, I want to focus on that "if your brother sins *against you*". In those early manuscripts the "*against you*" is missing. Why do you think that is?'

'Later scribes missed it out.'

'Thank you, Bede, yes, but why?' Bede went to speak again, but Daniel held up a hand. 'Anyone?'

The small black man put up his hand.

'Yes, Brother . . .?'

'Sebastian. I think it may be because the version in the more ancient manuscripts is too . . . general?'

'Go on.'

'If it read "If your brother sins, go and tell him his fault . . ." then that means you must correct him for anything he does that offends. "Sins *against you*" is personal.'

'And do you think that is significant?'

'Yes. Think how much easier it is to challenge someone who wrongs you' – he rolled the r sound in 'wrong' – 'than someone you have just seen doing wrong. If you drive into my car at the traffic lights then of course I will admonish you. But if I just see you drive through a red light then I will not . . .'

'Not a good example, actually,' said Bede a bit snap-pily. 'How could you admonish someone if they were driving away and you were stationary?'

'Yes, you are right,' said Sebastian. 'Forgive me.'

'There's your example of the general sense of the text,' said Father Paulinus. 'Bede admonishes Sebastian for an error in analogy, not for any offence against him.'

'Are you sure about that?' said Augustine. 'Sounded a bit personal to me.'

'And if we're talking about offending,' said Darren, 'maybe we should ask Colin? If you're after expert knowledge?'

Daniel raised his hand to hush them and used the trick parish priests presiding over fractious meetings soon learn: 'Let us pray,' he said. 'O God, from whom all holy desires, all good counsels and all just works do proceed; give unto thy servants that peace which the world cannot give; that our hearts may be set to obey thy commandments, and also that by thee, we, being defended from the fear of our enemies, may pass our time in rest and quietness; through the merits of Jesus Christ our Saviour.'

'Amen,' the room replied.

'You can see,' said Daniel, 'merely from our discus-sion so far, that these differences are not insignificant, these choices are not insignificant.'

'And especially for us,' said Father Paulinus, 'called to the cloister to seek God in this most exacting way. To us, Jesus speaks most searchingly, most challengingly, in the *imitatio Dei* – you must be perfect, as your heavenly Father is perfect.'

'It's rather a lot to ask, isn't it?' said Anselm, in a jocular tone, looking around the class for approval. Daniel realised who he reminded him of. It was Joyce Grenfell.

'That is why we spend so much time trying to clear some space for God to come and dwell within us,' said Father Paulinus. 'We do that through prayer, through confession, and through Chapter of Faults.'

Daniel suddenly felt a flash of dread at the memory of the Chapter of Faults, or rather the Lesser Chapter, nursery slope for the Greater Chapter, which monks only attended after they had completed the novitiate and joined the community as a full member. The two chapters took place four times a year, or when the abbot considered it necessary, and were forums for the declaration of the things you had done wrong. In front of the whole community you confessed a fault, expressed repentance, and the abbot bestowed his blessing.

Only it didn't always work out quite like that, because monks, like everyone else, are susceptible to self-regard, failure of understanding, prejudice and hard-heartedness. Sometimes the confession of a fault could be the coded accusation of a fault in another, and that would lead to a tit for tat, and an escalation of passive aggression, so common in cloistered life where there is nowhere to retreat, nowhere to avoid the person who has offended you or you have offended, who you will see all day and every day for the rest of your life. So you either become expert in reconciling the irreconcilable, or one of the forty suspects in the event of a murder.

'It is a mistake commonly made,' said Father Paulinus, 'that the novitiate is a training course and that at the end of it you will have acquired the skills to be a monk. It is not that at all. It is a warning of what is to come, the narrow and hard path that awaits you. It gets harder, not easier, and you will have to endure the unendurable to prevail, and you will be changed unimaginably. Cardinal Newman says, "To be perfect is to have changed often."'

'Yes, I like that,' said Daniel. 'The Greek word, which this Bible version translates as "perfect", is *teleoi*, and it really means perfect in the sense of complete rather than without fault.'

Brother Nicolai looked confused. 'Is there any difference?'

'I think so. How can we be without fault as the Lord is without fault when we are born into sin and He uniquely is not? It means, I think, that we must be whole, offer ourselves entire to Him, to live as our Lord wants us to live – life in its abundance.'

Daniel felt a rush of blood to his face.

'*Hina zoen echosin kai perisson echosin* – John, chapter ten, verse ten,' said Bede. 'So that you may have life and have it abundantly.'

Daniel started to cry.

★

Bernard had spent all day in his study 'working on family papers'. This enterprise was an excuse to retreat yet further from the world he was already in retreat from. As the present grew more disagreeable, the past appealed to him more, and he had plenty of that to hand, recorded in the letters and accounts books and diaries his ancestors had left behind. He had not been especially interested in his family history as a young man, and barely noticed his ancestors' portraits, which hung everywhere – flour-faced de Floures with their shorthorns and their dogs. In age he found their company, if not more compelling than that of his contemporaries, then less irritating.

Bernard had never sought the companionship of dogs. When he was a boy the usual complement of spaniels and retrievers had padded around the estate, but they were working animals, not pets. Pets came with his third wife, who adored cats and would have filled the house with them had not Bernard's behaviour been so intolerable. When she returned to her home city of Siena she left Jove – *Yovveh* as she pronounced it – the large white Persian cat, as a reminder and a reproach, but Bernard had come to appreciate the independence of his nature and the ferocity of his predation.

Now the infestation of dachshunds had driven Jove from his usual domain. The last Bernard had seen of him was a white ball of hissing indignation disappearing behind Mrs Shorely when she and Audrey left the dogs with him because of 'an emergency'.

It was really too much that he should have them forced upon him when he was trying to concentrate on his research, so to encourage Hilda and the puppies to settle down he moved their bed to the knee hole in his desk where they curled up and went to sleep, secure between his cavalry twill turn-ups and brown brogues.

Eventually the puppies shifted, squirmed and started to mewl for milk, a sound Bernard had not really heard since the nursery and the mewling of his own children, which he'd found so intolerable he had at once closed the nursery door behind him and left them in the uneven care of nannies. When they were old enough he had sent them off to school and the uneven care of masters and matrons. It was neglect, according to his second son Alex, which had ruined their chances of intimacy and love. But both his sons had managed to form attachments, albeit so unsuitable that he assumed they were intended as his punishment. His daughter's attachments were much more mysterious, thank God.

From between his feet the mewling stopped as the puppies attached to their mother and began to suck.

7

Daniel had felt too upset to come to Vespers. His unstoppable tears, bearable in front of Alma, unbearable in front of the novices, had plunged the class into absolute silence before the appointed hour. Father Paulinus had told them to study Matthew, chapter eighteen, with special attention, in whatever language they preferred, and herded Daniel out of the seminar room and into the cloister garth, where Daniel had assured him he was fine, made a joke about the charism of tears and made off.

He had gone to his room and instead of sitting at his desk praying, he had lain on his bed like an invalid. The light faded and in darkness he heard the big bell go for Vespers and then the little bell for dinner, but he had no appetite, either for the unappetising menu – mutton with caper sauce – or for the silent interrogation of the brethren, who would all know about his loss of composure and say nothing, for they ate in silence, save the scraping of cutlery and crockery, the awful mouth-symphony of careless eaters, and the recitation by the monk on reading duty that week, a portion of the Rule, followed by a couple of chapters of the book set for their edification and entertainment. He was so unlucky in love it would probably be *The Sorrows of Young Werther*, he thought, and he would lose his composure again. He decided to stay in his room until Compline, the last service of the monastic day, its unchanging texts said and sung in veiling darkness.

Compline was early in winter, at eight, so before the bell went he slipped into church and sat at the back, in a corner where no one else would sit, and did not move as the swish-swish sound of approaching monks came softly down the nave.

The brethren appeared in choir two by two, wearing their cowls with hoods up, like figures in a Caspar David Friedrich painting. It used to thrill him when he was a postulant looking for a monastic home, this sombre and Romantic spectacle, but now he found it a little bit showbiz, a self-conscious attempt to recreate a fancied past, like the medieval banquet Bernard had once hosted at Champton, only the hog roast hadn't cooked properly and everyone had to have a hot dog from the Braunstonbury van instead.

The monks bowed to the cross behind the altar and then peeled off left and right into their places in the stalls until Abbot Aelred, bringing up the rear, was in his stall too, and they sat as one and settled into silence.

But Daniel did not settle into the silence. Something

was wrong – not so wrong that he knew what it was, more a vague unease caused by something at the edge of sense. Was it something in the church? Something outside? Something in the mood? He could not tell. And then there was a rap as Abbot Aelred knocked on his stall as a signal to begin, and the monks stood.

'The Lord almighty grant us a quiet night and a perfect end,' said Aelred in his soft and even voice.

'Amen,' the brethren replied, and so did Daniel, the response producing itself involuntarily.

They said together the general confession, '. . . that we have sinned through our own fault, in thought and word and deed . . .', and asked for God's forgiveness. Then the precentor led the community in the singing of the first psalm, his voice so soft it was almost unrecognisable as it floated up over the choir. The monks responded and their hushed chorus flowed down the length of the nave to Daniel.

He managed to sing until the verse in Psalm 91, '*He shall call upon me and I will answer him, I am with him in trouble; I will rescue him and bring him to honour . . .*'

Where are you, he thought, when I call upon you? Where are you when I am in trouble? But instead of tears came anger and the comfortless words from 'Footprints': 'When you saw only one set of footprints, it was then that I carried you.'

'Keep me, O Lord, as the apple of your e-e-e-e-e-e-e-e-eye,' chanted the precentor, the last word drawn out and modulated in what Daniel thought the most unnecessarily complicated coda in plainsong. 'Hide me under the shadow of your w-i-i-i-i-i-i-i-ings,' came the response.

Compline ended with a blessing.

'In peace we will lie down and sleep,' said Aelred.

'For you alone, Lord, make us dwell in safety,' came the reply.

'The almighty and merciful God, the Father, Son and Holy Spirit, bless and preserve us.'

'Amen.'

The monks processed out, but some, instead of leaving through the double doors to the monastery, gathered in a semi-circle round the statue of the Virgin Mary, life-sized, looking down from her plinth at the brethren looking back at her, their beatific smiles copying hers.

'*Salve regina . . .*' sang one.

'*Mater misericordiae . . .*' sang the others, and the famous hymn to Our Lady, traditionally sung before retiring, floated up – or it did from those who liked that sort of thing. The Abbey of Sts Philip and James, being Church of England, had no uniform policy on matters as divisive as the veneration of the mother of God. Some were traditionalists; some were modernists; some, like Daniel, were in between. He rather liked the ceremonial opportunities Mary had bequeathed the Church, but rather disliked the more extravagant claims made for her by her most fervent devotees. Also, if he were entirely honest, over-extravagant devotion to the Holy Mother made him feel disloyal to Audrey.

He took a little candle, lit it with a taper, stuck it in the votive stand and asked Mary to give comfort to those who suffered and were anxious, and especially to those whose lives had been destroyed by murder and violence and madness. And for a blessing for his own mother – another stab of guilt followed – and for Neil, whom he loved before all people and all things, and could she intercede for him so his unrequited love might be bearable?

'Daniel?' Abbot Aelred whispered his name. 'Could I see you?'

'Yes, Father, of course. Where?'

He indicated him to follow and they slipped into the cloister. 'We'll go to my parlour. I know it's after Compline and we should all be keeping silent and you're on retreat, but I really must talk to you, my dear.'

They walked in silence and darkness to the cloister. On two sides were the reception rooms of the ugly mansion the monastery had originally been. They were now used for the public element of their existence: receiving guests, entertaining dignitaries and, on Sundays, Monk Tea, as it was called, when the brethren who could bear it had a slice of cake and cup of tea with anyone who wanted to come.

A couple of monks ahead of them quietly opened the French windows to the sitting room, the one where they kept the television set.

'It's nearly time for the programme they all like,' said Aelred. 'Do you watch it?'

'No,' said Daniel, 'not my sort of thing. *Birds of a Feather*, I think.'

'Yes, that's it.' He opened the next set of French windows to the abbot's parlour and went in. Daniel followed and stood in the indistinct room, lit in blue and red, from moonlight and the glow of the banked-down coal fire burning in the grate. Indistinct, but still awful, furnished with discarded pieces from the world outside, which had eschewed them in favour of G Plan or Ercol, so stepping inside was like stepping into a great-aunt's parlour, with tired chintzy sofas and horrible lampshades. Aelred went to switch on the standard lamp. It clicked, but no light came.

'Oh bother,' he said and tried it again. Nothing.

Daniel tried the switch next to the door. Nothing.

There was a knock at the door. 'Yes?' said Abbot Aelred, and one of the novices opened it.

'Father Aelred,' he said, 'the telly's not working, nor the lights.' It was Brother Anselm; Daniel recognised his voice and manner. 'I can't see anything on in the cloister, so I don't think it's a fuse. It must be a power cut.'

And then Daniel knew what had disquieted him when he was at Compline. It was the absence of the sound of the generator in the background. 'I think the generator is down,' he said. 'I can't hear it. I noticed it at Compline.'

'Who is *custos lucis* now?' asked Aelred.

'We don't really have one, Father Aelred,' said Anselm, 'but Bede looks after it.'

'Tell him to go and find out what's happened, and see if he can fix it.'

'I think he's already gone, Father Aelred.'

'This is God's judgement, Anselm, for looking at the television after Compline.'

'Yes, Father Aelred.'

'Well, run along.'

Anselm closed the door extra-quietly as he left, in acknowledgement of the abbot's mild rebuke.

'Sit down, Daniel. I'll light a candle.' Daniel picked, out of habit, the least comfortable-looking armchair while Aelred took a couple of those little chafing lights Audrey used to keep her terrible fondues viscous, placed them on a saucer, lit them, put them on the coffee table and sat down opposite Daniel. 'How atmospheric, no?'

Candlelight flickered weakly between them.

'You'll know why I wanted to see you, Daniel.'

'I thought you always waited for someone to come to you?'

'Normally, but I have to go away tomorrow for a conference . . . abbots' jamboree . . . and . . . I am your spiritual director, and you are suffering. Is there anything you want to tell me?'

'I don't know.'

'Not like you. You know *everything*.'

Daniel said nothing but thought for a moment. 'I

don't know what has happened. I don't know what to do. I don't know who I am.'

'Oh,' said Aelred, 'that's *good*. Would you like a glass of something? I think I have some of our mead, but I would hesitate to recommend it. Some whisky? I'm having whisky.'

'A whisky then,' said Daniel.

Aelred went to a cabinet and took out a bottle. He poured two splashy measures into tumblers. 'Would you like a drop of water?'

Daniel nodded.

'It's a Speyside, my favourite. Those smoky ones that are so in vogue make me think of dark Satanic mills.'

'Here, you mean?'

'Once upon a time. Not many mills now, and it was wool, not cotton, on this side of the Pennines.' He went to the fire, poked it, and tipped on a few little lumps of coal. 'And coal. That's why we came here. To be a light in that particular sort of darkness. Old Etonians among the urban poor.' He passed Daniel his drink and sat down. 'Chin-chin!'

Daniel said, 'I read somewhere that Blake did not mean industrialisation but the Established Church. Dark Satanic mills are churches, not factories.'

Aelred raised an eyebrow. 'An interesting idea. What do you think?'

Daniel said nothing but looked at his whisky and the firelight through it. It gave a faint tawny glow that wavered and turned. Then he said, 'Life in its fullness.

Isn't that what we are supposed to offer?'

'It's what Our Lord offered.'

'Quite. Do we?'

Aelred said, '"And Priests in black gowns, were walking their rounds, And binding with briars, my joys & desires."'

Daniel felt sadness rise within him – like nausea, he thought, only promising uncontainable tears rather than vomit, and he thought in a way he would prefer vomit – and then a sob came, and another.

Aelred said nothing until Daniel was done. Then he took a sip of his whisky and said, 'I hope you're not expecting a hug.'

Daniel laughed, which did nothing to improve his teary-snotty face glistening in the firelight.

Audrey was standing in the hall at Champton House in a pool of light that formed a circle around the telephone for guests' use, overlooked by a sad-looking Charles I on his horse.

'Miss March? Audrey Clement. I hope you don't mind me telephoning you at home and so late – I got your number from our phone book, salvaged from the flames – only when we spoke earlier I was so excited I forgot to mention that we are staying at Champton House, so there's no point in trying to telephone me at the rectory, not that you would, seeing as you were there when it burnt down . . . Yes . . . Quite splendid, I'm in Queen Charlotte's Bedroom. Do you know it?

Why would you, of course? . . . The one who was
married to George III, the mad one . . . Well, yes . . .
It's as if she had only just left! Her porcelain, her portrait – Zoffany, I think – and . . . Ah, yes, to business,
only you said you would telephone me later, so I've
rather jumped the gun. Have you had a chance to think
over our mutual interest, if I may put it that way? . . .
Oh, good! Shall I come to see you at the shop tomorrow? . . . Eleven it is. For elevenses . . . Oh, if you need
to telephone me for any reason, it's Badsaddle 264.
While I'm here! I'm sure I don't need to ask you not
to share that with anyone, but it is a *private* number . . .
Until tomorrow, Miss March. Goodbye!'

She replaced the handset with a satisfying ding. It
was one of the old black Bakelite telephones, the colour
of Bovril, with a plaited brown cord, no-longer-
functional silver buttons on the top, and Badsaddle 264
printed on a round piece of card at the centre of the
dial. As the ding faded the clock over the huge fire-
place chimed. It was nine. She and Bernard – he was
now definitely 'Bernard' – had dined in the old servants' hall on shepherd's pie and apple crumble, made
by Audrey in the kitchen, grudgingly conceded to her
by Mrs Shorely. 'A gesture of thanks, Bernard, for your
kindness in looking after the dogs this morning.' He
had insisted the dogs joined them as they ate, and then
in the library after supper, where Hilda and the puppies
lay in their bed, Cosmo curled up beside them. 'How
many dogs!' thought Audrey, looking around at the

family portraits of de Floures dressed luxuriously in silks and lace, sitting in pretty little dells or by tinkling brooks, with a servant or two behind and a spaniel or two in front. They reminded her of her own photo album, and of the snaps carefully mounted in it with glued-in corners and behind tissue paper, of her and her sisters sitting on the steps from the drawing room to the lawn at Crosskeys, with their little red spaniel puppy Rufus held on her lap. She remembered the occasion, her tenth birthday; she remembered her father taking the photograph; she remembered the smell of stocks, which grew in pink and white masses on either side.

She looked guileless, she thought, in the photograph. Guileless, like the simpering Georgian girls in their silks, who of course had more to come in their lives than their portraits anticipated. Audrey had quite a lot more going on in her life now too.

She had a plan. In fact, she had *two* plans.

Her eyes glittered.

This time there was no tap on the door. 'Father Aelred,' said Anselm, red-faced and breathless from running. 'You need to come!' He was holding a torch, its beam flickering around the room.

'What's the matter?'

'There's been an accident!'

'How bad?'

'Very bad. Someone's . . .'

Aelred held up a restraining hand. 'I shall have that conversation with the infirmarian, I think, Anselm. Has someone sent for him?'

'Yes, Father Aelred.'

Aelred fetched a little pouch and a prayer book from his desk drawer. 'You'd better come too, Daniel, if you don't mind?'

Anselm set off too quickly for the older men to keep up, so he kept having to slow down, but then speeded up again. Occasionally he would stop if they came to a rough section of path and guide them through it with his torch like a cinema usher. As they approached the turbine house more torch beams could be seen through the trees. It made Daniel think of a *son et lumière*.

When they arrived the infirmarian, Father Cuthbert, was waiting for them.

'What's happened, Cuthbert?' said Aelred.

'Someone's . . . gone in.'

'In the river?'

'No, the *turbine*.'

'Who is it?'

'I can't tell.'

'Get everyone to go back to the monastery. Daniel, come with me.'

The door to the turbine house stood open. Aelred took a torch from Anselm, gave it to Daniel, and they went in.

In the torch beams it looked even more like Dr Frankenstein's laboratory, but the horror the turbine house contained was not of that kind. The torchlight played over the control panel, but the dials were at zero, though the switches were down, and hanging on a peg Daniel saw the tool belt with its dangling array. The cogs and gears threw giant shadows onto the whitewashed walls, but they were still, not turning, because they had become jammed, jammed solid, and the system had shut down. But what was causing it? Aelred peered into the stilled machinery with his torch and flinched. In the jerk of torchlight Daniel saw something on the floor flash.

'Aelred, over there,' he said, pointing, and there in the torch's beam were a pair of spectacles, round and horn-rimmed, like Billy Bunter's.

8

'I will telephone his parents. And the police must be notified, and the brethren – that can wait if they don't all know already. I won't be attending the conference after all. And then there is the question, the problem, of retrieval.'

'And then, Father Aelred, what do we do with him?'

'Not much we can do, I am afraid, Cuthbert.'

'No, I meant his funeral, his burial.'

'I will discuss that with his parents. I know he would want to be buried here. We've buried novices in the Calvary before, you know. There's half a row from the Spanish flu, 1918. They may want to take him home, I don't know.'

They were sitting with Daniel in front of the fire in the abbot's parlour. A third glass of whisky had been poured for Cuthbert.

'We must phone 999,' said Daniel.

'So you said, dear . . .'

'We have to. Now.'

'Oh, yes, it's your area of expertise . . .'

'Should we perhaps wait until the morning?' said Cuthbert. 'I mean, what can they do? Except make an unnecessary fuss.'

'It's an unexpected death,' said Daniel, 'and they will need to send an ambulance and the police—'

'An ambulance?' said Cuthbert. 'I don't think even Elijah could do much for poor Bede.'

'. . . and it may, of course, be a crime scene.'

Aelred and Cuthbert exchanged a look. 'A crime scene, Daniel?'

'Yes.'

'Are you suggesting, Father, that this may not be an accident?'

'We don't know. And until we do know, one way or another, it is the police's business.'

Cuthbert put his glass down. 'You don't think . . .' He was silent.

'Think what?'

'You don't think . . . that perhaps recent experience has coloured your view of this?'

'It's what you have to do, not what I want you to do,' said Daniel.

Cuthbert shrugged his shoulders. Aelred said, 'Can I just call the police station? Sergeant Bainbridge comes to Mass here. We'll feel better if it were him.'

'He won't appreciate having to come out after *News at Ten*,' muttered Cuthbert.

'You could, but it won't make any difference, he'll

have to call an ambulance. Until death has been certi-
fied, Bede is a casualty.'

'It's hardly a flesh wound, Daniel.'

'Not the point. It's procedural. And let us not forget,
please, that we are dealing with a young man's sudden
death.'

'Yes, Father. We know,' said Cuthbert. 'We have our
procedures too.'

Daniel said nothing.

Aelred finished his drink. 'While we've been
talking, Daniel, the novice master has been praying
with the novices for his immortal soul in the crypt
chapel. Father Cuthbert, would you please dial 999 and
notify the authorities? From the office? And then please
call Sergeant Bainbridge and ask if he is able to help us.
Daniel, I have to telephone Bede's parents, if you will
allow me?'

'I'll go to the chapel, I think.'

'And then would you come back? In a few minutes?'

'Of course.'

Daniel followed Cuthbert out into the cloister, light
enough in clear moonlight for them to make their way
without a torch.

'Do you really think it might not be an accident,
Father?'

'Might not.'

'So someone contrived to get him into the machinery? Why would they do that?'

'I don't know. Nobody knows. Unless a person or

persons had a hand in his death, then they would know.'

Cuthbert said nothing for a moment. 'Why would anyone want to kill Bede?'

'You know Aelred's line about there being forty suspects if there were a murder here?'

'It doesn't seem so amusing now,' said Cuthbert. 'And it's ridiculous. One of his witticisms. Such a fund of them.'

They walked in silence. Then Cuthbert said, 'But really, it makes no sense.'

'Father, it is most likely an accident. But it could be murder, it could be suicide, and until we can establish the facts, we cannot make a judgement.'

'Suicide. A horrible thought.'

'It happens.'

'Oh, it's happened here. Father Hilary walked into the river. Like Virginia Woolf. Though there the resemblance ends. And several have drunk themselves to death. I don't think Bede was that type. But what goes on in the novitiate has always been a mystery to me.' He stopped. 'I'll leave you here. I have to telephone 999, like someone in *Casualty*. You seek refuge from the world behind the monastery wall, but the world just follows you in.'

'It was already there.'

'I suppose so.' And Cuthbert turned and walked away.

Daniel went through the double doors into the church, dipping his fingers in the bowl of holy water to sign himself with the cross. He made his way to the west end and then down the stairs, which led to the crypt chapel. He let himself in and sat at the back on a bench against the wall. The novices and some of the brethren were kneeling in front of the altar, on which the tabernacle now stood open, the Blessed Sacrament within it exposed and lit by half a dozen tea lights. Kneeling in front of it was Father Paulinus, he assumed, though could not tell for certain as he had his back to him.

There was silence, interrupted by a sigh, a cough, the rustle of someone shifting on their knees, the click of tiny beads, a sniff. Daniel noticed again the absence he had unconsciously noticed at Compline, the missing rhythm of the turbine house. But when had it stopped? It must have been after dinner, for the lights came on as usual between four and five, and were in use at Vespers and at supper. It must have been at Compline, or just before it, because the loss of power was only noticed when the brethren left the dark church and tried to put the lights on. But why would Bede, the most diligent of novices, miss Compline to go to the turbine house? And how had he come by his terrible end?

A voice suddenly spoke into the silence. 'Hail Mary, full of grace, the Lord is with thee, blessed art thou among women, and blessed is the fruit of thy womb, Jesus . . .'

It sounded like Noël Coward, only the 'thou' came

out as 'theow' – such a tricky sound to get right if you are trying to disguise your accent.

There was a frisson, a frisson Daniel remembered from his own novitiate. It came with a distinctive sound, the faint rustle of individually imperceptible flinching. It happened when someone did or said something especially controversial during worship. In his day a fellow novice, intoxicated with the spirit of the age, invited representatives of local churches to a Solemn Vespers for Christian Unity. It began with him running down the darkened nave to the altar where he turned to face the startled congregation and shouted, 'Come, Lord Jesus, look on Batley!'

After the frisson a small chorus responded to the Hail Mary in unison. 'Holy Mary, Mother of God, pray for us sinners now and at the hour of our death.'

The single voice repeated: 'Hail Mary, full of grace, the Lord is—'

Then another voice said, 'For God's sake, Darren, shut up. This is not the time or the place.'

'. . . THE LORD IS WITH THEE. Blessed art thou among women, and blessed is the fruit of thy womb, Jesus.'

'Holy Mary, Mother of God, pray for us sinners now and at the hour of our death,' came the uncertain response.

'Hail Mary, full of grace . . .'

One of the figures stood, then approached the kneeling novice who was leading the rosary.

'. . . the Lord is with thee, blessed art— Ow! Did you just kick me?'

'Shut up, Darren, shut up, shut up, shut up.'

'We're saying the rosary . . .'

'We're trying to pray for Bede. How dare you turn his death into a partisan protest?'

'It's the rosary! A prayer of the Church Catholic!'

'And we're the Church of England. Can't you give it a rest? For one moment? Someone has died. And I wonder if you . . .' He mumbled something.

'Wonder if I what?'

'I wonder if your gesture of mourning is as affected as your accent.'

Father Paulinus stood. 'Stop. Get out. Both of you. To your rooms. Stay there until I send for you.'

They were both silent for a moment. 'Yes, Father,' said the kneeling novice eventually.

'And shame on you both.'

The kneeler got up and Daniel thought for a moment he was squaring up to his enemy, but then, in a detente born of habit rather than goodwill, they both turned and genuflected together to the altar.

It was Darren the postulant who had been leading the rosary and Brother Placid who had complained. Not for the first time, Daniel noted that the name chosen by a monk could be dissonant with his nature. Placid pushed ahead and then, detente done, went through the door without holding it open for Darren, a glaring breach of the rules of performative hospitality, whereby you were expected to make gestures of consideration to those you especially disliked. Daniel saw Aelred on the other side, who stood by to let the postulant past, then saw Daniel and signalled for him to come.

Daniel turned back to face the altar, genuflected, and left, feeling behind him the silent buzz of discord so familiar to vicars, who pass through rooms where the darkest impulses of humanity have flared up and disarranged everything, like poltergeists throwing ornaments around.

'What was that about?' asked Aelred.

'An eruption of differing churchmanship.'

'Oh dear.'

'Darren started saying the rosary and Brother Placid lost his temper. I think he might have kicked him.'

'The Virgin Mary would have kicked Darren,' said Aelred, 'and he's on the same side.'

'We had our differences when I was here – west facing rather than east facing, prayer book or Roman Rite – but nothing like this.'

'It's because of the ladies,' sighed Aelred.

'The ordination of women?'

'It's divided the whole community. Some are resolutely in favour, others are no less resolutely against. It has got especially bitter in the novitiate. You know how febrile it can be.'

'But why so bitter?'

'I think it may be because some of them are rather scared of ladies, though they would not say so. Officially it is a theological disagreement, of course, an obstacle, perhaps an insurmountable obstacle, to the unity of the Church.'

'What unity?'

'Some of us, Daniel, have devoted our lives to working to restore communion with the Bishop of Rome.'

Daniel nodded. 'I think there are more obstacles to reuniting the Church of England with the Church of Rome than whether or not we ordain women to the priesthood.'

'But you see my point?'

'Yes, of course, but what I just saw was not simply an ecclesiological disagreement.'

'Blood has been spilled for less.' Aelred seemed to check himself. 'But would you fetch Paulinus? I need you both.'

'What for?'

'Counsel.'

At the north lodge to Champton park Alex and Nathan were hosting a kitchen supper. Theo had decided to postpone his return to London and was still dossing down with them. If required to give an explanation, he would say it was because he wished to make sure his mother was recovering from her scare in the burning rectory, especially now his brother had gone missing. Also, he had no urgent reason to return to London, for he was between jobs. Also, he was feeling ropey after the weekend and Alex had obtained from his sources in Braunstonbury a quantity of cocaine. It would have been bad manners to leave him and Nathan to snort it alone and so he had stayed, or rather not gone, in the endless midnight chimes of habitual drug use.

Alex, too, was between jobs, if what he did could be so described. He was on the fringe of a new movement, Long Pig, which had started at his art school, and faithful to its doctrines he had rejected the formalities of technique and tradition and created work that was to the Courtauld what Anarchy in the UK was to the Mozarteum in Salzburg. Violent, chaotic and infrequent, his 'performance pieces' had generated some interest and even some income, but like most who have never had to earn a living, he only worked when he wanted to.

It was the same for Honoria, whose 'job' was little more than persuading her smart friends to have their wedding receptions at the Motcombe Hotel and ensure that the most splendid were covered by *Tatler* and the *Daily Mail*.

Their mother's riches, acquired before Bernard, and intact despite his attempted raids on them in the short years of their marriage, provided them with an allowance of a generosity in inverse proportion to her maternal affection. Her distance was cash in the bank, a deal they had no choice but to accept, and better solvent and loveless than insolvent and loveless, or so thought Honoria. Alex was less content.

Their fortune had provided for this evening's

engagement, a kitchen supper for Honoria. It was a kitchen supper in name rather than location, for the kitchen was too small for such a gathering, so they had been sitting as usual at the lovely Georgian dining table, which was too big for its space, which had to do double duty as dining room and drawing room. It was laid with china and cutlery too big for the table, overlooked by portraits too big for the wall. The lodge was only slightly larger, Theo thought, than one of those aristocratic dolls' houses he had seen at the V&A, only the furniture in them was to scale, unlike here.

Nathan was in the kitchen clearing away. He had made a sort of pheasant chasseur – 'Pheasant poacheur, rather,' said Alex – with red cabbage and pommes dauphine, then they'd had a Viennetta, for Nathan had not really mastered patisserie – two Viennettas actually, for he thought a single box of the frilly confection, while suitably festive, insufficient for four. They had drunk a Bardolino and a Moscato, items from the rattling dowry their stepmother, the present Lady de Floures, had brought with her in a truck but left behind when she retreated to Siena.

The three were sitting in front of the fire smoking purple Silk Cuts and drinking a Calvados Alex had stolen, like the red and white, from Bernard's cellar on one of his smash-and-grab raids while Mrs Shorely was on her afternoon off.

'I don't know why everyone's making such a fuss,'

said Theo, trying to stretch out. 'It's not as if he walked out into an Antarctic blizzard.'

'Something to talk about. We love having something to talk about,' said Alex. 'And a disappearing rector is a novelty.'

'Not for much longer,' said Honoria. 'He'll be back before we know it.'

'And then we can all get back to talking about our favourite topic, which is you, Hon, and your lusty sergeant.'

'He's certainly that,' said Honoria. 'Came round for lunch and went off in a huff when I offered him nothing more exciting than a Penguin.'

'He's like a puppy when he's around you.'

'Yes. So sweet.' She was silent. 'Do you think they may be connected?'

'What?'

'The strapping sergeant and the case of the absent parson?'

Alex looked at her. 'Yes, I do.'

'Oh? How?' asked Theo.

'Hasn't the thought ever crossed your mind that Daniel's attachment to Neil might be about more than solving mysteries?'

'You mean . . . Daniel has . . . special feelings for Neil?'

'It solves a BIG mystery about Daniel.'

'Doesn't it?' said Honoria.

Theo burst out laughing. 'Daniel? A *truncheon*

muncher?' Honoria flinched at that. 'The last time – the only time – Daniel had a special feeling for someone was when he was a little boy and Granny took him to hear Kirsten Flagstad sing at St Matthew's, Northampton, when Father what's-his-name – Hussey – was in charge. He wet himself. Granny had to bring him home in a chorister's cassock.'

'And nothing since then?'

'I'm fairly sure Daniel is about as sexually active as a fish slice. Not so much as a pimple when he was a teenager. Not so much as a crusty sock under the bed. I know, I looked. I once found a magazine hidden under his pillow. It was a catalogue for ecclesiastical vestments.'

'But,' said Alex, 'just because he hasn't shown any sign of erotic desire in the past – and how would we know? – doesn't mean it isn't happening now. And if it *is* happening now, imagine what that would be like?'

Honoria said, 'We're talking about *two* people, aren't we? I don't know about Daniel, but let me assure you, Neil is no more gay than Henry Cooper.'

'You never *know* . . .' said Alex.

'Don't be ridiculous, Alex. If there is passion between Daniel and Neil, it's going one way.'

'Is it?'

'You love a scalp, you gays,' said Theo. 'But not everyone you want to be gay *is* gay.'

'You said this about George Michael, Alex,' said Honoria. '*George Michael?*'

'I don't think *everyone's* gay. But it needn't be that. They've become close.'

'I imagine solving murders together creates a certain bond.'

'No, more than that. And it's not just one way. They make me think of best friends at school.'

'Yes,' said Honoria, 'and Neil goes on about him. Endlessly. Daniel said this, and Daniel said that. He's started listening to Mahler.'

Theo said, 'I found a Marc Almond record on Daniel's radiogram.'

'What was it, "Tainted Love"?'

'No, that cover with Gene Pitney. But Daniel playing anything later than the Second Viennese School is obviously evidence of a *folie d'amour.*'

'Neil's got that Marc Almond record too,' said Honoria. 'He must have, because he keeps humming it under his breath – drives me bananas.'

'Maybe it's "their tune"?'

Nathan came in from the kitchen carrying a tray with a cafetière, which looked like something from a laboratory, and dainty jewel-bright coffee cups. 'I've done the washing-up, Alex,' he said, 'and I bruck one of these cups. Sorry.'

'Coalport,' said Alex, 'nothing *that* special.'

Nathan put the tray down and began to pour.

'Nathan,' said Theo, 'they think Daniel's secretly in love with Honoria's policeman and has been rebuffed and that's why he's gone away.'

'The rector?'

'Who else?'

'It's . . . never crossed my mind.'

'What?'

'That the rector would like anyone. I mean, he likes everyone, doesn't he? So picking one . . . it's not what he does, not to my mind.'

'But did you ever think he might be gay?'

'You all look gay to me. Not you . . .' He nodded at Honoria.

'Neil is definitely not gay,' she said.

'No, nor him. But Alex and Theo and the rector.'

'I'm not gay,' said Theo. 'Well, not *very*.'

'The things you say. The things you like. BBC Two. No overhead lights. Getting hay fever.'

'That's not the same thing as wanting to have sex with men.'

'You can do that without being gay, though,' said Nathan. 'Do you want cream in that?'

The three of them looked surprised. 'Sorry, say that again,' said Honoria.

'Do you want cream?'

'Not that.'

'Oh. Most men who like to do it with other men aren't gay. They don't go to the opera. Have sushi. Fall in love.'

'What do they do?'

'They end up sharing a bed with a mate after the pub. Or they go to lay-bys and toilets or the picnic area at Wythmail Woods. How do you think I got started?'

Alex said, 'I thought with me.'

'Not just you. Or they go out and get wasted and end up in . . . situations . . . Then they go home to their wives and their kids and drive lorries and go to the football. You know?'

Nobody said anything.

'I can't see Daniel in an HGV,' said Honoria eventually.

'Me neither,' said Theo. 'And I can't see him hanging around a picnic area looking for anonymous sex.'

'Daniel is not a wraith, a disembodied spirit,' said Alex. 'He's a man and he has all the component parts of a man. Sex. Desire. They may be unimaginable to us, but it doesn't mean he doesn't have them.'

Theo said, 'And they could be dormant – or repressed – and then someone comes along and they wake up. Maybe Neil reaches the parts other men can't reach and Dan's desire is roused and – he may not even realise what's happening – and before he knows it, he's falling for Neil and it's for the first time and he doesn't understand what's happening and he starts to think Neil is feeling the same thing too.'

Alex nodded. 'And Neil is feeling attraction and affinity too, just not in the same way, but Daniel's a polar bear that's just woken up from hibernation and all he sees is a fat seal waving at him and he thinks, hello, there's my breakfast.'

'Oh, God . . .' said Honoria.

'What?'

'Neil *was* falling in love. Not with Daniel, but with me. And that was a big secret. And Daniel, who misses nothing, saw it, but thought it was about him. And then Neil – yes, of course, this is what happened – confessed it to Daniel after the service yesterday and Daniel discovered it wasn't him but me. Oh, how devastating!'

'And that's why he went. Makes sense.'

'But where?'

Aelred and Daniel and Father Paulinus were in the abbot's parlour. They were sitting in the ugly armchairs around a coffee table. One of the novices had made tea and the whisky bottle had been put back in Aelred's cupboard. They did not need a stiffener, they needed something that would sustain them, for this was going to be a long night, and they needed to be alert. At least they weren't obliged to sit in candlelight. Father Paulinus had fired up the old diesel generator that provided power when the turbine was out of service, so the lights were on, not only in the monastery, but up at the turbine house, where an ambulance and a police car had arrived, flashes of blue through the night. These sudden illuminations made the darkness of what had happened at Ravenspurn seem all the more stark. Aelred had spoken to Bede's parents – to whom he was Adrian, not Bede, with a story from birth to adulthood and a place in a family – and hearing their shock, then grief, distantly by phone when he told them their son had died in an accident (he did not give much detail) made the awfulness all the more awful.

Monks are not sentimental people, and their affection for each other, where there is affection, runs cold. 'In this life,' Aelred used to tell the novices, 'it is not about what you feel but what you do.' Whenever he had to deal with deep human feeling, Aelred felt a sort of distaste, almost a revulsion when emotion was especially high. He had seen enough of passion in the war to prefer to keep it at distance, beyond the perimeter of the monastery wall preferably. Visitors brought theirs, of course – Daniel had, with his uncontainable and undignified tears – but the cause happened off-site, and the visitors left and the rhythm of Aelred's life was restored with barely an interruption. Of course, monks brought their passions with them too, and when they flared, and the cloister trembled with anger or fear, he felt most acutely the aloneness of his chosen life. And he felt most vulnerable when what happened in the cloister obliged the involvement of the outside world, with its different ways of doing things, and processes that did not match theirs or threatened the delicate balances on which the community's viability relied.

'There are a number of issues we need to consider,' said Father Paulinus with characteristic rigour. 'First, was the death of Brother Bede an accident? If so, then we need to discover how it happened. I have had a thought about that. The machinery is exposed and as far as I know we have not made many attempts to ensure that all steps were taken to mitigate the risk it might cause to anyone operating it. There is legislation, I am led to believe, and when we last had it serviced the engineer said that although it was of great historical interest to him, it was an accident waiting to happen, and if the Health and Safety Executive, which is the body established to ensure that working practices—'

'Yes, yes, Father, we know about that . . .'

'—if they were to inspect it, I do not know if we would be compliant, and if we would have to take immediate remedial action . . .'

'But the turbine house has been in operation without incident since long before the war,' said Aelred. 'We know more about it than they do.'

'Then perhaps we have been lucky, or lucky up to now. It is no defence for us to say that we did not think the rules applied. I will take advice on this, of course.'

'Are there exemptions?' asked Daniel. 'And if so, would we qualify?'

'I don't know. Like I said, I will take advice. But if we have been negligent, then we have to consider the legal consequences.'

'We've been using Wallace & Wallace for years,' said Aelred. 'I'm sure they would have said if there were the potential for exposure to *unnecessary* risk.'

'And there is another possibility,' continued Paulinus, 'or set of possibilities. Was his death caused by himself or by another deliberately?'

'Really, Father,' said Aelred, 'it seems in the poorest of taste to even say such a thing . . .'

'That may be so, Father Aelred, but the police officers on site are working with that possibility in mind. It is potentially a crime scene . . .'

Daniel shuddered, remembering the terrible night at Badsaddle Airfield when he had seen Josh Biddle's body in the old chapel there, lit in arc lights, surrounded by scene-of-crime officers and pathologists in their paper suits, logging every gruesome detail, the brutal mystery of his death.

'. . . we will hear from them in due course,' Paulinus continued. 'They will make their enquiries, but I think it important that we consider the whos, whys, whens, wheres and whats before we speak to them . . .'

'If someone has done harm to Bede,' said Daniel, 'can you think of a reason why, or a likely candidate?'

Aelred was stretched out in the armchair, his fingers pressed together in front of his face in an attitude half of prayer, half of thoughtfulness. 'As I've said so many times, in the event of a murder at the monastery we would all be prime suspects.' It did not seem so funny now and he waved his hands in the air as if to dispel an unpleasant smell. 'But of course, it is a ridiculous idea. He may have been irritating, sometimes unbearably irritating, but . . . kill him? And if somebody did, kill him like this? No, it is absurd.'

There was a knock at the door.

'Yes?'

Brother Placid opened it. 'I have Sergeant Bainbridge, Father Aelred.'

He ushered in a uniformed policeman, in his fifties, thought Daniel, with grey hair and a face set in the experienced officer's unchanging look of wry detachment. 'Father Aelred,' he said in a Yorkshire accent. 'Fathers,' he added, nodding at Paulinus and Daniel. 'Very sorry that we find ourselves in these circumstances.'

'Dennis, how kind of you to come,' said Aelred. 'I do hope we have not spoiled your evening.'

'A policeman's lot is not a happy one, Father Aelred, especially not when *The Amsterdam Kill* is on telly. But Mrs Bainbridge is on the video recorder. Don't be surprised if all the lights go out again . . .' He laughed at his own joke.

'You know Father Paulinus – he's the novice master, among other things – and this is Canon Daniel Clement, who was once a novice here. Many years ago.'

Sergeant Bainbridge looked puzzled for a moment. 'Not the Canon Clement who's vicar of Champton? The sleuth? You're all over the papers!'

'Rector of Champton. But what you read in the newspapers is mostly nonsense.'

'Isn't it always? But I believe you know one of my lads? Neil Vanloo? I helped train him when he was a young constable. How's he getting on?'

Daniel's stomach lurched. 'Very well – he's the detective, not me.'

'Talented young man, even as a probationer, but that

was a nasty business with your curate. I was sorry to read about it. That poor boy.'

'Yes, it has been horrible.'

'But what of our poor Bede?' interrupted Aelred.

'Very nasty too. A terrible sight.'

'We know. I didn't know where – or what – to anoint . . . So I just poured some holy oil in like . . . 3-IN-ONE on a bicycle chain.' Aelred shuddered.

Nobody said anything.

Then he said, 'But, Sergeant Bainbridge, do you have any preliminary thoughts about what happened?'

'I think he was working up there and he got his scapular caught in a cog and it pulled him backwards into the machine. Ker-chung!'

The monks looked at each other.

'We've never had an accident with it before,' said Aelred.

'Then you were lucky, Father Aelred,' said Sergeant Bainbridge. 'Unprotected moving parts like that? Health and Safety would have a field day!'

'Would have? Or will have?' said Paulinus.

'Doesn't apply to you.'

'Why not?'

'As I recall, the legislation only covers employers and employees. Health and Safety at Work Act. And you're not either.'

'But we are employers,' said Aelred. 'We have cleaning staff.'

'In the monastery?'

'Yes.'

'But not in the turbine house?'

'No, only the brethren go there.'

'Then I don't think the Act applies. I have to say, there are reasons why we've had Factory Acts and inspectorates and occupational health. Workplaces with this kind of machinery are dangerous. Safety first?'

'Well, you never think it will happen to you, I suppose. And we . . . we have always gone our own way here. As you know, Dennis.'

'I'm not looking to come here and tell you how to do things. You are the experts at living your life. But you are going to have to explain to his parents how their son came by his death. That might be a very difficult conversation if they come to feel that you have been . . . negligent.'

Aelred winced. 'Negligent? Negligent means liable?'

'I would have a word with your insurers.'

Paulinus pulled a face. 'We are not over-insured, as a matter of fact, Sergeant,' he said.

'Why not?'

'I suppose we have always acted consistently with our belief in providence. That the Lord will provide for our needs. And, actually, he does provide.'

'I don't mean to sound flippant,' said Sergeant Bainbridge, 'but the Lord has not provided casing for your turbine machinery. That's your job, I dare say, meeting God halfway? Like I said, you might want to talk to your insurers. And your lawyers. Anyway, I had better head up the hill, see what the lads are thinking. Any chance of a brew? It's a cold night.'

'Yes of course, Dennis, for you and for the men. Paulinus, could you get a novice on to it?'

Paulinus nodded and left.

'And you'll keep me informed of . . . anything I need to know?'

'Of course, if I can. You never know how it will go with an investigation like this. And if you have any concerns, Father Aelred, you know how to find me. Goodnight, Fathers!' he said with a professional cheeriness at odds with the sombre mood of that night.

Miss March had been looking forward to stopping at the Mandarin for a takeaway supper of sweet-and-sour pork with egg-fried rice after 'A Voyage into the Fjords', this evening's programme for Music Appreciation at Braunstonbury library. Then Margaret Porteous approached her in the interval between Grieg's 'Peer Gynt Suite' on the gramophone and Sinding's 'Rustle of Spring' on the pianoforte, played by Miss Wood, LRAM.

'Miss March! So lovely to see another Champton face at our soirée! Stella used to give me a lift, then Anne kindly offered after Stella died, but . . . well, no Anne tonight.'

So Miss March offered to take Margaret home in her Vanden Plas after the event, and then spent the next forty minutes wishing she had not because there were some navy suede and tan leather cross-body bags that looked like Liz Claiborne but weren't on the front seat, which she did not want Margaret to see before they were properly displayed in the shop.

Miss Wood at the pianoforte hoisted the Norwegian flag again with Grieg's 'Wedding Day at Troldhaugen', a very jolly occasion indeed and full of promise, which the soloist seemed to anticipate with tremendous energy.

There was applause and a vote of thanks, more applause, and a call went out for assistance in putting away the pianoforte.

'It's a Blüthner, Miss March,' said Margaret, 'a very fine instrument that belonged to Miss Wood's mother.'

It looked – and sounded – to Miss March like it might have belonged to Grieg's mother, but she made no comment for she was hungry and would now have to make do with a sandwich or something from the freezer. She gently shepherded Margaret towards the library steps.

'Wait here, Margaret,' she said. 'I'll bring the car round.'

She had parked her Vanden Plas, with its bronze livery and gleaming grille, in the council car park, the most convenient spot for the library, but it was also the most convenient spot for McDonald's, and now the spaces on either side were occupied, an Escort on the left and a Fiesta on the right. Both cars were heaving with young people, smoking and eating and drinking, and playing on booming sound systems what sounded to Miss March like an air-raid warning.

'POMP up the JYAAAM, POMP it UP!'

What is a jam that you might pump up, she wondered?

'Git the PWARTY STWARTED.'

The party had already started evidently, for as Miss March approached someone threw a greasy box out of the window of the Fiesta. It landed at her feet, always objectionable, but she was wearing a new pair of Ponticelli court shoes in blue leather and suede and the thought of a grease spot on them was intolerable.

She glared at the occupants and there was something about her that made them wind up the window as she drew level. She rapped on the glass, but the people inside ignored her. The driver turned up the volume and smirked to himself rather than to her, which so irritated her that she picked up the greasy box, with three cold fries still stuck to it, and fastened it under a wiper.

'TAKE YOUR RUBBISH HOME!' she said very firmly. Then she got into her car and sat absolutely still. She'd recognised the driver. She did not know where from, but it stirred something in her so powerfully that it took a minute before she was able to turn the key in the ignition and drive away.

'Just throw those things on the back seat, would you, Mrs Porteous?' she said when she pulled up at the foot of the library steps.

'Oh, the bags,' said Margaret. 'They're lovely . . . Are you all right, Miss March?'

'A contretemps with some louts. Nothing to worry about.'

'In the car park? It's like Gin Lane after dark. The police do nothing about it. And they know who they are.'

'Seat belt, please.'

Margaret buckled herself in, and Miss March drove away. There was a fiddly junction with Station Road, but once they were through that she spoke.

'Why?'

'Why what?'

'Why don't the police do anything about it if they know who they are?'

'What can they do? In the old days they'd get summary justice administered on the spot. If the constable tried that now, they'd arrest him.'

'So who are they?'

'Some of them are from Champton and the Badsaddles. Went to our school. You perhaps know I am a foundation governor . . .' There was a slight emphasis on 'foundation'.

'No, I did not.'

'Have been for years. One of those voluntary positions you take on and never seem able to give up. Like churchwarden. Anyway, we had a terror a few years ago, Brandon Redding. A terror at ten, a nasty piece of work at twenty. His mother chucked him out and he went to live with his father – I say father, I think it was a more casual arrangement than that – in Stow, but now he's back in Braunstonbury.'

'When was he in Stow?'

'Oh, must have been when he was sixteen? Yes, it was; it was after he failed his GCEs. Four years ago. He only lasted there a couple of years and then he came to Braunstonbury and got a job at the record shop. He's into that ghastly music.'

'I just heard some. Makes "In the Hall of the Mountain King" sound like Bing Crosby.'

'I suppose so. Also mixed up in drugs and goodness knows what, they say. I think he may have been involved with that poor Biddle boy. I wonder why you're going this way, dear?'

'This way? Oh, I've missed the turn. Silly of me. Autopilot. Thought I was going to Stow.'

Aelred and Daniel were now sitting alone in the abbot's parlour. Father Paulinus had left just after Sergeant Bainbridge and the whisky had come out again. They were sipping in silence, anxious rather than companionable, then Aelred said, 'You've been rather quiet, Daniel. What do you think?'

'About what?'

'What Sergeant Bainbridge said. Negligence. Liability.'

'I don't think we should be worrying about liability in the first instance.'

'No,' said Aelred with a testiness he could not conceal. 'Of course, it is Bede we must think of and his family . . . who are on their way.'

'I don't mean that, quite.'

Aelred looked at him and his eyes narrowed. 'What do you mean?'

'I'm not sure it was an accident.'

Aelred said nothing for a moment. 'Why?'

'I don't know.'

'What do you mean, you don't know?'

'There's something not right about it.'

'Hard to imagine a death of this kind any other way.'

'It's more specific than that. But I can't put my finger on it.'

Aelred looked thoughtful. 'Can you talk me through it?'

'What was he doing there?'

'I've been thinking about that. I wondered if it was to make sure the blasted thing was working properly. It's rather an unreliable system, you see. Well, you know . . .'

'When I talked to him this morning, he said it had been acting up.'

'So perhaps he wanted to check it before *Birds of a Feather*? The brethren wouldn't like it if the television set didn't come on and they missed it.'

'But why during Compline? Wasn't he diligent about liturgy?'

'Oh my goodness, yes, exceptionally so. You should

see him when he's thurifer, it's like he's handling uranium.'

Daniel in his time had been thurifer, responsible for the little silver bucket on a chain in which incense was burnt. It was a fiddly thing and required careful use to ensure smoke billowed when smoke was required. For a diligent novice, as he and Bede both were, high and holy days obliged performing splendid figure-of-eight swings while on the move, a necessary accomplishment if you wanted to be taken seriously as a contender by your fellow novices. It had not occurred to him at the time, but did now, that the monks were not really interested, and if they noticed at all it was with irritation at them showing off.

'If he was diligent about everything, and if he was worried about the generator, would he have thought that a priority? Or attending Compline? Or perhaps Paulinus asked him to go and check?'

'Might have. Paulinus is also diligent, as you may have noticed. He's precentor, novice master . . . and other things. A very capable monk.'

'Yes. Wasn't it him singing Compline earlier? One of those voices that's made for plainsong.'

'Like yours . . . but never mind that. So, if Paulinus asked him to go and check the turbine during Compline then he would have done it, I think. Obedience to the novice master in a particular matter would trump standing orders about attendance. But, Daniel, you haven't said what I think you might want to say.'

'No. You mean, I think it was murder?'

'Or suicide?'

'No, murder.'

'Why would you think that?'

'I don't know. I've seen a few now. And it feels like that.'

Aelred took a sip of whisky and absentmindedly rinsed his mouth with it as if it were Listerine rather than Balvenie. 'You've just been through a very upsetting experience – more than one very upsetting experience – and that inevitably will colour your perception of events.'

'But we need to inform the police of our suspicions.'

'*Your* suspicions. At the moment only that. It's too big a leap to make, from Bede being in the turbine house at an unwonted time to being the victim of murder. Can't you see that?'

'Yes, but . . . perhaps I've got a nose for these things.'

'I think you should get some sleep. Let's see how you feel after Matins. And after I've heard what the police have to say.'

The fire was low in the grate at the warrener's cottage when Honoria heard the sound of Neil's Escort arriving. His headlights swept across the drawn curtains and then he rather blundered through the front door, she thought, like a copper breaking into a drug den rather than a lover arriving in the dead of night. But she quite liked that, his physicality, his purpose.

'Hello, love,' he said and gave her a kiss on the cheek. 'Sorry it's so late, but . . . you know work.'

'I feel I should say your dinner's in the oven, or something like that, but it isn't.'

'I wouldn't want it to be. I had a horrible burger with the lads, anyway. But have I got news for you . . .'

'I need to talk to you too.'

Neil raised an eyebrow. 'That sounds ominous.'

'Not ominous, but you might need to brace yourself. Can I pour you a drink?'

'What are you having?'

'Probably a bottle of Daddy's claret. Want one?'

'Go on then.' He took off his jacket like a rugby player taking off his jersey and half fell onto the sofa. He let out a sigh. 'Has your dad found out about us?'

'Daddy? No, it's not that.' She handed him a glass of Saint-Émilion and sat next to him, curling her feet up and sliding her body against his. He smelt faintly of works canteen, grease and tomato ketchup. A note of changing room. Not entirely unlovely, she thought. 'I think we've – I've worked out what's up with Daniel.'

'We?'

'I've been to supper at Alex's.'

Neil nodded. 'What's the theory?'

'Neil, have you ever wondered why Daniel and you have become such close friends?'

Neil looked a little surprised. 'That's an unexpected question.'

'Have you?'

He was silent for a moment and then said, 'Of course I have.'

'And what do you think?'

He took a big slurp of wine. 'Honestly? Affinity.'

'Affinity? What, you have so much in common?'

'No, not like fishing at t'gravel pits and going down t'pub. The opposite. One of the things I like most about Daniel is that we aren't interested in the same things. I enjoy the difference. Through him I see the world in a different way. And he's so bloody clever. I love his scope, his insight. And he makes me laugh.'

'And?'

'This is really not the kind of conversation I'm look-ing for, to be honest.'

'Me neither. But there's more?'

He thought again. 'Yes, there is. He has something I want.'

'Go on.'

'A part of me that's missing. And I think it's the same for him. A different thing, but the same . . . I mean, I have something that he lacks.'

'What?'

'Daniel's all thought, all mind. But what about his body, his passions, his desire, his anger, his appetite for life? He shows nothing of that to the world. And I think he shows nothing of that to himself . . . and it must be in there, because I don't think he can do the things he does, or understand people, without knowing how blood and guts work. Not as an abstract theory, but as a person with a life. Am I talking a load of bollocks?'

'No, not at all. It makes a lot of sense. And that's you, of course. Very much flesh and blood. Fit, athletic, passionate. Perhaps that's what fascinates him?'

'But I'm not just flesh and blood, love; I think, I feel. We have an affinity of mind, not body.'

'You like his intelligence? But you don't lack intelligence. So what do you want from him?'

'Faith.'

'Oh . . .' That had not occurred to Honoria.

'I used to have it and it went. It was such a big part of me, and now it's such a big absence. Daniel is like – there's a line from one of the psalms, a river full of water. I want to get in it again. I want to swim in it again.'

'Blimey! Have you ever talked about this?'

'To him? No, we don't talk personal stuff. Well, sometimes we get near it a bit . . . then we pull away.'

'Example?'

'When we're driving. Both facing forward, looking out of the windscreen at the world outside, not at each other. Sometimes he'll say something, or I'll say something, and suddenly there's a feeling of . . . standing on the edge of something. But what do you do when you come to the edge of something?'

'Go over, or step back?'

'We're not Bonnie and Clyde,' he said.

Honoria got up and poured them another glass of wine. His had gone quickly, she thought.

'This is making you uncomfortable?' she asked.

'A bit. It's not the sort of thing . . .'

'Funny, because you're unusually eloquent when you do talk about it. You want to swim in Daniel's great big river again? What does that sound like?'

'I don't know. What does it sound like to you?'

'It sounds like something lovers say.'

Neil looked baffled. 'What do you mean, like lovers?'

'What do we look for in a lover? Completion. "You complete me," you know?'

There was a pause. Then Neil said, 'You complete idiot.'

Then Honoria looked baffled. 'Me?'

'Me,' he said.

'Go on.'

'Daniel. Not abstract. Passionate. About me?'

'Yes, about you. Nothing abstract about it. He's in love with you, Neil. Don't you see?'

'No. No, not at all. Why would I? Did you?'

'Not until today. Alex did. But then he's got a sixth sense for that sort of thing. But what about you?'

'What do you mean?'

'What do you feel about him?'

'Me? I'm not in love with him. Not in that way. I'm not made that way. But Daniel . . . is made that way?'

'Perhaps he is.'

'Why didn't he say anything?'

Honoria thought for a moment. 'It's not the easiest thing for a country parson in middle age to tell a young detective sergeant. It's more the kind of thing you'd hear taking a statement than in a tête-à-tête.'

'Why didn't he tell me? He could have told me. What did he think I would do?'

'Perhaps he didn't realise it himself at first. All those passions kept firmly at bay. And then suddenly they're not.'

'Bloody 'ell!'

'What?'

'After the All Souls service. I asked him to come with me to the rectory because I had something to tell him. And he thought . . . no, he can't have.'

'He thought you were going to tell him that you felt for him what he felt for you.'

'And instead I told him I was in love with you.'

There was a silence.

'That's an interesting way of declaring your love to someone.'

'I don't go around declaring my love for people.'

'People?'

There was another silence.

'Poor Dan,' said Neil. 'I need to see him.'

'We don't know where he is.'

'That was my news. I know where he is.'

'How?'

'He's at his monastery. It's near Bradford. He met an old colleague of mine today, station sergeant at Ravenspurn. Left a message for me at the station.'

'Cops and clergy. Everyone knows everyone.'

'I've got to go and see him.'

How interesting, Honoria thought, that the one he runs to is the one he is not in love with.

'Can you get time off?' she asked.

'I'm on my time off.'

'Can you at least fit me in tonight?'

9

Matins at Ravenspurn abbey was more splendid than usual on the Feast of St Willibrord, a local saint from Ripon, who left Yorkshire to evangelise the peoples of the Low Countries in the eighth century. He founded an abbey at Echternach, so Ravenspurn had a sort of twinning arrangement with it, and the celebration was fully observed, for nothing may interrupt the daily round of prayer, and the celebration of a life lived fully for God, even the death of a brother, and so horrible a death. Bede's sudden absence was not only in their minds but on display, for his stall in choir was empty, and there was something different about the plainsong chant; the subtraction of even a single voice thinned it, changed the texture.

Sitting in the visitors' pews were a middle-aged couple, set apart from the other guests. They were Bede's parents, Mr and Mrs Corbett, who had driven through the night from Telford in their new Mark III Cavalier – 'once driven, forever smitten', said Mr

Corbett out loud as they cruised past Rochdale on the M62, forgetting for a moment what awaited them. Their son's death awaited, explained by Abbot Aelred in the abbot's parlour, with cups of hot, sweet tea, and as many details omitted as their questions allowed. They had not slept but came to Matins, for where better to go when grief has crashed into your life than to the place which connects you to the life beyond?

You would think a community of Christian disciples would be good at bereavement, but monks are not, or not by the standards of the world outside, because they live on the threshold of heaven, and when someone crosses that threshold, it is not seen really as a loss, but more a change of routine. And, as Daniel had observed and experienced, monks tended not to be sentimental about those they lived with – they have seen too much of each other and revealed too much of themselves for that – so the Corbetts sat in their miserable purdah, with guests and brethren maintaining a distance.

'God, the Saviour of all,' intoned Aelred, 'you sent your bishop Willibrord from this land to proclaim the good news to many peoples and confirm them in their faith: help us also to witness to your steadfast love by word and deed so that your Church may increase and grow strong in holiness; through Jesus Christ your Son, our Lord . . .' and then he yawned an uncontainable yawn, 'who is alive and reigns with you, in the unity of the Holy Spirit, one God, now and for ever.'

'Amen,' they all replied.

After the blessing the monks processed out and the guests followed into the hall and thence to the refectory for breakfast. The Corbetts did not know what to do, so Daniel collected them and ushered them with as much silent politeness as he could towards a table. He showed them to their places and when Mrs Corbett said 'thank you' one of the older monks shushed her from reflex, and this seemed so harshly done that Mrs Corbett went red and started to cry. Mr Corbett tried to hush her, in that moment more embarrassed by her weeping than concerned for her distress. Daniel found it suddenly unbearable and said, 'Perhaps you would like to come with me? I can make some breakfast in the guest house.' Aelred gave him a nod of appreciation from the top table. He showed the Corbetts out and they followed him to the guest house where there was a kitchenette, offering 'tea- and coffee-making facilities', and a toaster, and some white sliced bread in a bread bin, and some little pats of butter and individual jams that looked like something that had seeped from a bandage. Mr and Mrs Corbett sat at a cheerless little table covered with a vinyl cloth.

'Would you like tea?'

Daniel made a pot and found some milk in the fridge. 'Toast?'

'Yes, please,' they both said.

'I thought they'd make their own bread,' said Mrs Corbett. 'You don't expect Mothers Pride in a monastery.'

'Father's Pride,' said Mr Corbett; 'they could call it Father's Pride,' and he smiled at his joke.

'We used to make our own bread,' said Daniel. 'When I was a novice here, but that was twenty-five years ago.'

'You were a novice here, Father?'

'Yes, I was Brother Crispin then. I'm Father Daniel now. Daniel Clement, rector of Champton in the diocese of Stow.'

'I thought I recognised you,' said Mr Corbett. 'You've been in all the papers. Because of the murder.'

'The *murders*,' said Mrs Corbett. 'How awful for you.'

'Yes,' said Daniel. 'I'm very sorry for your loss. I only talked to Bede – to Adrian a couple of times, but I found him very engaging.'

'He's an amazing lad,' said Mr Corbett. 'I don't know where he gets it from.'

The fact of his son's death had not yet altered the tenses of his sentences. And then it did. 'He's . . . he *was* very bright. Mind like a dynamo. We used to have to put on the wireless when we put him to bed when he was little or he'd never go to sleep. And then always reading. Grammar school, scholarship to Oxford . . .' He ran out of words as the realisation that the future promised for his talented son would not arrive. 'We are so proud of him.'

The toaster dinged and two slices jumped up like startled rabbits. Daniel put them on a plate and pulled up a chair at the little table with the vinyl tablecloth where he had seated the grieving Corbetts.

'I don't know that I can eat anything,' said Mrs Corbett.

'You must try, love,' said Mr Corbett and started spreading the slices with butter from the foil-wrapped pats. 'You can never . . . get it all on the knife, can you?' he said, and Daniel noticed that his hands were trembling.

The door swung open with the force used when the opener thinks the room is empty. It was Colin. He looked surprised. 'Are you using the toaster?'

'Evidently.'

'Only the controls are very sensitive, and I've set it precisely.'

'We haven't touched them,' said Mr Corbett defensively.

'Nothing worse than toast that's underdone or over-done. Damp or burnt.'

'Good morning, Colin,' said Daniel. 'This is Mr and Mrs Corbett. This is Colin . . .'

'Morning. Will you be long?'

'Long?'

'I usually get a clear run at the kitchenette after Matins.' He gave the forced smile of someone trying to be polite, but not too hard.

'Aren't you staying in the monastery, Colin?'

'Yes, but I usually have my breakfast here. It's a bit early for me over there.'

'Mr and Mrs Corbett are staying here. In the guest house. They are Bede's parents.'

'Oh, I see. I am sorry for your loss.'

'Thank you.'

'He had the makings of a fine scholar.'

Nobody said anything.

'But take as long as you want,' Colin said eventually.

He hesitated. For a moment Daniel thought he would lean against the counter and wait there. Then he gave the faintest shrug and left.

'That tea should be brewed by now,' said Daniel. 'How do you like it?'

'Milk and two for me, just milk for Joyce.'

Daniel made the tea in mismatched mugs, and they sat for a moment in silence as Mr Corbett ate a slice of toast and Mrs Corbett left hers uneaten and they all sipped their tea.

'He could have been a don, Father,' said Mr Corbett, 'but then . . . vocation, you know?'

'Dons were originally monks,' said Daniel, 'and anyone who's been a fellow of an Oxford college would feel at home in a monastery.'

'Were you at Oxford?'

'I was an undergraduate in London, then Oxford for theological college. Then Leeds for my PhD, when I was here. I didn't finish it, actually.'

'Why not?'

'I realised my future lay elsewhere.'

'Why? Sorry, I don't mean to pry . . .'

'I loved it here. It was to me what it was to Bede, to Adrian, I think. I saw myself in him.'

'But you left.'

'Yes, I came to realise – actually, Father Aelred came to realise first – that God had other plans.'

'How do you mean?'

'I think he saw that I was really made for parish ministry. It took me a bit longer to see it. I was so set on coming here.'

'So was Adrian. I remember when he came back from his first retreat here he couldn't stop talking about it. It was like when we took him to Disneyland.'

Disneyland, thought Daniel; he had sometimes thought Ravenspurn was like Disneyland, not that he had ever been to Disneyland – a place where fantasy became reality. Those who believed in this life said they were living in anticipation of heaven; but if you did not, wouldn't it look like that? Those who did live it, and were made for it, were not fantasists but realists, because they cannot live any other way. The thought flashed through Daniel's mind of Pluto catching and killing Donald Duck in an outbreak of cartoon violence.

'We were churchgoers, Father,' said Mrs Corbett, 'but not very religious. Adrian went to Sunday School, and he loved the Bible stories and at school he sang in the choir. And then he wanted to go to St Saviour's, very High Church, because they had a choir. So we took him and the minute he went through the door he knew it was for him. Smells and bells and everything. I found it a bit much at first, but we got used to it and then we got to love it. Adrian started as a server – he was boat boy—'

'That's how I started too,' said Daniel, remembering the anxiety of being tiny and dressed in a cassock and cotta, a tiny white sort of poncho, and having to follow the thurifer around carrying the brass incense holder, shaped like a little boat on a stand, with a hinged lid and a spoon. He had to open the lid and hold it very steadily when the thurifer needed to spoon out the fat grains of incense inside and pile them on the coals in the thurible so they would suddenly catch and start to burn, and scented smoke would billow out and make his eyes sting and his throat catch if he wasn't careful. The first job you get as a junior server, he thought, was really an introduction to the impracticalities of proper ceremonial, where nothing was designed with utility in mind and a child was required to stand in proximity to red-hot coals and smoke.

'. . . and then he went up the ladder, you see. He became a torch bearer, and an acolyte and then assistant thurifer and assistant crucifer . . . and he did Divinity at school and loved it . . .'

'But history was his best subject,' said Mr Corbett, taking over from his wife, 'and he was so clever he got a scholarship to Oxford, because he wanted to go to Magdalen for the music and Pusey House was just down the road, so it was seamless, really. Off he went to college and on Sundays – and most days – he went to worship at Pusey House. It was a perfect fit, really.'

It would have been a perfect fit, thought Daniel, for when he had been at Cuddesdon, the theological college just outside the city and the nearest thing the Church of England had to Sandhurst, he would go to Mass sometimes at Pusey House just to get a fix of proper Anglo-Catholic religion. There the True Faith was maintained, there in quasi-monastic discipline the rites and ceremonies of the Church were properly celebrated, buttressed with sound learning thanks to its library, and detached from the world, which flowed up and down St Giles'. Standing outside, facing that world, was a sign saying 'Pusey House Chapel, open to members of the University'. That was either an invitation or a barrier, and although Daniel was a member of the university he remembered pausing at the door and asking himself if he wanted to worship in a church that opened its doors only to such an exclusive clientele. He went in, and was beguiled, and worshipped, and loved it, and joined dozens of others like himself and Bede, but never forgot that feeling on the threshold. Years later, he discovered it had formed into something solid within him, and was why he was not in a cloister but a parish.

'Do you know it?'

'I'm sorry?' said Daniel.

'Pusey House?'

'Yes, I do, I used to worship there too.' He blushed,

not at the memory of the extravagances of his piety and worship when he was a student, but at having lost his concentration when he should have been paying attention to bereaved parents.

It was breakfast time at Champton and Bernard was sitting alone in the old servants' hall with a cup of coffee and a bowl of Alpen, which he thought good for his health, for it reminded him of the sawdust-like supplement he had been given in the war as a defence against the malnourishment caused by rationing. The door swung open and Audrey swung in.

'Good morning, Bernard!' she said.

'Good morning, dear lady,' he replied, thrown for a moment by the interruption and the brio of his guest. 'I hope you slept well? And the puppies?' He looked hopefully at the floor, but scampering came there none.

'With Mrs Shorely,' said Audrey, 'who has not only – very kindly – offered to mind them this morning so I can meet the decorators at the rectory, but also offered to boil me an egg.'

Bernard's defensive instinct rose. 'Decorators?'

'Decorators, and the insurance man from Ecclesiastical to assess what needs replacing. And what's covered.'

Bernard shuffled towards the sideboard and poured her a cup from the ugly stainless-steel coffee pot on the hot plate.

'Your coffee, Audrey. But why enjoin battle?'

'Oh, you know how it is with insurers. The cover, so

comprehensive when they sell it to you, turns out to be anything but comprehensive when you need to claim.'

'But I'm sure they won't quibble over arson. And water damage.'

'That's what I intend to find out,' she said. 'And if there are points we quibble over, at least I know there is the estate to turn to.'

'Well,' said Bernard, 'I feel sure that your insurers will make more than ample provision—'

'It is so very reassuring, Bernard, to know that you take your responsibilities as patron seriously, as so many de Floures before you also have. And that you will not see your rector and his widowed mother live in squalor . . . sounds like something from a Victorian novel, doesn't it?'

Audrey's eyes, he thought later, glittered as she said this.

'And to know we can rely on your very generous hospitality in our hour, or days, or weeks, of need . . .'

Jean Shorely appeared in the doorway with two brown boiled eggs in a double eggcup and two slices of toast on a plate. 'Four minutes and thirty seconds, Mrs Clement, give or take. Anything more, m'lord?'

'No, thank you, Mrs Shorely.'

As Mrs Shorely retreated, Audrey took the crown clean off the first of the eggs with one swing of her knife — what an efficient headsman she would have made, thought Bernard — and looked inside. 'Give or take . . .' she said.

★

After breakfast Daniel was sitting at the desk in his plain little room in the guest house. He was trying to think about Bede, trying to sort the details – some in focus, others blurred – that would tell him how and why he had died. Normally this took little effort; his natural gift for observation and the propellant of curiosity would produce hypotheses, or rather scenarios, that would run in his imagination until counter-arguments or lack of evidence stalled them. Eventually the scenarios would fail until one or two remained. He could feel it physically when the details began to fit together – a feeling of pressure in his sinuses. He sometimes wondered if this was what was meant by scenting victory.

But now there was nothing. It was as if his thoughts had stalled. The story of Bede's death was not as straightforward as the version he knew would soon be official. There was too much shadow, too much flicker, obscuring and blurring what had happened, and too much anxiety swirling round the community to allow so neat and swiftly confected a story to stand. He also knew there was little point in challenging it unless he had a better version to offer, and he did not. How could he come up with a better version when all he could think about was Neil, in the self-inflicted torture of unrequited love? Unrequited love. That was for governesses in Victorian novels, and it usually came right, or they walked into a lake.

It was not going to come right. He was not going to walk into a lake. He was going to do what he had done before, return to the life he was called to, without distraction, or indulgence. And that would start now.

He got up, left the silent loneliness of his room behind him, and went to the common room. He was reading the paper when the hebdomadary, Brother Sebastian, came by. 'There's a letter for you, Father,' he said, dropping onto the coffee table an envelope of pale-blue Basildon Bond, addressed to him in familiar writing and the royal-blue Quink the writer invariably used. Daniel left it there while he read the paper, which was full of speculation about events in East Germany reaching a crisis. There had been a huge demonstration in Alexanderplatz a couple of days before and no one had been shot, and there had been a change of leader, and if he were not so distracted by the letter on the table in front of him, he might have dared to hope that change of a kind and an order unthinkable for forty years was coming. But he could not read about epoch-defining events until he had read the rather more parochial contents of the letter in front of him, so he abandoned *The Times*, which was immediately taken, almost snatched, by one of the older monks whom he had not seen hovering, and opened the envelope.

Inside was a sheet of his own notepaper, but Champton Rectory and the address had been crossed out. Underneath, in capitals, Audrey had written CHAMPTON HOUSE and added in subscript, 'Badsaddle 264'.

Dearest Dan,

I think this will probably get to you because I think you are at Ravenspurn. I think this because I can't think of anywhere you would more likely run away to. And you have run away, I think?
I don't know why – but you must know, dearest Dan, that there is nothing you need run away from as far as I am concerned.
Will you let me know you are all right?
And when you will come home?
I think Bernard would also like to know when you are coming home.
Your loving mummy
xxxooxxx

P.S. I have a marvellous project underway, but you need not concern yourself with it.

P.P.S. It is this: I am rather pestering Bernard. I have breakfast with him and I sit up late with him in the library, not because I want to – I would rather be in bed – but because the more disagreeable he finds my presence in the house (and he's far too polite to avoid me), the quicker he'll be to cough up for repairs to the rectory if the insurance doesn't cover it.

P.P.P.S. I know you won't like this but you are NOT

GOOD at this sort of thing and I am, and you're not here anyway.

P.P.P.P.S. The Sedum spectabile is still out, just – amazing!

Irrepressible Audrey, he thought, who says what needs to be said in a dozen brief lines and what should not be said in stream-of-consciousness postscripts. He wondered what he should do. Reply by letter? Or telephone? He did not know if he would be able to manage a conversation on the telephone. Perhaps a message for Mrs Shorely to pass on?

There was a gentle cough. Aelred was standing just behind him.

'I hope I am not disturbing you, only Sergeant Bainbridge is in the parlour and would like to talk to you.'

Daniel followed Aelred into the cloister. 'What does he want?'

'I don't know exactly. How are the Corbetts by the way?'

'Exhausted. I gave them breakfast. I think they are sleeping now.'

'I hope they are. The infirmarian gave them some of Father Chad's Mogadons.'

'Is he meant to do that?' Daniel asked.

'He's responsible for the care of the sick, so I should say so,' said Aelred.

'But it's prescription only, isn't it?'

'It's not chemotherapy, Daniel.'

Aelred walked on ahead of him, to avoid any more conversation on this topic.

In the parlour Sergeant Bainbridge, in uniform, awaited. The fire was lit and he sat in front of it warming himself with a cup of tea and a plate of cheap biscuits.

'Canon Clement,' he said, and half stood as a gesture of respect rather than the full monty.

Daniel nodded – 'Sergeant Bainbridge' – and sat down opposite.

'Would you like something, Daniel?' asked Aelred, more as a nod in the general direction of Darjeeling rather than a firm offer.

'No, thanks. You wanted to see me, Sergeant?'

'To put your mind at rest, Father,' said the policeman. 'Father Aelred mentioned that you have concerns about Brother Bede's death?'

'I have many concerns about his death – who wouldn't? – but a question rather than a concern.'

'Go on,' said Bainbridge.

'Why are you so quick to attribute it to accident?'

The policeman's face set slightly. Daniel had seen the same with Neil when he was talking to 'concerned citizens'.

'It's the scenario that fits the known facts.'

'Are you sure?' said Daniel.

'No,' Bainbridge replied curtly.

'So what are you going to do?'

'We can never be sure, can we? But we play the odds,

Father. It looks more like an accident than anything else, and until someone has a good reason to question that, we are unlikely to commit more resources.'

That sounded like something people said at a press conference, thought Daniel. 'May I ask one more question, Sergeant?'

'You may.'

'What was he doing there?'

'Brother Bede? Inspecting the turbine,' said Bainbridge.

'Why?'

'Father Paulinus asked him to take a look at it to make sure it was working properly. It had been a bit erratic, and they wanted to watch telly.' The sergeant changed tack. 'Can I ask you a question?'

'Yes, of course.'

'Why would someone want to murder Bede?'

'I don't know,' said Daniel. 'But murderous feelings are not unknown in religious communities.'

Aelred winced at that.

'Do you think if he had been murdered it would be by someone here?' said the sergeant, with rather a steady look.

'Who else could it be?' said Daniel.

'Canon Clement, I know this community inside out. I was honoured to be made an oblate here a few years ago. I try to observe the Rule, I say my prayers, I contribute to monastery life. And I can assure you that no one here would want to murder Bede. Or anyone else.'

Daniel made to speak, but the sergeant held up a hand. 'Forgive me, Father . . . for I have sinned' – he smiled at his joke – 'but I just wonder if you may be . . . susceptible to thinking the worst of this because of your recent, and not so recent, experiences?'

Daniel smarted a bit at this. 'I don't think my state of mind, whatever it may be, has any bearing on the legitimacy of the question.'

Aelred said nothing but joined his hands at the fingertips in front of his face in his particular way of not saying anything.

'It was an accident, Father,' said Sergeant Bainbridge. 'The investigating officers and the medics all agree. He got his scapular caught in the machinery, it pulled him in, he broke his neck. That's the cause of death; the coroner, no doubt, will concur. Very unfortunate – tragic, in fact – but nobody else was involved.'

Daniel felt a moment's yearning for Neil Vanloo, not for his physical presence this time, but for his professional curiosity, and for his trust in Daniel's instinct for wrongdoing.

'I dare say.'

Aelred said, without looking at him, 'I'm sure I don't need to add, Daniel, that we would all very much appreciate it if you kept this conversation, and your question, to yourself? Everyone is already very upset, and you know how volatile the mood of a community can be.'

'And, if I may say so, your reputation precedes you, Father,' said the policeman. 'It's like having Hercule Poirot on your patch. You've only got to turn up and every death is suspicious.'

'It was just a question,' said Daniel. 'If it is as you say, then it is answered.'

'Good, good,' said Aelred, fluttering his fingers in that way of his when he was trying to dispel something unpleasant. 'Thank you, Dennis, for your time. Are your men finished?'

'Yes, Father, pretty much. Body's been retrieved, it's with the coroner. Inquest to come. It might be wise not to operate the turbine until its deficiencies are better understood.'

'We have the diesel generator as an alternative. Very expensive, but . . .' He waved his hands around again.

'Enchanting things, aren't they, Mrs Shorely?' said Honoria, as Hilda, exhausted, lay on her side while the puppies restlessly squirmed to get nearer to her, to get more of her.

'Yes, Miss,' said Mrs Shorely, but Honoria felt her agreement was not fulsome and perhaps contingent on their continuing enclosure in a sort of cage made out of Victorian border edging, which one of the gardeners had erected in the housekeeper's room. She had up-holstered half with old horse blankets from the stables, and the dogs seemed very comfortable there, and half with sheets of newspaper so they would learn how to do their business separately. 'Don't want them fouling the nest, do we?'

'No, we don't,' said Honoria. 'Very kind of you to look after them. I feel I should relieve you of the duty, but I have to be . . .' and she nodded towards the back door. She did not need to be anywhere, in fact, apart from somewhere where there were no puppies to look after. She could not admire them for long before tender feelings gave way to a cooler assessment of their beguiling charm and insistent needs. Neil Vanloo provided enough of those for her to be getting on with, and the benefit she derived from his athletic investment in her pleasure was balanced with the demands his romantic nature made on her patience. 'I can't remember the last time we had puppies at Champton, can you?'

'Her ladyship, the middle one, had spaniels, Miss. We had a bigger staff then and I was not obliged to have them in here. The gamekeeper did all that. And his lordship has always preferred cats.'

'Yes, he does, doesn't he? Unusual attribute.'

'I think he likes their independent nature, Miss. He's never been one for ties. If I may say so.'

'But he seems to be rather smitten with these. Mrs Clement tells me he was playing with them in the library after dinner.'

'Hard not to fall for a puppy, Miss.'

'And Mrs Clement? Have we seen her?'

'She's at the rectory. Gone to meet the insurance man and the decorators.'

'Is it an awful mess?'

'It's mostly water damage, or so I hear. Bob Achurch has been in and says its carpets and furniture that need replacing and a bit of woodwork, but nothing serious. Lost one of the portraits of the old rectors, but only the one. Thank goodness Miss March called when she did.'

'And that it was the night of the fireworks and the fire engines were all on standby.'

'Might be a blessing in disguise for Mrs Clement.'

'A blessing?'

'Yes, she'll get it all fixed up nicely and not have to pay a penny, now she's lost her . . . little business.'

Honoria was no longer surprised by Mrs Shorely's extraordinarily comprehensive and up-to-date knowledge of Champton's affairs. She knew everyone, at the big house, in the village and at church, and her phone's little dashboard pulsed red as intelligence was phoned in from her regular sources almost as soon as events occurred. Champton's affairs . . . she thought. Did Mrs Shorely know of hers with Neil Vanloo?

Honoria knew from the hotel trade that secrets, especially romantic secrets, are rarely watertight. When she had started at the Motcombe she had been surprised how guests who would be scrupulously discreet with their peers were wildly indiscreet in front of chambermaids, drivers, waiters, as if they could not hear or see or understand what was being said and done.

This could be complicated when she planned an event for someone she knew. Honoria, with her Smythson notebook, was not like a shop assistant, but someone you went shopping with, and the attitude of the brides-to-be and their retinues immediately changed when they realised who she was. When she was at Champton deference was paid to her, if only because it had been for so long. No one apart from the very old actually touched their caps to Bernard any more. It had always been a formality, from the bob of a parlourmaid to Mrs Shorely's 'm'lord', and behind it there could be lively intelligence, a lookout for the promotion of one's own interest, dislike, sometimes hatred, sometimes indifference, sometimes affection.

Mrs Shorely was not only a collector of intelligence, but a sharp-eyed observer of things. She had her network of informers, principal among them Norah Braines at the post office, but she also ran the house-keeping and that meant laundry and emptying bins, and Honoria – the last person to advertise her private life – was no more prepared to wash her own sheets, or dust the warrener's cottage, than Margaret, Duchess of Argyll. For her, like hotel guests or anyone who has their mess cleared up for them, there was a line where discretion gave way to convenience, and at that point she slackened her normal caution.

But now Honoria's radar was activated. 'I hope Mrs Clement won't miss the income too much. I understand it was considerable.'

'She won't be stony broke, Miss. She's got a job.'

'A job?'

'At Elite Fashions. Miss March sacked Anne Doll-inger – no one knows why, but she's taken on Mrs Clement three days a week. It's not quite the wages she was getting for fortune telling, but it should keep her in scarves.'

'I wonder if she's ever had a job before.'

'Yes, Miss, she was a nurse before she married Mr Clement – nursed all through the Blitz as a girl.'

'Oh, yes,' said Honoria, 'I think I knew that. I don't imagine she would have been particularly daunted by a mere Blitz.'

'I dare say not. So, it looks like it'll be me having to look after these dogs after all.'

'Oh, Mrs Shorely, I wish I could help. Only I'm here, there and everywhere at the moment.'

'Yes, Miss. Will you be needing the warrener's changing?'

The bluntness of that answered Honoria's question. She could have flustered but went cold instead.

'Yes, I think so. A thorough clean. And some logs for the fires too. I'd like it kept cosy.'

After the conversation with Aelred and the police ser-geant, Daniel had gone out for a walk. There was High Mass at midday for St Willibrord, and he wouldn't miss that, but he had some time and he wanted to think, so he put on a coat and borrowed some boots and walked up the hill behind the abbey to the moor that glowered down on the valley beyond the monastery.

He loved it with an austere love, for it was a bleak place, with pale, stringy grass, the odd wind-warped tree, dark dry-stone walls and farmhouses that looked from a distance like Second World War defences. He had loved walking on the moor when he was a novice, for a bleak landscape is the proper setting for monastic life, or so he thought then. He had once been to stay with a community of Benedictine monks in northern France who lived in a monastery as beautiful as Mont Saint-Michel and had oysters for lunch on feast days. They seemed unusually sunny for Benedictines, almost cheerful, the chant jaunty, and he wondered if that was because they lived in a place of plenty rather than in a fort on a hill surrounded by thorns and an unforgiving wind, and the cry of curlews, with collops on the menu every Monday.

It was one of the first things he noticed when the enchantment began to fade – the thinness of the diet, the thinness of the life, the cold wind and fortifications, the curlews crying. So he had left, and after billets in the Fens and in the city, he had come to Champton, with its plenteous rivers and wide-skirted meads. He thought of his house, so handsome and dignified, beside his church; the path from the rectory through the park to the big house, *so* big and yet somehow packed with an abundance of architecture – the spiky medieval heart, the red-brick Tudor range, the baroque extravagance of the facade, the orderliness of the Georgian wing overlooking the lake; the estate, glowing in summer, the fields waving with wheat, the trees thick and gently restless, the birdsong, the meadows, the butterflies. A land of plenty, which he loved, and in which he grew and thrived and sat in the sun and felt the wind on his face and smelled the roses.

And yet here he was, at Ravenspurn. All enchantments fade, he thought, they have to, and when they do, where do you need to be? His first instinct when his latest enchantment failed had been to return here, an instinct so powerful he'd packed half a bag and driven without stopping until he did. But to return to what? The familiar round of prayer, the endless song of plainchant, the unchanging routine, the sense that he had stepped off the bus, and the bus had come round, and he had just stepped on again.

But he was not the same person he had been when he was last here. He looked around at the moor and his eye landed not on the thorn bush, the outcrops of stone, the huge sky, but on the M62, its distant traffic like blood in veins.

Suddenly he wanted to pray.

He turned to make his way back to the monastery, but someone was on the path coming towards him. It was Colin. He seemed uncertain what to do and turned as well, but then he turned back and started walking towards Daniel again. There was an awkward couple of minutes as they drew closer, neither of them sure when to acknowledge the other with a wave, a nod, a word, or whether to maintain the English habit of pretending somebody is not there.

Daniel spoke first. 'Colin, we seem to have had the same idea.'

'I take a walk up here most mornings. It helps me to get my thoughts in order when they are tangled.'

'What, if I may ask, is tangling them?'

'Oh, the Guelphs and the Ghibellines, the Bayonet Constitution, the Concordat of 1801 . . .'

'I imagine that could easily cause a tangle.'

'Yes. But one of the advantages of having no full-time occupation is the leisure to study widely.'

Daniel thought for a moment how to phrase his next question. 'Weren't your opportunities rather restricted?'

Colin looked surprised, then said, 'There are always limits. But I have no one holding me back. No tortoises to my hare, if you see what I mean. I can go at my own speed. I can go where I want to go. I am not subject to groupthink.'

'Groupthink?'

'You know the term? It is from social psychology.'

'It sounds like Orwell.'

'Derived from Orwell. But it refers to the tyranny of consensus.'

'The consensus of the scholarly community?'

'Yes. What does it do to ideas, to argument, to keep everyone cosy in ivy-covered colleges, with gowns and snuff and codes of behaviour?'

'That's a good question,' said Daniel.

Colin rather puffed out his chest and said, 'I go where they cannot go. I see connections they cannot see.'

Daniel thought of Mr Casaubon in *Middlemarch* and his impossible quest for the key to all mythologies. 'Most interesting,' he said, nodding, and made to leave.

'Yes. But I just wanted to say . . . that was awkward this morning at breakfast. I hope I did not seem insensitive. It was just a surprise, and you know how easy it is to get into habits in places like Ravenspurn. How are Mr and Mrs Corbett?'

'In shock and in grief and at the very beginning of having to get used to a world without their beloved son.'

'Very difficult, but if anything can prepare you for that I suppose it is losing a son to the cloister.'

'Not the same thing. At the very least, there are visiting rights.'

Colin flinched. 'Yes.'

'Did you know Bede well? His period – the end of Austria-Hungary – that would have been of interest to you?'

'I did know him. But he was not a collaborator. Not a collaborator at all. I don't think he took my research seriously. He was typical of his type.'

'His type?'

'If it wasn't Oxford, it wasn't worthy of serious consideration.'

'Ah, yes.'

'And he was not generous in sharing the library. And he was . . . I'm going on, aren't I?'

'That's all right. He was what?'

'He had irritating habits. He muttered when he was working. Very distracting. And sometimes he was just there when I wanted him not to be there. And I was no less entitled to be there than he was.'

'It is sometimes difficult for novices to work out where they fit in. Not yet brethren, but not visitors either, if I may say so.'

Colin sounded a little stung. 'I meant as a scholar.'

'It is a competitive calling.'

'Yes. Well, I think I will carry on untangling, Father.' He nodded at Daniel, turned again, and walked away.

The abbey church was empty when Daniel pushed open the big double doors from the outside rather than from the cloister. He wanted to come in this way, like someone who was just passing rather than someone who had a place. He did not want to sit alongside anyone else, so he made his way to the oratory, a little-used chapel at the back of the church, under the organ loft where the brethren would leave photocopying and umbrellas, which infuriated the sacristans, who would leave the intruding articles on the big table in the hall with neither an explanatory nor accusatory note.

They must have just done a clear-out, for the room was completely empty apart from a few prayer stools against the wall – Daniel took one – and an icon stand with a shallow bowl in front filled with sand and spent tea lights. There was another smaller bowl with fresh tea lights and one of the coloured disposable cigarette lighters priced three for a pound at Bradford market.

Daniel took out from his wallet the playing-card-sized reproduction of the icon of the Anastasis. It was a little creased and worn at the corners now, but he had kept it with him wherever he went for a long time. Paisie had given it to him. The original was in his monastery in Romania, although it did not really make sense to speak of an icon as being 'original', because they were copies of copies of copies going back to St Luke himself, patron of painters, according to the tradition that Paisie believed without question and Daniel thought highly doubtful.

But they agreed that icons were not paintings, but windows, an impermeable surface in this world but giving onto a vision of something beyond if you had eyes to see. You had to look, really look, and look again, and the icons would look back at you and you would feel that you were being seen, not the other way round.

Especially with *this* icon; the Anastasis meant 'resurrection' and it showed Jesus in an unfamiliar setting for Christians of the West. He was not rising from the tomb but on the threshold of the underworld, the Harrowing of Hell as it used to be called. He had thrown down its gates, trampled them under his feet, and now reached into its pit to pull out of the darkness those who were condemned, for redemption had yet to come. Finally, here it was. Adam and Eve were usually at the head of that queue, Jesus pulling them up so the chains and padlocks that bound them shattered and fell away as they rose into the new life thanks to this cosmic hero, who stared out of the image directly at the viewer.

Daniel propped it up on the icon stand and lit a tea light in front of it so the little image seemed to glow, almost to grow. And then he let go of everything that was on his mind, troubling his spirit, fretting his sleep, and he let out a sigh.

Then there was nothing, just silence and the glowing image, and the tinnitus in his right ear that was always there, but that, too, started to fade, or rather he stopped noticing it, for he started noticing something else. Something began to form and come into focus. It was the image he was looking at, of Christ yanking the yet-to-be-redeemed out of the pit of Hell itself, only it wasn't a pit, it was a turning engine; he heard through the tinnitus its gears grind, and Christ was yanking out not Adam and Eve, but Bede.

A bell began to ring, the bell summoning the community for Mass, but it resonated deeply within Daniel, and sounded like a call not only to the Eucharist, but to everything it offered and demanded.

He slipped out of the door and saw Aelred standing between the two ranks of stalls that faced each other along the middle section of the church. He was at the lectern putting bookmarks in the large Bible that was kept there. Then he looked up and saw Daniel and nodded towards the sacristy, an oddly informal gesture.

He was waiting for Daniel just inside the door, next to the vestment chests, which stood in a line along one wall. Three of them had vestments laid out in the meticulous way of that community, in reverse order for the convenience of the officiant putting them on. Ooh, thought Daniel, apparelled amices, cinctures in the shape of the omega, stoles in the shape of the alpha, and he felt the sort of background glow that came whenever ceremony was done properly. He did not want to be charmed at this moment, though, and he made to speak, but before he could Aelred said, 'Daniel, you're playing the organ, yes? Nothing fancy, English Kyriale V, three hymns and a short – short – voluntary?'

'Paulinus has asked for rather a novelty. But it's been a while since I played at a High Mass at Ravenspurn.'

'Like riding a bike. You'd best get going.'

Neil Vanloo drove in through the monastery gates – 'The Abbey of Sts Philip and James at Ravenspurn VISITORS' CAR PARK' announced the sign. He got out and stretched. It had been a longer drive than he'd expected, and there had been a horrible accident on the A1, and he had been stuck for half an hour thinking what he was going to say when he got there. After a while he'd stopped rehearsing that conversation because he did not know what Daniel would say, or even if he would want, or be able, to say anything. He knew also that what we do matters, not what we say, and that just to come and be there was the important thing. But where had he come, and where was Daniel? How did it work here, and how could they meet?

He was obviously round the back, where the deliveries came. There was a door with a keypad and a latch, which he tried, but it didn't move, and a doorbell, which he rang, but no one came. He felt like he was trying to break into a prison. Then a bell began to ring. If it rang, it must be for something.

He followed its sound, round the side of the building, and there was what looked to him like a stately home converted to institutional use. He had seen lots of these before – police headquarters, children's homes, young offender institutions – but this was a monastery, and the only monasteries he had ever come across had been in films, and they were normally ghostly with chanting hooded figures, or swashbuckling with swordsmen in tights. A real monastery was a new environment for him, and he did not know quite how to proceed, so he took a minute to look and think. At the end of the range of buildings stood the church; the bell was tolling from one of the towers and a large double door stood half open. He walked towards it, but saw no one coming or going, so he waited outside and listened for a moment and heard doors opening and closing and the scraping of chairs, so he stepped in through the porch and into the church.

It looked so large and yet so empty that he felt he

was in another sort of outside. It could have had its own microclimate, he thought, and the odours – such strange odours – made him think of a tropical forest, but then he gradually began to see that it conformed to the pattern of Daniel's church: an altar, an organ at the other end, pews. He saw people in normal clothes at the back, so he walked tentatively towards them, not knowing if he was meant to be there. No one stirred or even looked at him as he slipped into a pew next to the pillar as inconspicuously as possible. Suddenly a monk appeared by his side with a heap of leaflets and books and murmured some incomprehensible instructions. He was about to ask if Canon Clement was anywhere around, but the monk slipped away on pattering feet. He was wearing, Neil noticed, a pair of black leather mules under his cassock, which looked more like orthopaedic clogs than the sandals he expected monks to wear.

The bell stopped tolling and there came the sound of organ music from above. Neil was not expert in the organ repertoire. He had grown up in the Moravian Brethren in Oldham and sung a hundred hymns a thousand times before surging hormones precipitated his departure. He probably still knew all thirty-three verses of 'The Saviour's Blood and Righteousness', but he realised that, though deep, the musical menu was not wide. One of the discoveries of his friendship with Daniel – he flinched as he wondered if there was anything left of it – was the variety of ways in which people worshipped God and how they did it, and how they wanted to live, and what they believed.

He had heard the organ at St Mary's Champton played dutifully, if not beautifully, by Jane Thwaite, he had heard it played more expertly by Daniel, but the sound that came out of this organ was quite different, not like a town band on Oak Apple Day, but sweet, flutey, soft and unassertive. It hung in the air, like the smoke that rose from the far end of the aisle to the left, a pillar coming out of a little silver bucket on a chain swung by a pyrotechnic handler, or something like that, who was accompanied by candle bearers preceding a procession of monks in their black habits. At the end were three in vestments, the kind of robes Daniel wore on Sundays, but with variations. Everyone stood. The music shifted without stopping into something he recognised as a hymn tune, but if in the mass of literature the monk had handed him there was a guide to whatever the hymn was, and an indication that he was to sing it, he had no idea where to find it.

Everyone started to sing:

'From Greenland's icy mountains,
From India's coral strand,
Where Afric's sunny fountains
Roll down their golden sand . . .'

It was male voices, thrilling like a Welsh choir, splitting into harmony by the second verse, and sung with familiarity and skill, so although it was not loud it seemed to fill the space of the church like wind filling the billowing sail of a ship. A ship, that was what it felt like, he thought, a ship on calm seas, like the ark at the end of its journey. He felt suddenly that feeling of complete security he had known as a child, that the bears waiting behind the settee and the skeleton in the airing cupboard and the thunder and lightning could not harm him. He was suddenly deeply moved and thought he might start to cry. Why was he feeling like this? What was moving him so profoundly?

He pretended to sing as a way of masking his effort at self-control and concentrated on the choreography of the monks entering the sacred space at the centre of the building two by two, then peeling off, one to the left, one to the right, and into their stalls. The three in vestments approached the altar and another, younger monk in a plain robe handed the middle one the smoking bucket and he took it all round the altar, which was set up with silver vessels and lit with six candles, until the whole thing was wrapped in a sweet-smelling fog. When that was done, and everyone was in their place, they bowed simultaneously towards the altar and then turned to face each other. Neil wondered for a moment if he should turn and face someone too, but no one else did, so he mouthed half-remembered words.

'Waft, waft, ye winds, His story;
And you, ye waters, roll,
Till, like a sea of glory,
It spreads from pole to pole;
Till o'er our ransomed nature
The Lamb for sinners slain,
Redeemer, King, Creator,
In bliss returns to reign.'

After the music had slowly faded in the church's vast-ness, the service proper began with words that were again half familiar, from Champton he supposed, or some faint echo from childhood. Then the monks stood and one of them led the others chanting a melody to words he thought must be Latin or Greek. It was sinuous, dramatic, almost erotic, he thought, and it wrapped itself around him like the smoke wrapped the altar, beautiful and strange. And then familiarity again, when a monk read from the Old Testament words he recognised.

There was a psalm – he half knew that too – then the monks rose and sang another chant with an *alleluia* at the beginning and another at the end and one of the three in special vestments wreathed the Bible in smoke and read from it another passage he knew, from the Gospel of Mark:

"And these signs will accompany those who believe: in my name they will cast out demons; they will speak in new tongues; they will pick up serpents, and if they drink any

deadly thing, it will not hurt them; they will lay their hands on the sick, and they will recover.'"

He felt again a pang of nostalgia for his childhood so keenly it was almost a pain. And then another feeling hurried along behind, of resentment, that this promise of freedom from harm and suffering, which he had taken on trust, had not been fulfilled. He had seen enough of suffering, both caused and endured, to find pious statements denying those blunt realities unendurable. Beyond that, there was now a deeper, more difficult resentment, a growing resentment, that the gift of that promise came with a demand – to make bad things better. Did he make bad things better? Did he, in word and deed, proclaim the greatness of Christ, and widen the kingdom of God? He had been brought up to welcome sinners to the threshold of heaven, but really, for years now, he had been on patrol on the borders of that other realm. He suddenly thought of Section 1 of the Theft Act 1978, obtaining services through deception, and wondered if that applied to him.

One of the brethren shuffled out from the stalls and went to the lectern. A sermon, Neil thought, on a Tuesday before lunch; another reason not to become a monk.

The monk was very old and his voice weak, and he had to lean into the microphone to be heard, and onto the lectern to stand. He had no notes, nor did he look at the Bible open before him. He said nothing at first, just looked around at the people looking back at him with an air of mild surprise. Then he spoke.

'I once met a snake charmer's daughter,' he said, 'which sounds like the beginning of a rugby song, but in this case it is factual. She wasn't from India, though we've all seen men there sitting cross-legged in front of a basket beguiling a cobra with a pipe. She was from Tennessee, and this snake charming, if that's the right phrase, was not a street entertainment, but a demonstration of faith in God. There was a custom in that state, in the wildest of its backwaters, where she grew up, for evangelists to take this text from Mark literally. Her father was one. He would stand in front of the congregation and produce rattlesnakes from bags. Then he would take one into his hands, allow it to slide and slither over his body' – there was the sound of a chair scraping and footsteps rapidly disappearing from the back of the church – 'provoke it, and allow the snake, if it was so minded, to bite him. The venom of the rattlesnake is highly poisonous. It is not a bite to be taken lightly. But, St Mark tells us, a believer will come to no harm.

'"What happened to your father?" I asked her.

'"He died."

'He *eventually* died, after suffering years of injury, the loss of fingers, atrophied tissue, getting iller and iller until one day a particularly vicious snake bit and killed him. Of course it did. No matter how unshakeable your faith in the literal promise of that Scripture – or, with an eye on today's date, in the healing power of St Willibrord, famous for curing nervous disorders, and perhaps even the neurotoxic effects of snakebites – it offers no protection from its venom.

'Was that a great disappointment to his congregation?

'"Not particularly," she said; it happened from time to time. But what of the promise Our Lord makes in Mark? "Well," she said, "he survived several others, so perhaps it was just his time?"

'I became fascinated by the snake-handling evangelists. They still meet today and over the years have suffered dozens of deaths. So many the authorities have occasionally intervened to try to curtail this highly specialised homiletical enterprise.

'But people keep coming, people keep getting bitten, people keep dying.

'Why?

'Because, she said, to her father faith was more important than anything. And if Our Lord promised they would be safe from snakes, then safe they would be even if they lost fingers and hands or died.

'For safety was faith, not life. And the only life worthy of the name was the life of faith.

'Few of us will find ourselves obliged to handle snakes. If offered one, we would probably, rightly, say that in our tradition the literal reading of such a Scripture is not only ill-advised but unnecessary, for we place authority in other sources than the Bible alone, and certainly not the Bible read in this way. Some say that is a fault, and we owe the Bible our most faithful attention. And they are right about the latter part. But I think that means we owe it not to surrender to the venom of serpents, but our best reading – careful, informed, thoughtful – and that is not a literal reading. We know too much about the world, about the evolution of snakes, and the methods of their predation, and – this is no less important – about the evolution of the Bible, not as dictation from God, but as a library of fragmentary and slowly assembled accounts of the mystery of our encounter with the One who made us and sustains us and redeems us. Why would you not want to give that your best attention? And if we do, is it not better to say that the truths of the Bible are not literal, they are far, far truer than that. To paraphrase that great theologian of the Scriptures, St Paul, they are truths that overflow the meagre vessel of our understanding and exceed the dimensions of the universe itself.'

And with that, the old monk turned abruptly and shuffled back to his stall.

Silence followed, for so long that Neil started to think something had gone wrong, or the old monk's words had so startled the community that they were shocked into silence. But then they all stood as one – Neil had given up standing and sitting himself by now, for it was too complicated – and the monk who led the singing began a line of chant, the others joined in, and the service got underway again. The show must go on, Neil thought, whatever happens.

There were prayers, and some complicated business with wine and water at the altar, and more standing and kneeling and sitting, and a bell dinged, and more smoke rose into the air, and then the members of the community shuffled up and formed a semi-circle in front of the altar, looking a bit shabby in front of the glittering splendour of the vestments and ceremony. Communion came to them, in the form of bread and wine carried by the three principals, and then, as the brethren returned to their stalls, the visitors sitting around him shuffled and got up and formed an uncertain crocodile up the aisle and towards the altar. Neil did not go with them. A part of him wanted to, because it felt discourteous not to accept the invitation to share, if he had understood it correctly, and also because he'd liked the little sermon, which had surprised him by speaking to his thoughts and feelings rather than the proper thoughts and feelings he knew he did not have when he had sat through so many sermons before.

Daniel preached like this too, about God not as a sort of implacable lawgiver to whom he owed an account of his actions, but as a mystery to be embraced. Something like that. It challenged him because he was a detective, solving mysteries was his trade, and as a police officer he knew better than most that life could not be lived without regulation.

The visitors formed another semi-circle around the altar and the three ministers went round again, with a plate of bread and a cup of wine, which they doled out to the communicants one by one. The first to receive was the first to turn and walk back down the aisle, and it was Daniel.

When he received communion in his own church, as a priest at the altar, Daniel would call to mind the needs of the community, for he was at that moment not only a sinner before God in need of grace, but the shepherd of a flock, and the nourishment was not only for him, but for them.

It was different here. As he received communion he asked God for strength and courage, like a soldier before a battle, for he had to haul Bede out of darkness, and that would cause a shaking and a rattling and a harrowing; and monasteries, like public schools and prisons, did not always absorb harrowings so well.

He walked back down the aisle to ascend the organ loft again to play the final hymn and a voluntary – 'a *short* voluntary' – and to begin the task that he had to begin.

And then he saw Neil sitting at the end of a pew looking at him. If he had been carrying something, he would have dropped it. He saw something flit across Neil's face too, a mixture of surprise and concern. Daniel looked away and kept on walking, with a parish priest's discipline of not exchanging bespoke looks with individuals in the pews. When he got to the organ loft he was a bit breathless, not from the steepness of the spiral stairs but from adrenaline, a fight-or-flight reaction, which he was so unused to it left his hands trembling. He took a moment to turn up the final hymn, 'We Have a Gospel to Proclaim' to the tune 'Fulda' – a belter for the benefit of the visitors; congregations loved it, but it was not often sung in the monastery because the brethren preferred a more muted palette and most of them had long ago grown tired of everyone's favourite hymns and would rather have something French in G minor.

He made a mistake playing the solo first verse, which was most unlike him, and he noticed Aelred look up from his stall.

'*We have a gospel to-o proclaim* . . .' sang the community and visitors, with a gusto from the latter that made the musician in Daniel slightly wince.

It was one of those hymns that built to a climax and a testing E flat for the word 'glory', which, when it came, was too much for many of the congregation and sounded disappointingly underpowered.

For the voluntary, in acknowledgement of the saint's day and Willibrord's connection with Yorkshire, Daniel had a nice idea, the sort of thing that those in the know would appreciate. He had decided to improvise on Ernest Bullock's setting of the anthem 'Give Us the Wings of Faith', words by Isaac Watts, one of his favourite hymnodists, and especially apt for the celebration of the saints:

Give us the wings of faith to rise within the veil,
And see the saints above,
How great their joys,
How bright their glories be.

Bullock was apt too, organist at Leeds Parish Church, just down the road, where under his direction Yorkshire's great choral tradition had been gruffly maintained.

The clever part was to improvise around the tune as if it were plainsong rather than set in four-part harmony, acknowledging both an anthem familiar to anyone who spent their time around Anglican choirs, and the custom of the house.

He would have allowed himself to feel pleased but was so put off by seeing Neil that his improvisation was so improvisational it started to sound like something else entirely, and he noticed Aelred look up from his stall again.

He kept playing, relentlessly, until the church emptied and he was sure no one was there. He finished with a sketchy little cadence, pushed in the stops and switched off the blower. The organ gave a long, tired sigh as the air escaped.

At the bottom of the stairs, sitting on a bench against the wall, was Neil.

10

'Hello, Dan.'

'Hello.' Daniel waved in a pointless way.

'Can we talk?'

'Of course.'

'I don't know where to . . .' Neil trailed off.

'Not here. After lunch?'

'Lunch?'

'Yes, I'm signed in to lunch, it's now. Are you signed in?'

'No, I'm not. But bugger lunch,' Neil said.

'I'm signed in . . .'

'I don't care. We can go out.'

Daniel hesitated, then said, 'I don't know that I can.'

Neil said, 'I think I've worked out what's happened. We need to talk. Sooner or later.'

Daniel eventually nodded and said, 'OK. Come with me.'

They left the church, still filled with the sweet, smoky fragrance of burnt incense, through the main doors and out into the monastery garden. It was raining and Daniel said, 'There's a pub not far from here that does lunch.'

'How far? A walk or a drive?'

'A drive. Shall I?'

'No, I'll drive,' said Neil with a firmness that was either a judgement on Daniel's terrible driving or in anticipation of a difficult conversation. Daniel suddenly wanted very much to say he'd take his own car too in case it became unbearable and he had to bail out. And then he thought the pub was not a good idea as a venue for potentially the most difficult conversation of his life, so he said, 'Or we could just find somewhere to sit?'

'Let's get out of the rain.'

'There's a squash court,' said Daniel, 'infrequently used. We could go there?'

They walked along a path through rhododendrons, their leaves gently shaking off raindrops. A vale of tears, thought Daniel, but he was so nervous he could only make small talk.

'How was the drive?'

'OK.'

'Did you come A1, M62?'

'A1. Then I cut across on the A57. At Worksop.' Neil was nervous too.

They walked in silence.

'Did you know there are twenty different kinds of rhododendron here?' Daniel said.

'I didn't, no. They look like evergreen bushes to me.'

'They're glorious in the spring. And some flower later. There's an *auriculatum* that flowers in August. Even September. Lovely creamy white flowers. I think we got ours from—'

'Daniel, I would rather you said nothing than talk about rhododendrons.'

They walked on in silence until they got to the squash court. It looked like a garage with an oddly sloping roof and stood isolated in a clearing in the woods. It had been built by some of the younger monks in the 1970s. This new generation, however, was no more likely to play squash than Australian rules football, and the court had instead become useful as a venue for encounters that were necessarily private – not easy to find in monasteries.

The door was fastened with a padlock, to which the code had always been the date of the publication of Newman's Tract 90. It released and Daniel invited Neil in.

'It's like being back at school and going for a crafty fag,' said Neil.

Daniel switched on the light and closed the door and they looked at each other for a moment, an unlikely pair, dressed inappropriately for squash on a court that looked as infrequently used as a bar in Mecca.

'How did you know I was here?' said Daniel.

'My old mate, who you know as Sergeant Bainbridge, told me.'

'But I only met him last night!'

'Jungle drums,' said Neil.

'Not hugely discreet of him.'

'Maybe he wanted me to know.'

'What did he tell you?' asked Daniel.

'Nothing yet. He left a message at the station. But it's you I want to see, not him.'

They looked at each other for a while, unsure how to begin. In the end it was Neil who broke the silence.

'I think I know why you are here. Can I say?'

'Yes.'

'I think I might have hurt your feelings, Dan. Unintentionally. I . . . this is difficult to say but . . . well, over the past few months you and I have become close, and I'm really glad we have. You know that. But I think maybe you have become close to me in a way that was not just as a friend?'

As Neil spoke, thunder drummed distantly. Daniel felt wretchedness fall upon him like a wet towel.

'I suppose I should say,' Neil went on – he'd been thinking about this all the way in the car – 'if I'm right, that I'm flattered you should feel that way about me, but I'm not flattered, I'm frightened.'

Daniel said nothing but stood there miserably, just taking it.

'I'm frightened that it puts our friendship in jeopardy. Our friendship means a great deal to me, Dan . . .' Neil grimaced. 'Christ, I've never spoken to another man this way.'

'How do you think I'm feeling right now?'

Neil nodded. 'Excruciating. Excruciated? Can you feel excruciated?'

'I don't think so.'

'But I need to say two things: firstly, I could never love you that way, Dan. I just couldn't feel about another man what I feel for a woman, like what I feel for Honoria. Sorry, but that's just how it is. And secondly—'

'Second,' snapped Daniel. 'Don't say "firstly" and "secondly". Say "first", "second".'

'I'm not here to argue grammar—'

'Linguistic prescription, but we can leave that for now.'

'Thank you. Second, I have never met anyone like you. You dazzle me with your intelligence. You impress me with your dedication. You move me with your compassion. You make me laugh. You understand me. I trust you. Since I met you, I think I have become a better person, I can live more truthfully, more fully, and I really don't want to lose that. You know that I love you too? Not in the same way, but . . . there it is.'

The rain was falling harder now, rattling on the corrugated roof like distorted applause. Objective correlative, is that what it's called? thought Daniel, wanting to dissolve into rainfall and rise in acclaim simultaneously.

'Thank you, Neil,' he said. 'How did you work it out?'

'Talking to Honoria.'

'What did she say?' Daniel asked.

'She told me. I had no idea. And you had no idea about me and her?'

'No, I thought . . . I got the wrong end of the stick.'

'When I told you about her it was a big surprise?' said Neil.

'You could say that.'

There was silence again.

Neil broke it. 'Is this the first time you've felt like this about someone?'

'Yes.'

'I see. That must be painful.' Neil looked puzzled. Then he said, 'Why me?'

'I don't know. I could list your qualities' – he would not list ALL the qualities that most appealed to him – 'but I know other people who are intelligent and dogged and tough and loyal and not like me. With you it's different, it's . . .' He couldn't speak so touched his hand to his heart twice.

'I feel that too. Only not with a bedroom scene. I kind of wish there was one, but' – he tried not to look uncomfortable – 'I wouldn't be able to manage it. Sorry, I feel I've let you down.'

'Of course you haven't. What is there to apologise for? It was a misunderstanding on my part. That's all.'

'I want us to be all right. Are you all right?'

'No, I'm not all right,' said Daniel. 'I've never felt such a loss of self-control. And there's nothing you can do about that, because I know now it's something that's happening in me, not something that's happening between us, and I need to understand what it is.'

'I'm here for you.'

'That's very nice to know, but I was hoping you would be here for me in the way you are for Honoria . . . Doesn't it sound ridiculous, saying it out loud? And when I think of you being with someone else in that way, I feel like I've been punched in the stomach, not that I have ever actually been punched in the stomach. I suppose it will take me a while to get over it. But, Neil, more difficult is coming to terms with what it has revealed about me, about who I am. My sexual orientation, I suppose. If I am of homosexual orientation.'

'You make it sound like a disability.'

'No, I don't think it's that, it's just not what I thought I was, and I don't know if that is something that has changed within me or – and this is more compelling – if it has always been there and I've repressed it, or denied it, or ignored it. If I have, I must be damaged by that. I've seen the damage that does. And if I am damaged, how good am I to others who are damaged?'

'Don't you have a thing about wounded healers?'

'Yes, but I didn't think I was wounded. I need to understand the wound.'

'Where does that leave us?' Neil asked.

'I don't know. Ideally, I should take some time so I can sort myself out.'

'That's why you came here. To stay at Ravenspurn. To take a sabbatical?'

'There's a problem with here,' Daniel said.

'What?'

'I think there's been a murder.'

Audrey felt rather a sense of achievement as she arrived at Elite Fashions later that morning. She had issued instructions to the decorators, had a searching interview with the loss adjuster, in that order, which was unusual, but the wind was in her sails and like Vasco da Gama's caravel rounding the Cape of Good Hope, she felt destined for glory.

Hilda and the puppies were corralled in Mrs Shorely's office. Cosmo had taken to following Bernard around, observed by Jove from vantage points inaccessible to anything but a cat. So the dogs were in the care of others, the repairs to the rectory were assessed, the necessary letter to her son was written and posted and by now received if her hunch was correct, and Audrey was about to be initiated into the mysteries of fashion retail.

'Good morning, Mrs Clement,' said Miss March in her cool and even way.

'Good morning, Miss March. Where would you like me to begin?'

'With elevenses, I think. I like to have a tray with a Camp coffee for me and a . . . perhaps the same for you?'

'Camp coffee?'

'That is what I like. You may have whatever you like. Mrs Dollinger once made me Lift. It's a sort of instant lemon tea but made of something from a test tube rather than a citrus grove and so distant from anything organic it glowed in the dark.'

'I might have ordinary tea,' said Audrey. 'Indian or China?'

'PG, I think.'

'Very good,' said Audrey and then regretted it, for it sounded like the kind of thing Mrs Shorely would say to Bernard, and she did not want to have that kind of relationship with Miss March. She suspected that Miss March did not want it either, and would prefer to see her new assistant as more like a proprietor's favoured heir learning the elements of the business than as a hired hand.

In the tiny kitchen she found the jar of Lift and looked inside. Long past its best, its crystals had formed into a lump, which seemed even less likely to yield up the tartness and freshness of lemon, so she threw it away. Lemon tea, whatever its provenance, reminded her of a favourite song of Daniel's when he was a little boy, 'Know'st Thou the Land Where the Lemon-trees Bloom' by Schubert, or Schumann, sung on a scratchy old 78 by Nellie Melba or someone like her. As Audrey waited for the kettle to boil she hummed it, then lah-lah-lahed it, and quite forgot herself attempting to soar to the higher notes until Miss March's lower-pitched voice interrupted.

'Is that a wireless on somewhere, Mrs Clement? It's very intrusive.'

Audrey returned from the kitchen with a tray. On it was a cup of Camp coffee for Miss March, a cup of tea for her, and a plate of biscuits from a tin of Rover Assorted.

'Is this how you like it, dear?'

'Perfect, thank you. And biscuits too!' Miss March took a pink wafer. Audrey took a Bourbon and placed it daintily on the saucer next to her cup.

'Cheers!' Audrey said, proffering the cup to Miss March.

'Don't chink, Mrs Clement,' she replied, 'it's . . .' She was going to say 'common' but restrained herself.

Audrey wasn't having that. 'Oh, we chink at the big house, Miss March, and I don't think anyone would mistake the silk drawing room for a tavern in the town.'

Miss March blushed. 'I didn't mean it like that. Isn't it bad luck to chink unless it's an alcoholic drink? Unless you've added a drop of something?'

Audrey laughed her most dismissive laugh. 'No, I was just hoping to acknowledge our understanding with a sort of toast!'

Miss March gave a little smile. 'No need. I think we are on the same wavelength in this. And so many things.'

'A murder?' said Neil.

'I think so.'

'I suppose I shouldn't be surprised.'

'It's not a theory that has attracted universal support,' Daniel said. 'Or any support.'

Neil pushed the hair back from his forehead, a gesture he often did when he was thinking. Daniel sometimes thought it was to air-cool the workings of his brain. 'Is there somewhere we can go?' Neil asked. 'Somewhere we can sit? Off-site is best.'

'The pub. You can drive.'

They drove out of Ravenspurn in Neil's white Escort – not so white after a long, wet drive up the A1 – up onto the moor, along the road that went over the top with measuring poles every few hundred yards for when the snows came. It was still raining, but not heavily, and while it was not beautiful, it was not as bleak as it could be.

'"*Out on the wily, windy moors . . .*"' sang Neil in a squeaky falsetto.

'What's that?'

Neil turned to look at him. 'Oh, Dan, you must have heard of Kate Bush? "Wuthering Heights"?'

'Emily Brontë? The Brontës lived not far from here. We could visit the parsonage if you'd like to see it?'

'Never mind. Can you tell me about this murder?'

'Over a pint. For you. A shandy for me.'

They drove in silence, higher and higher, where the grass was yellow and tussocky and the crumbling walls moss-covered on one side.

'She was dead at thirty,' Daniel said.

'Who was?'

'Emily Brontë. They all died young. The five sisters and poor Branwell.'

'Dying young was not unusual for those days. Not round here,' said Neil.

'Oh, but it was, and for a specific reason.'

'Which was?'

'The graveyard,' explained Daniel. 'It was at the top of the hill, with the church and parsonage below. Rainfall – and there was a lot of it – passed through decomposing corpses before it got into the water supply. Put a lot of parishioners in their graves, which compounded the problem.'

'Imagine that? Poor lasses,' said Neil.

'Actually tuberculosis and pregnancy did for the sisters. Alcohol and laudanum did for Branwell. Next right.'

A smaller road, more of a lane, with a weather-beaten signpost, went at right angles to the road, then down an incline to a crossroads. The pub stood in the north-western quarter and it looked exactly like every other building nearby intended for habitation, long and low and grey, built from stone that seemed to have risen spontaneously from the landscape rather than having been quarried and cut.

'The Black Bull,' read Neil. 'Inviting.'

They parked in front, next to one of those new Land Rovers that was intended for prestige rather than utility, with a personalised number plate, which made

Daniel inwardly tut twice. It was quiet inside, just a couple of people at the bar talking rugby, a man in a tracksuit on a fruit machine, and one other couple in the dining room. A waitress brought them the menu. 'It's hearty fare,' Daniel said, and he chose a lasagne.

'Rice or chips or rice *and* chips?' asked the waitress.

'Neither,' he said, 'but do you have anything like a salad?'

'Salad?'

'Yes, just something on the side. And a half of lager shandy.'

'And you?' she said, addressing Neil.

'I'll have the same, but with chips, please, and a pint of mild.'

The waitress left them, and they stayed for a moment in silence punctuated by the whirr and ding of the fruit machine.

'A murder?' Neil asked again.

'I think so. I could be wrong. Everyone thinks I'm wrong, but I have a feeling about it.'

Normally someone suspecting murder because they had a feeling about it would not merit Neil's urgent attention, but this was Daniel, and if Daniel had a feeling, it would not be due to the workings of a suspicious mind, or indigestion, but because something not yet seen had snagged him like a thorn in a jumper.

'Tell me,' Neil said.

'One of the novices at the abbey, Brother Bede. He was working in the turbine house – there's a hydro-electric turbine there, runs from water coming off the moor, it's been there for years. Well, the power failed last night and when someone went to see what the matter was they found him dead. He'd got his scapular caught in the machinery . . .'

'Shoulder blade?'

'Not that sort of scapular. It's the long sort of pinny monks wear over the cassock. Anyway, it seems to have got tangled in the turning gears and dragged him in and broken his neck.'

'Nasty,' said Neil. 'But murder? More like gross negligence, manslaughter at worst, from what you say. You can't have that sort of machinery running without it being made safe. Health and Safety at Work Act 1974, I think.'

'Only applies to employees in a workplace, apparently. Monks aren't employees. But that's not my point.'

'Which is?'

'I don't think it was an accident that he got dragged into the machine,' said Daniel.

'Why?'

'I wasn't sure at first, but I think I've worked out why.'

'Explain,' said Neil.

'It was just now, playing the organ. When I sat on the stool I went to swish my scapular over my shoulder so it wasn't hanging down in front of me.'

'Why would you do that?'

'The pedals – I can't see them or play them if my scapular's in the way.'

'You're not wearing a scapular,' said Neil.

'No, it was a reflex from my time in the novitiate. I spent so long at the organ console it just became habitual for me to sling it over my shoulder.'

'And this novice?'

'I don't think he would have gone anywhere near the machine if his scapular was flapping about.'

'Maybe he forgot? Something distracted him?'

'There's something more. I saw him there earlier that day. I was out walking and the door was open so I went in to have a look – nostalgia if you like – and Bede was there. And he was wearing a tool belt over his scapular. It's where he kept spanners and a screwdriver and whatever it takes to keep a turbine running. It seemed so incongruous around a monk's waist. And it was such a big waist he'd had to punch an extra hole in the belt. It was the belt that kept his scapular from flapping around.'

'And?'

'When we found the body the tool belt was hanging up on a peg, not fastened round his middle. I noticed it especially because of the extra hole. You see, I think the first thing he would have done when he went to check the machinery was put on the tool belt. Creature of habit, like any monk. Also, diligent.'

'So what happened?' asked Neil.

'What do you think happened?'

'I don't know. I take your point, but I don't see how you get from there to murder.'

'Someone was waiting for him,' Daniel mused. 'And contrived to get him into the machine.'

The waitress appeared with their drinks. 'Pint of mild and a shandy?'

'Yes, thank you. The shandy,' said Daniel.

'Thought you were the shandy,' she said. 'And you the pint,' to Neil.

Where do they get it from, thought Daniel, the slightly comical, slightly rude, say-it-like-it-is manner of Yorkshire people?

'You were saying?' said Neil.

'I think someone pushed him in. I think he was murdered.'

'Who would want to murder him?'

'Why does anyone murder someone?' said Daniel.

'Money, sex, fear, jealousy, hate?'

'Yes.'

'I hope I'm not being thick,' said Neil, 'but a monastery is surely a place you go to get away from that sort of thing?'

'People often think that until they get there.'

'Really?'

'It's not a refuge from the world,' Daniel said. 'It *is* the world. And you're stuck in it, with the same people, for ever.'

Neil was silent for a moment. 'Do you know what it reminded me of when I arrived?'

Daniel shook his head.

'A prison. It has the same feel. Institutional. Inaccessible. Smells slightly of frustrated men.'

'Yes. And sometimes it seethes.'

The waitress returned with the food. 'Two lasagnes. And your salad. It's piccalilli, best I could do.' She put down a ramekin filled with bright-yellow slime covering some mushy chunks of vegetable matter.

'Thanks, love,' said Neil, sounding more northern than he usually did. As she left he said, 'I don't like the look of this.'

'Me neither,' said Daniel, 'burnt lasagne and piccalilli from a jar . . .'

'I meant . . . how are we going to do this? Investigate a murder – suspected murder – on a slender hunch. What did Dennis make of it – Sergeant Bainbridge?'

'Unpersuaded. I got the impression he thinks I am in shock because of Josh Biddle's murder. And the police don't like non-police telling them what they're missing, or not many do. I think he felt it was a straightforward death by misadventure. Medics too.'

'What did Dennis make of your theory about the tool belt?'

'I didn't tell him. I hadn't worked it out when I spoke to him. And . . . it's not like talking to you, Neil. I don't think he's much interested in what I have to say.'

'Not many of us would be when everything points the other way. He'll be glad to get it done and dusted.'

'And there's something else,' Daniel added.

'What?'

'The community. They don't want to think un-comfortable thoughts. Or admit to thinking un-comfortable thoughts. They're delicate systems, monasteries – like prisons – and even little things can get magnified wildly and out of control. We had a ter-rible fight when I was there over whether it was kosher for the deacon and subdeacon to wear folded chasubles instead of tunicles and dalmatics in penitential seasons. It ended in a fist fight. Well, more a slapping fight.'

'I don't think it was such a contentious issue in Moravian Brethren circles in Oldham at the time.'

'So if we can come to blows over vestments, imagine what allegations of a murder would do?'

'So you think the boss at the abbey would prefer not to confront it?' said Neil.

'No one would. There's nothing like monastic life to incentivise doing nothing when you should be doing something. There is a lot to be said for doing nothing, by the way.'

'Murder isn't folded jezebels, or whatever you call them.'

'It wasn't about the chasubles,' said Daniel. 'It was about much more profound matters than what you wear. How you get to heaven and how you get to hell. Literally worse than a matter of life and death. And there's another thing.'

'What?'

'They don't like outsiders getting involved. It's a natural consequence of enclosure.'

'Enclosure?' Neil said.

'Living behind a wall. In the old days it was much stricter than it is now, but they're still used to doing things their own way, and their instinct is to hide when people look over the wall.'

'But they're open to visitors?'

'Part-open,' said Daniel. 'We see what they want to show us.'

'The police are involved now, and the coroner, whether they like it or not,' Neil pointed out.

'The police are Dennis Bainbridge. He worships there. He's an oblate of the community.'

'A what?'

'A sort of lay member,' Daniel explained. 'He won't want to do anything to upset them unnecessarily.'

'You make it sound sinister.'

'It's not sinister, or not intended to be. It's just how separated communities work. And they are separated for a reason – to live a life of discipleship to Christ in a world which doesn't understand what they do. It makes them suspicious about anyone beyond their circle. You must know something about this from your childhood.'

'I didn't choose to be Moravian Brethren,' said Neil. 'I was born into it. And I didn't realise we were different until I was a bit older at school. At first, I thought we were just chapel, like lots of other kids.'

'What made you realise you were different?'

'Pacifism. No toy guns, no war games. No flag waving. And we were more interested in what was going on in Zanzibar than Rochdale.'

'Why Zanzibar?' asked Daniel.

'Mission. We had a link with Tanzania. I went when I was a lad. And . . . well, this is not the time . . .'

'Go on,' Daniel pressed.

'We didn't have social class, or distinctions of money and status. Everyone was the same. I think it's what Honoria likes about me – I don't care that she's posh.' Daniel must have flinched, because Neil looked down at his drink. Then he blushed. 'But that's nothing to do with the matter in hand. What do you want to do?'

'I want to find out if I'm right. And if I am, to do the right thing.'

'How are you going to do that?'

'Softly, softly.'

Neil drained his pint. 'I could be Watt to your Barlow.'

'I don't follow.'

'Could you use a hand?'

II

Bernard had ordered lunch to be served in the Rudnam Room. It was his favourite room for luncheons of the second degree, not the grandest, but not plain, with views of the park on two sides and French windows that opened onto the terrace. It was also the favourite of his ancestor, Lord de Floures, when the eighteenth century became the nineteenth, known as Farmer Hugh. The room's name came from the de Floures' estate in Norfolk, which Farmer Hugh infinitely preferred to Champton. Although his birth and inheritance obliged him to spend most of his time at the family seat in the Shire the family had dominated since the Norman Conquest, he had always been happiest at Rudnam, among farmers and cattlemen, doing what he loved before all things: breeding shorthorns. His achievements in this enterprise looked out at Bernard today. Farmer Hugh had commissioned more than two dozen paintings of his finest specimens, and hung them on all four walls, from floor to ceiling, for they were dearer to him than the sons and daughters who hung on the more formal walls of the library, drawing room and picture gallery. With windows on two sides and overlooked by comely cattle, the room felt more outside than in, which was why Farmer Hugh had chosen to die in it, with the French windows open to the park grazed by distant deer, in the year of the Great Reform Act, having mitigated the more alarming effects of that legislation by instructing his newly enfranchised tenants-at-will to vote as he and his heirs and successors instructed.

Farmer Hugh's latest successor sat at the head of the dining table, a splendid four pillar specimen from the reign of Mad King George, which could easily seat a dozen, but today was set for three: the place on his left was laid for Honoria and the place on his right for Canon Dolben, former rector of Champton, who had been installed before Bernard was born and resigned the living more than fifty years later. The ancient cleric now lived in an old folks' home, the Old Vicarage at Pitcote, which Daniel would visit once a month to bring him communion, and four times a year to collect him and bring him 'home to Champton' for tea at the rectory he had occupied for so long.

Today it was Honoria who had gone to collect him and complete the nursing staff's slow and delicate handover, like porters at Sotheby's handling a late-Ming bowl. When they arrived at Champton she had to run into the kitchen and get Mrs Shorely to help manoeuvre him out of Bernard's Range Rover. This was a longer procedure than either woman had planned for, and by the time they had helped him to shuffle through the saloon, into the library, Mrs Shorely's pork chops turned out of the Aga so overdone they looked like warped ammonites.

They slithered onto their plates when Mrs Shorely deposited them in front of the diners, and made so little concession to the old canon's dental capacity that Honoria had to cut them up for him and wedge them against the mashed potato Mrs Clement had advised Mrs Shorely he was especially fond of. After this dole, carrots and peas followed. She laved the whole ensemble with gravy and finished it with a large spoonful of apple sauce. How much simpler it would have been, she thought, to assemble all this in the kitchen rather than at his place setting, with cutlery and china that belonged to an age of butlers and underbutlers, but Canon Dolben, as former rector of Champton, merited a measure of ceremony, and especially today, because Bernard wanted to raise a difficult issue: the unnegotiated absence of the present rector.

'Called away, Canon Dolben, a great emergency, in the middle of the night, so urgent it seems the rector had insufficient time to make any arrangements for his absence.'

'Oh dear. That sounds most unlike Canon Clement. It must have been something unusually pressing. And, I suppose, private?'

'I wouldn't dream, naturally, of speculating about what it might be, but—'

A peremptory bark sounded from behind the door.

'—nevertheless, it has left us rather in the lurch, and with the dreadful business of the man at the Badsaddles . . .'

The bark sounded again.

'Honoria, would you?' She got up and went to open the door.

'It makes things very difficult, and as patron of this living, if not quite that of the Badsaddles, though that's never been made clear . . .'

Cosmo came barrelling into the room, then skidded across the last few feet of polished parquet and collided with Bernard's lower leg.

'Oh, Cosmo, you dreadful beast,' he said, and leant down to ruffle his ears. 'I am mindful of my responsibilities, under law – *under law* – to ensure Holy Communion is celebrated in at least one of our churches, and to me that means St Mary's rather than the Badsaddles, every Sunday, but the bishop, I dare say, disagrees?'

'It does not matter what the bishop thinks, or does not think, the canons of the Church of England require precisely that,' said Canon Dolben.

'So if the good people of Champton turn up for Holy Communion on Sunday at eight and there is no parson to oblige them, what am I to do? Surrender myself to the police?'

'I don't think that would be necessary, my lord,' said

Canon Dolben. 'Hardly any parish clergy say morning and evening prayer in church every Sunday, as the canons also oblige us to do, but I don't think many are picking oakum at Dartmoor.'

'But I am led to believe that you do not need to be a parson to lead those services,' said Bernard, 'though you do if its Holy Communion?'

'That is true, but your problem regarding Holy Communion is unlikely to result in your prosecution.'

'Then what am I to do about the problem?'

'I would advise trying to ascertain the whereabouts of the rector and establishing when he intends to return,' said Canon Dolben. 'Isn't this his dog?'

'It is. Cosmo.'

'After Cosmo Gordon Lang?'

'I don't know.'

'The first bachelor Archbishop of Canterbury in a hundred and fifty years. How apt.'

'The rector abandoned not only us, but his dogs, which have just had puppies,' continued Bernard.

'That is extraordinary. He has always struck me as devoted to them.'

'So you see . . .'

Bernard took a chunk of scorched and fibrous chop from his plate and offered it to Cosmo, who snatched it from his hand like a sparrowhawk taking a pigeon.

'Gently! Gently! . . . Not to mention his mother, who is living here . . . very comfortably, one might say immovably . . . while repairs to the rectory are made. So, as you surmise, it must be something very significant to have made him behave in such an out-of-character way. And that, of course, makes me only worry more about what will happen, or not happen, on Sunday.'

'But he will be back for Sunday, I am certain he will,' said Canon Dolben.

'But what if he has had a moment of madness or is incapacitated in some way?' said Bernard. 'What then?'

'Then . . . Ah, I see.'

'I do not wish to impose on you, Canon Dolben, in your retirement, but there is no one at Champton, let alone the Badsaddles, better qualified to step into the breach – if breach there is – than you, and you are so fondly remembered . . . *loved* . . . by so many here that I cannot think of anyone . . .'

'You have spoken to the archdeacon?'

'I never speak to archdeacons.'

'Then you are at a disadvantage in this situation.'

'I will never speak to that ridiculous man ever again. And before you suggest it, nor the bishop. If it wasn't for them and their harebrained scheme to bundle us in with the Badsaddles, we wouldn't have got into the mess we're in today.'

'I don't think you can lay the blame for that at the door of either the bishop or the archdeacon. Most unfortunate, but not deliberate.'

'I'm not saying it was deliberate, I'm saying it was short-sighted and offensive. My family has held the advowson of this living since the twelfth century.

Godfrey de somewhere or other, *our* man, put in at our expense and – I need hardly remind you – it's been looked after by my ancestors and by me ever since.'

'I feel I must also remind you, my lord, that the right of presentation does not convey the right to press an incumbent into your service, and—'

Honoria interrupted. 'Dear Canon Dolben, could you possibly help us out? You are so beloved in the parish and with the awful shock of the murder so soon after last year, we think it would be very reassuring and comforting for people to know that you would be at the helm if Daniel's absence continues, don't we, Daddy?'

She said this with a hint of vehemence, which checked Bernard's angrier impulse, and he breathed heavily a couple of times before collecting himself.

'Sunday service, Holy Communion and Choral Evensong here at St Mary's. Two bottles of Latour '78,' he said.

'Half a case,' said Dolben.

'If you do Matins as well.'

'I will do Holy Communion and Evensong. And only for half a case.'

Bernard was so annoyed he could only nod.

'And I shall look forward to seeing you there, my lord. *Pour encourager les autres?*'

Daniel knocked on the door of the guest master, Father Dominic. Like every other monk he had two jobs, succentor to Father Paulinus's precentor and this – not one of the most sought-after jobs in the monastery, for it obliged the holder to engage with strangers.

Father Dominic did not wish to engage with strangers at all, for he was unusually shy, even for a monk. It was shyness that had made him a schoolmaster, for he was least uncomfortable when he was in the society of people junior to him, and the part he played in their life was not negotiated but given. Prep-school master had been an ideal choice, especially because he had taught at his old school and so there was an additional benefit of familiarity. Had it not been for the nervous breakdown – or, rather, the unfortunate events that led to his nervous breakdown – he would have stayed, but he could not stay, and so he sought a safer refuge in the cloistered silence of a monastery.

That had not worked out as he'd expected either, or not entirely, because Aelred's belief was that it is the duty of an abbot to do the opposite of what the brethren wanted him to do. Better to test them beyond endurance for the benefit of their immortal souls than merely accommodate the obvious for reasons of convenience. And so the congenitally untidy were made sacristans, the physically idle gardeners, the dyspraxic masters of ceremony. 'It's not about what you want, but what God wants,' Aelred would say to disappointed brethren who were hoping to get the library but got the chickens instead.

It was the 'firm expectation' that any job would be

accepted without demur, complaint or refusal, for it stated in chapter sixty-eight of the Rule, in a phrase Aelred had long ago committed to memory, 'If a brother be assigned a burdensome task or something he cannot do, he should, with complete gentleness and obedience, accept the order given him.' 'It is not about us,' Aelred would add. 'It is never about us.'

The cleverer monks, seeing this coming, would sometimes try to manoeuvre themselves into the job they wanted by pretending it was the last thing they wanted – 'Oh, Father Aelred,' they would say, 'I've made a terrible mess of printing the Advent booklets, I just can't get the hang of the photocopier . . .' to enhance their chances of being appointed liturgical publisher, which meant a nice warm office, as much tea as you wanted, and playing around with layout.

Aelred was not stupid, however, and he knew his powers, and his rights under the Rule. When one particularly wily senior monk saw the position of prior – perhaps the most onerous in the monastery – coming his way and attempted to dodge it not by saying how much he would dislike the job, but by saying he was actually incapable of doing it, Aelred reminded him that if the weight of the burden was altogether too much for his strength, then the brother should 'choose the appropriate moment and explain patiently to his superior the reasons why he cannot perform the task without pride, obstinacy or refusal. And if after the explanation the superior is still determined to hold to his original order, then the junior must recognise that this is best for him. Trusting in God's help, he must in love obey.'

You could often tell those who were in love obeying Aelred's decision by their gritted teeth, but the Rule was the Rule and the abbot's decision was final.

Which was why Father Dominic, who would have found the incessant socialising of a desert island a trial, was guest master.

He did his best to be out when people needed him, and his best never to answer a ring on the bell at the gate, and some guests arriving had waited there so long they had eventually lost heart and gone home. The more persistent would track him down, sooner or later, as Daniel had that afternoon, to arrange accommodation for Neil, who was waiting in the bookshop at the main door.

Daniel did not wait for Father Dominic to invite him in but knocked and entered, which rather startled him.

'Crispin! I hope everything is satisfactory. Only Father Aelred put you in without consulting me due to the very late hour of your arrival. Fortunately, there was a room available, but I did not have time to air it or put one of those little milks on your tray . . .'

'It's fine, Father. It's Daniel now, by the way.'

'Oh, yes.'

'And I want to book in a guest, if I may?'

Father Dominic opened his desk diary and tilted it

towards him as if the contents needed to be protected from another's scrutiny.

'Who and when? Only we have the Companions' Retreat coming soon and then we're always busy with retreatants in Advent . . .'

'Mr Neil Vanloo. And he's waiting outside.'

'That's rather . . . instantaneous?'

'A spiritual crisis, Father. I would not ask, only Mr Vanloo is known to me and I can vouch for him.'

'But we have you here, and Bede's poor parents . . .'

'There is room, Father. And the abbot was—'

'Yes, the abbot, the abbot . . .' Dominic shrugged in a very Aelred way and said, '*I should so very much dislike to cause you any inconvenience, Father, but as the ark was obliged to find room on board for every living thing of all flesh, two of every sort, so we are obliged to accommodate the ladies of the Batley Mothers' Union on their Advent retreat . . .*'

Dominic's imitation was so well observed that the pleasure it gave was immediately tempered by the thought that what he could do for Aelred he might do for you.

Dominic closed the desk diary. 'Can he pay?'

'Yes.'

'Is he a student or a pensioner or on benefits?'

'None of those.'

The guest master sighed. 'Well, I suppose he had better have Room 12. It's the same floor as you. Vanloo, you say?'

'Neil Vanloo.'

'Is he a Dutchman?'

'No, from over the Pennines actually – Oldham.'

'Oh dear. Does he need me to explain things to him?'

'No, I can do all that.'

'I hope I can get him on the list for supper tonight. Only I noticed you were not at lunch today, although you were signed in, which caused some inconvenience.'

'My apologies, Father, but Mr Vanloo arrived unexpectedly and . . . well, pastoral necessity, you know?'

'Only we're having salmon, it being a feast day, and I don't know if there's enough to stretch. Such short notice. But I shall try. Help yourself to the key.' Dominic pointed at a board with rows of hooks, from which dangled keys on wooden fobs marked with numbers in marker pen. 'It is an awkward time, Crisp— Father. That poor novice dead in an awful accident. I have half a mind to ask Father Aelred that we close to guests. It's very disruptive when something like this happens.'

'I know it is, Father,' said Daniel. 'I have had more than my share of disruption in the past little while.'

Father Dominic frowned. 'Well, yes, you would know. I hope this doesn't follow you around.'

'What?'

'Murder, mayhem, mishap.'

'I don't think it works like that,' said Daniel.

'Don't you?' said Dominic. 'I've known clergy who were like lightning conductors for evil. Wherever they went, awful things happened. It's as if the devil was following them around waiting to pounce.'

Daniel took the key for Room 12 from the board. 'Do you think the devil has pounced here?'

'Wouldn't be the first time,' said Dominic.

'In what way?'

'In what way what?'

'Murder, mayhem, mishap?' said Daniel.

Father Dominic suddenly looked even more deflated than usual. 'Oh, mishap, mishap, mishap.'

Daniel said nothing. A few seconds ticked past.

'Mishap,' said Father Dominic finally, but he sounded slightly hesitant.

Daniel went to leave, but then stopped. 'Do you think, Father, that there may be more to Bede's death than a simple verdict of death by misadventure?'

'Nothing is ever simple, is it, Father?' said Dominic.

'But do you have any suspicions about Bede's death?'

'I thought you were here on retreat?' Dominic stood up and smiled. 'Good day, Father. I hope Mr Van Dyke—'

'Vanloo.'

'—has a peaceful and fulfilling stay with us.'

Daniel nodded, and left.

Neil was browsing the community's publications in the little bookshop. There was a history of the abbey of Ravenspurn, books of plainsong chants, *Spiritual*

Exercises for Single Persons, and one that had caught Neil's attention, *Keeping Hens*.

'Something for everyone?'

'The monastery has always kept hens. We used to keep sheep and cattle too, though not any more, but the hens stayed. We all had to take a turn looking after them. One of my more hated duties.'

'Why hated?'

'Have you ever kept hens?' Daniel asked.

'No. It was more pigeons when I was a lad.' Daniel could never be sure if Neil was joking when he spoke about his northern roots. 'Are they difficult to keep, then?'

'No, not really, quite easy, but like everything here, it's a question of balance. Some of us got quite involved with the hens. More involved than we should. They became more like pets. And singular attachments are frowned on in a monastery.'

'Singular attachments?'

'Getting too fond of someone.' Daniel blushed. 'That's the hardest balance to keep. It upsets everything if two of the brethren become particularly close.'

'Brethren, yes, but chickens?'

'Lonely people form attachments. Spinsters and cats. Widowers and terriers.'

Neil frowned. 'I just don't understand why anyone would come here.'

'Love to the loveless shown, that they might lovely be.'

'I know that. What's it from?'

'A hymn.'

Neil half sang, half muttered, 'My song is love un-known . . . my Saviour's love to me . . . love to the loveless shown, that they might lovely be.'

'Yes, different tune from ours, that's "Rhosymedre", a lovely old Welsh tune. Ours is more recent, by John Ireland. He lived at Deal—'

'We sang it at church,' Neil interrupted. 'It was in our hymn book. Number 145. Good Friday?'

'Passiontide.'

'I've never thought of it like that,' Neil said.

'How do you mean?'

'So . . . wretched.'

'I don't think it's wretched,' said Daniel.

Neil nodded. 'Hens? People getting too close to hens?'

'It wasn't the hens; it was undermining the detach-ment we need to function. Because we ate them as well as their eggs and that was too upsetting for the younger novices who had looked after them and given them names. It caused one of the worst rows we ever had.'

'A poultry matter.'

It was one of those jokes Daniel did not at first recog-nise. 'To an outsider, that's . . . oh, Neil.' He produced the key. 'Let me show you the guest house.'

They left through the side door that led from the car park to the bookshop and the offices, and beyond them the monastic buildings. It was secured with a coded push-button lock.

'The code is C1841X. Press each button till it clicks. Then the handle will turn and the door will open. Try it – it's a bit difficult at first.'

Neil jabbed at the buttons with fingers that looked too big for the job, but he got it and the handle turned.

'That's it,' said Daniel, 'and you'll remember 1841 because it was the year Tract 90 came out, which caused all the fuss.'

'I'm not going to remember that.'

'I'll write it down for you. Same code to open the door to the guest house.'

The guest house stood at the other side of the car park, made from the same grey stone as the monastery with windows made of diamond panes set in black painted iron. Inside the floor was laid with red-brown lino and a plain flight of stairs led to a plain landing. A door, painted in institutional cream, opened onto a lino-floored corridor with doors on either side.

'It's not quite the Hilton,' said Daniel.

'It's just like the place where I trained,' said Neil. 'Which one are you?'

'I'm eight,' said Daniel. 'You're twelve. Here's the key. The bathrooms and loos are through the doors opposite. Do you want a minute to settle?'

'It won't take a minute.'

'No, you don't have anything with you.'

'I do actually, a bag in the car.'

'You thought you might be staying?' Daniel asked.

'I didn't know. But I came prepared. Clean shirt and a razor. I can get them later.'

'Don't you have to be in Braunstonbury?'

'I took some leave. I'm owed weeks,' said Neil.

'But what about the Biddle murder?'

'Man arrested and charged. Full confession. He'll plead guilty. There's not much to do. You did it all.'

'What about Honoria?'

'She made me come.'

'Out of pity?' said Daniel.

'For me,' said Neil.

'Why you?'

'Dan . . .'

Daniel nodded eventually, then said, 'Let's concentrate on what we're going to do.'

It was a drizzly afternoon in Champton. After Honoria returned from Pitcote and reversed the delicate handover of Canon Dolben – Aubrey to the nursing staff – she decided on a walk in the park. There was something stuffy, with the awful suggestion of incontinence, about an old folks' home that she wanted to dispel, so she took the wet, wind-tousled Holly Walk from the north side of the house through the garden to the park and the lake beyond.

She took Cosmo for company, and he raced ahead of her through the ragged avenue of holly and ivy – how Christmassy, she thought – towards the badgers' setts that lay along the banked sides of the path, irresistible temptations to dachshunds, bred to hunt these creatures, an aptitude of which Honoria was unaware.

She wanted not only to clear her head of the clinging atmosphere of the old folks' home, but also to think through what she was going to do about Neil Vanloo, or PC Bod as Alex had started calling him. While she quite liked having a sexy cop for a lover, she had no more interest in the Police and Criminal Evidence Act than Lady Chatterley in the husbandry of grouse.

In her friendships and family relationships Honoria was not incapable of kindness or empathy or generosity, but there was a manageable distance to them, a distance she did not want to surrender to Neil as lovers are supposed to do.

She sometimes wondered if this meant there was something wrong with her. So many of her romantic attachments were malformed in comparison with those of most of her friends, but if this ever worried her, it was not enough for her to do anything about it, apart from bail out when irritation overtook desire.

A rush of wind came funnelling up from the lake as Honoria reached the end of the Holly Walk. She sat on one of the uneven stone steps that led down to a field, blue or yellow in spring with linseed or oilseed, but now ploughed, and the iron-rich deep-red earth lay in shiny furrows like thick corduroy. Then she realised she was more alone than she wanted to be, for Cosmo had not reappeared from the bushes.

'Cosmo! Cosmo!' she called, but nothing came scampering towards her through the holly and the ivy.

Daniel was showing Neil round the monastery grounds. The turbine house was still out of bounds, but he took Neil to the perimeter as far as he could, then reapproached the monastery through the Calvary, where departed brethren lay in lines under their wooden crosses, awaiting the Resurrection. Each cross was carved with their name – just the name they were known by in the community – the date of their death and the simplest prayer:

WILFRED
1934
Jesu Mercy

ODO
1949
Jesu Mercy

WALTER
1922
Jesu Mercy

BRUNO
1970
Jesu Mercy

DOMINIC
1906
Jesu Mercy

'Didn't we just talk to Dominic?' said Neil.

'A different Dominic,' said Daniel. 'The name gets reused when a monk dies. Or leaves. I replaced a Crispin and a Crispin replaced me. Everything is reused when a monk dies; we don't waste anything. When we clear their cells all their possessions, pens, socks, toothbrushes even, are left out in the hall and we help ourselves to anything we need.'

'Toothbrushes?'

'Yes.'

'That's disgusting.'

'I think it was more of a gesture than an effort at oral hygiene,' said Daniel. 'We own nothing, we have no possessions, everything is the community's. When we go someone else picks up where we leave off. My cloak – you know the black one I wear for funerals?'

'The big Dracula cloak?'

'It's a Melton actually, but yes. That came from Boniface.' He pointed at a grave.

'Did you know many of them?' asked Neil.

'Most of this row. Hugh, Benedict, Ambrose . . . I thought I would take my place in the middle of the next row or the next row. I would have liked that.'

'Why?'

'Belonging,' Daniel said simply.

They walked on through the Calvary towards the orchard and the vegetable gardens.

'What are these?' Neil was looking at a row of little crosses, miniature versions of the ones they had just looked at in the graveyard but planted near the base of the Calvary wall.

'I don't know,' said Daniel, and bent to look at them.

THEODORA
1988
RIP

ROSE
1988
RIP

KYLIE
1988
RIP

EUNICE
1988
RIP

'They look like pets' graves,' said Neil.

'I don't think we would do that,' said Daniel. 'It's not very Ravenspurn.'

'Hens,' said a voice behind them. It was the jolly-looking young novice with freckles and untamed curly dark hair.

'Hello . . . it's Anselm, I think?'

'Yes, Father.'

'Call me Daniel, please.'

'Yes, Father.'

'This is Neil. He's come here for a few days. A sort of informal retreat. Neil, this is Brother Anselm.'

'Hello,' said Neil.

'Well, you won't find much peace and quiet here, I'm afraid,' said Anselm, 'not at the moment.'

'I was sorry to hear of . . . your brother's death,' said Neil. 'Is that the right way of putting it?'

Anselm nodded in acknowledgement. 'Do you know if Bede will be buried here, Father?'

'I don't,' said Daniel. 'It's for his parents to decide. They may want him near them.'

'I hope he does end up here. I think he would have wanted that.'

The three were silent for a moment, then Neil said, 'What happened to the hens?'

Anselm flinched. 'A fox. Got into the coop last year. In Passiontide, which I suppose is apt.'

'Nasty,' said Neil.

'Horrible. I discovered them. The coop was . . . it was awful. And they were just left, not eaten. I could have forgiven the fox if he had been hungry or had cubs to feed. But it was just a slaughter.'

'How did it get in?' said Neil. 'I saw you had a fence.'

'I don't know how it got through the fence. Or over it. But someone left the coop door open. They were helpless. There was one survivor, our cockerel, David. You must have heard him?'

'Funny name for a cockerel,' said Neil.

'He arrived on St David's Day.'

'We used to give them saints' names when I was here,' said Daniel.

'We have a rule that whoever looks after them gets to name them,' Anselm explained. 'Rose after Rose of Lima, a favourite of one of my predecessors. He also chose St Theodora – Byzantine empress, I think. She was a naughty one. The hen, I mean. I don't know about the empress. I imagine she was not naughty if they made her a saint.'

'Afraid not,' said Daniel. 'She was a . . . I suppose we'd call her an exotic dancer, before she married the emperor.'

'Oh, well. They were challenging times.'

'What about Eunice? Who's St Eunice?' Neil asked.

'Not exactly a saint,' said Anselm. 'Father will know better than me, but I think she's in the Epistles?'

'The Second Epistle of Timothy. She's his mum.'

'I think that sounds much more suitable for a Dumpy,' said Anselm.

'A Dumpy?' said Neil.

'The breed, Scots Dumpies,' said Anselm. 'A rare breed. Eunice sounds like a Dumpy, don't you think?'

'And Kylie? I can't believe there's a Saint Kylie?' said Neil.

'Not that I know of,' said Anselm, 'but I chose that one because I ADORE Kylie, and she looked a bit like her. Manner rather than appearance. Dumpies are not the pin-ups of the poultry world.'

Daniel said, 'I'm sorry you had such a loss. May I ask why they are buried here?'

'Oh, there was a *major* sadness. I mean, they were like pets to us, not just egg layers. They all have personalities – well, you'll know, Father. We were devastated. So we couldn't just put them in the rubbish.'

'We ate them in my day,' said Daniel, 'until there was a revolt. Same reason.'

'I don't know how people could do that,' said Anselm.

'It caused a big debate,' said Daniel, 'rancorous, in fact, and in the end it was decided that we wouldn't eat them any more. And they lived their natural lives. Hildegard of Bingen got to twelve or thirteen, I think. But this is . . . rather splendid' – he indicated the row of little graves – 'I don't think we went to all this trouble.'

'We had a big debate too, Father, and it was also rancorous, and some of us had been reading Father Linzey on animal rights and there was a split between us, and the brethren too, on whether we should go vegetarian. Some of us have. But it got more complicated when the fox got the hens.'

'I can imagine why,' said Daniel.

'Why?' said Neil.

'Some of us wanted them to have a proper burial,' said Anselm. 'But others thought that was a step too far. Theologically.'

'I don't understand.'

'Traditional theology,' said Daniel, 'is clear that animals do not have souls – only we do – so there is no afterlife for them to live.'

'No pets in heaven?' said Neil.

'Afraid not,' said Daniel. 'Well, I say afraid not; it's not a matter of bliss or hellfire. If they don't have souls that are capable of answering for themselves before God then how can there be a place for them in heaven? Or hell? Which are the consequences in eternity of sin and salvation. But you try telling that to a little old lady whose cat has just died. I did once, as a matter of fact, when I was young and zealous. She said, "No cats in heaven, no me in church. Goodbye."'

'There's a school of thought now,' said Anselm, 'which would not be so quick to banish animals from heaven. All God's creatures, all precious to God, all made from God's . . . stuff. Is that just lost when they die? Did you know Aquinas thought women didn't have souls? But they seem to be able to get into heaven.'

'I don't think that's quite right, Anselm,' said Daniel.

'Didn't he argue from Aristotle that women were imperfect creatures?'

'He argued that there were different kinds of souls,' said Daniel. 'Vegetables had vegetative souls, animals had . . . I think he called them sensitive souls . . .

and humans had corporeal souls, capable of existence beyond death.'

'We argued this all out after the Chapter of Faults,' said Anselm. 'Father Dominic was on our side, Father Paulinus was against. It got very bitter and there was a big fallout, not in the brethren so much, but the novices. Some of us were pro eternal life for animals – I was – some of us weren't. Bede, Augustine, Sebastian, some others – Bede was the leader of that faction. He could be very rigid theologically. The abbot had to intervene and came up with a *via media*.'

'A what?' said Neil.

'Middle way. A sort of compromise. We could give the hens burials and remember them and pray for their eternal rest – see, RIP? – but they could not be buried in the Calvary alongside the brethren. So that's why they're here.'

'Do you think you will see Kylie in heaven, then?' asked Neil.

Anselm looked a bit stung. '"How often have I desired to gather your children together as a hen gathers her brood under her wings." Luke, isn't it? Nothing good is ever lost, that was what Father Aelred said.'

'Very Church of England,' said Daniel, 'and so is the "RIP" rather than the "Jesu Mercy" the brethren get. But I noticed there are no hens now?'

'There's a moratorium. It got so nasty – you know how these places can be – the abbot said we should have a year of prayer and reflection and work out something we could all agree on. I don't think we're there yet.'

'What about David the cockerel?' said Daniel.

'Celibate, like the rest of us. For now.'

Alex, Nathan and Theo had decided to have a leisurely afternoon at the lodge. They were all three lying on the sofa with the curtains drawn against the feeble November afternoon light watching a video of *Top Gun*. Alex was expounding what he thought were obvious references to the Sacred Band of Thebes and the symbolism of riding front and back in an F-14 Tomcat with a fatal ejection when suddenly Honoria burst in without knocking.

'I need your help.'

'What's happened?' said Alex.

'I've lost Cosmo. I took the idiotic beast on a walk with me in the park and he ran off and he won't come back. I've been calling him for half an hour – three-quarters of an hour.'

'He'll probably just come back when he wants to,' said Theo. 'They usually do.'

'But back where?' said Honoria. 'To the house? To the rectory? To Holly Walk?'

'This was in Holly Walk?' said Nathan.

'Yes, he was with me one minute then gone the next.'

'I know where he'll be. Come on.' He gave Alex a kick.

'Now? But it's the homoerotic volleyball scene next.'

★

Daniel and Neil were waiting in the hall when Brother Sebastian, hebdomadary, came to ring the bell for tea.

'Helloo, helloo,' he said in his sing-song voice and went to pull the rope that hung by the front door. The dings rang out from a little bellcote on the roof, summoning the brethren to church for services, and to the refectory for meals, but not to be confused with the Angelus bell and the sacring bell, rung not for time-tabling but to focus prayer in a particular way. Daniel knew the difference between the sound of the bells; it was so deeply imprinted on him that he felt, like one of Pavlov's dogs, saliva beginning to juice in his mouth in anticipation of the treats to come. Brethren arrived and guests, and when the hall clock struck four the most senior of the brethren present, which was Father Paulinus, said, 'The eyes of all wait upon Thee, O Lord, and Thou givest them their meat in due season. Lord God, Heavenly Father, bless us and these Thy gifts, which we receive from Thy bountiful goodness, through Jesus Christ, Our Lord.'

Everyone responded with 'Amen' and Paulinus invited the guests into the refectory – a gesture of honour to visitors, which, while faithful to the Benedictine tradition, was not logistically sensible, for new visitors did not know what to do, and experienced visitors followed the example of the monks, holding back so that those newest to this complicated hospitality took precedence, which only compounded the problem. It caused a bottleneck in the doorway and usually it was impatient pressure from the older monks – who had long ago stopped bothering about inconveniencing the guests to satisfy form and were hungry for their crumpets – that forced them through.

Tea at Ravenspurn had not undergone much of a revision since the community was first established. Everything else had, from governance, to liturgy, to the timetable, but tea had endured pretty much unaltered. There were Brown Betty pots, so large they had an extra little handle at the front as well as the back, and white china mugs in rows with stainless-steel jugs of milk. There were hot crumpets in piles on platters that had just been brought in from the kitchen, with bowls of butter and, in a concession to those with cholesterol issues, little pats of Flora too. There was jam in bowls, and jam in jars with handwritten labels, and there was sliced white Mothers Pride in a Tupperware box waiting to be toasted in the three institutional toasters, which clicked and whirred, the descent and ascent of the slices operated by a sort of gear stick. There was also Patum Peperium to make anchovy toast and two kinds of cake – a chocolate cake and a Victoria sandwich – sliced generously and set out on large plates.

By now the older monks were ahead and those capable of pouring the tea from such big pots were helping themselves, while the novices went round to see to the very old monks who were already seated at the refectory tables, whom they treated with the same solicitude tempered with impatience that Daniel had noticed at old people's homes.

Not only were the refreshments plentiful, at least outside Lent, but the regulations also permitted conversation, so those monks who wanted to could talk to the guests, some of them with the obvious enjoyment of people who could do with more society than their way of life allowed.

Daniel poured himself and Neil mugs of tea, while Neil took a plate and loaded it with crumpets and cake as lavishly as if he'd scored a century at a cricket tea.

They found an unoccupied table and sat at the top end.

'I thought it was poverty, chastity and obedience,' said Neil as melted butter oozed from the holes in his crumpet. 'I don't know about the other two, but this seems quite lavish to me.'

'Not particularly by the standards of those who started this place,' said Daniel. 'Old Etonians. Edwardians. Tea in those days was eleven courses, maybe ten in Lent. And when I was here we still had monastery servants – kitchen staff in white jackets and gloves – but they were redeployed in the reforming zeal of the late Sixties.'

'"We",' said Neil; 'you say "we" when you're here.'

'Do I?'

'You do. You still feel part of this, don't you?'

'Yes, in a way. I do when I'm here.'

'Do you ever wonder what you would be like if you had stayed?'

'Yes. You know the problem of Schrödinger's cat?'

'I don't think I do,' said Neil.

'He argued that a cat could be simultaneously alive and dead,' said Daniel.

'Eight times.'

'No, not like that. But . . . I don't really understand it properly, but he imagined a cat in a box and proposed that there was really no way of knowing whether the cat was alive or dead until you opened the box. So it follows that until you know definitively one way or the other, the cat is both. And there's a refinement of this, which theorises that there are two coexisting universes, one in which the cat is dead and another in which the cat lives. Not just two universes, as many as you like. I sometimes think there's another world which coexists with this world we happen to be in now, in which I am still here.'

'And I am not?'

'Well, you wouldn't be. But you have your own limitless universes in which to exist.'

'Would you rather I didn't exist?' Neil asked.

'Oh,' said Daniel, 'this conversation is turning in an alarming direction.'

'Let me put it another way. Does it bother you that I am here?'

'Why would it?' said Daniel.

'Safety,' said Neil.

'I don't know.'

'This is a place of safety for you, Dan. No singular attachments. Nothing to mess you up, disrupt your routine.'

'I suppose that is part of the appeal.'

'Resistible appeal,' said Neil.

'Yes.'

'Why didn't you stay?' Neil asked.

'I started to feel – faintly at first, then more strongly – that God had other plans.'

Neil took another bite of his crumpet. 'Plain is best, right?' he said. 'Just butter, no jam . . . Is that about what you're good at? You're more suited to one way of life than others? Or you can't hack it? The demands?'

'I think I am fundamentally suited to this life,' replied Daniel. 'But that's not enough.'

'I don't understand.'

'That's why I left. Because it suited me so well.'

'Most people look for a life that suits them,' said Neil.

'It would require no sacrifice.'

'No sacrifice? Except poverty, chastity, obedience, getting up at the crack of dawn, dressing like a vampire, and never going anywhere else?' said Neil.

'That would not be so hard for me. And I don't think God calls us – he doesn't call me, certainly – to a life that does not involve sacrifice. A real sacrifice, something hard and unforgiving and impossible, which could cost everything else.'

Neil took another crumpet. 'These are damn good, Dan.'

'Yes, that's what gets us through the day. Elevenses, tea, cake and crumpets. It's the feast that makes the fast.'

'So, you're a monk who's in exile from the monastery.'

'In a way,' said Daniel. 'I'm pretty sure God wants me in the world, not the cloister. But not for my comfort.'

Neil finished his crumpet and took a sip of tea. 'Not sure what I make of that.'

'It's not your problem, Neil.'

'I'm not sure what that makes of me.'

'I don't understand,' said Daniel.

'Am I something God sent to mess up your life, but it's a different story in a parallel universe somewhere?'

Daniel blushed. They sat in silence as he thought what to say, but before he could Father Paulinus approached with a mug of tea in his hand. He did not ask to join them but just sat down.

'Hello, I am Father Paulinus. You are?'

'Neil. Neil Vanloo. But excuse me, Father, we were just—'

'Vanloo? A Belgian?'

'No, from Manchester, other side of the Pennines. But from Hesse originally.'

'Manchester? Was it textiles that drew the Hessians to Lancashire?' He smiled at his own joke in the way of someone who is not witty.

'No, religion. We're Moravian Brethren. But I was

just discussing something with Canon Clement—'

'Oh, the Unitas Fratrum! How interesting. When did the Moravian Church arrive in Manchester?'

'Oldham, Greater Manchester. The 1780s, but—'

'From Herrnhut originally? I am fascinated by Zinzendorf, such an influential man, a great evangelist for Christ to some, to others an arch-heretic. Did you know, Father, the Wesleys attended the Moravian Church in London before Methodism became systematised?'

'I think I did know that,' said Daniel.

'I have been to Herrnhut. I lived in Saxony – passed through – when I was a boy.'

'My family came here from Herrnhaag, the notorious one,' said Neil.

'Ah, that was where Zinzendorf's son – or grandson, was it? – practised his theology?'

'It was the son, Christian. You probably know more about it than I do.'

'He believed he was the hole in Christ's side?' said Paulinus.

'He proclaimed himself to be the side wound, yes,' said Neil.

'Yes, the hole in Christ himself, made by the soldier's lance as he hung on the cross, the wound into which doubting Thomas put his hand to know his Lord was alive again, and through which the brothers may pass to be united with Our Lord. All souls were female, you see, according to Zinzendorf Senior, and all – men and women — were called to be brides of Christ. The way in was through a hole in the body. Zinzendorf the younger believed he was the wound — in fact, he believed he was of Christ himself. He conflated the theological with the sexual. All were brides waiting to be filled — so flesh and blood, so personal, so contrary to the refinements of the Counter-Reformation — and there was . . . a great scandal?'

'There was,' said Neil. 'And the community dispersed, and some of us ended up in Oldham, where life was nothing like so interesting.'

'And what brings you, then, to Ravenspurn?'

'I'm one of Canon Clement's flock. I'm here on a . . . well, a break. I don't think it's really a retreat.'

'And you arrive by day and come in through the door. Unlike Father Daniel, who comes by dead of night and jumps over the wall?' Paulinus made a little jumping gesture as he said this and spilled some tea on his scapular.

Neil took another gulp of his. 'You make him sound like the wolf in the fold.'

'"*The Assyrian came down like the wolf* on *the fold . . .*" Byron, I think? Recalling the story of Sennacherib in the second book of Kings.'

Neil was beginning to find Paulinus a little trying. 'I hear you've had some real problems with predators?' he said.

There was a look of suspicion in Paulinus's eyes. 'Predators?'

'A wolf in the fold. Or on the fold. Or a fox in the hen house?'

'Ah, you heard about the massacre. Last year. All our hens were taken.'

Daniel said lightly, 'Yes, we saw the Chicken Calvary.'

'Silliness, of course,' said Father Paulinus, 'but the novices were . . . what do they say now? . . . From *träume*?'

'Traumatised?'

'Traumatised. Like a silly dream!'

'It's not from the German,' said Daniel. 'It's not *träume*. It's from the Greek, *traumas* – a wound.'

'Oh. I did not know that. A wound. But they do not know what it is to be wounded. How could they? But they should.'

'They should?'

'They have not suffered. They do not know what it is to be wounded. Or to wound.'

'I hope they never do,' said Daniel.

Paulinus snorted. 'Well, there we disagree. Anyway, there was a great falling-out. I thought it should be ignored, not indulged, but the abbot thought reconciliation a better way, and he chose, as you would expect from him, a wily compromise. He could have been a great Jesuit, you know?'

'Which of the novices?' asked Daniel.

'Which of the novices?'

'Which of the novices was traumatised?'

'It upset Anselm. He looked after them and he had

got fond of them and sentimental. I find this hard to understand.'

'The English love of animals?' said Daniel.

'Oh yes, that, certainly – but I mean allowing yourself to be sentimental about animals that provide you with eggs and meat to eat. A week or two of privation and they would overcome such delicacy of feeling. We who lived through the war, you know?'

'You were in Germany?' asked Daniel.

'For some of it. Like Mr Vanloo's, my people are a bit of a jumble. Swabian originally, but settled in Czechoslovakia, Hungary, Yugoslavia. My grandmother was in Saxony, near the Czech border. I remember her as a typical *oma* – apron, baking, singing in the kitchen, you know? But in 1945 her husband was in the army – he had died in Russia, but she did not know it – and the Red Army was near, and she had managed to keep a pig in the cellar, just, fed on potato peelings and scraps, undiscovered. And she realised she had to kill it before it became food for the Russians. She had never even seen a pig killed. You know what she did?'

'What?' said Daniel.

'She took two bricks, jammed one in its mouth and beat it to death with the other.'

Neil and Daniel were silent.

'Sentimentality is one thing. Life and death is another. It made me impatient with Anselm. He named one of the hens after a pop star. When Kylie was found decapitated he cried like a child. And then the non-sense over a funeral . . .'

'He's young, he's sensitive?'

'Others were not so silly. Bede – a sound theologian as well as a most able historian – he thought it nonsense. That was where it all blew up. Often it is not the obvious ones, the hot-tempered ones, the most passionate, who cause the problems; it is the amenable and the mild.'

'What happened?' asked Daniel.

'Nothing at first. It just simmered for months and then there was an argument during the Mass. It was only a few weeks ago, St Francis's Day. And as you may not know' – he looked at Neil – 'St Francis has this association with animals, and – this was perhaps a mistake, *mea culpa* – I had put Bede down to do the intercessions that day and he prayed for all involved in the care of animals, and he prayed for those who raised them to provide meat for our tables and so on . . . and something broke in Anselm. And then at the Peace he refused Bede's hand. In front of everyone. And then they could not receive communion, of course, and then they clashed in the sacristy and there was a physical fight. I mean, it was hardly Siegmund and Hunding, but I remember a set of cruets flew through the air and smashed against the wall.'

'What did you do?' asked Daniel.

'I had to take it to Father Aelred and there was a mini Chapter of Faults.'

'What's a Chapter of False?' said Neil.

'Not false, faults,' said Daniel.

'Yes, *faults*, my accent . . .' said Paulinus.

'It's when the community meets formally and we declare our sins to the abbot and each other,' said Daniel, 'and then the abbot pronounces absolution.'

Neil raised an eyebrow. 'A court of self-incrimination?'

'And accusation. You can accuse others too,' said Daniel.

'You are a lawyer?' asked Father Paulinus.

'No,' said Neil, 'not exactly.'

'Not exactly?'

'No, I'm not a lawyer. If I were, I would wonder if the culpable are reliable confessors of their sins.'

'Oh, well, that is a discipline for every day here,' said Paulinus.

'You confess your faults to each other every day?' said Neil.

'Not in that formal way, no, but we have to give an account of our actions to God every day. And we confess our sins together at Mass every day – generally, not specifically.'

Neil grimaced. 'Don't you ever think there is something indulgent about this . . . lavish repentance?'

'No,' said Father Paulinus, 'it is the opposite of indulgent.'

'Is it? There seems to me to be something precious about it.'

'That is the Protestant in you talking.'

'I couldn't really call myself a believing Protestant any more,' said Neil.

'Maybe so, but you are a Protestant non-believer. You don't like . . . fuss.'

Neil considered this for a moment. 'You're right about that. I don't like fuss. I prefer directness. And you have just made me think that maybe that has something to do with being taught that grace and truth require no mediator but come to us directly from God.'

'Through your side wound,' said Paulinus.

'I have never thought of it that way. But there is something in me that recoils from all this ceremony, from Latin, from fancy business with smoke and bells and living like this.' Neil finished his tea. 'I am going for a walk. When's showtime, Dan?'

'Vespers, Neil, at six. Shall I collect you from the guest house? Half past five?'

'OK. Father.' Neil nodded to Paulinus, and left.

Paulinus watched him go. 'What an interesting person, Daniel.'

'I think so, yes.'

'And so . . . strapping.'

Daniel said nothing.

The Holly Walk, thick with evergreen, was already anticipating nightfall when they got there. Nathan parked the Land Rover at the top and left the head-lights on. He gave a spade each to Alex and Theo and a torch to Honoria.

'He'll have gone down a hole after a billy. I know where they are.'

They hurried down the walk, the car headlights casting long shadows before them, and stopped at a bank where badgers had dug uneven holes surrounded by the exposed roots of bushes and trees. 'Shut up!' said Nathan. 'Listen!'

They kept silent for a second and Nathan put his ear to one of the holes. 'He's in here.' He took the torch and shone it down the hole, then shoved his arm in as far as he could go. They heard, faintly, a whimpering sound and a snort.

'He's too far in, I can't reach him. We're going to have to dig.'

After a few spadefuls, the earth began to move, and Nathan got on his knees and with his hands dug further in until they hit a tangle of roots.

'It's like a cage,' said Honoria, holding the torch, 'how the hell will we get him out?'

'If he went in, he can come out,' said Nathan. 'Let me see if I can get him.' He reached in and felt for Cosmo's tail, which was wagging until Nathan yanked hard. Cosmo squealed but did not shift, so Nathan lay down and gently got both hands around his hind quarters and dug away at the surrounding earth with his fingers. Eventually the dog began to wriggle and suddenly was free, dirty and blinking and nervous, but released from captivity in the web of roots and dirt. He barked, and sneezed, and barked again.

'Let me just check him.' Nathan shone the torch in Cosmo's face, which made him try to pull away, but there were no gashes or cuts that Nathan could see. 'Lucky. I had a terrier lose half his snout to a billy here once.'

When they got Cosmo to the Land Rover Nathan wrapped him in a blanket. 'He'll need a bath,' he said.

'I'll do it,' said Honoria.

'Dear Mrs Shorely,' said Alex, 'what would we do without her?'

'No, I'll do it.'

And Honoria did attempt to do it, although not without help. As they arrived at the back of Champton House, where the kitchens and the laundry stood round a courtyard, Audrey was returning from her first shift as shop assistant at Elite Fashions. She had decided she did not really like the sound of 'shop assistant'. Miss March had proposed 'floor manager', but that did not feel quite right either so Audrey had counter-proposed 'retail consultant'. Miss March had raised an eyebrow but then thought Audrey could call herself what she wanted provided she did the job for the pay agreed. Audrey nevertheless felt, rather than thought, that she should perhaps use Champton's kitchen entrance rather than the front door. The front door would do if she were arriving as the rector's mother, but arriving that way from her employment in trade would seem somehow not right, so she chose a humbler one.

Nathan had Cosmo, still wrapped in the blanket,

under his arm. The dog gave a little yap when he saw Audrey. She peered into the bundle, which started to wriggle.

'That hound is filthy,' she said, 'where's he been?'

'He went after a badger in the Holly Walk, Mum,' said Theo. 'We just had to dig him out.'

'You utter fathead, Theo—'

'Not me – Honoria,' said Theo, happy to point out his mother's misdirected insult.

'Oh,' said Audrey, and gave a tense little laugh. 'Perhaps best to keep him on the lead where there are burrows?'

'My fault, Audrey,' said Honoria, 'but to be *fair*—'

'Let's get as much of this muck off him as we can. Have you a hose? Then it's bathtime for Cosmo.'

'But he's been through an ordeal,' said Honoria. 'I think more delicate handling?'

'He's a dog, dear, not the infanta of Spain.'

There was something in Audrey's tone that Cosmo recognised. The moment Nathan put him down he shot out of the blanket and ran as fast as he could past Honoria and through the kitchen entrance into the house.

'Catch him,' snapped Audrey. 'I don't want him bringing badger doings into the house! I know whereof I speak!'

Honoria and Alex and Theo ran after him, leaving Audrey and Nathan in the courtyard.

'Aren't you going to help, Nathan?'

'I . . . don't like to,' he said, and nodded towards the house.

'Oh dear, I suppose not. But you were so good with Hilda when she had her puppies . . .'

'I'll find a hose,' he said and went off to the line of sheds at the end of the range.

'And a brush, if you can find one? And a tin bath if there is such a thing?'

Audrey carefully closed the kitchen-entrance door behind her, lest Cosmo, anticipating his watery fate, should try to bolt again, and went through to Mrs Shorely's office. The housekeeper was sitting at her desk reading *Woman's Realm* and wondering if anyone in the real world had any use for a fruit kebab.

'Mrs Clement?' she said, glancing up.

'Mrs Shorely, I am so sorry about Cosmo, the mucky little pup, leave him to me.'

'We've not seen Cosmo,' she said. 'Not the most attentive of new fathers.' She nodded towards the little whelping enclosure where Hilda was lying, while the puppies, wrinkled and squirming, relentlessly fed.

'He just ran into the house. From the courtyard. Honoria and Alex and Theo in pursuit?'

'They carried on past. Try the hall. Mucky?'

'Yes, went down a badger sett, they had to dig him out.'

Mrs Shorely sighed. 'Why did they let him in?'

'The door was open. He was through it before you could say "sausages". But I'll take care of it.' Audrey hurried to the hall just as Jove scooted across the tiled floor, which was marked with muddy paws, visible on the white squares, invisible on the black. Audrey followed them to the far corner and the corridor that led to Bernard's study.

Bernard was sitting in his armchair, a tumbler of whisky knocked over on the fender and Cosmo curled up on his tweedy lap. When Cosmo saw Audrey he tried to burrow into the crook of Bernard's arm.

'He's trembling, the poor little brute,' said Bernard.

'Bathtime, Bernard. Oh, look at your *shirt*! Cosmo loathes bathtime.'

'Perhaps it's being hosed down with freezing-cold water that's making him nervous?' said Bernard, sounding peeved. 'It would make me nervous.'

'And poor Jove,' said Audrey, 'he just scooted past me looking like a . . . terrorised cloud.'

'You seem to have rather a gift for frightening animals, Audrey,' he said.

'It's not me. Dogs hate cats, cats hate dogs. They are, as you put it, brutes, and incapable of anything but the most rudimentary hygiene. Cosmo needs a bath.'

'Then I shall give it him,' said Bernard.

Neil and Daniel were up in the organ loft, looking down on the length of the abbey church. It was half an hour before Vespers, when Daniel would normally be on his knees, saying his prayers, turning the beads of his *metanoi* through his fingers. But it was Second

Vespers for St Willibrord and therefore Solemn, which meant a coped celebrant and smoke and music, and Daniel was playing the organ.

He had asked Neil to be with him in the organ loft as his page turner, which as he said it sounded like one of those euphemisms the clergy like to use to explain their proximity to another when that proximity requires explanation, like 'confirmation candidate' or 'organ scholar'.

His proximity to Neil on this occasion really did need some explaining, not to the community but to himself, for he had left his normal life in the middle of the night to escape Neil, to seek sanctuary in the cloister from his unbearable passion, where so many others had sought the same, or to break free from asymmetrical attachments, or despairing of a life lived fully in the world. But he had to admit that he liked to have Neil near – his presence, his warmth, even his smell, which was faintly of Old Spice, though Daniel did not know that was what it was. He did know this was a weakness on his part and one he should not indulge, but he had – he hesitated to call it an excuse – a reason, and that was to do what they had done before: discover a murderer. They were on the scent of something, or someone, and their attachment to each other in that was, if not symmetrical, complementary.

'What do I have to do?' Neil asked.

'Stand on my right, and when I nod turn the page. Do it quickly but efficiently, and keep your arm out of the way of the music so I can see it. It's St Willibrord today, so I'm playing the Fugue à la Gigue by Bach – German, like him – and a jig, because he's associated with dancing. There's a lot going on.'

'How many turns?'

'Two.'

'Not that demanding, Dan.'

'No, but I don't really want you here to turn the pages – well, I do, but mostly I want you to keep watching the community, and when I say so tell me if anyone looks up.'

'Why?' said Neil.

'I want to see who notices when I make a mistake.'

'Chapter of Faults?'

'No,' said Daniel, 'something I want to confirm. But have a go at a page-turn. Stand there to my right but behind me. When I nod, turn.'

Daniel played the first voice of the fugue, a jaunty little figure that jumped around like a gambolling lamb, and then added the second voice with his left hand, no less jaunty, and the two did their little dance until another voice joined, still jaunty, but this was in the pedals, and trying to be jaunty with your feet rather than your fingers is challenging. He was concentrating hard when Neil's shadow fell over the music and he lost his place, which made him snap.

'Don't stand so close, Neil . . .'

'Sorry,' said Neil. 'Where do you want me to be?'

'Not in my light.'

'Here OK?'

'I just need you not to get in the way of what I'm doing.'

'In art and in life,' said Neil.

'What does that mean?'

Neil sang, *sotto voce*, '"*Don't stand so-o close to me . . .*"'

'Neil, I'm trying to concentrate. Just turn the page when I nod.'

Daniel started again and this time, as the lambs were gambolling away, when he nodded Neil leant over and flicked the page at exactly the right moment for a flawless shift. The lambs gambolled without stumbling to a satisfactory end.

'That's a very jolly number,' said Neil. 'I see what you mean about dancing.'

'It's also very difficult. I'm going to make a mistake in the pedal part at the end – only a little one, you won't notice it – and it's after the last page turn, so I won't need you here. I want you to watch the community and tell me what happens.'

Second Vespers for the Feast of St Willibrord, Apostle to Frisia, went without a hitch. Aelred, vested splendidly in his abbatial mitre, was assisted by two novices who held open the two sides of his cope so he could swing the thurible and wreathe the altar in scented smoke during the singing of the Magnificat.

At the end of the service, after the abbot pronounced a blessing, he returned to sit on his stool, his two servers on either side, and Daniel struck up with the organ voluntary. There was a little ripple of approving nods from those in the community who got the reference to St Willibrord in his choice of the fugue, a silent version of the polite laughs from those who get the jokes in Shakespeare. Then, after two faultless page-turns from Neil, he arrived at the last entry of the pedal part, when everything comes together for the big finish. And then in the fourth bar from the end he changed a pedal triplet so it went up a major second, rather than down a major sixth – a change so tiny and inoffensive to the ear no one would notice it.

One person noticed it.

'Aelred,' said Neil, 'looked up just before the end.'

'Ah,' said Daniel, 'I thought so.'

'But that wasn't the interesting thing,' said Neil.

'What was the interesting thing?'

'What everyone else was looking at.'

'Which was?' Daniel asked.

'The two lads on either side of Aelred having a spat.'

The lights were on in the courtyard when Audrey appeared from the kitchen entrance. Nathan was waiting dutifully with a tin bath and a hose.

'Stand down, Nathan. Bernard is bathing the dog.'

'His lordship? Give a dog a bath?' He laughed.

'I know, but that's what he intends to do.'

'Jean Shorely more like.'

'No. Well, she's to bring him towels and Honoria's

got some baby shampoo, but now he intends to bathe the dog himself in his own bathroom.'

Nathan started to coil the hose, then said, 'You want to be careful about that, Mrs Clement.'

'Careful?'

'It's like that with dogs. If they don't get the attention they want from someone, they'll look for it from someone else.'

'Cosmo is *smothered* with attention,' said Audrey.

'Often happens with dogs when bitches whelp. It's all about the mum, see, and the puppies.'

'But they've hardly been out of my sight.'

'I know, but what about Cosmo? The rector's not here, the rectory's out of bounds, he's in a strange place. And what with you helping out at Miss March's shop . . .'

'Consulting, dear, not helping out.'

'He's attaching to his lordship. And his lordship may be attaching to him.'

'Bernard and Cosmo? Like John Noakes and Shep?' said Audrey.

'Dogs and humans attach. Always have. It's in the blood,' said Nathan.

'Well, that's not what I'd planned *at all*.'

12

After Vespers, Daniel switched off the organ and put away the music in accordance with the meticulous shelving system Aelred had invented when he was the community's organist. He and Neil then made their way to the hall to await the supper bell. They passed the sacristy, empty by now, save Paulinus and the two novices, now derobed, one in a cassock and a blue scapular, the other in a plain cassock – Brother Placid, he remembered, who had seemed rather abrasive at their session on the New Testament, and Darren the postulant with the sinister semi-shaded glasses.

'You serve the abbot,' said Paulinus, 'not your own liturgical prejudices. And it is the Holy Mass, not a forum for your squabble.'

Brother Placid blinked and said, 'I must say, Father, that I wouldn't dream of disrupting the liturgy—'

'But you did,' said Darren. 'You placed the mitre on the abbot's head for the censing of the altar during the Magnificat. By what authority?'

'Does it matter?'

'By what authority? You should know these things!'

'Don't speak to me like that,' said Brother Placid.

'Don't mess things up, then,' Darren shot back. 'Do your job. It would help if you knew what it was.'

'Darren, I have been doing this since long before you were born,' said Placid. 'Yours is not the only way—'

'It's in Fortescue!'

'Fortescue is not one of the historic formularies of the Church of England.'

'So just do what you like?' said Darren. 'Give him a top hat? A fez?'

'Do you think Our Lord minds particularly if I get the hat rules wrong?' said Placid.

'Yes, I think he does. Why not give your best when you could give your best?'

'Darren,' said Father Paulinus, 'compose yourself.'

'Father, not only did he mitre the abbot for the censing, which is wrong, he also ignored me when I said so, and at the end for the blessing he put it on the wrong way round.'

'That was unfortunate,' said Paulinus.

'Try exercising oversight of the Church when your lappets are flapping in front of your face,' said Darren.

The bell for supper went.

'We will continue this conversation after supper,' said Paulinus. 'You will come to my office—' He saw Daniel and Neil standing in the doorway. 'That was the supper bell, Father,' he said.

Daniel nodded and motioned to Neil to follow him down the corridor towards the hall.

'What was that all about?' said Neil. 'Hat wars?'

'It's complicated. I'll tell you later.'

After Miss March shut up the shop for the day, she popped over the road to the post office. She had started taking the *Braunstonbury Evening Telegraph*. It was a good source of intelligence for business because it alerted her to forthcoming events in the town's social calendar, for which ladies might be persuaded to buy a new frock.

The Beagle Ball was held on the first Saturday in January at the Assembly Rooms, perhaps the most splendid gathering of the year, and as Christmas approached, with its mood of largesse, she was thinking about what her ladies might like to wear. Everyone under forty wanted to look like Princess Di, who had created a sensation on a trip to New York earlier in the year wearing smart Catherine Walker suits by day and a gorgeous Victor Edelstein white beaded gown with a bolero by night, but Miss March's ladies were of riper years and no more likely to wear something like that to the Beagle Ball or the Braunstonbury Chamber of Commerce Dinner Dance than a leopard-skin bikini. Jacques Vert, she thought, Windsmoor, were the key to unlocking their purses, and Audrey Clement, who had an almost supernatural feel for these things, agreed in general, but added highly focused specifics. 'Frank Usher,' she said, 'long dress with a bit of Lurex in a geometric style with a three-quarter-length-sleeve jacket. So you can fold it over the arm with the label showing.'

Miss March had also grown to like the personal columns in the *Evening Telegraph*, especially the rhyming obituaries, which were sometimes surprisingly bold. 'You thought the driver waved you past,' went one; 'you weren't to know you'd breathed your last.' It made her laugh all night.

She also liked the paper as a source of intelligence for Braunstonbury's shadow life, which expressed itself through vandalism and shoplifting, summarised by a reporter at the magistrates' court. The more nefarious infractions – assaults inflicted, contraband seized, frauds perpetrated – were written up more vividly, under pictures of the sort that appeared in the rogues' gallery on *Crimewatch*. These she read with particular interest.

The bell dinged as she pushed the post office door open to find Norah Braines at the counter in conversation with Dot Staveley. As soon as they saw her they were silent.

'Good evening, Mrs Braines, Mrs Staveley,' said Miss March.

'Miss March,' said Mrs Braines in coldish acknowledgement. 'The post office is shut so it's shop only.'

'Just the paper, please, and a packet of Mintoes, if you have one.' *Dad's Army* was on at eight, her father's favourite, and she liked to watch the repeats and suck a

Mintoe – also one of his favourites – in his memory. She kept an old Mintoes tin in the cupboard, from the Sixties, she thought, 11*d*. for a quarter-pound, into which she decanted the packet. She found it comforting.

'You're making the news today, Miss March,' said Dot Staveley rather boldly as Mrs Braines handed over the folded copy of the paper.

'In the paper?'

'No, dear, parish pump. Personnel change at Elite Fashions, we hear.'

'You mean that Mrs Dollinger has left my employment?'

'I do. Anne's a friend of ours,' said Dot.

'I'm sure she is. But I don't see what business this is of yours, Mrs Staveley, or anyone else?'

'Only a lot of us spend money in your shop and . . . you know, ill feeling?'

'The old order changeth, yielding place to the new,' said Miss March. 'At Elite Fashions as well as the Communist Bloc. I'm sure you understand.'

'And we hear there's already a replacement,' Dot went on.

'Mrs Clement has kindly offered to assist me as floor manager.'

'How clever of you to snap her up. Such a head for business,' said Dot.

'And such a sure sense of fashion. So important to have someone who has an instinct for what customers like. Not just now' – Miss March looked at Dot with an appraising eye – 'but what they will want to wear when others have blazed a trail.'

Mrs Braines intervened. 'That's 67p, Miss March. You know, I could get my lad Christian to deliver your paper, if you prefer?'

'No, thank you, Mrs Braines, I like to call in. Catch up on the news that isn't fit to print. Mrs Staveley' – she nodded at her – 'my regards to Councillor Staveley.'

The door dinged as she left.

'You really don't like her, do you, Dot?' said Mrs Braines.

'She was horrible to Anne. Made her cry.'

'It's not hard,' said Norah.

'I know, but . . . Miss March just seems to think she's better than the rest of us. Goodbye, Anne; hello, the rector's mother.'

'Retail consultant.'

'I'm free!' Dot trilled like Mr Humphries in *Are You Being Served?* 'And the rector's mother has always got something up her sleeve. A plan. Some ulterior motive.'

'Everyone's got a plan, Dot.'

Supper in the refectory was silent, or rather without conversation, for as in the ancient custom of the Benedictine tradition, one of the monks, appointed as lector for that week, sat at a stool in front of a lectern.

The abbot said a particularly mean grace – 'Forgive us, Lord, for feasting while others starve' – and the lector began with a portion from the Rule of our Holy Father Benedict.

'Chapter twenty-five. "A brother guilty of a serious fault is to be excluded from both the table and the oratory. No other brother should associate or converse with him at all. He will work alone at the tasks assigned to him, living continually in sorrow and penance, pondering that fearful judgement of the Apostle: Such a man is handed over for the destruction of his flesh that his spirit may be saved on the day of the Lord. Let him take his food alone in an amount and at a time the abbot considers appropriate for him. He should not be blessed by anyone passing by, nor should the food that is given him be blessed."'

The abbot rapped the table and the monk put away the Rule and produced the book they were reading through for pleasure rather than instruction. They all sat – Neil looked at Daniel and said, '*Bon appetit*' – and the novices, wearing white scapulars to serve dinner, appeared from the kitchen pushing trolleys from table to table.

The lector announced his text. '*Imperial Twilight: The Story of Karl and Zita of Hungary* by Bertita Harding. Chapter twenty-three: "Farther down the river bronzed colliers plied their oars and turned sullen eyes from the passing enemy craft, while fishermen drew back their nets before the rampant White Ensign of Britain . . .'"

Dinner was not a considerable meal – there was a

sort of hash, followed by bread and jam – and no wine was served, as it had been with lunch to mark the feast. Weak beer instead was poured from jugs that smelled faintly of the detergent used in the dishwashers. It was the cellarer's job to provide for the brethren's alcoholic needs, which in Daniel's day, when that duty fell to him, meant going once a week to the cash and carry at Owthorne to stock up on Watney's Party Seven, Emva Cream sherry and a gin so coarse William Hogarth could have cleaned his brushes in it. It was revealing, however, to know who was drinking what, because individual orders, as well as community orders, were placed with him. What do you buy a monk for Christmas or his birthday? Gin, probably, and because mixers were not a monastery staple, gin and ice was the signature drink, usually sipped after Compline when the house was in Greater Silence and the monks in their quarters. Some, the irredeemably social, failed to uphold that item of the Rule and drank quietly together; others drank alone. Drink, indiscipline, jealousy, sex – worldly vices not left at the gate but admitted to what Aelred once called 'laboratory conditions'.

Neil, meanwhile, was enduring another of the trials that come with monastic life. He was sitting opposite one of the older monks whose management of the intake of food and drink was so incomplete that half of what was intended for his inside ended up on his outside, on the scapular, which looked like Mount Everest's death zone.

Dinner was mercifully short, business-like. After the bread and jam had gone silently round, and the monks had offered more to guests with enough of a suggestion of perfunctoriness for them to understand that acceptance was not expected, Aelred rapped the table again.

The lector concluded, marked his place, closed the book and they all stood.

'We give Thee thanks for all Thy benefits, O Almighty God, who livest and reignest world without end,' said Aelred.

'Amen.'

'May the souls of the faithful departed, through the mercy of God, rest in peace.'

'Amen.'

Everyone crossed themselves, except Neil, who wasn't sure what to do.

They turned to face the abbot, who led out the diners at the top table, followed by the older monks who could walk, and the rest of the community, and then the novices, who assisted the monks who could not walk, including the one who sat opposite Neil. When they helped him up a small cascade from the smorgasbord of his scapular tumbled onto the floor, and words came to Neil's mind that he had not thought of for years, about being unworthy of the crumbs under the table.

He followed Daniel out into the hall. The abbot was waiting for them. 'Daniel,' he said, 'introduce me to your friend?'

'Father Aelred, Neil Vanloo. Neil Vanloo, Father Aelred.'

'I hope dinner was not too much of an ordeal. Father Sylvanus is not always the prettiest of dining companions.'

'No problem,' said Neil. 'Thanks for your hospitality.'

'You are a parishioner of Daniel's?'

'Not exactly. A sheep of his flock,' said Neil.

'I see. Would you like to join me for a sherry? It's marginally less undrinkable than the beer.'

'That's very kind of you, Father,' said Daniel, 'but we're seeing Paulinus.'

'Well then, you must see Paulinus. How long are you with us, Mr Vanloo?'

'Another couple of days, I think.'

'Then sherry tomorrow?'

'Thank you.'

The abbot glided away.

'Are we seeing Paulinus?' Neil asked Daniel.

'I hope so. I didn't want to get into a conversation with the abbot about why you're here.'

'I can understand that.'

'I don't think you do,' said Daniel.

'You don't want to discuss our personal stuff in front of a monk?'

'It's not *that* I'm concerned about, it's him discovering you're a policeman. Let's find Paulinus.'

Daniel led Neil along the corridor to the cloister. It was empty, save a couple of monks having cigarettes outside the offices on the east side. In one office, Daniel could see Paulinus at his desk, using a sort of typewriter. That's not a typewriter, thought Daniel. That's a Panasonic KX-W900.

Paulinus looked up. He seemed puzzled at first to see Daniel looking in through his window. He got up and opened the glazed door to the cloister. 'Mr Vanloo? Father?'

'I'm sorry to disturb you,' said Daniel, 'but is that a Panasonic KX-W900?'

'Ah, you are an aficionado? Come in, come in.'

They stood around Paulinus's desk. 'I wouldn't say aficionado, but I've read about them. I've never actually seen one.'

'It's a typewriter,' said Neil.

'It is not a typewriter,' said Paulinus. 'It is a word processor.'

'Strictly speaking, it is something between a word processor and a typewriter,' said Daniel. 'It does what a typewriter does but with the functions of a word processor. You see, you type, and the text appears on that little screen – you can edit it and even save it to a floppy disk – but then press a button and it prints it like a typewriter. How did you get one?'

'Responsibility for office supplies is mine, Father.'

'May I see?'

'Of course.'

Paulinus sat at his desk and gave what Neil very quickly found to be an impenetrably technical account of the characteristics of the device. After a while he said, 'But what's it for?'

'What's it for?'

'What are you using it for?' Neil specified.

'I am writing a sermon.'

'Why do you need a word processor to do that? Can't you just write it the normal way?'

'This allows me to write it line by line and correct it if I make a mistake. I can fix it, or find a more felicitous word, I can change it . . . there is something to be said for writing in a rush, if you are in the Spirit, rather than hesitating as the Spirit's breath blows through your conscious mind. Do you see?'

'That's interesting,' said Daniel. 'I've often thought about the way the materials we use affect how and what we write.'

'Quite so, think of the shift from scroll to codex.'

'Oh, yes—'

Neil interrupted. 'What's the sermon about?'

'It is about a saint of the Middle Ages, Elizabeth of Hungary. It is her feast in a week or so. I asked to preach in her honour, for she is a great favourite of mine. A queen who lived like a slave.'

'She was so harshly treated by her confessor that she died of exhaustion while she was still practically a girl,' said Daniel.

'Without a word of complaint, or a twitch of resistance,' said Paulinus. 'She obeyed. Blessed is she among women!'

'Sounds like the victim of a domestic.'

'That's what some of the brethren say. And the novitiate. But she was a queen, not a cowed girl.'

'Still sounds like abuse to me,' said Neil.

'To the judgement of the world, perhaps,' said Paulinus.

'Yours is a more violent world than I thought,' said Neil.

'No more here than anywhere,' said Paulinus. 'Just different.'

'What was that fight at Vespers about?' asked Daniel.

Paulinus looked and blinked. 'There was no fight, Father. There was a little squabble between the acolytes – there often is when Darren is on duty.'

'The postulant. He seems very keen. Very certain.'

'He is. Weren't we all?'

'We had our fights too, when I was in the novitiate. And it was usually the postulant.'

'What's a postulant?' said Neil.

'An applicant to join the community,' said Daniel. 'First, they come as a postulant, then, if they are considered suitable, they join the novitiate. Then, if they can survive that, they become what is called a professed monk. Full membership.'

'The postulancy is often difficult,' said Father Paulinus, 'for people come with unrealistic expectations, or with psychological damage of some kind. We don't know who they are until we find out, and we can only do that by living with them. So there's a trial period and if they seem suitable, they continue; if not, they leave.'

'Darren seems to rub people up the wrong way,' said Daniel. 'He caused a row at Benediction after Bede died.'

'You were there?'

'Yes. He started a Hail Mary and, I think it was Placid, lost his temper with him and walked out. He kicked him. Accidentally on purpose.'

'He clashes a lot with Placid. He did again today. Darren knows the ritual to the smallest detail. Placid doesn't really care about that sort of thing. Neither does Aelred, now. He used to be so diligent, but it faded. Poor man, called to be an abbot when he'd much rather be left alone in a library to read . . . Placid gets impatient with Darren for his obsession with ceremony and Darren gets frustrated with Placid for messing it up.'

'I'm with Placid,' said Neil. 'Why fuss about a hat when half the world is starving?'

'Because the big things are in the small things, Mr Vanloo,' said Paulinus. 'It is not really about a hat, as you call it. It is about doing things the right way. And what the right way is. We are the Church of England. We can't agree about biscuits, let alone salvation.'

'But we manage our differences,' said Daniel, 'the middle way, with reason and moderation.'

'We like to think so, don't we?' said Paulinus. 'The English love of moderation. But if you look at that from the outside you see that being so doggedly moderate, refusing to take a position, is itself taking a position. What is the reasonable middle way between right and wrong, good and evil? And we have now the highly divisive' – he pronounced it *deeveesive* – 'issue of the ordination of women to the priesthood. To Placid, it is a simple matter of justice that must be put right, repented of. To Darren, it is to destroy the Church.'

'Can't the pope just say something?' asked Neil.

'We have no pope, Mr Vanloo, we are Church of England, so there is no final authority of that kind. And if there were, we wouldn't obey it. I sometimes think trying to be *anything* – high, low, in between, liberal, Catholic evangelical – in the Church of England is impossible.'

'Why?'

'Because we are neither fish nor fowl nor good fresh herring.'

'*Red* herring,' said Neil.

'Red herring. It is not a Church, it is a personality disorder.'

'Then why not leave it?' asked Neil.

'I could not leave it,' said Paulinus.

'Why not?'

'Can you leave your family?'

'But you weren't born into this,' said Neil. 'You're not C of E.'

'No, my family are what you call Old Catholics. Union of Utrecht.'

'That's Holland.'

'Yes, but my family were in Swabia, Czechoslovakia, Austria-Hungary. There are Old Catholics in many places, not just the Netherlands.'

'So you are Catholic?' said Neil.

'We are ALL Catholics here, just not Roman Catholics. Anglo-Catholics mostly, if you believe such a thing can be, but I am Old Catholic. We are not in communion with Rome. We were, but we went our own way after the First Vatican Council. It is a very complicated story. We are now in communion with the Anglican churches, which is why I am here.'

'In the Church of England or in Ravenspurn?'

'After the war we were all displaced, you know, and I came to England. I found my way here and knew at once I wanted to stay.'

'Do you have family, Father,' asked Daniel, 'in Germany or Czechoslovakia?'

Paulinus closed his eyes. At first Daniel thought he was praying, then he said, 'It is the past, Father. A terrible past. Many lost, many scattered. The turmoil of war. The younger brethren get so anxious, so worried about . . . the ordination of women. I lived through the descent of nations into the madness of war and the collapse of the Reich. I know chaos, and it is not ordaining women priests. Darren would think differently.'

'And Bede?' said Daniel.

'Bede is . . . *was* opposed to the ordination of women, yes, but if anything it made his relationship with Darren more difficult. Darren thought Bede should be his ally, but he drove him round the bend.'

'Why?'

'Bede could be irritating. You saw that in class. He was a clever boy, he always knew better, and very often he did know better. He was a brilliant student at Oxford, and Darren went to a technical college in Ipswich, and Bede was not always patient with him.'

'But they were of one mind on the issue of women priests?' said Daniel.

'Both opposed, but Darren's opposition was instinct-ive. Bede's was theological. Darren could not keep up with that. So Bede was an ally who made him feel weak, not strong. But I wanted to ask you something about Bede, Father.'

'Yes?' said Daniel.

'I wonder if you would offer some spiritual support to his parents. I have left them an assurance of my prayers, and the intercession of St Elizabeth.'

'Patron of those who have lost children,' said Daniel.

'One of them.'

'And widows?'

'And the homeless, and lacemakers, and the Order of Teutonic Knights also,' said Paulinus. 'And Budapest.'

'Busy lady,' said Neil.

'But you have pastoral gifts for the consolation of the bereaved that I do not have. Perhaps you could spend an hour with them?'

'Yes, of course,' said Daniel.

'Now, would you like to have a turn on the KX-W900?'

13

Audrey and Theo were in the library at Champton House. The fire was lit but had not yet given much warmth, so they were sitting on opposite sofas at the end nearest the grate, where logs popped and hissed as the flames intensified. They were drinking aperitifs, to which they had helped themselves from a tray on the sideboard. Audrey's was a Noilly Prat, which Bernard had got in especially for her on Honoria's advice, and Theo was having a Campari and soda, because that was the only thing on the tray he felt able to drink.

'Then you and Neil came to the same conclusion,' Theo said. 'Ravenspurn.'

'I think so. Where else would he go after disappearing in the dead of night? I have written to him there,' said Audrey.

'I think you're right. I know Neil's gone up there to see him. Honoria told me. Rather an extravagant gesture, I said, from someone in the middle of a murder investigation.'

'Has he? I wonder if that is wise.'

'They got their man, so I suppose Neil took some time off.'

'That's not what I meant.'

'Oh.'

'Darling, why do you think Daniel has disappeared?'

'I couldn't say, Mum.'

'I think you could. Don't say on some mysterious Church errand.'

Theo looked towards the door in the hope that someone would come in and he could escape this conversation. No one came. 'Dan's inner life, Mum — always been inscrutable to me.'

'Yes, I know, he is rather a sphinx, but it is not what he chooses to reveal about himself that I am wondering about. It is what he unintentionally reveals about himself.'

'You sound like him,' said Theo.

'Perhaps something of his method has rubbed off on me.'

'Or he got it from you. No one can parse the subtleties of a peep-toe on a court shoe like you.'

'It so depends on the toe, dear. And knowing one's feet.'

'I suppose I must ask you what he has unintentionally revealed.'

Audrey had thought about being asked this question and how to answer. 'I think perhaps he has a crush on his new friend.'

'Why?' said Theo.

'He comes alive when Neil walks into the room. Neil looks at him like an adoring younger brother, like you used to. Only this is not brotherly love.'

'No.'

'I don't think Daniel has ever felt like that about anyone before. And he's a priest. I thought celibacy was as natural to him as thrift to a Scotchman. So to see him doe-eyed over anyone, let alone a young policeman, is unexpected. Didn't you notice it?'

'Can't see what you're not looking for,' said Theo.

'What's the view from the lodge?'

'Alex saw it coming, but sexual proclivities of any kind are so unremarkable to him he wouldn't think it worth mentioning.'

'Sexual proclivities?' said Audrey. 'A crush, don't you think?'

'A crush certainly, but a crush on another man.'

'It doesn't mean he's a homosexual,' said Audrey.

'Doesn't it?'

'There's nothing of that in the family.'

'Uncle Harry,' said Theo.

'He wasn't your uncle, he was your father's cousin. And anyway, he wasn't a homosexual.'

'He was convicted of gross indecency in a lavatory at King's Cross.'

'He was under a lot of stress.'

'Mum, what do you do when you're under a lot of stress?'

Audrey said nothing and took another sip of vermouth. 'He was a sensitive man.'

'He was a bachelor who collected Georgian enamel pill boxes.'

'*Men,*' said Audrey, 'such lazy creatures.'

'What does laziness have to do with it?'

'Can't be bothered to get out there and put some effort into courting. Did Honoria know?'

'I don't think she saw it coming,' said Theo. 'Neither did Nathan.'

Audrey took another sip of her Noilly and admired what it came in – a vessel somewhere between a tumbler and a wine glass, with a lovely diamond-cut band round the middle, something she imagined was made specially for vermouth in the Edwardian era. So many lovely things at Champton.

'A priest is tricky enough,' she said. 'Imagine having that conversation with the bishop? But a policeman?'

'I would quite like to think a bishop would look more favourably on a priest having a passion for a policeman than, say, a gypsy.'

'No, I don't mean that. I mean, can you even have a homosexual policeman? Hello, Super, I've something to tell you . . .'

'Neil's not a homosexual,' said Theo.

'Oh – gay then, whatever we must call it.'

'He's not gay. He's not homosexual. He's not that way.'

Audrey at first could not think of anything to say.

She put her glass down and breathed out through her nose – not quite a sigh. 'So Daniel's feelings are unreciprocated?'

'Yes.'

'Are you *sure*?'

'Absolutely sure,' said Theo. 'Well, a qualification: his *sexual* feelings are not reciprocated. Neil definitely feels *something* for Dan.'

'Yes, he must. Look at them. Like love-stricken swains. Perhaps Neil has not yet discovered where his interest lies?'

'Oh, he has, and it is not towards his own sex.'

'You sound like you speak from knowledge?' said Audrey.

'Yes. He and Honoria have been having a passionate affair for months. Top secret, by the way.'

'Why the hell didn't you tell me?'

'There's something in me, Mum, that wilts at the thought of discussing sexual intimacies with you.'

'Good Lord, what will Bernard make of it? A bent gypsy, a squaw and a plod for in-laws!'

'I am the least censorious of people, as you know,' said Theo, 'but we really don't say things like that now.'

'Does Neil know Daniel has fallen for him?'

'He does now. Honoria worked it out and told him.'

'Of course. So they *were* love-stricken swains, only not for each other.'

'Think so,' said Theo.

'Poor Dan. No wonder he's fled to the cloister again. And now that fathead's gone after him,' said Audrey.

'I think that's rather sweet.'

'Oh, stab him in the heart and then go and open the wound.'

There was a burst of energy suddenly as Cosmo came hurtling into the library just behind Jove. The cat leapt onto a sofa and from there jumped onto a shelf. Cosmo skidded on the polished parquet and disappeared under the sofa. Jove stood, his back arched, his fur on end, making a sound like someone with a laryngectomy trying to scream.

'Cosmo!' shouted Audrey. 'Come out AT ONCE!'

The little dog emerged from under the sofa, but not in obedience to Audrey's command. A little wolf, who looked like a toy, he was concentrating on his prey, hackles up, and stamping his paws like a bull in a ring.

'Cosmo! COSMO!' shouted Audrey. Cosmo did not even twitch. Then Bernard appeared in the doorway. 'Cosmo,' he said, 'you brave soldier!' The dog unstiffened and turned towards him, looked back at Jove, still *en garde*, and turned again to trot towards Bernard, then followed him to the drinks tray. Bernard poured himself a whisky – Teacher's, Audrey noticed, not the single malt that stood next to it – squirted it with soda and sat down on the sofa opposite Audrey, at the other end from Theo. Cosmo jumped up into the gap between them.

'Cosmo,' said Audrey, '*not* on the furniture.'

★

Neil had quite soon had enough of the demonstration of the capabilities of the KX-W900 and suggested he and Daniel leave Father Paulinus to his sermon.

At the door Daniel said, 'Oh, one thing . . . if you don't need me as relief organist, would you mind if I joined you in the choir to sing? I'd forgotten how much I miss it.'

'Mind? I would be delighted. And we would be honoured. In fact, why don't you deputise as pre-centor?'

'You have a succentor – shouldn't he do that?'

'Dominic? He won't mind. And it means I can play the organ. I hardly ever get to play since I've been precentor.'

'It's been a long time since I cantored here.'

'You have done it a thousand times. And your voice is beautiful. You know you sing like a monk? But, of course, you learnt how to here. Why don't you lead Compline later? It's not difficult, it's the same every night. You have your cassock? I could find you a scapular.'

'I'm not a novice any more,' said Daniel.

'But you were, Father, you were!'

'Thank you, I'd like that.'

'Do you need me to go through it with you?' Paulinus offered.

'I don't think so.'

'Everything you need is in my stall – it's just Compline

with an antiphon for the Nunc dimittis because of Willibrord. It's at the back of the book. But you know your way around that. I'll leave a scapular for you in the sacristy. Now I must get back to St Elizabeth, if you will allow me?'

'Thank you, Father. See you at Compline.'

Paulinus saw them out, then drew the curtains before he returned to his desk – a declaration, thought Daniel, of closure. Aelred's curtains too were drawn and Daniel held his finger to his lips as they passed. They stopped at the south-west corner to the cloister where there was a bench. 'Let's sit,' said Daniel. 'I want to be sure Aelred won't see us.'

'It's very like a prison, isn't it?' said Neil.

'In what way?'

'Having to find a corner where you won't be seen. Big Brother is watching you.'

'Like a panopticon.'

'What's that?'

'The old lock-up prisons, with a central section where the guards sit and wings radiating off it. So the prisoners could be observed all the time. It was invented by Jeremy Bentham in the eighteenth century and was supposed to be for their own good. No let-up in the reformation of their character.'

'No let-up in the reformation of their souls here?'

'Something like that. Only it presupposes the good intentions of those doing the reforming. And the benign character of the institution.'

Neil thought about that for a moment. Then he said, 'Explain the hat problem, Dan.'

'You witnessed a liturgical crime in Vespers.'

'A what?'

'There are rules about what we wear, when we wear it, what we do while we wear it. You know why?'

'Tell me,' said Neil.

'How do we know a bishop is a bishop?'

'He has a shepherd's crook and the pointed hat – the mitre. There's a pub called that in Stow.'

'Yes. The crook – the crosier, we call it – to show that he is a shepherd of the sheep; the mitre is more complicated – it's meant to represent the Holy Spirit as a flame over his head, like the apostles at Pentecost.'

'Is Aelred a bishop then?' asked Neil.

'No, but he's like one. Some abbots are given mitres and crosiers too, and rank as bishops. They can't do all the things that bishops do, though – confirm or ordain, or not nowadays. You know how you can tell if someone is a bishop or an abbot in a stained-glass window?'

'Beard?'

'No,' said Daniel, 'the bishop's crosier points away from him, the abbot's towards him. One is shepherding out in the world, the other in the fold.'

'So why were those lads arguing about the mitre?'

'The mitre is worn in church only for certain things. Processing, blessing, confirming. It is not worn for censing the altar.'

'I think the abbot did wear it when he did the altar,' said Neil.

'He shouldn't have. But it would have been presented to him by one of the novices, the mitre-bearer. Was he wearing sort of oven gloves?'

'Yes, long and orange and silk, I think. And the other lad with the crook had them on too,' said Neil.

'Vimpas.'

'What are vimpas?'

'They protect the bishop's sacred regalia from the soiling fingers of lesser mortals, I suppose.'

Neil was silent for a moment. Then he said, 'I've seen that in Egypt.'

'The Copts?'

'No, an old tomb. I was there on holiday and saw a carving of the pharaoh with his attendants, and they were carrying his things and wearing those sort of oven gloves. I think it was more than a thousand years before Christ.'

'Perhaps some distant relation of what we do here,' said Daniel.

'The ritual handling of a demigod's kit? Sometimes I don't understand what you're about at all.'

'Ceremonies tend to get more complicated and more defined over time. And these ceremonies are very old. If you went to Holy Communion in Jerusalem in the fourth century it would still look recognisable, I think.'

'But why was that lad holding the crook so angry about the mitre?'

'He knew what he was doing. The other didn't. He stood and offered the mitre to the abbot at the wrong time, but once he'd done it there was no undoing it, and Aelred wouldn't really mind anyway, so he put it on and he censed the altar in his mitre. To the traditionalists that's an arrestable offence. Especially the younger ones, who are keen and know better and would no more make a mistake putting a mitre on an abbot than turning right instead of left at a roundabout.'

'There was another row at the end,' said Neil.

'Same reason?'

'The lad – actually, he wasn't a lad, he was older; my age, maybe your age – offered the abbot the mitre, but I think it was the wrong way round, because when the abbot put it on his head the two little tails that hang down at the back were at the front and fell down over his face. It was quite funny. That's when the other one lost his temper.'

'Oh dear.'

'I have to say,' said Neil, 'looking at this from the outside, it doesn't seem very important.'

'When you were at police college did you learn drill?'

'Yes, we did.'

'Did you take it seriously?'

'Yes, we did. But it wasn't Trooping the Colour. We're plods, not the Grenadier Guards.'

'This is the Grenadier Guards,' said Daniel. 'Or some of them like to think they are. Getting it right, getting it perfect, is of supreme importance. How would you feel if you were a Grenadier Guard and a copper turned up at Trooping the Colour and dropped his truncheon during the royal salute?'

Neil was a bit stung. 'Why does any of this matter? I can't imagine Jesus flipping out if a disciple passed the port the wrong way round at the Last Supper.'

'No, but what did Jesus say when the disciples criticised him for letting a woman pour expensive ointment on his hair?'

'"Leave her alone," as I recall.'

'"*Kalon ergon ergasato en emoi . . .*"'

'I don't do Latin, Dan.'

'It's Greek: "She hath wrought a good work on me."'

Without thinking, Neil said, 'And you wonder why you've never had anyone close in your life.'

Daniel flinched.

'Dan, I'm sorry,' said Neil. 'I didn't mean it seriously.'

'No, you meant it flippantly.'

'Dan, please . . .' Neil reached out to him, but Daniel flinched again.

'Please don't,' he said.

'What can I do?' said Neil.

'Nothing. It would be better if you left.'

'I don't want to leave.'

'This is torture.'

'Dan, I don't know what to say. I don't understand.'

'How would you feel if Honoria was the first person you had ever been in love with – the first person you had ever wanted to be . . . close to in your life – but she rejected you?'

'It's not the same thing,' said Neil.

'How would you feel?' Daniel pressed.

'Pretty bad, I guess.'

'What would you do?'

'Pick myself up, dust myself down, start right over again.'

'You see my point.'

'But we're not the same, Dan. It's not the birds and the bees, it's friends.'

'For you. Not for me. What you feel for Honoria, I feel for you.'

It was Neil's turn to flinch a bit. Then he thought about it. Then he said, 'Do you?'

'I'm in love with you,' said Daniel.

'Yes, I understand that bit. But I don't know that it's the same,' said Neil.

'What's different?'

'It's not just passion, Dan. It has consequences.'

'That's different?'

'Marriage, kids, home, grandchildren . . . You see?'

'I wouldn't plan your wedding to Honoria just yet, Neil.'

Neil looked at him, then said, 'It's not like you to say something like that.'

'You're having an affair, a clandestine affair.'

'Yes, but if it goes somewhere, that's where it goes.

It's the way of the world. It's nature. It's . . . the meaning of life.'

'But not for people like me,' said Daniel.

'Maybe not. Maybe this is the meaning of life for you. Priesthood. Here.'

'I've never felt less secure than now.'

'You've never felt this sort of attraction before,' said Neil. 'You've never felt desire. I understand desire. I've even felt desire . . . we were teenage boys, Dan, we had wanking competitions. And once . . . Well, you could say I lost my virginity twice, in a very mild sort of way. But then we met girls and . . . what is it? When I became a man I put away childish things.'

'Childish things?' said Daniel.

'I just got interested in girls, Dan, and that other stuff just faded away. Like gobstoppers and Meccano.'

'You think I'm trapped in childhood?'

'No, of course not. I don't know. I do know I wish I wasn't having this conversation.'

'Sorry to be so disobliging,' said Daniel.

'Can't we just put this behind us?'

'All I can think about now, Neil, is how you lost your virginity in a mild way.'

Then Neil said, 'You know, if you stand back from this, it's a comedy, isn't it? Not a tragedy.'

Daniel said nothing. If Neil had been looking at him, he would have seen the flush rising in his cheeks.

'It's a comedy as old as time,' Neil went on. 'Man barks up wrong tree. You can see that, can't you?'

'Can you see how wounding that is?'

'Come on, Dan.'

'Come on? I feel utterly broken. Foolish and ashamed.' He crumpled.

Neil started to say something but checked himself. Then he said, 'I don't want to make you unhappy. But I can't leave.'

'Look at me, Neil. It would be better if you did.'

'But we have to catch a murderer.'

'That's not the difficult thing.'

Miss March sat at the little table in the kitchen of her flat over the shop. She had been looking for somewhere suitable to live since she took over the lease, somewhere with character, somewhere near enough to Champton for a little of its lustre to shine on her. But there was nothing quite suitable and she found she quite liked living over the shop, as she had in Stow, where March & March shod the better-heeled ladies and gentlemen and clergy of their cathedral city.

But she could not stay there after the death of her father in the ruckus in the street, so she had switched shoes for frocks, Stow for Champton, and was eating her supper, a Sainsbury's Simply Heat & Serve Traditional Beef Hotpot. The *Braunstonbury Evening Telegraph* was propped up on the cookery-book stand she used only for reading the paper, and never for cookery books, for she had not so much as boiled an egg since her father died. Even so, she raised an eyebrow over

Sainsbury's describing its beef hotpot as traditional. Lamb was traditional for hotpot, for her mother had made it, frugally, with potatoes and onions and water – a sort of cheerless soup she and her father had tried to enliven by shaking Lea & Perrins into it after she'd splashed it onto their plates.

Her parents had got divorced, shockingly, in the Sixties, causing her both embarrassment and relief. Embarrassment that her mother had met a physiotherapist at her origami class, found a satisfaction she had not found with her husband, left the family home and moved with him to Northumberland, where they now ran an owl sanctuary. Relief, too, that she had her father to herself, a man whose modest manner matched her own, along with a horror of emotional display and an aptitude for providing saleable items for the better class of customer.

Miss March finished her plate of hotpot and decided to let it go down while she flicked through the paper before pudding – a Prize hazelnut yoghurt that was a day past its sell-by date. *Dad's Army* with an accompaniment of Mintoes would be her after-dinner entertainment.

She sat on the new sofa she had bought from Habitat, grey like her, but boxy and modern. It looked like a prototype rather than a finished item of furniture, but it fitted the small space and achieved what she considered the proper balance between comfort and discomfort. There was one comfort she enjoyed without mitigation: the fluffy pink slippers she had put on after leaving her loafers at the door, as incongruous on the impeccable Miss March as rugby boots on Princess Michael of Kent.

She turned the pages of the paper. The Towns-women's Guild had enjoyed a display of hand-painted porcelain, a six-year-old's vanished kitten had not been found but had been replaced by a mistreated equivalent courtesy of the Snorscombe Cat Sanctuary, and a Mr Hughes of Westmead Road urged readers to be on the lookout for the second coming of Christ.

She turned another page and was suddenly alert. It was the rogues' gallery of those convicted in the magistrates' court. One who had assaulted his girlfriend, not for the first time, stared out of the page at her, and stirred the memory that had last been stirred when she encountered the loutish youth in the car park outside Braunstonbury library. His name was printed beneath his picture: Brandon Redding.

Brandon Redding. Local tearaway. Drug dealer. Nasty piece of work. The rector had a run-in with him on Bonfire Night; Audrey had told her about it 'in the strictest confidence' as they sat in the back of the ambulance on the rectory lawn, not because of suffering the effects of smoke, but of climbing out of a sash window that had not opened generously enough to allow a dignified escape. Audrey had wondered if it had been him whom Miss March had seen loitering in a dark hoody before the fire was started, but it wasn't. Miss March was a bit disappointed. She rather liked louts; they confirmed her narrow view of the world, and if she had an ambition, it would be to sit on the bench as a magistrate and deal with them as they should be dealt with. Only that never happened, for it was mere scoldings nowadays, and fines paid at a pound per week from Income Support, rather than the brisk corrective of the rod.

It was a lout who had done for her father, who had woken them up by shouting in the street with his loutish gang, then relieved himself in the shop door-way, and when her father had confronted him the lout had treated him so roughly he had suffered a heart attack and died. She had watched it happen from the window.

Brandon Redding. Miss March, like any retailer worth her salt, knew that memory did not always arrive in one coherent scene, like a snapshot. More often it was not so obvious. A phrase, a gesture, a match of colours, a way of walking. Something connected with something in the unconscious, or barely conscious, and suddenly you would know. Not to a standard of proof that would pass the test of a courtroom, but you would know.

Brandon Redding.

'Not the difficult thing?' said Neil. 'Do you know who did it?'

'Not sure yet,' said Daniel, 'but I have an idea.'

'So tell me.'

'I need to make sure. And I have a job for you, please: to renew your acquaintanceship with Sergeant Bainbridge.'

'Why?'

'He might know something about someone.'

'In the community?'

'Or connected with the community,' said Daniel. 'Do you think he would talk to you if there were someone at Ravenspurn with a past?'

'What sort of a past?'

'A past that might have resulted in a criminal investigation?'

'He might.'

'Could you find out if there had been a criminal investigation?'

'Depends,' said Neil.

'If I were to give you an outline of the matter, and a location and a date, would that help?'

'Yes, probably. But do you want people here to know I'm police? Might that not sound the alarm?'

'It doesn't matter now, or it won't very soon,' said Daniel. 'I, meanwhile, have to make my own enquiries. And I need to see Aelred.'

'OK, I'll call in on Dennis Bainbridge. What name, what date, what offence?'

'I've written it down,' said Daniel, and he reached into the pocket of his cassock and passed Neil a folded piece of paper.

Neil looked at it and nodded. 'I see.'

'In part. Don't jump to conclusions. Any questions?'

'Yes,' said Neil. 'Are you all right now?'

'No. But we can make something right.'

'Leave it with me.' And Neil went one way, Daniel the other.

Above them, on the upper floor to the cloister, a window, which had been quietly opened an inch or two when they had sat on the bench to talk, opened wider. A head, white and wispy, like a dandelion clock, peered out.

There was a light on in Aelred's room; Daniel could see it in the gap under the door. He tapped on it.

'Come in,' said Aelred in a flat tone.

He was sitting at his desk looking at a file. He quickly closed it when he saw Daniel. 'Oh, hello. Are you alone?' He peered to look behind him to see if Neil was there.

'Yes, Neil's gone for a pint at the Junction. After High Mass and Solemn Vespers, he's had enough religion for one day.'

'He's Moravian Brethren, I hear.'

'Brought up Brethren. But who told you that?'

'Paulinus. He loves that sort of thing. He's quite a mix too. Old Catholic, but an offshoot or something – I can't really remember.'

'He was just telling me about it,' said Daniel.

'He brings a Germanic thoroughness to everything he does.'

317

'Flashes of spontaneity, though.'

'Do you think so?' said Aelred.

'He just asked me to deputise as precentor.'

'Strictly speaking, he should ask me first. And the succentor should replace him.'

'I will, of course, do whatever you ask,' said Daniel.

'You'd be the only one who does.' Aelred sighed. 'I have authority *ex officio* but none *ex persona*, if I can put it like that.'

'The servant-king role is difficult, isn't it?'

'I don't mean that,' said Aelred. 'I mean my personality. When I was a boy my people had a house in Norfolk. Wells-next-the-Sea, do you know it? They were horsey people and so I had riding lessons. On the beach there. I remember I was put on a little black pony called Polly. We went out into the sands and everyone trotted away in a group except Polly. She just ambled along at her own pace. I suppose I should have spurred her on, but it seemed so unkind to do that and I didn't want to hurt her, so I tried to urge her into a trot by saying . . . encouraging words. To no avail. She just went her own way in her own time. I still remember the contemptuous look the groom gave me. I don't have the kind of personality that conveys authority.'

'Spiritual authority?'

'*That* never got someone to do what they didn't actually want to do.'

'But they elected you abbot.'

'Because they knew they could run rings around me.

And, of course, you'll do a marvellous job as precentor. Dominic will have to lump it. And it will make Paulinus happy.'

'So he can play the organ?'

'Yes.' Aelred pulled a face. 'That means a *feast* of Max Reger.'

'No voluntary at Compline,' said Daniel.

'Oh, you're starting tonight?'

'Yes. With your permission.'

'Of course. Is that why you wanted to see me?'

'No,' said Daniel. 'I wanted to ask if you think it might be a good idea to hold a Chapter of Faults.'

'Why?'

'For the novitiate, I mean.'

Aelred looked thoughtful. 'I had wondered about that. But why do you ask?'

'I think there are anxieties that need to be aired – or earthed.'

'There always are.'

'But Bede has died, and you know better than me how these things blow up. Like depth charges. Better a . . . controlled explosion, surely?'

'Of what?'

'All the usual things.'

Aelred gave him a look. 'And the unusual things?'

'Like what?'

'Murder,' said Aelred. 'I do wish, by the way, you wouldn't keep bringing it up.'

'It's not an everyday thing.'

'Oh, but it is. I don't mean murders themselves, though they are surprisingly frequent – and very often undetected, wouldn't you say?'

Daniel nodded.

'I mean the effects. You know this from the parish. You know this from your prison ministry. And you know this from here. We have always given refuge to those who have been away – put away – and then one day, after years of being behind bars, they are discharged and sent back into society, but society most definitely doesn't want them. So they come here. And, of course, you know this from your friend. The policeman.'

'Oh. Did Sergeant Bainbridge tell you?'

'No, I worked it out. And then asked Dennis. Why didn't you say who he is?'

'I did,' said Daniel.

'You most certainly did not.'

'I did. He's not here on official business. He's here on personal business.'

There was a pause. Then Aelred said, 'I see. *That's* who he is.'

'And he's leaving tonight,' said Daniel.

Aelred gave a little sigh of relief. 'It's rather unnerving, you see, to have the police here, especially when they're . . . not exactly undercover, but—'

'Well, he's going.'

Aelred nodded. 'About another Chapter of Faults . . .'

'Yes?'

'It's good to dampen the fires of rage, but hasn't it occurred to you that it might stoke them?'

'I know monastic life, and I think you have a problem that needs to be faced. There is a method for doing this. Tried and tested. Objective. Call a chapter.'

'Thank you for your most helpful advice, Daniel, and the inestimable benefit of your long experience as an abbot.'

'I remember from the Rule, Father – I paraphrase – that if any commit faults, they must come before the abbot and community, admit the fault and make satisfaction. Isn't that right?'

'I know the Rule – and I don't paraphrase – "If someone commits a fault while *at any work* . . . the monk must at once come before the abbot and community and of their own accord admit the fault and make satisfaction." It goes on, "When the cause of the sin lies hidden in their conscience, the monk is to reveal it only to the abbot or to one of the spiritual elders."'

'Hens.'

'What about them?'

'They are the work of the community, are they not?'

'Indeed they are.'

'And you held a Chapter of Faults when the fox got into the hen coop, never got to the bottom of that, and then there was the row over whether it was orthodox or not to have little hen funerals for them, about where they should be buried?'

'There was.'

'Paulinus seemed to think the Chapter was effective at neutralising the enmities that caused.'

'Perhaps it was. Paulinus rather likes neutralising enmities, he's a rigorist in these things. The trouble is, in neutralising some, he can cause new ones.'

'And what about squabbles in church between acolytes over vimpas and crosiers and mitres? Isn't liturgy the work of the community? Aren't those faults at work?'

'Oh, *that*. Yes, I suppose so.'

'I think it would be good for the novitiate, if they were to air any grievances, to admit any faults and receive pardon.'

Aelred thought about that. His eyes narrowed. Then he said, 'I will speak to Father Paulinus about it. Only I don't want to make anything worse rather than better.'

Dinner at Champton was served in the Rudnam Room. Bernard sat at one end of the table, shortened to its most intimate proportions for the three who dined on it tonight; Audrey on his right, Honoria on his left. Cosmo was curled up at his feet, Audrey observed when she pretended to drop her napkin to see, and it made her think for a moment of those monumental sculptures of dead knights on tombs resting their armoured feet on a favourite whippet.

Mrs Shorely was off, so Honoria had made another pheasant casserole, a dish frequently on the menu in the autumnal months of avian carnage – a carnage so catastrophic that the households on the estate that qualified for a dole of game started to lose their taste for those savoury flavours before the last conkers fell. Honoria had enriched Mrs Shorely's rather plain version of the dish with bacon and Calvados and cream and apples from the orchard. It was delicious and Bernard, already in an unusual mood of content-ment, produced from the cellar two bottles of Grand Cru Alsace Riesling and grew so much more con-tented after drinking a whole bottle himself and eating half an Arctic roll that he announced he was going to bed.

'Honoria, see to coffee and brandy in the library, will you?'

He got up to leave and nodded to his guests in the cursory way of someone in whom hospitality had become formalised and made for the door. There was a scrabbling of claws on parquet and Cosmo started to follow him.

'No, Cosmo, stay. STAY,' said Audrey in a tone of firm expectation.

The little dog paused and looked first at Audrey, then back at Bernard, who was closing the door behind him, and gave a little whimper. Then he ran to the closed door and shoved his snout into the gap at the bottom and took a great sniff, and then another, his whole body suddenly a device for processing the re-treating scent of that which he most desired. He gave another little whimper and scratched at the door, which alarmed Audrey, for it was Georgian and made from a glossy toffee-coloured mahogany.

'Stupid beast,' she muttered, as she did when the dogs did something vacantly vandalistic, like pee on a rug or grub up her hydrangeas. She picked Cosmo up and tucked him under her arm, which made him suddenly submissive. 'Shall we go through to the library?' she said. Honoria thought how very much at home Audrey had made herself in so short a time.

'We think they're like us, don't we?' said Audrey as they crossed the chequerboard flags of the saloon, 'like children, or faithful retainers, and then they do something bestial and you realise they're no more civilised than the fox killing your chickens.'

They shut the library door to keep Cosmo in and settled in front of the fire, which was burning low but warmly. Cosmo lay on the rug but with his head up, looking at the door through which he hoped Bernard would reappear. Honoria poured Audrey a *déca*, which Mrs Shorely grudgingly had to provide from her weekly shop at Braunstonbury Sainsbury's. It was called Café HAG, which Mrs Shorely thought well named, for Audrey's chatelaine tendencies were beginning to try her patience.

'Would you like a brandy or a whisky or something, Audrey?'

'Are you having one?'

'I'll have a whisky.'

'Then I'll have a brandy. Not a large one.'

'You won't want a large one,' said Honoria. 'It's nothing special. Unlike the wine we had with the pheasant.' She poured a treacly measure from a lovely late-eighteenth-century decanter that wore round its neck a silver gorget engraved with the word 'BRANDY'. In anticipation of guests, Mrs Shorely had filled it from a bottle of Three Barrels VSOP, which she had also bought from Braunstonbury Sainsbury's rather than Bernard's wine merchant in St James's.

'What was it?' Audrey asked.

'An Alsace Riesling. Apparently you can tell the really good ones because they smell faintly of petrol.'

'So many lovely things hover, don't they, on the edge of palatability? Like game.' She quickly added, 'Not your pheasant, Honoria, that was delicious. But people like it high, don't they?'

'Like blue cheese and truffles. The hint of something pungent and earthy.'

Honoria handed Audrey her brandy in a proper brandy glass, heavy crystal, engraved with the de Floures circlet of flowers. Such lovely things.

'Apropos things pungent and earthy, your father did a very good job of cleaning up Cosmo,' said Audrey. At the sound of his name the dog looked at her for a second, then turned back to the door.

'He smelled lovely,' agreed Honoria. 'Floris No. 89, I think – Daddy's favourite. Extraordinary devotion, I've never seen anything like it.'

'It seems out of character.'

'I've never seen him so beguiled by a dog. Perhaps he's getting soft in old age.'

'Dachshunds are fiercely devoted. Tirelessly devoted,' said Audrey.

'To their owners? Cosmo seems to have betrayed his first love and found another.'

'It's the puppies. Nathan told me. When a bitch whelps, dogs tend to wander. And with Daniel absent . . .'

'Any idea when he might return?'

'He's on retreat. I'm not sure how long they last. There's a thirty-day retreat he always wanted to do, but I think you have to go to Wales to do that and he's in Yorkshire.'

'Yorkshire?'

'Yes. But you know that, dear.'

Honoria nodded and took a sip of whisky. 'Theo?'

'Yes, but I'd guessed.'

'He told you why?'

'Yes,' said Audrey. 'That I *hadn't* guessed. Did you know?'

'No, until I worked it out. Daniel's not the sort of person you can easily imagine having a passion.'

'You've never seen him in a Ryman. Like Tiny Tim at the poulterer's. But a *folie d'amour* is something new.'

'Nothing in his youth?'

'Not that I knew about. But as Daniel so often observes, unpredictable passions can surge anywhere.

And he's not the first person to have an unpredictable passion. Even in sleepy, settled Champton.'

'You mean me?'

Audrey turned the brandy in her glass so it caught the firelight. 'I was thinking of your brother and Nathan. But you have had rather a glow lately.'

'I've been having a fling with Neil.'

'So I gather. What is it about that policeman that sets all hearts aflame?'

Honoria thought about that for a moment. 'He's not like the usual type of man I get to meet. He's clever, he's different, he has . . . how to put this? Considerable gifts.'

'I see. Pungent and earthy.'

'Yes. But . . .'

Audrey looked up.

'But?'

Honoria swirled her whisky in its glass, unconsciously imitating Audrey. 'It's a fling. Could it be more than that? No. Not just because I don't really see myself keeping his sausages and mash warm until he comes home from the station, although naturally I don't. It's more . . . well, Cosmo.'

The dog stirred again at the sound of his name and looked up at her.

'Such doggy devotion. So touching, so innocent, so uncomplicated. Like Greyfriars Bobby, sitting on his master's grave waiting for him to come home. A pretty story, isn't it, but would you really want someone waiting around for you eternally with his tongue hanging out, panting?'

'What do you want?'

'A bit more of a battle. Do you see?'

'I've always preferred total compliance. That's why I married Daniel's father. But it's not for everyone. It's not for you, and now he's in love with you and Daniel's in love with him.'

'Yes.'

'And you're not in love with him and he's not in love with Daniel.'

'No.'

'One of those situations when you wish someone would come along with a love philtre and it would all work out, like in Shakespeare,' Audrey said.

'It would take quite a philtre,' said Honoria.

'What are you going to do?'

'Break another heart, I suppose.'

Ten minutes before the bell for Compline tolled, Daniel made his way to church. It was dark, lit only by pools of light over the entrances and the side aisles, so he switched on the desk light in Paulinus's stall to find the Compline book and turn up and mark the antiphons for a saint's day. It felt like he was invading his privacy slightly, for a stall is the equivalent for a monk of a work desk, and like most work desks an element of personalisation occurs, even if it's rather frowned upon.

In a way, we are quite like the German Democratic Republic, Daniel thought, where the desire for one's own things was at that moment contrasting so sharply with collectivist virtue that the world order seemed to be trembling; and he thought again of his friend Paisie in Romania. In his last letter he had said resentment of Communism there was rising; there had been a strike in a tractor factory, and a diatribe critical of Ceauşescu, the beloved and unbudgeable leader, was circulating.

The human aspiration to have one's own things is strong, he thought, even if it's a condition of our fallen state. For some of the brethren it was customised bookmarks, postcard-sized reproductions of beloved works of art, a tiny secondary relic *ex cilitio* of a doubtful saint in a locket, or silk ribbons in different colours to mark the places in complicated volumes full of variations for seasons and feasts, terminating in a bead, or a blob of clear nail varnish, or stitched to prevent fraying. Small works of devotion, 'The Dark Night of the Soul', a book of Latin psalms, a Greek New Testament, Vaughan's *Pious Ejaculations*, which always made the novices laugh when it was set as a text, were also stowed away in stalls on both sides of the aisle.

As Daniel took out the Compline book from the shelf in Paulinus's stall something fell onto the floor. He could not see what it was at first but bent to pick it up and hold it under the desk light. It was a rosary, rather like a *metanoi*, only longer and more complicated, with beads of pearl strung in sets on a silver chain, terminating in a cross.

It was not a normal cross, plain or crucifix, but a design he thought he had seen before, though he could not remember when or where. It was small, made of plain metal, had arms of equal length, but each terminated in an arrowhead. At the centre was a cipher that looked like a capital I – for *ichthys*, the fish, ancient symbol of the faith? He was sure he had seen it before. Old Catholic? Something from Paulinus's past? It was old and worn, so maybe it had accompanied him on his pilgrim's progress from central Europe to Ravenspurn? Daniel was suddenly afflicted with a sense of trespass again; handling another monk's rosary seemed to overstep the mark, like someone using your favourite pen, so he replaced it on the shelf carefully, coiling it in a circle with the cross on top as a gesture of respect.

The Compline book, which also contained the order for the midday offices, was marked up and it took a moment for Daniel to work out what was what. The black ribbon, appropriately for a night office, marked the Order for Compline, and the red, he discovered, marked where the different texts for the saint's day feast were printed, words first, then the plainsong, notated in little black dots on four lines. On special days the little black dots formed complicated clusters, for the chant would be more ornate than usual, more melismatic – a word Daniel liked, for it was derived from the Greek word for song, *melos*, but also carried the connotation of the Latin word for honey, *mel*, as the chant poured slowly and sweetly.

Daniel looked around but could see no one in church, so he practised the special antiphon, a plainsong preface, for the Nunc dimittis, the Song of Simeon, sung at every Compline.

'Lord, now lettest thou thy servant depart in peace,' it begins in the lovely Book of Common Prayer version, and used to be known only to those who attended Evensong. It was now known to lots more because a setting of it for boy treble and plangent trumpet had been used as the theme tune for John le Carré's *Tinker Tailor Soldier Spy*, so was more widely heard at nine o'clock on a Monday evening coming out of the television as a prelude to Alec Guinness as George Smiley, wiping his thick glasses to see what he needed to see before he could hang up his hat.

The antiphon was full of leaps and clusters, and to practise it Daniel had to vocalise it fully, rather than in half-voice. By the second bar he was transported back to his days in his stall, singing chants, which he loved almost more than anything, not only for the art, but as a foretaste of what he imagined heaven would be, individual voices joined in perfect praise. He finished the last note and the sound of his voice rang in the empty church, decaying slowly in its space to nothing. Or it would have been nothing had not a voice said, 'Bravo!' from the darkness, which made Daniel cough with embarrassment, for it was not intended as a performance, nor for applause.

A figure emerged out of the dark. It was the novice Brother Augustine, the one who looked like Friar Tuck. He was so big he moved like darkness itself. 'That was lovely, Father, you sounded to the manner born.'

'I was a Cantor when I was in the novitiate.'

'I am meant to be one now.' He pulled a rueful face.

'No strong singers?'

'A small pool. Bede could sing. Anselm has a nice voice. Sebastian tries. But Placid and Darren . . .'

'I suppose you get what you get. We had some fine voices when I was here.'

'Oh, they can sing. Or they could if they didn't hate each other. You know how it is, singing plainsong reveals the man, exposes the secrets of the heart, and all that.'

Yes, it does, thought Daniel.

'It will change, I suppose, with Bede's death. Get worse probably.'

'Why?'

'They both hated Bede. Now he's gone, there's nothing to dilute their loathing for each other.'

'Unusual for a brother to alienate two such different personalities.'

'Bede could annoy anyone. So top-of-the-class, so lacking in self-awareness.'

That sounded like something he had read somewhere,

thought Daniel. 'Not the sort of thing that is usually unmanageable. It takes more than that.'

'Oh, yes. Well, Anselm hated him because he left the door open to the hen coop and all his pretties were killed by the fox, and then he argued against having a hen funeral. It was bitter. And Darren hated him – well, Darren hates everyone – for not being solid enough on priestesses. I think the vote on that subject is too much for him. I think he'll cross the Tiber. What about you?'

'I'd quite forgotten about it,' said Daniel. 'What happened at Synod?'

'It voted in favour. The way ahead is clear. First priestesses should be up and running in a couple of years. So, will you?'

'What?' said Daniel.

'Cross the Tiber?'

'Become a Roman Catholic? No.'

'Me neither. I'll stay if I can. Why should I leave the Church I love because it has . . . what do they call it? A moment of madness? But they'll have to work out something solid for us. Some sort of provision. Protect us from the apostasy of our turncoat bishops. But imagine a Church of England communion lady trying to ordain someone?'

'It will come,' said Daniel. 'Change always does. Look at East Germany. Look at the Soviet Union. The old order changeth yielding place to the new . . .'

'But this is the Church, Father.'

'Which changes like everything else.'

'Not on something as fundamental as this.'

'Actually, it does. Lending money at interest was condemned by Scripture and the teaching of the Church for centuries, unequivocally. The sin of usury. Change was unthinkable. And then trade and capital and banks remade the world, and it became expedient and necessary and the Church profited from it even while the popes continued to condemn it. The Reformation could not have happened without it, for the rise of the merchant class followed, a fact conveniently forgotten when people condemn things for not being biblical.'

'That may be so, I couldn't say, but unlike priestesses, it is not a first-order issue, Father.'

'That's my point. It was, once. And then things changed.'

Augustine looked affronted. 'So, you're *in favour*?'

'It's not like that for me. It's like joining the EEC. I don't have passionate feelings about commercial and political convergence in Europe; if it happens, it happens. What difference does it make? God is still God. Jesus is still our Saviour.'

'But how will he save us if the Sacraments of the Church are made worthless?'

'By the agency of women priests?'

'Precisely.'

'I used to get worked up about these things, but now whenever I stand at the altar and hold in my hands the broken body of Christ, entrusted to me for the salvation of souls . . . if God wills it that I can, anyone can.'

'I am disappointed in you, Father.'

'I'm not here to appoint you, Augustine.'

Augustine trembled. Then he said, 'I am the hebdomadary this week, Father, and I have to ring the Compline bell. Some traditions we still uphold,' and he turned in a rather Bette Davis sort of way, which did not really work, for it required a sort of brittleness he could achieve in temperament but not in stature.

Daniel stepped back slightly as he left, feeling the force of his anger, but it receded and as Augustine started to ring the bell it faded to the point where he no longer felt even the hint of the anxiety confrontation normally provoked in him. Daniel was no longer a member of this community, and its passions, both obvious and obscure, were not his. He had his own passions to deal with. He was heartbroken, devastated, beside himself – he liked that expression for its explicit out-of-body-ness – in a predicament that was causing him self-doubt he had never experienced before.

No longer a member. So why, when he settled into the precentor's stall, did he feel immediately at home? He had felt the same way in the novitiate when he served as precentor there, as if he had discovered who he was. But this was not an arrival, it was a return. 'Always we begin again.' I should be here, he thought. I should always have been here. I've never really left.

Augustine went and lit the candles on the altar, and

then extinguished all the lights in the church one by one until only one shone faintly over the entrance from the cloister. Daniel heard the sigh as the organ bellows inflated on the balcony at the west end.

Then came another sighing sound as the double doors from the cloister opened and then the swish-swish of the brethren arriving, hooded according to custom, with the abbot at the rear. When all were in their places Aelred rapped on his stall and the service began in darkness, for all knew it by heart, save Daniel, who kept the desk light on in his stall so he could read the antiphon for the Nunc dimittis.

When it came Daniel opened his mouth to sing and something unexpectedly beautiful happened. The words and the plainsong and his voice and spirit joined and rose into the darkness of the church, alone at first – 'let your light so shine, O Lord, upon us' – and then the brethren joined their voices with his, a bit ragged at first, and in-dividual, with startling variations in tone, accuracy and beauty, but Daniel's line was so strong and true that he hauled the others with it so that by the time they reached the little cluster of notes around 'that the darkness of our hearts being wholly done away', they were singing as one. As one? There was no loss of individuality – he was who he was, Aelred was Aelred, Augustine was Au-gustine, Sebastian was Sebastian – but they had become gloriously one in singing the praise of God.

You silver swan, Daniel, thought Aelred, which opened its throat to pour forth melody before expiring, because there was nothing lovelier left for it to do.

'In peace we will lie down and sleep,' Aelred said.

'For you alone, Lord, make us dwell in safety,' the community replied.

Daniel was sitting at the desk in his room. He had the little icon of the Anastasis in front of him, Jesus hauling the souls of the lost out of the pit of hell, lit by a tea light.

There was a rap on the door. Daniel opened it and let Neil in.

'How was Sergeant Bainbridge?'

'Forthcoming. Suspicious, but forthcoming,' said Neil.

'And?'

'You were right. There's more than one, actually. But it is as you thought.'

'Who knows?'

'Aelred, I suppose, as Abbot. Maybe our suspect has a confessor among the brethren too? Sergeant Bainbridge, of course. What do you want me to do?'

Daniel indicated to him to sit in the armchair. 'What I said.'

'I don't know what you mean.'

'Leave,' said Daniel.

Neil looked surprised. 'Why?'

'Better that way.'

Neil was silent. Then he said, 'I thought we had got beyond this, Dan.'

'That's because you want to be beyond this. I am not. I want you to go back to Champton and Honoria.'

'But what are you going to do?'

'I have to make some decisions,' said Daniel.

Neil said, 'Hang on. We are trying to establish a murder. And find a murderer. Personal stuff will have to wait.'

'I want you to do something for me on the way home.'

'Now you're being mysterious,' said Neil.

'I need you to visit someone – I'll tell you who and where, and I want you to show him something.'

'What is this about?'

Daniel handed him a piece of paper. On it there was a sketch of a cross with equal arms terminating in four arrowheads. In the centre of the cross was a cipher that looked like a capital I.

'What are you going to do?'

'I shall spend tomorrow morning talking to Mr and Mrs Corbett and suggest they wait a while before deciding the burial arrangements for their son.'

'OK. Any messages for home?' asked Neil.

'Warmest regards. Fondest wishes. Assurance of prayers.'

'Got it.'

Neil made to go, but when his hand was on the doorknob Daniel said, 'More than one?'

'Yes. According to Dennis that white-haired little gnome has form too.'

'Colin,' said Daniel.

'Colin Cummings.'

'Yes,' said Daniel. 'He says he's a scholar on sabbatical.'

'He may be a scholar but he's on licence, not sabbatical,' said Neil.

'So I gathered. What for?'

'Manslaughter. Long-running argument with a neighbour about motorbikes. Kept him awake when he revved them. So Colin set fire to their garage. Whole house went up. Killed the neighbour and his wife and their two-year-old.'

'How long did he serve?' asked Daniel.

'This was in the early Sixties and he hasn't been out that long. Finished up at HMP Ford with more degrees than you. Do you think he's . . . a person of interest?'

'I do,' said Daniel. 'Don't you?'

'Why would he want to murder Bede?'

'He burnt a whole family alive for keeping him awake at night.'

14

Neil arrived at Braunstonbury Police Station after his long drive back from Ravenspurn, a journey made longer by the diversion to Oxford, where he had called in at St Kilda's College, identified himself to the porter and enquired if he could please speak to Dr Keschner on a matter of high importance. Fortunately, Dr Keschner was in his rooms trying on a pair of shoes he had just collected from Ducker's, made to order for a considerable sum.

He sat down on the sofa opposite the detective sergeant, whom he had installed in the armchair in which he usually put students for tutorials, poured two cups of tea, offered his visitor one of the Bahlsen Jubilee biscuits he had brought back from Germany on his last visit, and spread his feet in a rather overdone V to show off the perfect loveliness and soft gleam of his conker-coloured Oxfords.

Neil did not notice the shoes and Dr Keschner soon forgot about them after Neil told him of the death of

Brother Bede. When he had collected himself, Neil showed him the sheet of paper with the peculiar cross drawn on it and then asked him the questions Daniel had asked him to take down in his notebook.

They spoke for twenty minutes. Dr Keschner went to his study and found some papers. 'I shall get them photocopied for you. The secretary will do it for me now if I ask nicely. If you would like to come with me?'

'Thank you,' said Neil.

They made their way down the staircase and across the quad to the college office. Ten minutes later they stood at the gate, Neil holding a manila envelope. 'You've been very helpful, Dr Keschner, thank you. And if anything occurs to you, could you please call me?' He gave him his card.

'Can you tell me what this is about, Detective Sergeant? If I knew more, I may be able to tell you more.'

'Not at liberty at the moment, Sir.'

'I have an idea what it may be about,' said Dr Keschner.

'We'll be in touch, Sir. Thank you for your time.'

Neil drove back to Braunstonbury feeling a peculiar mix of urgency – the hunter closing in on his prey – and calmness too, because the kind of trap Daniel was setting was not the kind he could imagine the murderer escaping. They never escaped, they never tried to, because whenever Daniel was after someone, or something from them, he would use neither carrot nor stick, but rather mobilise the essential qualities of the person concerned to reveal who they really were; and then all was revealed, all 'the secrets of the heart' as Daniel called them, and there was nowhere to go after that.

Neil remembered a conversation he'd had with Daniel about the devil, a lively and terrifying presence in his childhood growing up in a religious community that renounced 'the lies and deceits of Satan', but which he now saw as a sort of folk superstition designed to make evil explicable. He assumed Daniel, whose piety was more pilot light than furnace, would think the same, but he did not. 'Sometimes,' he'd said, 'I have thought I have encountered active evil, an evil of purpose, evil with agency. Not an absence, a presence. I feel it prickle, like the witches in *Macbeth*, when people destroy themselves and others not through wickedness, but through having their goodness turned against them. It is the deadliest of weapons. What turns good into that? It takes *something*.'

Back at the station, Neil waited until three for Daniel to call. The phone rang as three o'clock struck.

'Hello, Daniel,' he said, 'looks like you were right. I talked to Dr Keschner and he gave me some documents that you need to see.'

'Urgently,' said Daniel. 'There's a Chapter of Faults for the novitiate tomorrow after Matins. Can you come back?'

Neil sighed. 'To Ravenspurn? Dan, I've . . . got something to do.'

'Honoria,' said Daniel.

'I am summoned to her presence. But look, I can fax them.'

'How?'

'There must be a fax at Ravenspurn?'

'Which everyone has access to,' said Daniel.

'Same at Ravenspurn Police Station. Any ideas?'

Daniel thought for a moment. 'Yes. Can you hang on till I call back? Say half an hour?'

'Like the fookin' bus, but slower,' said Alma. 'Pardon my French, love.'

Daniel and Alma had just made the quarter-to-four train from Ravenspurn. It was misleadingly called a Sprinter and rattled slowly along the Calder Valley line connecting York to Manchester. Daniel remembered taking its less immodestly named predecessor once from Leeds to Preston, and as it heaved itself over the Pennines a terrible thunderstorm broke. In flashes of lightning, a howling wind and drumming rain, the driver's Yorkshire-accented voice came on the PA to say, 'Ladies and gentlemen . . . welcome to Lancashire.'

They would not be going so far today, just a couple of stops to Hebden Bridge, where Donna, Alma's niece, awaited at the library.

'Mytholmroyd,' said Alma absentmindedly as the train pulled out of the station. 'Sounds like something from Dungeons and Dragons.'

'What's that?' asked Daniel.

'It's a game the lads are all playing, like Monopoly only with wizards and dwarves and mortal combat.'

'Ted Hughes's hometown,' said Daniel. 'Doesn't he write about the cliffs?'

'Scout Rock,' said Alma and nodded towards the window, 'that's it over there. It overhangs the town, like Aberfan.' She made a gloomy face and Daniel thought of his mother, who shared with Alma a relish for disaster, and wondered if that was one of the reasons why he liked her so much.

After he had spoken to Neil, he'd found the piece of card on which Alma had written her telephone number and called it. Was there a fax machine at Hebden Library and would Donna be able to receive an urgent fax for him? Alma said to call her back in a minute. As he replaced the receiver, he saw there was a lady waiting outside the phone box in the intensifying gloom and strengthening rain. She rapped on the glazed door with her ten-pence piece.

'I'm waiting, love,' she said.

Daniel politely stepped aside and held the door open for her. 'Will you be long?' he asked. 'Only I've got to call someone back and it's urgent.'

'It will take as long as it takes,' said the lady and put down her bag with the air of someone settling in. 'If it's that urgent, there's another phone box at the station.' She produced from her bag a cache of ten-pence pieces, which she proceeded to stack as the door closed behind her.

Daniel had rushed to the station down the long lane that led through the town and over the canal. The phone box outside was one of the old ones, lit the colour of pale urine, smelling of the same, and empty. The handset was battered and sticky, but it worked, so he called Alma back.

Yes, she said, there was a fax at Hebden Library, and this was the number. Donna would make sure it all came through, and he would have to fetch his coat and meet her at Ravenspurn train station. 'Already there,' he said.

He had called Neil at Braunstonbury Police Station to give him the fax number, but he had used up all his ten-pence pieces and had to use a fifty, an extravagance that he thought in an absentminded way he should justify by having a conversation about the weather, but Neil, with a note of testiness that Daniel felt more keenly than he should, had said he had to go.

Alma had been quiet for a while. Then she said, 'Tough place.'

'Mytholmroyd?'

'The whole valley. "Valley" sounds like something from England's green and pleasant land, doesn't it?' said Alma. 'But there's a dark, wet wound in the rock round here. Good place for a monastery.'

'Why do you say that?' Daniel asked.

'Dark and wounded. Monks are drawn to all that, aren't they? And so many of you lads had darkness and wounds of your own, right?'

345

'Why do you think that?'

'I don't know. All that time staring at a man with a gaping gash in his side, dead on a cross. Why don't you just . . . live your life? *This* life, the here and now, like our Donna?'

'I don't know, Alma. I suppose because of what lies on the other side of the cross. New life. Life transformed.'

'I'll tell you what lies on the other side of the cross, Crispin. Hebden Bridge.'

'Of course. It's not magic; it's not the back of the wardrobe opening onto Narnia, with elves and kings and queens and Aslan waiting . . .'

'. . . Dungeons and Dragons . . .'

'. . . yes, fantasy, but actually what you find on the other side *is* Hebden Bridge – the town hall, pattern cutters, the picture house, the factory at Acre Mill . . .'

'. . . that closed, love, asbestos . . .'

'. . . it's still Hebden Bridge, but *we're* different, and we can start living that new life there, or anywhere.'

The train slowed, although it was already going so slowly it was difficult at first to tell that it was about to arrive at the station.

'Here we are,' said Alma.

They walked over the footbridge that crossed the river and the canal and then through the little town to the library, a square and solid building produced from the industrial wealth of the last century. The interior was a contrast, not municipal grandeur, but blond wood and strip lighting, like, he imagined, a Norwegian youth court. A woman came down the corridor to meet them holding a thick scroll of paper. She was shorter than Alma, twenty years younger, what his mother would call 'handsome', and was wearing a stripy top like a Frenchman, but with jeans and trainers.

'It was like the Dead Sea Scrolls coming through, I thought the paper would run out!' she said as she approached.

'Donna, this is Crisp— Well, it's Daniel, but I call him Crispin.'

'Hello,' he said. 'I can't thank you enough for this.'

'What am I to call you?'

'Daniel.'

'That's a relief,' said Donna. 'I never know what to say to vicars, even if they're in mufti. And if they're one of Auntie Alma's, it's Father this and Father that.'

'We had a lad come through Ravenspurn,' said Alma, 'called Jonathan Christmas, and now he's Father Christmas.'

'Archdeacon of Bowick now,' said Daniel.

'It's like Shakespeare,' said Donna, 'everybody's a place as well as a person. Have you time for a brew?'

'That's most kind, Miss . . .?' He immediately regretted the faux pas.

'It's Ms, if you're going to be formal about it, but if you're Daniel, I'm Donna.'

'Of course. A quick one? I need to go over these documents . . .'

'Good luck with that,' said Donna. 'It's quite faint in

places, and the photos haven't come out very well at all. Not that I was really looking.'

Donna showed them into the library office where there was a tray with mugs and lidded jars on a small fridge.

'I'll just fill this,' she said, taking a kettle. 'Make yourselves comfortable.'

Daniel and Alma sat in the two chairs facing the librarian's desk, which felt a little formal, as if they were being called in to explain the late return of *The Remains of the Day.*

'What *is* that?' said Alma, nodding at the scroll, which Daniel was holding a little too tightly.

'Just some research I'm doing.'

'Pretty urgent research,' said Alma. 'What's it about?'

'Church history,' said Daniel. 'I need it for tomorrow – something I'm doing with the novitiate.'

Donna returned with the kettle and switched it on.

'You're our first celebrity visit since John Kettley.'

'Celebrity?'

'On the telly every day, doing the weather. He's more famous than Ted Hughes up at Heptonstall and he's the Poet Laureate.'

'I meant me.'

'You've been in all the papers! Because of the murder of that lad. Second murderer you've caught, it says. "The Hymn-singing Detective" according to the *Daily Mail*, not that I read it.'

'That's nonsense, I'm afraid,' said Daniel.

'Perhaps he's on the scent of another one, Donna, perhaps you've played your part in bringing a murderer to justice!'

'A fax that long from the police? The thought did cross my mind.'

'Police? Ooh, Crispin, you fibber!' said Alma.

'Not fibbing, Alma. The documents were from Oxford. A friend of mine faxed them from work.'

'Which happens to be the police station?'

'Yes,' said Daniel.

'Is it your fella?' Alma asked.

'No. I don't have a fella . . .'

'It's all right, Crispin, she's a gay too.'

'He's not my . . . anything.'

There was silence for a moment. Then Donna said, in a neutralising phrase she had learnt from her aunt, 'Are we to have cake?'

Honoria was lying on the sofa in the little sitting room that was part of the Champton Suite at the big house. It was reserved for the use of the heir to the title and estate, and her father had once told her, indelibly, that he had spent his wedding night there deflowering her mother in much the same way as his parents, grand-parents and great-grandparents and so on had done before him. 'What do you mean, "in much the same way"?' she'd asked. 'Dutifully,' he'd replied.

Partly for that reason she had chosen the sofa rather than the bed to lie on, although the creaking ark of dynastic congress would soon be occupied by Neil. She had decided that their last assignation should end on a climax, literally, partly because it seemed an act of generosity on her part, which might soften the blow of rejection that would follow, and partly because she thought it might cheer the place up a bit to have sex for fun rather than obligation. What had to be done had to be done, but it might as well be done in the right spirit.

Neil had called earlier and left a message with Mrs Shorely for Alex. The content of the message was not important; it was a code for her to call his pager with a number where he could call her back. She went to the lodge to take it and he told her he was back in Braunstonbury and would call round to the warrener's cottage later. But the warrener's cottage was suddenly out of bounds, for Bernard, provoked by the imposition of guests, had, in a fit of unusual expenditure, initiated a programme of improvements, lest he was again obliged to accommodate dispossessed clergy and their dependants and to endure talking at breakfast. The repairs to the rectory, to Audrey's unreasonable and exacting specifications, were soon to be underway, and the warrener's cottage was also to be upgraded so that, in the event of future mishaps, long-stay visitors could be suitably and sufficiently accommodated there.

So Honoria had arranged to meet her soon-to-be ex-lover in the house, but with all discretion, for the Champton Suite was separate from the family rooms and could be accessed discreetly by a set of back stairs, a humane improvement added in the reign of one of the Georges – she could not remember which – to allow for such comings and goings as an eligible bachelor or newly-wed might require. The stairs connected with a convenient entrance too, just along the kitchen range but beyond the sight and hearing of Mrs Shorely, who sometimes reminded her of the babushkas who sat at a desk opposite the lifts on every floor of the Rossiya Hotel in Moscow and noted arrivals and departures.

There was a creak on the stairs.

'In here!' she called.

The door opened and there was Neil, looking, she thought, arrayed in sexiness, or rather lambent with sexiness, for he had come straight from work and was actually arrayed in one of the Marks & Spencer suits that comprised half his small wardrobe. The sexiness was the man within, put together well, full of beans, and completely unaware of his own radiant desirability, which made him so desirable that for a moment she wondered if her decision to end their affair was the right one.

'And all because the lady loves Milk Tray,' he said, and produced from behind his back a box of chocolates that he had bought at a petrol station on the way home. 'It's not actually Milk Tray,' he said. 'They didn't have any.'

She knew she had made the right decision.

★

As Daniel walked through the gates at Ravenspurn the bell began to ring for Vespers. He was so absorbed in the documents he had started to read on the train he had forgotten he was temporary precentor and had to run to change into his cassock and scapular. 'A good monk never runs . . .' and he decelerated to a monastic *lento* as he came into the cloister and then into the church, where he took his place in Paulinus's stall just as the brethren were lining up to process in. Paulinus was playing something spare and breathy on the organ, with a peculiar open sound on the edge of acceptability – the kind of sound only organists who know their instrument inside out are able to find.

There was nothing special in the calendar today, so the chants and antiphons were all straightforward and the hymn serviceable. Daniel liked the plainer services best, the business-as-usual services, which came round and came round and came round, and you did not have to think about what you were doing, you just let it happen; the best work of monks, he thought, was done in that happy, unself-conscious state.

He bowed for the blessing at the end and remained standing as the community processed out to another improvisation by Paulinus, this time with a wobbly reed stop, which must have sounded truly celestial when the French organ builders who had made the abbey's instrument first created it, but which to modern ears sounded more like a stylophone.

Daniel was marking up the Office Book for the services to come, remembering as he went along the complex but reliable logic of the slips of paper that told you where to sing, what to sing, when to sing, and then pulled out Paulinus's rosary and looked again at the curious little cross at the end of the chain.

'Cross barby,' said Paulinus, who had silently arrived beside him. Daniel started slightly, for he felt that he had been caught snooping, which in fact he had. 'You know it?'

'I've seen it before,' Daniel said, 'but remind me?'

'The cross barby – or *barbée*, more properly – the fisherman's cross. Those are supposed to be fishhooks, barbs, at the end. For we are fishers of men.'

'And the cipher?'

'What do fishermen catch?'

'Fish,' said Daniel.

'And what is the Greek for fish?'

'*Ichthys*. Is it very old?'

'The symbol is,' said Paulinus. 'The cross not so old. It may seem to you an indulgence, but it is of personal significance to me.'

'I have something like it,' said Daniel, and took the *metanoi* Paisie had given him from his pocket.

'Ah, a *metanoi*,' said Paulinus. 'You have been to Romania?'

'No, it was given to me by a monk from Iaşi who was a student here when I was in the novitiate.'

'It looks well used.'

'It is. Repaired so often I don't think anything of the original survives apart from the cross. A habit I got into here, which I can maintain outside. It's so difficult to do what we do here outside the cloister.'

'Impossible,' said Paulinus.

'Yes. Impossible.'

They were silent for a moment. Then Paulinus said, 'You are haunted – is that too strong a word? – by the version of you that did not leave.'

'Perhaps you can come back and be haunted by the version you became after you left?' said Daniel.

'I don't think so. What is it Aelred says? You choose this by unchoosing everything else. And vice versa. When I was young I entered a community, near where I grew up. It was not a wise choice, just a convenient one, but . . . I decided halfway through the novitiate to leave. I saw the abbot and he released me, and I packed my little suitcase and the novice master showed me to the door. As I left, he said, "You have abandoned heaven and chosen hell, goodbye!" and slammed the door shut.'

'Where was this, Father?'

'The past. And then eventually I found here, and I chose this. And I unchose everything else. And we must stick with our choices, yes? You and I. And everyone. But this is not what I wanted to say. We are having a Chapter of Faults tomorrow in the novitiate, after breakfast. The abbot will preside. We will sing the litany.'

'Do you want me to lead it?'

'No, Father Dominic and I will take care of that. Precentor and succentor in role, business as usual, yes? But I wanted to ask if you would attend and hear confessions afterwards? Best to have someone from outside for this sort of thing.'

'Yes, of course.'

'Crypt chapel. No Mass after Matins for obvious reasons.'

'Obvious?'

'Who will come to receive communion – or, more to the point, who will *not*? – before a public examination of conscience? Those not in a state of grace, or not until you have absolved them.'

15

Audrey was already at breakfast the next morning when Bernard came down, followed by Cosmo, who was now sleeping in his lordship's bedroom, indeed on his bed, though Bernard did not think it necessary to share the details of their arrangements. For Bernard, dogs were more often outside than inside, had a job to do, and if inside they had their own billets near the kitchen. Cosmo had other ideas and followed Bernard everywhere, and if Bernard were to close a door on him, he would sit outside intermittently giving a single identifying bark. At first, to stop it happening, Bernard had opened the door and the little dog had settled at his feet once Jove had left the premises, and gradually, as dog adapted to human, human adapted to dog. There was something about Cosmo that fitted Bernard and something about Bernard that fitted Cosmo – two displaced alpha males, Honoria had suggested – and the thought of Cosmo departing to his bed in the kitchen when Bernard departed to his in the family wing had become unthinkable, though Bernard did not want it to be known, for there was something about having a dog on the bed that suggested the nursery, and neediness.

He flinched when he saw Audrey, an involuntary reaction, for it meant conversation at breakfast. In Bernard's regiment, if you did not wish to speak or be spoken to at breakfast, the convention was to wear one's cap in the officer's mess, and a very civilised convention he thought it, but he might have been wearing the helmet of Skanderbeg for all the difference it would have made to Audrey that morning.

'Bernard, Cosmo, I have NEWS!' and she held up a letter, slightly stained by buttery fingers.

'Yes?'

'The wanderer returns!'

'Daniel? When?'

'He will be with us on Sunday.'

'But I've arranged for Canon Dolben to take the service,' said Bernard.

'He doesn't want to take the service, he won't be back in time, but he will be home!'

Mrs Shorely appeared in the doorway. 'It's sausages, m'lord, and I've got mushrooms from the park if you want some?'

'Thank you, Mrs Shorely.'

He waited for Mrs Shorely to retreat, which she very slightly hesitated to do, for she had recognised the handwriting on Audrey's letter, could sense with unusual accuracy shifts in her employer's mood and knew the ways of the world.

Audrey, too, was sensitive to such things, and no stranger to the ways of the world either, so she put on her brightest smile as Mrs Shorely left.

'He's in Yorkshire, Bernard, at the monastery. He's been on retreat.'

'His job is not to retreat. His job is to appear.'

'And he will, on Sunday,' said Audrey.

'To watch another padre do *his* job?'

'They are taxis on the rank, Bernard. There's always another perfectly good one behind, Canon Dolben no less than Canon Clement.'

'But Canon Clement is *my* rector. And thanks to *my* rector going AWOL, Canon Dolben diddled me out of half a case of Latour.'

'Well, how nice for him to have such a lovely going-home present to take with him after the service, and what a model of generosity you are as patron.'

'What's he on retreat from, anyway? The armies of Babylon? The Assyrian wolf? The Hittites, the Jebusites and the Amorites?'

'How ever do you remember all those funny Old Testament names?'

'Because diligent padres drilled them into me. I don't recall them going on retreat when we landed at Anzio.'

'You served in the war, Bernard? As a child prodigy?'

'Not me, Mrs Clement,' he said icily, 'my regiment.'

Audrey was tempted to reply in kind, but mindful of

her obligations and her aspirations, she moderated her tone. 'You and I, Bernard, are not troubled by what Daniel calls the inner life.'

'What's that?'

'Quite. Personally, I find the outer life is more than enough to keep me occupied, but for people like Daniel, and those of his calling, a certain introspection is necessary.'

'Why?' asked Bernard.

'I don't know – to understand better the nature of man, or the doings of God? He got it from his father, I think, who also had an inner life . . . all that Mahler . . . and his brother has a dash of it too, in a different sort of way – an actor sort of way.'

'But why *now*?' said Bernard impatiently.

'Who can say? Do you know what's going on in the lives of your children?'

'Rarely, if ever. And when I find out I wish I hadn't.'

Audrey picked up her teaspoon and unnecessarily stirred her cup of *déca*.

'Are you trying to tell me something, Audrey?'

She continued stirring for a second or two, then said, 'If I wanted to tell you something, Bernard, I would tell you.' And she tapped the side of the cup with a tinkling sound.

The professed brethren of the community of Sts Philip and James at Ravenspurn looked up from their breakfasts as the summoning bell rang at an unwonted time.

And then they returned to their Weetabix and their boiled eggs when they remembered that the novitiate was having a mini Chapter of Faults that morning. They had prayed for its reconciling aims five minutes earlier, but bells going off trigger reactions. Some of the older brethren were so accustomed to the summoning bells that they started to get to their feet until restrained by those with a livelier awareness of that day's horarium, and soon the sound of scraping chairs faded and the crunching of toast was restored.

In the crypt chapel, Daniel sat at the back. He had been there at half past four that morning to pray without interruption and happily alone until the Matins bell. When it rang he discovered that his knees in middle age had lost the flexibility of youth and he staggered like a drunk until he found the wall. He had prayed to find a break in the urgent clamour of this world's concerns and a way through for grace, and its gifts of enlightenment, strength, clarity, generosity, compassion.

He was going to need these, he thought, as he pulled on a cotta ('like a virgin's negligee', Neil once said) over his cassock and hung a purple stole round his neck, the kit of a priest going to the confessional, to act as the conduit of judgement and mercy. All are in need of judgement, for without it there is no mercy, and all need mercy, for none of us is without the shadow of sin. This, like vestments, bothered Neil, who thought it more a racket than a business, and that God's grace needed no mediator. But Neil did not offer remedies for sin, more methods of compensating for its effects, and as Daniel waited for the arrival of the novices he thought of what had been brought to him by penitent and sometimes impenitent souls: the faint grey sins of the meek and mild, like misted breath, and the fiery sins of the fierce, and, from the least likely of people, the most terrible of sins. The membership of that last group was about to grow, he thought, and for this he had been preparing.

The novices arrived and took their places in the stalls facing each other across the floor, the altar at one end, an organ at the other, in a miniaturised version of the great abbey church above. Dominic, Paulinus and Aelred were already there, seated in front of the altar in plain cassocks and scapulars, the precentor and succentor flanking the abbot in a way that made Daniel suddenly think of the Beverley Sisters. All sat in silence for a few minutes, a silence punctuated by the unofficial sounds of Darren sniffing, so irritating it could make Snow White slap Bashful, and then the irregular and heavy tread of the habitually late Brother Augustine descending the steps outside. He was breathing so heavily when he sat down that the whole congregation, in unspoken concord, waited till he had recovered before Abbot Aelred stood, and everyone followed.

'In the name of the Father, and of the Son, and of the Holy Spirit. Amen.'

Paulinus, on Aelred's right, struck a tuning fork and held it to his ear.

'*From all evil and mischief,*' he intoned; '*from sin; from the crafts and assaults of the devil; from Thy wrath, and from everlasting damnation . . .*'

The novices sang the refrain: '*Good Lord, deliver us.*'

Then Dominic, on the succentor's side, responded: '*From all blindness of heart; from pride, vainglory, and hypocrisy; from envy, hatred, and malice, and all uncharitableness . . .*'

Uncharitableness, thought Daniel, what a tricky poly-syllabic word to try to match with plainchant meant for Latin.

The novices sang the refrain: '*Good Lord, deliver us.*'

And so it went on, from Paulinus, to Dominic, then back again, beseeching God for deliverance from the deceits of the world, from lightning and tempest, from sedition and rebellion, heresy and schism. It concluded with a blessing. They sat and Aelred spoke.

'The sacrifice of God is a broken spirit; a broken and contrite heart God will not despise . . . My dear broth-ers, it is an ancient custom of the Benedictine tradition, in which we try to live, that sins *against* the community are remedied by, first, accounting for them *to* the com-munity. In ancient times this was done in especially emphatic ways. Novices who erred – made a mistake in the chant or perhaps kicked over a bucket of milk – would be whipped for their transgressions. In our time, and in our idiosyncratic appropriation of those customs as Benedictines in the Anglican family, such methods, though almost irresistibly attractive, are not enforced. But the need for rendering an account is no less emphatic. Our sins are no different from those of our predecessors, and no less injurious to the common life we are called to lead. So allow me to remind you – us – of our obligations by reading from the fourth chapter of the Rule of our Holy Father Benedict.

'In the first place, you must love the Lord God with your whole heart, your whole soul and all your strength, and love your neighbour as yourself . . .'

Daniel noticed a movement; someone – something – flickered in the gap under the door beyond the altar. The door led to a winding stair, faintly lit, which went to the sacristy above, rarely taken for it was used now as a repository of old candlesticks, prayer books, and wire and oasis for flowers.

'. . . bind yourself to no oath lest it prove false, but speak the truth with heart and tongue. Father Paulinus?'

Paulinus also stood. 'When you are ready,' he said, 'stand, admit your fault, and Abbot Aelred will acknowledge that. Repent, make right what you have done wrong, and remedy will follow. Father Daniel is here also and is ready to hear your confession, if you need to do that. And I think you do, or some of you, most urgently.' He sat down.

'OK,' said Abbot Aelred. 'Brethren, it's over to you.'

'Jesus Christ,' said Honoria, waking up semi-wrapped in the sheets and blankets of the Champton Suite's deflowering bed. What time is it? she wondered, but then the clock over the stables chimed four quarters and then the hours, and there was a short moment of suspense when it got to six and she wondered if it would strike once or twice or thrice more.

Once. It was 7 a.m. The door opened and Neil walked in from the bathroom – a luxury afforded the son and heir – in a T-shirt and boxer shorts. Even then she felt stirred.

'I need to get off home,' he said, 'wash and brush-up before work.'

'Your toilette,' she said.

'Shit, shampoo, shower and shave, love. Twenty-five per cent of that mission is accomplished. I wouldn't go in there for a while if I were you.' He started to get dressed.

What had to be done had to be done.

'Neil,' she said, 'this has been ever so much fun, but I don't want to do it any more.'

She waited for him to say something. He said nothing but gave a grunt and a nod, made a mess of doing up a shirt button and had to start again.

'To be honest, the excitement of sneaking off to the warrener's cottage has rather dwindled for me – you'll be pleased to know the excitement of what we did there hasn't at all – but I think we both know it's not going anywhere.'

He found his trousers and pulled them on.

Honoria tilted her head to one side so a coppery garland of hair unfurled. 'Aren't you going to say anything?'

'I didn't know it wasn't going anywhere.'

'Oh.' She untilted her head. 'I see.'

'I thought we were definitely going somewhere.'

'Really?'

'Yes. It's not unheard of.'

'But, really, Neil? Me and you? Walking off into the sunset hand in hand?'

'Do you have to make it sound so . . . insignificant?'

'It would never work,' she said.

'Why?'

'Because you have your life . . . and I have mine.'

'I'm aware of that,' said Neil.

'Could you honestly see me living in Braunstonbury in a semi, cooking you bacon and eggs before a shift?'

'Stranger things have happened.'

'They really haven't.'

'Alex and Nathan?'

Honoria lay on her back and looked up at the ceiling rather than at him. 'That sort of proves my point. What's going on in that relationship? What do they want from each other? I know what Alex wants. A shag. A valet. A nanny.'

'But they've been together for a while now. And they've been through a lot together. It must be more than that. Don't you see?'

'In Alex's world, getting a gay gypsy outlaw boyfriend is like winning the jackpot.'

'In the end, it's two people in a room, Honoria. All that other stuff . . . is just incidental.'

'Maybe in your world.'

'You keep saying that. My world, their world. What about your world?'

'What do you mean?' she asked.

'What is it?'

'My world . . . is my family, my . . . you know . . . all this.' She pointed at the walls where the likenesses of her ancestors looked back at her.

'So why do you long to escape it?'

'I don't,' she said. 'Where do you get that idea from?'

'I don't think you and me was just animal attraction, Honoria.'

'Don't be ridiculous.'

'What am I then?' he asked.

'Oh, this is a conversation I so much don't want to have. And, to answer your question, I have my work.'

'You don't do anything.'

'Yes, I do.'

'Your job? When was the last time you were there?'

'I don't have to be there. Not every day. You don't understand. I'm not on duty. Look, can't we just say it's been fun, thank you, see you around?'

He was not easily thrown. He could look on disappointment and misfortune, even his own, without losing his balance, but no words came to him now, or not in a form he was able to say.

Honoria unwrapped herself from the bedclothes and found her cigarettes and lighter on the bureau. As she lit one, she looked at the portrait above it of one of her great-great- – she did not know how many greats – grandmothers, a famously pious reformer. She was dressed in sober black and white, and was wearing one of those stiff pleated bonnets, which made her look half-parson, half-chef. Ridiculous, she thought. This was the Lady de Floures, she remembered, who had a dozen children, half of whom had died of scarlet fever before they grew up, a husband who grew cold, and a memorial where she was lodged among the de Floures tombs, which looked very plain, as she did, but was comically extravagant in praise of her wifely, matronly and homely virtues. Honoria wondered what she would have made of a life like that, had she been born into it, and then saw that the old lady's mildly smiling face was overlaid by the reflection in the glass of Neil tying his shoelaces, which perhaps gave an answer to that question.

He let himself out without saying anything.

It was like a sort of auction, thought Daniel, when you start off with the smaller lots, an incomplete set of sherry glasses, a Malacca cane, a small sketch in pencil that looked a bit like something by one of the Glasgow Boys, then suddenly a silver marrow scoop from the reign of George III was brought before the bidders and the atmosphere changed.

First to speak was Sebastian.

'Father Aelred,' he said, 'I wish to confess the sin of a careless remark. I was on kitchen duty last week and

I remarked to Brother Bede that we throw away more food in a day than my family sees in a month. It was an exaggeration . . .'

Not much of an exaggeration, thought Aelred, who had spent a year with the Rhodesian community before he was made abbot.

'. . . and I did it because I was in that moment angry.' Sebastian genuflected towards Aelred, who responded by making the sign of the cross at him in his neat and tidy way. Such a contrast, thought Daniel, to his expansive hand-waving habits in conversation.

There was silence again. Placid spoke next.

'Anger, too, from me. I kicked Darren during Benediction. I lost my temper. I thought he was being deliberately provocative, saying Hail Marys like a hooligan at a football match, as if he—'

Aelred held up a restraining hand. 'Just a confession of sin, please. Save the explanation, if you must, for later.' Placid knelt, Aelred made the sign of the cross, and Placid sat down again.

There was silence, then it was Anselm. He stood and said, 'I'm afraid I made rather a mess of the liturgical printing for Advent. I got some of the margins wrong, but I bound the booklets anyway because I couldn't be bothered to work out how to make them right.'

He genuflected and Aelred made the sign of the cross.

This was not going how Daniel thought it would.

The rising energy of resentment was in danger of stalling, but then Darren stood.

'It wasn't Bede who left the chicken coop open so the fox got in. It was me.'

'Bede told me he had done it,' said Augustine.

Father Paulinus said, 'Do not speak, Augustine.'

'No, it was me, but I blamed him for it, and he was so dizzy he couldn't remember what he had done and I . . . I suppose I wore him down with my insistence and he—'

Anselm, suddenly not mild, said, 'You bastard.'

'Anselm—' said Aelred.

'You *absolute* bastard. I blamed him for that.'

'I was angry with him,' said Darren. 'He'd let me down, he let the side down.'

'He was on your side, you idiot,' said Placid.

'He was *not*,' said Darren. 'He was weak. No, worse, he was a traitor.'

Aelred stood. 'Enough. Confess your sin. That's all.'

'Father Aelred,' said Paulinus, 'for clarity, if I may?'

Aelred looked a bit surprised but yielded.

Father Paulinus went on: 'We are not talking about hens, I think we can all see that . . .'

'I'm talking about hens,' said Anselm, his voice shaking a little.

'No, I think we need to confront what has really divided us,' said Paulinus, 'and it is the decision of Synod that we have women ordained to the priesthood.'

Darren snorted.

'You may not like it, Darren – I do not like it – but it is coming . . .'

'I like it,' said Placid, 'and so does Sebastian, and we are not the only ones . . .'

Darren gave a sneering laugh. 'You might as well ordain an owl. Or a pillar box.'

'People, Darren, made in the image of God,' said Placid, 'not wildfowl, not . . . ironmongery.'

'And so God gives us Our Lady,' said Darren. 'She is the Mother of the Church. She is the model of women. We should look to her.'

'The *theotokos*,' said Nicolai, breaking his silence, 'the one who bears God Incarnate. Why do you Protestants not see this?'

'We're not Protestants, Brother Nicolai,' snapped Darren, 'we're Anglo-Catholics.'

'Anglo-Catholics? You say this but it does not mean anything. Catholic is with the pope. You are no more with the pope than we Orthodox. But we do not pretend to be something we are not. To me, your Church looks like it is trying to be the Communists and the Social Democrats at the same time. *Şi dacă o casă este dezbinată împotriva ei însăşi, casa aceea nu poate dăinui . . .*'

'A house divided against itself cannot stand,' said Paulinus.

Aelred said, 'Yes, to get back to the original point, the community only holds together when it accounts for its sins to itself. So?' He waited.

Placid stood again. 'I hate you, Darren. I don't want

370

to. I don't think of myself as someone who hates people, I think of myself as compassionate and generous and tolerant, but since you've been here I have realised I am not.'

Augustine knelt, then said, 'It's worse than that, actually . . .' He paused. 'I hate you not only for your nasty views, your narrow-mindedness, your malice. I hate you because you are depriving me of something I have cherished all my life – my niceness.'

'Now we're getting somewhere,' said Aelred and made the sign of the cross at him again. He sat down.

Anselm then stood up. 'I *am* nice, and I hate you too, Darren. I used to just find you hard work and a bit embarrassing, with your views, and your refusal to listen to anyone else, but I *really* hate you now. The chickens . . .' He paused to collect himself. 'How could you have left the coop door open? And then blamed Bede for it? What sort of a person does that?' A thought struck him. 'If he closed it then why did you open it? You must have opened it and left it open after he closed it. Why would you do that?'

'It's just chickens,' said Darren.

'What?'

'It's not the Massacre of the Innocents.'

'But that's exactly what it was! What's wrong with you?'

'Chickens,' said Darren. 'With little funerals and headstones. Dumb creatures without souls. What's wrong with me? What's wrong with *you*?'

Suddenly Anselm launched himself at Darren. It was as unlikely as a volcano erupting in a rockery, so unlikely that for a moment no one knew what to do. And then bathos, for when Anselm actually got to Darren he did not know what to do, for he had never hit anyone in his life, so he sort of flapped his hands and then beat him on his chest like a helpless young thing in a black-and-white film confronting an indifferent husband. Darren was so taken by surprise that he lost his glasses, which broke with a satisfying crunch on the floor under Augustine's feet when he and Sebastian intervened to separate them.

Aelred waited for the moment to pass. Everyone sat down. The energy, discharged, left a sizzle, an electrical odour. The little hairs on the backs of necks and forearms were still standing up. 'Anselm?'

Anselm stood. 'Forgive me for my outburst, Father.' He kneeled and Aelred gave his blessing.

'Darren?' said Aelred.

Darren did nothing.

'Darren? Are you not sorry?'

Then he stood. 'I did it deliberately to get Bede into trouble. I can't say I am sorry for that. He needed to be . . . contained. Augustine – who takes him seriously? – but Bede was clever and sound, or so we thought, and we need people like him to fight the good fight.' He flashed a look at Anselm. 'But he wasn't sound, after all. So I had to do something about that.'

'What are you saying, Darren?' said Aelred.

'We're in a dirty fight, but victory is worth it.'

'Darren. What *are* you saying?' said Placid.

There was silence.

'Did you hurt him?' Placid asked.

'I just told you what I did,' said Darren.

'No, did you . . . have a hand in his death?'

There was a long pause. Darren's eyes, unobscured by the sinister shaded lenses of his glasses, looked unusually bright.

'I don't know.'

The atmosphere was suddenly again charged.

'I don't know . . . if he topped himself. He wasn't stable. When the chicken thing happened . . . people turned on him. Maybe that had something to do with me?'

Darren went to kneel and Aelred lifted his hand in blessing, but before he could make the sign of the cross a voice came out of the dark.

'Bede did not kill himself,' said Daniel.

'Why do you say this, Father?' said Paulinus, peering into the darkness at the back of the chapel.

Daniel walked out of the gloom and into the light. 'Because he was murdered.'

Aelred gave a tut of irritation.

'I didn't *murder* him,' said Darren, in an understandably unguarded way, pronouncing 'murdered' in his original Scouse accent.

'I know you didn't. I am not the only one who knows you didn't.'

'Oh, Daniel, *really*,' said Aelred.

'As our Holy Father Benedict says, "We must speak the truth with heart and tongue." So now is the time,' said Daniel. 'An offence against the community must be made good within the community. Father Paulinus?'

'Yes. That is so, but why are you so insistent that the poor boy's death is murder? It was an accident. The police say so, the paramedics say so, the coroner will say so.'

'What do you say?'

'Me? An accident. Why would I doubt the police or the medical people? Why do you see murder everywhere?'

'Because this is a monastery,' said Daniel.

'Light and shade, Father. Sometimes deep shadow, but murder?'

Then Daniel said loudly, 'Colin!'

Aelred winced. 'This is a Chapter of Faults for the novitiate, Daniel. Could you keep that in mind.'

'Colin! I know you're there.'

The door behind the altar opened and there he was, rubbing his hands on his trousers, with a look of contrived surprise. 'I was just . . . I wanted a prayer book.'

'Really?'

He shrugged.

'You and Bede had a row. I heard you,' said Darren.

'More than one,' said Augustine.

'We had our disagreements,' said Colin. 'He was a very irritating man. *You* shouldn't need telling.'

374

'Was the argument about Austria-Hungary?' asked Daniel.

'Oh dear,' said Aelred, 'the cause of many a row.'

'Arguments!' said Placid.

'He . . . interfered with my research. It was *intolerable*.'

'How?' asked Daniel.

'We were both interested in the same period, as you say, Father, and he was always in the library. And whenever I looked for a book he got there first. You know he kept them on a separate shelf, as if they were his, and when he wasn't there, if I took one, he would lose his temper?'

'He's not the only one to have a temper,' said Augustine. 'I heard you shout at him.'

'We all have limits,' said Colin.

'And we know what happens if someone crosses yours,' said Placid.

Colin looked startled. 'Whatever do you mean by that?'

'We all know where you came from, Colin. Your alma mater. The one with bars on the windows. Not a lot of competition for the A. J. P. Taylors in Dartmoor.'

Aelred snapped, 'Placid. Remember yourself.'

'We all know,' said Placid. 'Why pretend we don't?'

'We do not hold people to the past,' said Aelred. 'What's done is done. The consequences were faced. It is over. Which is why we observe the strictest discretion about where our visitors come from.'

'Fat chance of that,' said Placid, 'this place is gossipier than a Sultan's harem.'

'An impulse we must learn to bridle,' said Aelred. 'Far worse is the impulse to judge. If we judge, we come under that same judgement ourselves. Do you need reminding?'

'I was not at Dartmoor,' said Colin, in rather a disparaging tone, which made Daniel wonder if some prisons had an academic cachet that others did not. 'And I am not a murderer,' he said. 'Manslaughter. Diminished responsibility.'

'No one is accusing you of murder,' said Aelred.

No one said anything.

'My research is everything to me,' said Colin. 'Everything. It's all I have. But I would not kill Bede over it.'

'I know,' said Daniel.

'How do you know?' said Placid.

'Because Colin cannot have killed Bede. He can't have been in two places at the same time. At Compline and at the turbine house.'

'You saw him at Compline?' said Placid.

'No. It was far too dark.'

'Even if you had, wouldn't it have been easy to slip out from the back without anyone noticing?'

'I didn't see him,' said Daniel. 'I heard him. He has this rather noticeable habit of joining in the congregational sections a fraction of a second after everyone else.'

'Oh, that's Colin, is it?' said Aelred. 'It is, as you say, noticeable. As is your tiresome repetition of the word murder, Father. I wish you wouldn't . . .'

'I would rather not, Father Aelred, but you did say that we are to speak the truth with heart and tongue.'

'Sometimes, Daniel, you make me think of a clever chorister trying to catch out the chaplain,' said Aelred.

'But he is right,' said Paulinus, 'we are under an unusually firm obligation here to speak the truth.'

'With heart and tongue,' said Daniel.

'Yes, of course,' said Aelred.

'Where were you when Bede died, Paulinus?'

Paulinus, suddenly on the spot, stumbled. 'I was . . . I was in church. With you, and everyone. At Compline.'

'I remember. In the precentor's stall, in the darkness, in your hood. "Keep me, O Lord, as the apple of your eye."'

'As usual.'

'As usual. We did not overlap here when I was a novice, and I don't know your voice – but when you sang, I heard something that wasn't right. You learnt your chant elsewhere, I realised that, and each tradition is different – but it was not just that. It sounded like . . . a copy. A caricature almost, as if you were not doing it seriously. But I was in deep distress and thought perhaps it was me. Then I realised the sound of the turbine, that perpetual background to everything we hear, always in the background, always, had stopped and I thought perhaps that was making the chant sound different. But now I think there is a more obvious explanation. It was not your voice at all.'

'Father,' said Paulinus, 'are you quite well?'

'No, not really, but . . .'

'Of course you are not well, Father. We all saw it. We thought it must have been the pressure of the last few days, your curate, the murder. A child too. Your personal life. Everything must have seemed strange. But it was me singing, of course it was. If not, then who?'

'Father Dominic.'

'Me?' said Dominic. 'What have I got to do with this?'

'I think it was you,' said Daniel. 'You are the succentor, deputy to Father Paulinus; you know how he sings better than anyone. You sit in for him when he's away.'

'I sound nothing like Paulinus.'

'But you could if you wanted to. Your impersonation of Aelred is exemplary. Quite the gift for mimicry . . .' A thought came to him. He turned to Paulinus. 'So that's why you asked me to deputise for you. So I would not hear you singing and perhaps notice the difference?'

Paulinus snorted. 'This is ridiculous! Even if Dominic could, why would he?'

'Because you forced him. And he knew that if he didn't do what you wanted him to do, there would be consequences.'

'Consequences?'

'You know his past,' said Daniel.

Aelred suddenly snapped, 'Stop!'

Daniel did not stop. 'What did you do before you came to Ravenspurn, Father Dominic?'

'I was a schoolmaster.'

'And why did you leave that profession?'

Dominic looked desperately at Aelred.

'This is not something for this chapter,' said Aelred, 'and we will hear no more of it. Let us pray . . .'

Before anyone could, Daniel interrupted. 'Speak the truth with heart and tongue. Dominic?'

'I had a breakdown. Do you have to be so cruel?'

'Rather, before you were Dominic. When you were Neville Banks. Housemaster at Calcott Prep until you moved on, and agreed to come here and live quietly, away from children.'

There was silence and then Dominic said, 'I never hurt anyone. My offences . . . such as they are . . . are not as great as some. We all sin, do we not? I repented and was absolved of mine. And now all I want is a quiet and holy life. But I have a tormentor who would deny me that unless I do what he says.'

'Repented and absolved,' said Paulinus, 'and yet the old Adam is difficult to entirely subdue. Yes? Your private habits, I mean. Your continuing fascination with youth culture? Your interest in pop music? The repertoire of Bros, for example, so very different from plainsong. But perhaps it is pop singers you are interested in?'

'I can see why you use such things to your advantage, Father, but do you really have to torment me with them?' said Dominic.

'How apt, that you come here to escape your past but find yourself now not the tormentor but the tormented,' said Paulinus. 'And are forced to do things you do not want to do.'

Dominic suddenly turned towards Aelred and kneeled. 'Father Aelred, forgive me, for I have sinned. I have behaved . . . unchastely . . .'

Aelred winced. 'Yes, yes, yes . . .' he said before Dominic could continue, and made the sign of the cross. 'Perhaps you could . . .?' He made a little patting gesture, as if to restore calm. Dominic stood up, went to sit down, but then stopped, turned, and walked out. There was, if not a sigh of relief, a sense of tension relaxing slightly; but not for long.

'Dominic is not the only person to seek escape from the past in the cloister,' said Daniel, 'and not the only one to find himself in danger of exposure.'

Aelred could not contain his impatience. 'This is beginning to get very irritating, Daniel. May I remind you that we are at Ravenspurn abbey, not St Mary Mead, and you are not Miss Marple.'

'It's why Bede died,' said Daniel. 'Why he was murdered. By you, Paulinus. Bede uncovered your past too. He knew what you are pretending to be.'

'I am not pretending to be anyone,' said Paulinus.

'It would be better phrased "who you are pretending

not to be". What is the first line of the Rule of St Benedict?'

'"Hearken continually within thine heart, O son, giving attentive ear to the precepts of thy master."'

'*Előírásai,*' said Daniel.

'What?'

'You were quoting from the Rule in our Greek class and could not remember the English word for precepts, and I remember you said – correct me if I misheard – *előírásai.*'

'I don't remember, but you are right about the word. It means precepts.'

'In Hungarian.'

'The community when I was first a novice was Hungarian speaking,' said Paulinus.

'Bede noticed too. He spoke Hungarian,' said Daniel.

'I am aware of his field of study, so I suppose he knew a little.'

'Expert, I think, as you would have to be if you were reading primary sources of that era. Hungarian is your first language?'

'German. I am Schwowe. Ungarndeutsche, a German-Hungarian. Danube Swabians in the history books – they emigrated from Swabia to the Danube Valley after the Ottomans retreated. So I grew up in Hungary. And, of course, I speak Hungarian.'

'Romanian too,' said Daniel. 'You recognised Nicolai's quotation from the Gospel.'

'We crossed borders along the Danube Valley – there are Schwowe in Hungary, Romania, Yugoslavia. So Romanian, a bit of Serbo-Croat too. It is not unusual for someone with my background. And so what? I speak Hungarian, Bede understood Hungarian.'

'I knew finally when I found your rosary.'

'The cross barby.'

'The Arrow Cross. With the cipher.'

'The fisherman's cross,' said Paulinus. 'An I for *ichthys*.'

'But it was not an I for *ichthys*,' said Daniel. 'It is an H. For *hungarizmus*.'

Paulinus sighed, then nodded. 'Yes. A relic of my youth. Sentimental of me.'

'You were a member of the Arrow Cross.'

'You make it sound like the SS. It was more like the Scouts. All of us youngsters joined – we had to.'

'It was nothing like the Scouts,' said Aelred in a low voice. 'It was a vicious, murderous gang of thugs.'

'What do you know of the Arrow Cross?' Paulinus snapped.

'I served with the army, Paulinus, in the war. No. 2 Commando. I know that sounds unlikely, but I was a padre. After the invasion of Italy, we went to Yugoslavia. And there I heard about the Arrow Cross Party. And its units.'

'Heard about it from the Communists.'

'And from our own intelligence,' said Aelred.

'You would know, Father, if you served in the war, what it was like. And what was at stake.'

'Yes, I think so. I saw how it reduced men to beasts. How men reduced other men to beasts. The terrible things they did. I don't mean in combat. I mean in domestic operations. Jews, gypsies. It is what brought me here.'

'It is what brought me here also.'

'But for different reasons,' said Daniel.

'Not to look at Christ on the cross,' said Aelred, 'but to hide from him.'

'To hide from him?' shouted Paulinus. 'I *fought* for him. To save him and his flock from the terror that would extinguish his light forever. The wolf bearing down on the fold. What would you do to protect those you love? What would you do to protect the Gospel of Christ from . . . nihilism? What would you do? You cannot know.'

'What did you do?' said Daniel.

'I joined the party. I fought. For family, for *Volk*, for Christ.'

'In the gendarmerie.'

Paulinus looked at him. He blinked twice.

'Interior Ministry Gendarme?' said Daniel. 'Csendőrség, is that how you say it?'

'Your pronunciation is terrible.'

'In February 1945 you were at Várpalota, I think,' Daniel continued. 'Where the gypsies were rounded up. A hundred and twenty? You made them dig their own graves and then you shot them. Were you the gendarme who shouted "For Christ!" before you murdered them?'

'Where did you hear this?'

'From Bede's supervisor at Oxford. A Dr Keschner.'

'I know his work.'

'Bede was working on the collapse of Horthy's government, the Nazi occupation, the aftermath. Dr Keschner says the atrocities perpetrated by the Arrow Cross were so appalling the SS refused to have anything to do with them.'

'You cannot know what it was like. The Bolsheviks were far worse than anything on our side. We killed them, but they would kill God. The Bolsheviks, and behind them their hordes, the Jews and the Slavs. And the gypsies.'

'The gypsies weren't Bolsheviks,' said Daniel.

'They were the same. A threat to stability and order. An impure people, a pollutant, is as dangerous in its way as those who set out to destroy us quite deliberately. And the opportunity came to deal with both at the same time. If you could save civilisation from its enemies, if you could cure it of a fatal disease, what would you do?'

'I wouldn't round people up and gun them down in the name of Jesus.'

'What can you know?'

'Bede knew. He suspected you. And after more than forty years hiding from the consequences of your crimes, the thought of facing them was too much. You told him to meet you at the turbine house to check the generator. And once he was there you pushed him into the machine . . .'

'His scapular was caught in the gears, it pulled him in.'

'He would never have done work on the turbine without his tool belt. I don't think his scapular would have got caught if he was wearing it.'

There was another silence as Paulinus thought. Then he let out a sigh and turned to the abbot. 'Father, I killed Bede.' He genuflected.

Aelred seemed bewildered for a moment, then made the sign of the cross over him.

Paulinus stood up. '"You are not to kill", and I did, so that is done. Are we to go to the police?'

'Yes,' said Daniel, 'but it is not quite done. Aelred, you knew about Father Dominic's history?'

'Yes.'

'What did you do about it?'

'Offer him a life. A way to grace and holiness. In a place where he cannot be a danger to little boys anymore.'

'But no calling to account, no reckoning for their sins in front of the whole community?'

'You are actually beginning to sound vindictive, Daniel. Perhaps you have become distracted from your true vocation?'

'What about the boys – men now – he treated so wickedly?'

'That was the responsibility of others,' said Aelred. 'My responsibility is to give Dominic his best chance of heaven.'

'Salvation.'

'God's salvation.'

'Repent, make right what you have done wrong, and remedy will follow,' said Daniel.

'Yes,' said Aelred.

'Do you think you are better at repenting than remedying?'

'I can't say I've ever really thought about it.'

'Do you find it easier to admit a fault than correct a fault?' Daniel asked.

'The two are indivisible,' said Aelred.

'You knew Paulinus was not at Compline when Bede was killed.'

'Did I?'

'I think so,' said Daniel.

'Why?'

'You did not look up when Dominic started to sing instead of him.'

'I'm not sure I understand your point.'

'You always do when something is wrong – a misstep in a procession, if someone mispronounces something. You'd look up if somebody ate a boiled egg with a teaspoon. You looked up when I was playing the voluntary, the Fugue à la Gigue, after Vespers and I altered a triplet in the pedal part. No one else would notice that.'

'Oh, yes, missing that major sixth. It had gone so well up to then.'

'But no reaction when Dominic started to sing instead of Paulinus. I just wonder why.'

'I don't remember.'

'Try.'

Aelred thought for a moment. Then he said, 'You are like Samson in the Temple, Daniel, righteously pulling down everything around you.'

'Why didn't you say something? You knew Paulinus was not in church when Bede was killed. Didn't you ask yourself where he was?'

'No,' said Aelred. 'When you are the shepherd of the flock – you should know this, Daniel – you take care over the questions you ask.'

'Because the answer might inconvenience you?'

'Because one has more important concerns than the – I think it almost a vanity – solving of puzzles. And that becomes habitual. Do I want to know everything? No, it doesn't serve. There are wolves, and foul weather, and ditches, and I must bring all safely into the fold.'

'Speak the truth with heart and tongue. Not just with the tongue, but with the heart.'

'A counsel of perfection, Daniel. No one does, no one *could*.'

'I'm not asking for perfection, Aelred. Just for truthful witness when someone has been murdered.'

'I did not know Bede had been murdered.'

'But you suspected. And you knew Paulinus was

not in church when he died. What did you make of that? Or did you turn away from a truth too difficult to contemplate?'

Then Aelred surprised Daniel. He was silent for a moment, then stood and turned to face him. Then he knelt and bowed his head.

Daniel made the sign of the cross over him.

16

Canon Dolben, while well-beloved, had never felt it necessary to introduce elements of captivating interest in services. This Sunday morning there was the added misfortune of him forgetting it was Remembrance Sunday, only realising his mistake when everyone arrived at church wearing their red poppies. 'Oh dear,' he said, when Margaret Porteous reminded him that it was the custom, initiated by him between the wars, to read out loud the names of those who had gone out from Champton to fight for king and country and not returned.

Bernard, unaccompanied by his kin, endured the service from a sense of duty but without good grace, miserably thinking of the half-case of claret this dreary ordeal was costing him, until he realised no sermon would be preached that day. He perked up so much he let out a satisfied grunt when the old canon started reading out the names of the glorious dead and then felt uncomfortably disloyal to their memory.

Then they had to rush to the war memorial to meet Gilbert Drage, representative of the Royal British Legion, in time for eleven o'clock and the Last Post, which Christian Staniland used to play on his trumpet (but he had become an atheist after his O levels and would have no part in it now). So after welcoming the faithful few who had come to remember 'the fallen of two wars' Canon Dolben started the hymn that they sang only on this day, obscure when he first chose it and now all but forgotten. It was not only unmemorable, but also pitched unhelpfully high, so nobody at all joined in until the big finish of the national anthem.

Daniel timed his arrival at Champton House to co-incide with tea. He left his bag at the bottom of the back stairs and in a spirit of meekness looked round the door of Mrs Shorely's room to check in, but she was not there. Hilda and the puppies were, and he knelt over their enclosure and cooed at them. Hilda stirred from her exhausting motherly duties and licked his hand, which made him suddenly sad again and he had to compose himself, then brace himself, before walking into the library.

It was nearly a full house. Bernard, Honoria and Alex were there – no Nathan – his mother and Theo were there, and Canon Dolben. All conversation stopped when he appeared in the doorway, but *toujours la politesse*, and Bernard said, 'Ah, the return of the prodigal!' and was so pleased with this unusual flash of brilliance that it mitigated the resentment he had yet to express.

Audrey came scooting over. 'Dan, Dan,' she said. 'Oh, we've *missed* you!' He bent to kiss her on both cheeks. She put her arm through his as the others enclosed him in a circle of welcome in front of the fire, which glowed red and crackled.

'Good to see you, Dan,' said Theo, punching him on the arm with gruff affection.

'*So* much to tell you,' said Alex, making wide eyes.

'Thank God you're back,' said Honoria.

'Dear man, dear man! Will you be officiating, then, at Evensong?' said Canon Dolben, with the unmistakable anticipation of a clergyman hoping to get out of something.

And then Daniel was suddenly attacked at rug level by Cosmo, who hurtled across the floor yelping with excitement, ran around him in circles, and jumped up almost as high as his knee in his delight at their reunion.

'We're hearing the most EXTRAORDINARY stories about your adventures in the monastery,' said Alex. 'You seem to be as adept at sniffing out murder as a pig after truffles.'

'It was not quite the retreat I had in mind. But . . . I never cease to be surprised by what one discovers in monastic life.'

'We're glad you have returned to parish life,' said Bernard. 'It's felt like an age since you disappeared. That's a quarter to five striking and I don't suppose you really have time for anything before you need to get ready and resume your duties?'

'I have a sermon that has gone unpreached, Father,' said Canon Dolben. 'It is not on the theme of remembrance, but you might like to preach it if you have not had time to prepare one of your own?'

'Let us savour the moment for what it is, Canon Dolben,' said Bernard quickly. 'The wanderer has returned – and on this day when we remember the many who did not return – no need for gloss or paraphrase.'

Daniel certainly felt no need to preach during that Evensong, for he knew no one minded a sermon not being preached, and Remembrance Sunday rather took care of itself, with no need for commentary from the pulpit. Theo read the lesson from the Old Testament, from the fifth chapter of Nehemiah. which he pronounced to rhyme with 'anaemia' (Daniel, like Aelred, looked up). '"So God shake out every man from his house,"' declaimed Theo, in a way that made Audrey think of *I, Claudius*, '"and from his labour, that performeth not this promise, even thus be he shaken out, and emptied. And all the congregation said, Amen."'

The less attentive among the congregation thought this an instruction, rather than a recitation, and repeated the 'Amen'.

Something would need to be said, Daniel knew, sooner or later; an explanation for his disappearance, and perhaps an indication of his intentions, once he knew with clarity what they were. He felt a sudden surge of feeling for his parishioners, whose welcome home was generous and unaffected, his absence making their hearts fonder.

The Magnificat followed, Dyson in D, sung so long and so frequently by the choir, and the choirs that preceded them, that everyone more or less finished together and in the same tonal world, but Daniel was not really listening, for he was thinking about the lesson, and what befalls us if we do not perform our promises to God, and how he had been shaken out as thoroughly as a dog's bed after its moult. Back within the cloister he quit before he made his vows, he had discovered what it was to be empty. But always we begin again, and he had begun again, picking up the plainsong thread he had put down a quarter of a century ago. There it was, waiting for him. Where would it lead?

After the service, he stood just beyond the church porch in the chilly darkness receiving the good wishes and welcome-backs of his parishioners, from Dora Sharman in her crocheted bonnet, and Anne Dollinger, who asked to speak to him at his earliest convenience, from Councillor Staveley with the politician's insistent handshake, and Miss March, who held back a little, shook his bare hand with her gloved hand and gave a modest smile – as effusive an expression of warmth as she could manage, he thought.

He was looking at his watch to calculate his chances of mustering the traditional Sunday-night supper of soup and a sarnie from Champton's kitchens. Maybe he would also cast an eye over the TV repeat of that morning's ceremonies at the Cenotaph? The last to leave filed past, his mother, and Jane Thwaite, who had given an element of support for the singing of the hymns and canticles at the organ, clutching two shopping bags of wizened medlars she had been bletting in the flower room since Harvest Festival.

'Hello, Daniel, lovely to have you back,' said Jane. 'Fancy some medlar jelly? Your mother and I have heaps!'

'Thanks, Jane,' he said. 'I would.'

'What a few weeks it has been! I hope you are going to have a chance to just . . . relax, regroup . . . re-engage?'

'I hope so. But we have to go – Mum, if we're quick we can make the Cenotaph. I think it's on at a quarter past seven.' He offered Audrey his arm.

'Darling, I think I'll make my own way back,' she said.

'Why?'

She looked down the path towards the lychgate, where Neil was sitting on the low wall under the lamppost, which cast its illumination over the threshold between Champton's sacred and secular jurisdictions. Daniel's heart gave a lurch.

'Let me give you a lift, Audrey,' said Jane. 'I've brought the car.'

Daniel found his cloak, switched off the lights,

locked the church door behind him and walked down the path to the lychgate.

'Glad you're back,' said Neil. 'But well done, Dan, another mystery solved, another killer collared. And what a collar!'

'Thank you, Neil. But it's not what I'm really for, is it? That's enough collaring for me. I need to get going.'

'Can I walk you home?'

'Yes, of course,' said Daniel.

'Come on then.'

Neil launched himself off the wall with his easy grace, a quality that Daniel loved and desired, and it was a bittersweet thing to behold. So was Neil's off-duty appearance, in jeans and a bomber jacket, like someone from the SAS poorly disguised as a civilian. That was stirring, too, until Daniel considered the contrast with him, in his high collar and long black cloak. 'Who Dares Wins' walking beside the minister endued with righteousness. Whatever had he been thinking?

'How's the rectory coming on?'

Neil was looking across the churchyard at the dark mass of Daniel's house.

'The decorators are in tomorrow. Mum is flushed with triumph. Insurers, Bernard – all in line.'

'She's amazing.'

'She is.'

'How did you leave things at Ravenspurn? I guess not business as usual.'

'Actually, yes. Pretty much. It is not every day a

community's novice master is arrested for murder – and possibly war crimes – and the abbot offers his resignation, but . . . well, whatever it is, it doesn't interrupt the routine. Nothing does. War, terror, want, epidemics, power cuts. They just keep going.'

'Yeah,' said Neil, 'but you don't go through something like that without it taking its toll.'

'But they endure, because whatever happens they carry on doing what they've always done, like a ship sailing through a storm. Steady as she goes. Can you see that?'

'Yes, I think so.'

They walked further into the park. It was a dark, clear night, the sky was full of stars, and the moon, nearly full, was reflected in the lake.

'Beautiful,' said Neil.

'"And spangled heavens, a shining frame. Their great Original proclaim."'

They carried on towards the house. The lights were on in the library. Drinks, thought Daniel, and he wondered if he could skip that and find somewhere to sit with his mother and the dogs and watch television and sip Heinz tomato soup from a mug, and things would be back to normal. Steady as she goes.

'It's very you,' said Neil.

'What is?'

'Ravenspurn.'

'How do you mean?'

'You come into focus when you are there.'

'That's interesting,' said Daniel.

'Like you said, there'll always be a part of you that's still there.'

'Yes.'

'Seriously, what would your life have been like if you had stayed?'

'I've been thinking about it a lot.'

'Do you think you would have been an Aelred? You're very alike.'

'That doesn't feel like a compliment right now,' said Daniel.

'I don't mean it like that, I mean . . . horses for courses.'

They walked on.

'Why did you leave?' Neil asked.

'I thought I knew, but I'm not sure now.'

The house loomed before them, mismatched roofs and battlements and chimneys and pediments and cupolas, bluish in the moonlight.

'Dan?'

'Yes?'

'Could you imagine going back?'

'Unanswerable question, Neil.'

They stopped at the door that led to the back stairs.

'Are you coming in?' Daniel asked.

'No.'

'Ah. The warrener's cottage?'

'No. I came to see you, Dan.' Neil knew what he was going to do.

'Oh. Thanks.'

There was a scrabbling at the door from the inside, and Cosmo's yelp, and then a deep sniff, and then more scrabbling, and more yelping.

'I'd better . . .' said Daniel, but he did not finish what he was going to say because Neil pulled him towards him, took his head in his hands and kissed him.

In the study, Jove softly jumped from the bookshelf onto the floor. He made his way across the rug to Bernard, who was sitting in his armchair looking at the fire, on his second brandy and soda. The cat brushed against his leg, once, twice, and started to purr.

Acknowledgements

I would like to thank the following:

Theodore Keschner.
Ross Campbell.
Kyle Sutherland.
David Fairley.
Euan Keatinge.
Stuart Palmer.
Katy Albert.
Catherine Muirden.
The Earl and Countess Spencer.
Deb Price.
Fr David Povall SSC.
The Community of the Resurrection.
Juliet Annan and all at Weidenfeld & Nicolson.
Tim Bates and all at PFD.
Hebden Bridge Local History Society.

Discover the
Canon Clement series

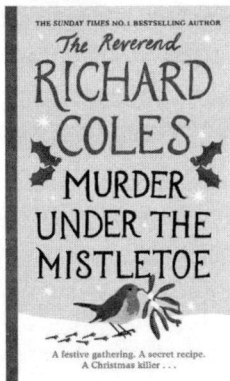

From No. 1 *Sunday Times* bestselling author,
The Reverend Richard Coles

www.richardcoles.com

Discover the Canon Clement Christmas novella . . .

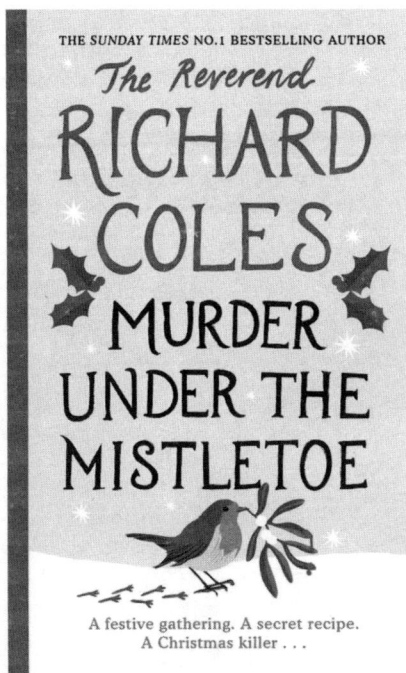

A social dilemma. A family emergency. A secret recipe. A murder . . .

From No. 1 *Sunday Times* bestselling author,
The Reverend Richard Coles

www.richardcoles.com

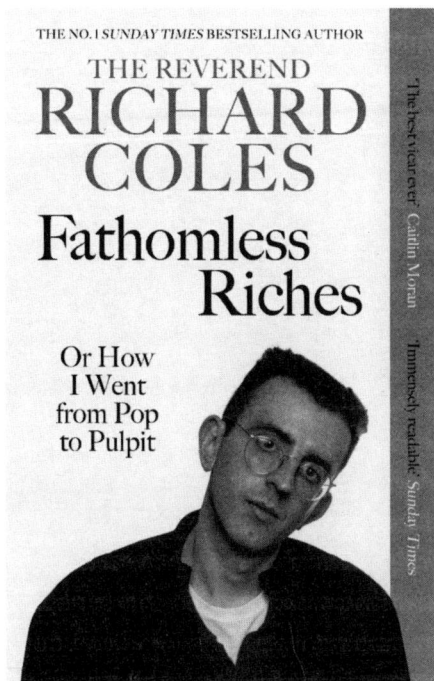

Discover the non-fiction from the No. 1 *Sunday Times* bestselling author, The Reverend Richard Coles

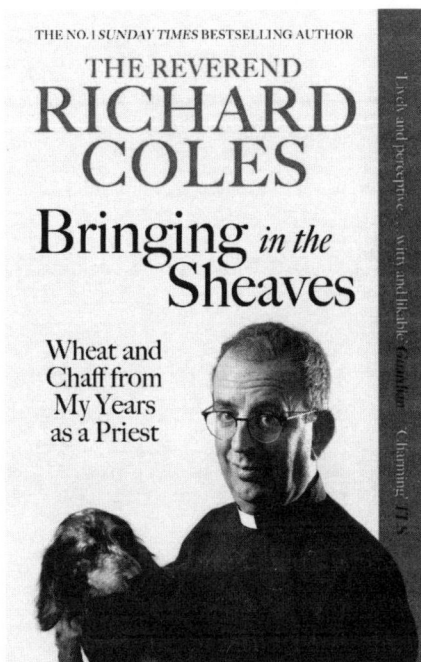

THE NO.1 *SUNDAY TIMES* BESTSELLING AUTHOR

THE REVEREND

RICHARD COLES

Bringing *in the* Sheaves

Wheat and Chaff from My Years as a Priest

Bringing in the Sheaves guides us through a year in the life of The Reverend Richard Coles against the backdrop of the Christian calendar – and the multitude of weird and wonderful characters he encounters along the way.

www.richardcoles.com